Anthem
OF THE
Cursed Empire

AUSTEA E. KETTE

Gold & Fire & Blood series
Book I

Anthem of the Cursed Empire
Gold & Fire & Blood Novel
by Austea E. Kette

Copyright © 2023 Austea E. Kette

This is a work of fiction. Names, places, characters and incidents are the product of the author's imagination and are fictitious. Any resemblance to actual persons, living or dead, events or establishments is solely coincidental.

Cover Design by MiblArt

ISBN: 978-609-08-0172-7

Bibliographic information is available on the Lithuanian Integral Library Information System (LIBIS) portal

All rights reserved. No part of this book may be reproduced, stored in or introduced into a retrieval system, or transmitted, in any form, or by any means (electronic, mechanical, photocopying, recording, or otherwise) without the prior written permission of the author.

CONTENT GUIDANCE: This novel contains depictions of sexual assault. Please read with care.

To my one and only superhero, my mum, who, despite not being able to read the story, has never discouraged me and never stopped believing in it.

Believing in me.

Anthem
of the
Cursed Empire

PROLOGUE

I was dying again.

The first time I faced death, I escaped it with the help of a man who later became the person I hated the most. Now, I doubted whether I was lucky enough to survive twice.

This was it. The end.

He told me to hold on a little longer, his irritatingly calming tone cutting through the chaos. Despite the blood gushing from my stomach, I wanted to punch him. If it hadn't been for him, I wouldn't be here, bleeding in his arms with a heart he'd played with and shattered. If it hadn't been for him, I wouldn't be fighting for my life.

I tried to hold on, compelled by the need for vengeance against those who had wronged me over the past six months.

But my eyelids drooped, and the light faded away.

Part I

Notes of Family & Sacrifice

The new boots would be great for the autumn; if I could afford them, that was. I didn't have a pair of shoes that weren't scuffed for the season, but when I put my hand into my pocket and felt a few coins, the desire to buy them vanished into nothing.

I couldn't spend the remaining coins I'd earned from my last piano performance. What if I needed them for something more important than a pair of new shoes?

The vendor noticed the direction of my stare and lifted the boots off the stand. "Five shillings. It used to cost six. For a beautiful girl, I'll give you a discount." He flashed me a toothless smile, and I repressed my disgust.

"Maybe next time."

I turned and resumed my amble.

"Are you sure?" he called behind me. "There might be no next time!"

Pretending not to hear it, I didn't slow down my pace.

Today had started off terrible enough. I didn't have time to deal with lousy vendors or to walk through the market, but I did it anyway. It would be surprising if I left it without spending at least a coin.

Although the sun was a warm touch against my skin, it didn't comfort me as it once had. Last year, I would have smiled as summer was my favourite season and warm days like this felt like a blessing from the Gods. But now, the increasing heat only reminded me that my younger sister, Gen, would be offered at the Summer Solstice.

"Elynn!"

My heart jumped when two girls hooked their arms through mine. I wasn't surprised to find Alise on my left and Irisa on my right, as usual.

"Shall we go shopping for dresses?" Alise asked.

"Yes, dresses!" Irisa exclaimed in joy. "It's the perfect afternoon for it. I heard the shopkeeper received new models this morning."

"Yes, Elynn, let's go. You should have bought one a long time ago, and the wedding is just around the corner."

The wedding. The mere thought of it made my stomach churn.

"Not today." I managed a pleasant voice. "I have other plans."

Alise smoothed back her blonde hair. "Oh, come on. If you're always so busy, when are you planning to buy a gown? I'm sure Chase already has a suit. And a bride not having her outfit before her husband? Shameful."

Irisa nodded. "Very shameful."

I internally rolled my eyes.

Alise and Irisa might have been born with the same souls, but when it came to their looks, they were the opposites. Irisa possessed much darker features than Alise, who looked like she hadn't seen the sun in years. But it was the start of the summer, and the season was hot in the Mortal Region.

They were pretty girls, as long as it concerned their outside. Gen liked to call them two-faced nuisances, which wasn't polite, but it emphasised their true colours.

"Well?" prompted Alise.

Yesterday, I'd told my mum that I was going to look at wedding gowns today, perhaps even buy one. That was my plan until Kris mentioned that more books were coming from the city tomorrow. More books meant more chances to find a solution to save Gen from the annual offering to the Empire of Beasts.

Kris and I planned to go to the library together this morning, but when I woke up on the couch clutching my sketchbook like a teddy bear, I found no one in the cottage. Gen had already left for summer school, and Kristian hadn't even bothered waiting for me. Now, since I woke up in the afternoon, I had to hurry to the library before all the new books were gone, leaving me with no time for shopping.

"I'm sorry, but—"

The loud clatter of hoofs interrupted me, and a horse stopped nearby, grabbing everyone's attention. I strained my neck to see, but the bright sun behind the rider made it difficult to recognise them. It wasn't until they got off the horse that I finally saw who it was.

A man dressed in brown shook his head, causing his light brown hair to fall across his sun-kissed face.

"Good afternoon, Chase," the girls said in the same cloying tone, almost purring like kittens.

He didn't acknowledge them with anything more than a curt nod as his emerald eyes landed on me.

I gulped.

"Hello, Ely," he said.

It was strange to see my fiancé in town on a Friday, especially in the morning ... or afternoon. To me, it still felt like morning, as I had only been awake for less than an hour.

I forced a smile. "I thought you were going for a hunt?"

After all, he was hunting every day but somehow still found time for me in the evenings. Secretly, I prayed that he would get so busy that he would forget about his fiancée and leave me alone for at least one day. Alas, that never happened.

"You mentioned you'd be buying a gown today and needed money for it." He reached into his pocket and withdrew a pouch. "Here. Get the prettiest one, and make sure it undoes easily."

Ignoring the queasy feeling gripping my stomach, I accepted the pouch. "Thank you."

"Also, I'll be away for the weekend."

I stifled a cry of joy, feeling a wave of relief wash over me at the fantastic news.

"Where are you going?" I asked, feigning genuine interest in the reason for his absence.

"It's not important where I'm headed, Ely." A furrow formed between his bushy eyebrows. "All that matters is that I expect you to be well-dressed at my manor on Monday morning."

Again, my stomach twisted. I swallowed, smiling like the obedient soon-to-be wife I was. "Of course." I then inhaled surreptitiously, just to add another lie so he wouldn't be suspicious. "I'll be waiting for you, my darling."

His pleased smile confirmed that I had said exactly what he wanted to hear. Without saying goodbye, Chase turned to his horse and mounted it. He guided the horse towards the sun and rode off, drawing admiring stares from the townsfolk until they disappeared from sight.

I almost breathed a sigh of relief, feeling the tension ease from my muscles. But I refrained, as two more pairs of eyes continued to watch me.

"He's so handsome," Alise remarked. "You're so lucky, Elynn."

Irisa nodded enthusiastically. "So, so lucky."

Lucky.

Perhaps I was lucky. It was rare for a man to propose to a woman without the traditional wife skills. Cooking, gardening, and homemaking didn't come naturally to me, and despite multiple attempts, I failed at each.

I'm lucky. I had to keep reminding myself of that or else I might bail when the wedding day came. I ignored the persistent inner voice that I constantly pushed to the back of my mind, unable to bear hearing it say:

But Chase isn't the man you felt in your trance, Elynn.

II

I pretended I was feeling unwell, escaping Alise and Irisa. They watched me until I disappeared in the direction of my home. Little did they know, I opted for a different, longer route to the library, winding through the buildings.

The lovely lady librarian welcomed me with her usual contagious smile. It was impossible not to smile back.

I neared her desk. "Kristian told me more additions were arriving. Are they here already?"

"Yes," she said. "Do you want to see them all?"

I nodded.

"Come this way."

I followed her to the small table standing before one bookshelf with two unpacked cardboard boxes on it.

"All the new books are here. None have been shelved yet."

"Can I go through them?"

She chuckled. "Of course. I'll leave you to it and hope you find what you're looking for."

As I watched her go towards the desk, I wondered if she knew why I was so eager to go through the new books. She must be suspecting it, at least, as it wouldn't take a fool to figure out why a girl was entering a library once a week and inspecting all the bookshelves, only to leave empty-handed. Especially when everybody in town knew the names of the sixteen-year-olds who'd be offered this year, Gen's name included.

I opened the boxes and started the search. There were gardening and cooking books that I would never pick up, and then there were two novels. One was a romance; the other was a mystery. I picked the mystery one for my mum. However, there weren't any that could have an answer I'd been looking for all along.

Hiding my disappointment, I came back to the desk and put a mystery novel on it.

"Is this what you were looking for?" she asked.

I chuckled aloud without meaning to. If my problems revolved around finding a perfect mystery book, my life would be simple to live.

"It's for my mum."

"Oh." She smiled, but there was something sympathetic about her smile. "Well, I have to register it first, then you can have it. Meanwhile, you can explore. Maybe you'll find something you missed."

Doubtful, but I didn't object and disappeared between the bookshelves.

I wished there was something I'd missed, but there was no book with a loophole that could save Gen from the offering. I'd investigated every nook and cranny of this library many times, and my chances of finding something worthwhile remained practically non-existent.

And yet I stayed here, hopelessly expecting that a new book with the answer written in it would fall into my hands, even if that had never happened before.

Sometimes I wondered if the offering wasn't a deception. Teachers had said we offered minors because it was the sign of peace, an agreement between the Mortal Region and the Empire of Beasts that they'd reached years and years after the ending of the Hundred Years' War. But what if it was a lie? I'd done my investigation, finding no written proof of it being true.

I halted at my favourite spot and brushed my fingers down the book's spine of the most horrifying tales ever written. There was a time when Mum used to read them to me. I was just a child then—a careless child living its best irresponsible life. More than anything, I longed to come back to that life and be irresponsible for a few more years to lose this weight upon my shoulders, but it would always remain as nothing more than a desire.

I reached the end of the aisle, but it wasn't empty. A figure was engulfed by the shadows. Reading a book with the help of a faint light filtering through the shuttered window, being so absorbed in it that he didn't notice me.

I plucked out a book from his hands, and the boy flinched, round glasses sliding down his nose. He had to shift them with the push of his finger to get them back in place.

"Lynn," Kris whispered, respecting the silence in the library even if I'd stolen a book from him, and his tone wasn't exactly pleased. "Give it back."

"Why?" I gave a quick look at the pages he was reading and read something I wished I hadn't. "Is that why you left without me? To read this ... unseemly thing?"

He flushed, rosiness crawling from his cheeks up to his ears. "I ... I was not."

"Right." I plopped my bottom down beside him and offered him the book, which he snatched from me. "Rude."

"As if you didn't do the same thing."

I rolled my eyes. "I don't think reading a cliché romance novel will help you get a ..." I made a thoughtful face. "Never mind. Maybe it would help you get a girl, after all."

"Please stop."

"Don't worry. You're young. You'll find someone who would be worthy of you. So far—"

"All right, I get it, Lynn."

A reflective smile touched the corner of my lips before I ruffled his neatly brushed brown hair.

He began fixing it right away, shooting me an annoyed look. "What's the matter with you today?"

I shrugged, resting my head against the wall while Kris adjusted his reading glasses once again. We couldn't afford the ones that would be a perfect fit for him. Luckily, these had been on discount since there was a little crack on the side.

"Oh, um ..." he began. "Don't tell Mum what I'm about to tell you, but Gen didn't go to summer school this morning."

I shut my eyes for a moment and let out a frustrated sigh before reopening them. "Where did she go now?"

"Didn't tell me."

Gen had become more and more distant these days. Uncharacteristically quiet, laughing less than usual, just like making her sarcastic puns. None of us talked about the forthcoming event in two weeks, but we were all aware of it. Ignoring it helped avoid the despair it'd bring upon us until we had no choice but to face it.

"We should head home." I rose and extended my hand to help Kris up. "Mum must be waiting for us with lunch."

Acting like a tough man, Kris ignored my hand and sprang to his feet by himself. I playfully rolled my eyes, pulling my hand away. Once he returned the book back to its place, we stopped by the librarian's desk. She gave me the book while Kris was taking off his glasses. We chirped our goodbyes to her before leaving.

Shouts of the vendors promoting their goods and people's chatters burst through as soon as we stepped outside. A group of giggling kids ran past us with the old lady behind them shouting to give her back her apple.

Now the market was buzzing with activity. Although we were strolling behind market stalls to avoid the persistent vendors, some of their helpers still managed to disturb us. Every time one introduced their product, Kristian shyly lowered his head while I waved them away, rejecting their offer, not even minding hearing half of it.

"How is the search for sorcerers going so far?" Kris inquired. His hands were in the pockets of his brown tweed trousers, and his shoulders were hunched as if he aimed to shrink and shrink until he disappeared.

During my determined year-lasting search, I was bound to discover something that could be Gen's salvation, like powerful sorceresses who had once existed in our region. I'd assumed some of them might still be alive, and when I found them, they could help me rescue Gen from the Summer Solstice offering. But I did a thorough investigation, questioned townies about them, and they all declared their eyes had never beheld them in their lives.

"I think they're dead," I said. "Or could be hiding somewhere for some reason."

"Have you tried to go to the pledgers' office and talk to them?"

Despite hosting the offering in the town hall every Summer Solstice and sending information about every youngest sixteen-year-old of the family to the Empire of Beasts three months before the day, I was surprised to learn pledgers didn't know much.

"Yes. They seemed like genuine people, but they couldn't help me when hardly anything depended on them. They could forge the lists, but they don't want to risk morphs finding out it is a lie and come here and slaughter us all."

Townies nearby fell into silence, casting us wary glances at the mention of shapeshifters.

Hardly ever could one hear someone talking about morphs. It wasn't forbidden, but it was like an unwritten rule not to discuss them in public, since mentioning them made people apprehensive. Unlike many, I didn't fear them, even if I should. My sister was going to be offered to the world teeming with them in a mere fortnight and nobody knew what happened to an offered kid there. But based on the tales featuring morphs, we were inclined to believe the worst.

The way Kris strained under townies' scrutiny caused me to lower my voice. "I'm thinking about travelling to the city's library. The book assortment is wider there. Perhaps I'll find something that might be helpful."

"How are you planning to get there? We don't have any transport, and the city is miles away."

"I'm planning to borrow one of Chase's horses."

Kris nodded without catching the strain in my voice. And I was glad Kris was the only one who didn't care about my engagement, or he did but didn't show it. He didn't have to know that Chase would never willingly hand his horse over with nothing in return. Not even to his soon-to-be wife.

As soon as we reached the forest and took a turn to the right, entering the footpath leading to our home, Kristian relaxed. We were safe from the vendors' helpers' harassment at last.

"You know why I'm not trying to find anything to help Gen?" he asked after a while.

"Because you secretly hate that she's smarter than you?"

His pointed look spoke volumes.

I laughed, nudging his arm with my elbow. "I'm joking," I said, and his eyes narrowed into slits. "Go on. Tell me why you're not trying to help her."

He sighed, letting go of his firm expression. "Because she's been preparing for it ever since she learned about the risk of her being the one to go. Have you forgotten her plan already?"

"Once she gets through the portal, she flees back home?" I remembered laughing at the nonsense of Gen's plan I'd heard a year ago, taking it as a joke rather than a plan based on reason. "We don't have a map of the empire, and even if we did, nobody has taught us how to navigate with it. Even if she somehow magically found a way home, do you think she wouldn't be killed as soon as she steps out of the portal? We don't know what morphs are capable of, and they're immortal. Anything can be lurking in their minds. She has no chances of surviving there."

"I wouldn't underestimate her. She can pull all kinds of surprises."

"She's too young to be on her own. She still needs someone to guide her. I'm not giving up."

"I know," he said with a sigh. "Mum said you'd fight until your last breath to keep us safe and lacking nothing. You are a hero, as she says."

I smiled faintly. "I'm not a hero."

Tweeting birds snatched the silence settled between us, and in approximately twenty minutes of walking, the wooden house appeared behind the trees' gaps. Our cottage. My home.

I *could* call it my home or admit to myself that sharing it with three people with no personal space had been getting on my nerves. I tried to make peace with living in a cramped room with my siblings, reserving the desire for a larger place to reside in for another life. However, Chase had a manor where he scarcely showed up. Perhaps marrying him had a bright side for me, after all.

Kris pulled open the door, and once we stepped inside the claustrophobic corridor, Mum's voice rang from inside the kitchen. "Who's there? If it's not my pesky kids, I will not be afraid to use a pan!"

I appreciated her honesty. *Sometimes.* And this was not one of those times.

"Rude!" I shouted back.

Her harmonic sound of laughter came afterwards.

As soon as Kris kicked off his shoes, he darted into our bedroom, leaving his footwear thrown on the floor. Sighing, I placed them neatly beside the entrance along with mine.

Hiding the book behind my back, I headed to the kitchen, where my mother was already preparing lunch, as expected. The divine smell tickled my nostrils, and my tummy growled in response to the tasty food's presence in the room. She was chopping some carrots, her chocolate brown hair tied into a bun to prevent it from falling into the food.

She glanced at me over her shoulder and smiled. "How was your day, honey?"

"Decent just as any other day." I brought the book from behind my back. "I got you a mystery novel." I put it on the counter. "Fresh from the city."

"What is it about?"

I shrugged, causing Mum to huff out a laugh and shake her head. I slid into one of the wooden chairs at the square table, glancing at the bee crawling on the window in a futile attempt to escape.

Mum raised the lid and pushed the diced carrots into the pot. The sight of burnt wallpaper above the stove sent a pang of guilt through my chest. Every time I saw it, I felt guilty, albeit it was over a year since the incident.

Once, when I'd attempted to cook for the family, a sudden burst of fire flared up, putting the kitchen and the entire house in danger. Thank Gods above, Gen was nearby to put the fire out as I'd panicked. I hadn't dared to touch a stove ever since. If it hadn't been for my sister, we wouldn't even have a place to live anymore.

I didn't notice that Mum was observing me this whole time while stirring whatever was in the pot. Faint wrinkles had newly appeared on her forehead, as if she knew where my thoughts had wandered too, but she didn't speak about it. She never did. She wasn't even angry when she'd come back home from the market, only to find one of her favourite pots damaged and a patch of her dainty wallpaper gone. But the fleeting shadow of sadness that had crossed her face didn't elude me, and it was worse than getting yelled at.

"Did you buy a dress?" she asked.

"No."

"Good."

Her declaration puzzled me. "Good?"

"We need to have a serious talk, my honeybee."

"How many times do I have to ask you not to call me honeybee?" I whined.

"But it's adorable." She gave me an appraising look-over. "Suits you well, too."

"Am I that fat?"

She huffed out a laugh. "Oh, please! But you could gain some weight. Mostly bones, hardly any meat."

I rolled my eyes.

She placed a lid on the pot and approached the table where she took a seat before me. As she clasped her hands on the table, she raised her head; her look was grave.

I squirmed in the chair.

She parted her lips, ready to speak, but before she could, I blurted out, "Gen didn't go to summer school today."

She frowned. "I'm thankful for you telling me this, but you're not deflecting away from the topic, Elynn."

"Can we discuss it later? I'm famished."

"No, you've been avoiding the talk about your wedding long enough," she said steely. "Now tell me, what do you think you're doing by marrying a man you don't love?"

"Food smells amazing, Mum. What—"

"Elynn."

I sighed, looking down.

"If you don't love him, why bother sacrificing the rest of your life for him?"

I forced a short laugh. "You've got it all wrong, Mum." I managed to raise my eyes at her. "I do l-l-*loooove* him."

But the words had come out wrong from my mouth. They even carried a bitter aftertaste.

She, of course, didn't believe me, not after that unforeseen stutter. "Don't sacrifice your happiness for us, Elynn. We don't need his fortune. We're doing just fine. I get orders to sew clothes from townies once a week. They give me a fair amount of money for them. Kristian is clever enough to move into the city and find a well-paid job. And you ... you are invited to play the piano at their parties sometimes. Together, we'll survive, so you don't need to marry someone you don't love, honey."

Mum, Kris, and I. No mention of Gen. As if she'd already accepted that Gen would be gone soon. But I still had time to prevent it.

"I'm sorry for being the one to tell you this, but you're getting old, Mother." She scoffed at my statement, a half-smile touching her lips. "You know you won't be able to sew clothes for anybody in this town, eventually. My playing isn't popular. I get requests to play in parties like three times per year—"

"Last year you played five times."

Ignoring her, I went on. "Then Kristian, no matter how smart he can be, he might not find himself in the government's heart. It didn't work out well for Dad, now did it?"

From the altered look in Mum's eyes, I registered what words had left me. How easily they had come out of my mouth with no conscious thought that I should have shut it once the topic had switched to her husband. My deceased dad.

She dropped her stare, but I'd already seen the heart-breaking look in her eyes: longing and boundless sorrow.

My father used to fish outside the Mortal Region and sell his catches in town to maintain us. Many people were willing to purchase his fish as he was not only trustworthy but communicative and convincing. He used to make a great businessman. But one day, when he left for his daily fishing, he didn't come back.

We'd waited. A day, two had passed. A week, but he'd never returned. He was gone along with his boat.

"Sometimes I dream about him," she admitted quietly.

I looked down at my hands, feeling uncomfortable.

"That he's alive, and ... and for a moment, I keep forgetting that he isn't in that ... state. That when I'd wake up, he'd be next to me ..." She trailed off. At least she didn't weep, but her low, barely audible voice told me she tried her best to avoid it.

She dragged in a shaky breath. "But he never is."

I pursed my lips.

Dad's death had hit each one of us differently. Mum had fallen into a deep depression, seeing no purpose in getting out of bed anymore. Kris had sealed himself in the studies, coming back home late from the library. Gen had started using baking as her coping mechanism while I'd worried about surviving, since our primary money provider wasn't with us anymore, whereas the other was unavailable. But then I'd tasted Gen's baked goods.

They were so delicious that an idea had struck me. I'd advised her to sell them in the market. At first, she was reluctant, thinking nobody would buy them, but as I secretly opened the market, it didn't take long to attract townies. They became obsessed with her creations, and soon requests were sent to us to bake cakes or other goods for their events.

This way we survived without our mum. It also helped Mum to battle her grief, for once she learned we had something to eat because of Gen, a sense of guilt must have surfaced because the next day, she was out of her bed. Mum compelled Gen to stop accepting the orders since she missed one year of school to keep us fed.

Then my time came to contribute to the family's welfare. I wasn't as gifted as Gen with baking skills, and not everyone in town could splurge on music, but I had my beauty I could make use of, which I had.

When Chase proposed to me in the stables, I didn't waver. He had enough money to build a better future for my family. It wasn't a loss of my life. It didn't matter whether butterflies fluttered or my heart skipped a beat when I was around him or not. It didn't matter, as long as my family was safe and maintained.

"You can't bail on your education like that!" Mum yelled from within the kitchen.

"What's the point?" Gen's voice came next. "I'm not going to be here in two weeks anyway. So, what's the point of getting an education if I'm going to die?"

"You are not going to die."

"How can you know that?"

"Elynn is—"

"Oh, Gods, seriously? Elynn is looking for a needle in a haystack. If there was some way to avoid this, she would have found a solution months ago. And if I get murdered, death won't care if someone dies with an education certificate or not."

"Don't you dare walk away from me, Genette."

The door flung open, and my sister stormed inside, shoving the door with such force that the walls shook slightly. Kris barely raised his eyes from his book, but other than that, he showed no reaction to Gen's outburst.

I'd stopped sketching once the argument had initiated.

Gen raised her hands near her head, close to clenching them while groaning, "Ugh."

Surprisingly, our mother didn't follow Gen. Perhaps she'd understood what Gen had said was true. Death wouldn't care about an education certificate to welcome her to its claws.

Gen fell prone on her bed, burying her face in the pillow.

I parted my lips to say something, but my voice failed me. I wasn't sure what words could put her at ease, so I resumed shadowing a gown with an orange crayon to distract myself, but after a while, I sensed her steel-blue gaze on me.

Unable to ignore Gen for long, I met her sulky face. I wondered whether she would throw her anger at me. If she did, I would handle it. It wouldn't be the first or the last time.

But she remained silent. A moment later, she looked at Kris. She stared at him for a while, but he either ignored her or didn't notice. Then she released a loud sigh, looked down at the bedsheet, and started to pick at it.

"Just say it," I said. She didn't respond. "Say what's on your mind," I prodded.

"Nothing."

"You're lying."

"You don't say."

I patiently waited for her to open up, but Gen didn't utter another word. I put the sketching book beside me and left the bed. I approached hers, which was only one step away, and perched on the edge. As I clasped my hands together, I turned my head to her. "You are not getting offered in two weeks."

She huffed, not buying my words.

"I'm serious, Gen," I said. "You are not getting offered."

"Did you find anything?" Her eyebrows rose. "A solution? A way to avoid it?"

It was a challenge to look her in the eye and say, "No."

She scoffed.

"But I'm working on it."

"You've been working on it for an entire year, Lynn!" She threw up her hands. "And what did you find? Bloody nothing!"

"Nothing *yet.*"

"Why are you so eager to find a way?" Her watery eyes were almost burning. "Why don't you focus on yourself, on the people you surround yourself with?"

"We're not talking about me now. We're talking about you."

"I'm not a child. I can take care of myself."

"Actually," Kris chimed in, pushing the glasses up on his nose, "sixteen-year-olds are still regarded as children."

Gen cast our brother a murderous look. "Oh, shut up. Nobody asked for your opinion."

Kris focused back on the book, smiling smugly.

"Child or not, you're not going anywhere close to that portal." Gen returned her gaze to me. "And it's the end of this conversation."

She didn't say anything back, to my astonishment. Gen could be as stubborn as a mule and quarrel all day long until she reached her win. Perhaps she was worn out of the fight with Mum and considering everything else that was going on ...

"Do you know that those two-faced nuisances are gossiping about you?" she inquired after a short period of quiet.

"Yes."

"Are you aware of what they're saying about you, though?"

"No," I responded. "But you're not telling me. I'd rather not know."

Whatever lies Alise and Irisa were spreading, there were far more essential matters I had to deal with. Perhaps a part of me prodded me into learning what they were gossiping about, but my mind demanded that I shouldn't.

I had to show strength and bravery. If not for myself, then for the sake of my sister.

Only for a little longer.

"I know the market that sells poison," she revealed. "Maybe I can slip some into their morning tea."

I let out a laugh.

"Or I can grab a knife," Kris joined in. "Attack them in the alley. I saw Alise leaving the bar late at night once."

My eyes widened. "You two are insane."

Kris grinned.

"As Dad used to say ..." Gen began.

"When someone hurts a family member, the family pays back," we recited childishly in unison. "And no questions asked."

Quiet, unbelievable chuckles came from us, and a thoughtful silence followed. After a while, I took Gen's hand in mine. "I'll find a solution." I looked her in the eye. "I always do."

I'd found a way to cheat on my tests, how to avoid eating broccoli without Mum's awareness, how to steal pastries from the bakery without getting caught ... And Gen was conscious of all of it.

"This is different, Lynn."

I smirked. "That's why it is more fun now. It's dangerous. More exciting."

"I swear if Elynn finds a solution to this," Kris said, "I'm moving to the city and getting into the government."

"You truly think I won't succeed?" I asked playfully.

"Obviously," Gen confirmed for both of them.

"Very well, then." I jerked my chin up, unable to resist a grin. "Watch me because I'm not giving up."

A beam of sunlight streamed through the window, jolting me awake with the realization that it was Monday. I'd spent the weekend assisting Mum in sewing clothes for the townsfolk, but now, anxiety gripped me as I approached Chase's manor.

When I went inside, he wasn't here. I wasn't relieved. He would be here eventually, and in the meantime, I admired paintings on the walls as though I hadn't seen them already. But it didn't take Chase long to show up.

"Here you are."

I put on a smile before I turned to him, finding him shirtless and adorned with weapons. "Here I am." I took in his outfit. "Were you on a hunting spree?"

He took a step closer. "I was."

I acknowledged his bare, clean hands. "I suppose hunting didn't go well?"

"It didn't," he said half-heartedly and reduced the remaining distance between us by putting his hands on my hips and pulling me closer to his half-naked body. "It's your fault I came empty-handed, Ely."

"How is it my fault?"

His eyes sparkled. The bile rose in my throat while my

stomach churned with nausea.

"I couldn't stop thinking about you. You were always on my mind, and I couldn't focus for two days." Chase leaned closer to my ear, and his tongue touched my earlobe. Disgust filtered through me, but I fought back an impulse to shrink back. "Do you want to know what I was thinking about?"

Absolutely not.

"Maybe."

His lips brushed against the skin below my ear. My body remained rigid. But I had to react or else he would know something was—

Oh, who was I trying to fool? Even if he realised something was wrong, he would ignore it. It was his forte to turn a blind eye to everything that was happening around him.

"I thought"—he spun me around. His hands were on my hips as he pushed me against the wall, lips close to my ear—"how pretty you would look like if I—"

I turned my head to look at the end of the corridor where the charcoal-black door was, almost knocking his face, but I didn't, to my disappointment. "What is behind that door?"

Ever since the first time I had stepped into his manor and seen the mysterious door, I'd been speculating on what was behind it. When I was alone, I attempted to get inside, but it was always locked. Whatever was in there, it must be of great value to consider locking it.

"Nothing you should concern your pretty head with." His strong hands went lower until they rested on the back of my thighs. "Now, where was I?"

"Chase," I crooned. "what's in there?" I batted my eyelashes.

"Nothing. To. Bother. Yourself. With."

My hair bristled at his rough tone. I shouldn't have asked him. I shouldn't have—

"If you show me ..." I turned to him and dragged my finger down his chest in a slow, seductive way while biting my bottom lip. He was frowning, but his breathing heaved. My seduction was working like a charm. "I'll do anything you wish."

The lines in his face softened. "Anything?"

I leaned in and whispered, "Anything."

I earned a satisfied smile from him.

He removed his hands from my legs, and when he pulled away, suddenly, I was able to breathe. I could only hope my offered services wouldn't be for nought, and whatever was behind the door was something noteworthy.

Chase walked in front of me. My heart was pounding as we approached the door. My curiosity had made me sell my dignity, but perhaps it was all for the better.

He fished out a key from the back of his pocket. Of course, I should have been wiser. I could have borrowed the key when he was asleep instead of humiliating myself. But what had been done was done. There was no going back now.

Chase inserted the key in the padlock and twisted it. "There is nothing interesting to see for a woman's eye," he muttered, and the padlock clicked open. "I don't get why you are so eager to see what's in there."

I didn't respond, and he opened the door, letting the faint light pour in. We stepped inside, and as Chase closed the door behind me, another wave of fright rippled across my already bedecked with gooseflesh skin.

I wasn't sure what I'd anticipated seeing. Perhaps something sick that would make me throw up. But it wasn't anything close to it. Crossbows, swords, and various other weapons, along with shields and armour, adorned the shelves, filling me with a strong sense of regret.

I questioned why an animal hunter would need to have so many weapons and outfits but came up with the theory that it must have been a family collection passed down through generations. And now Chase was their possessor, since his parents weren't alive, whereas his youngest sibling had already been offered a long time ago.

I shifted closer to the shelf with swords in different sizes and materials, but only the golden one snagged my attention the most. But the more I stared at it, the more my heart rate grew, the more I was paralyzed, the more I felt dread.

"This is Goldy," Chase announced, and I nearly jumped out of my skin. I'd failed to notice him standing so close to me.

He hefted a sword by its hilt. I stepped back, for the first time obeying my instincts to stay away from the sword and the man holding it. "It's about two centuries old."

My eyes never left the shiny sword. Its gigantic and fascinating blade reflected my face, as if warning me I could be its next victim.

"That's a long time."

My voice hadn't come out brittle. I applauded myself in my mind. However, I couldn't say the same about my quivering fingers, which I had covered behind my back.

He nodded. "It is." His forefinger brushed down the blade. My blood ran cold, but I didn't wrap my hands around myself to quell the shivers. "It's used for killing morphs."

I blinked twice. Three times. Chase's eyes moved from the sword to me, a hunter's smile playing on his thin lips.

I had to collect myself or else I might faint.

"I thought they were immortal."

He laughed. What was so amusing, I couldn't fathom. "Morphs are stronger than us. They have powers humans could never dream of. It's a fable that morphs are immortals. They have a life span as we do, but they live longer than us, for about a thousand years unless someone thrusts the golden weapon into their heart and they"—he swung the sword in the air with an attempt of showing off, and I backed away more—"dead."

With another step back, my back hit something. I turned my head and faced the other shelf loaded with more golden weapons, such as knives, hatchets, daggers, and a collection of arrows. My inner voice was screaming at me to flee, but I stood stock-still.

"W-why do you have so many weapons that could kill a morph?" I turned my head to him, who had finished flaunting his swordplay.

He laughed, oblivious to the subtle change in my tone or the pallor that must have painted my face.

"Aren't you too curious, Ely?" He put the sword back in its place. But I still felt tense, no matter if the fatal weapon wasn't in the hunter's hands anymore. It was still here, threatening to hurt me, potentially *kill* me.

But there was another one that caught my interest, too. Behind Chase was hanging a longer and sharper sword of the colour of silver on the dull grey wall.

"Is that sword used for killing morphs as well?"

I couldn't compare the feelings that were simmering within me when I'd seen Goldy to the ones stimulated by this sword. As intimidating as Goldy as it was, the silver sword affected me differently. As if some child within my head cowered into the ball and shuddered. I couldn't understand why my blood curdled and why my body tensed at the sight of those specific swords but not at the other ones in the armoury.

He followed my stare. "That?" He turned and slid closer to the wall. "It's for dragons."

Dragons. All I knew about them was from the bedtime stories Mum used to read to me.

In tales, dragons were depicted as fiends that were a danger to other living kinds. Their variety was boundless, but only the most powerful ones breathed lethal fire and could set the world on fire whenever they desired. However, dragons hadn't been seen for a long time, which implied they weren't among the living anymore. If it was true, and they were all gone, it was better for the world.

"What is it made of? Aren't gold weapons used to kill a dragon?"

"Gold doesn't kill dragons, Ely," he said in a rather patronising tone, but I was too interested in learning more about dragons to pick up on his speaking manner. "Only weapons covered in platinum do. It isn't as common as gold, though."

"But it doesn't matter because dragons don't exist anymore, right?"

Chase's doubtful expression didn't elude my eyes.

"You believe dragons are still alive."

"Enchanters obliterated them about ten years ago. They are all dead." But he seemed to convince himself more than me. "Even if some of them could still be alive, dragons aren't the worst creatures a human could cross his path with."

Chase knew quite a lot about other species, which was unlikely for any human, and it got me doubting his claimed profession. I wouldn't be surprised if he turned out to hunt other species and not just for the fun of it.

"And who is far worse than morphs or enchanters?"

"Half-breeds." His voice was scarcely audible. "Creatures who are a mix of both kinds. They are the ones any creature would fear the most in this world."

I was hearing about half-breeds for the first time. The possibility of someone existing who had morphs' powers to shapeshift and enchanters' powers to enchant and do only the Gods knew what else didn't sound appealing to me.

"How are enchanters killed?" I asked him, pushing the thoughts of half-breeds temporarily away.

"With iron."

"And what about half-breeds?"

An amusing smile pulled the corner of his mouth. "I don't think anybody apart from the Gods knows an answer to this question, Ely."

I surveyed the armoury yet again, rummaging through my head in search of more questions to avoid Chase as long as I could, but he had already approached me. His hands were on me, but before he leaned in to kiss me, I spoke. "There's something I have to ask you."

"Questions later," he said, leaning closer. "Now, fun."

But I pressed my finger to his lips before they could reach my own. "I'll be quick. I promise."

The ominous shadow entering his eyes made my heartbeat quicken again.

"What is it?" His tone was just as intimidating as his stare. I tried to swallow the fright, fend it off to ask what I must.

"Can I borrow your horse for a few days?"

His eyes narrowed into slits. "What for?"

"For a trip to—"

"No."

I stared at him, but ignoring my mad heartbeat yet again, I tried. "Please. I would do anything."

"You were already going to do whatever I pleased before I showed you this room, Ely."

"Please, I—"

"No, Ely," he almost growled, his hands tightening on my hips. "Now hush your mouth. I don't want another sound escaping your throat if it doesn't involve pleasure."

He was close to smashing his disgusting lips against mine when I interrupted him again. "I'll do it."

He winced. "Do what?"

"You know what."

Chase's confused stare was buried in mine until his eyes lit and his mouth curved into an expectant smile. "Really?"

"Yes, if you lend me your horse for a few days."

His smile broadened. I forced myself to smile, too.

"I'll lend you a horse, Ely." He planted a kiss on the corner of my lips and then whispered, "But if you don't give me a boy, consider your family homeless, my love."

Mum was reporting to me gossip she had heard in the town's market today. I found it hard to listen to her when I was drowning in my heart-aching thoughts while stirring a mixture in the bowl.

I was trying to be useful by helping her out in the kitchen. I *needed* to be useful for something since I'd been becoming more and more disappointed in myself lately. What was I even good for? I could only thank the good genes because, apart from my beauty, I had nothing.

Squeezing the spoon tight, I glowered at the stirring mixture as if attempting to burn it. The poor dough had to put up with all my emotions I kept locked inside me under a gazillion locks.

"Honey," Mum said, bringing me back to reality. I looked over my shoulder. She was standing on her tiptoes, trying to reach for a bottle filled with dark liquid. "Could you help your old mother?"

With a deep sigh, I paused my work. "You're not old." I approached her. Then I raised my hand and reached for the bottle with no effort. "Just don't put products where you can't reach them."

As I extended a bottle to her, I met her face, which had turned incredulously pale.

"Mum?"

Before I could trace what was happening, she grasped my wrist and pulled the sleeve up to my elbow. I attempted to yank my hand from her grip, but she held it with an impressive strength.

Her eyes were fixed on the blue and purple marks marring my bronze skin.

I didn't react or say anything.

Then she looked up at me, puzzled and beyond concerned.

I playfully rolled my eyes. "It must have appeared after I hit the edge of the piano." I winced at the bruise. "Harder than I thought."

I met her unbending stare and held it while ignoring my conscience.

"Why are you lying to me?" Her voice was as mild as a caressing summer breeze and as brittle as a fallen thin branch.

She didn't believe my lie. She never did. My mother could read her children as easily as tales. And it got me wondering if I'd also be able to make out what was wrong with my future progeny as well.

But I didn't want to think about it. Not this way. Not ever.

"I'm not lying," I mustered a low but a certain reply.

She released my forearm and pulled away, shaking her head. "You are not marrying that man."

"What?" I frowned. "No, Chase didn't do it," I hastened to say. "I hurt myself by accident. I swear."

But she kept shaking her head, dodging all my words, refusing to believe my lies.

She stepped towards me, close enough to bring my face into her warm and rough hands. "My dear, dear honeybee, you are worth so, so much more than him. Don't submit yourself to us. Life shouldn't be suffocating you but the opposite. You should breathe through it. You should swim through it. You should be happy."

"Mum, he's not—"

"Oh, cut the crap," she said fiercely, shocking me. It was, perhaps, the first time I'd heard my dearest mother using a dirty word. "You. Are. Not. Marrying. Him." Her steely voice sent shivers skidding down my spine. "You deserve better. A man who would never say a bad word about you, who would never, *never* lay a hand on you, who would treat you like a goddess. Mark my words, Elynn."

Tears were already leaking through, and I pressed my quivering lips together.

"You only live once. Don't waste your time on people who don't deserve it," she continued. "You're only nineteen, Elynn. There's a whole world ahead of you. Don't waste it on men like your arsehole fiancé or for saving your family. Live. Just live for yourself, for heavens' sake."

I fought back the urge to sob, refusing to falter before her, determined not to show weakness because I must stay strong and—

"Elynn, promise me you'll break off the engagement and follow your dreams, live the life you want to live."

But my lips didn't part. I couldn't make a promise. At least, not from the bottom of my heart, as it would be yet another drop of a lie in the lake of thousands.

"Elynn." With her thumbs, she brushed the tears off my cheeks. "Promise me."

It was hard to lie to her, to my own mother. But I tried to put all my effort into my lying skills and do my best to fool her so she'd be relieved.

"I promise."

She studied me, seeking a lie. I kept my face straight and did not avert my gaze.

Eventually, she sighed as if a heavy rock had slid off her chest and brought me into a tender, tight embrace. I buried my face in her shoulder, wishing for someone else to hold me so I could show my weakness and succumb to sobs.

But I did not have that someone.

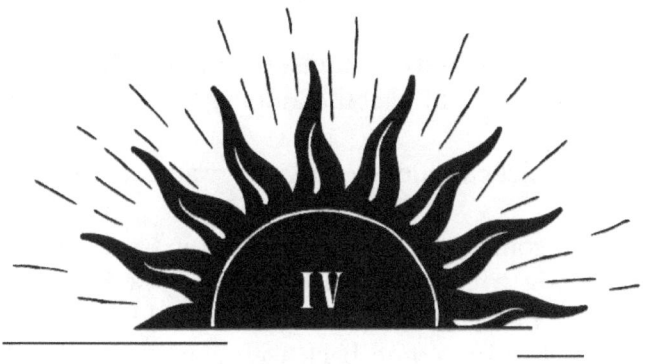

I'd been going through the city's library books for four days. Even if the assortment here was broader, like I'd predicted, I found nothing.

The coins Chase had given me were running low. The accommodation and food in the city couldn't have been priced higher. And yet, on the fifth day of my arrival, I continued to wander through the same library like a desperate beggar in search of something edible. Repeatedly going through the shelves, hoping there was something important I missed.

Or maybe I didn't try hard enough. Maybe I should have travelled to the Empire of Beasts and begged whoever ruled the empire to spare my sister from whatever awaited her. But it would have been lunacy. If I'd travelled there, I wouldn't have survived a day in their world.

No human could survive. And my sister was going to die there or be used for Gods knew what.

What if I smuggled my family somewhere overseas? It wasn't like it was something new. People smuggled their children who were about to be offered. They also sent away their newborns who had been born after they had already offered their youngest that turned sixteen. They feared morphs would come after them, too.

Nobody knew why morphs were so specific with the offering. And I doubted if someone who didn't go through the portal ever would.

But paying somebody to transport my family... it would be costly, and where would I get the money? Smuggling them wasn't feasible.

I almost kicked the bookshelf, wanting to scream in frustration.

How was I going to face Gen once I came back? She knew the purpose of my trip. She might not ask how it went, as she questioned none of my research. But I could tell she still had faith. And if I didn't come back with something, the flame of hope still burning in her would go out.

There was still something I hoped I wouldn't have to do, but I'd officially run out of possibilities ... and hope.

I'd gotten wind of people selling their souls in exchange for their deepest, darkest desires to come true. I could sell my soul to save my sister. But first, I needed to learn how to make the Gods below listen to me.

I found myself in the aisle of books about Gods. In a matter of minutes, I held the book about the merciless Gods ruling below. I opened it and sought the keyword of the soul until the sound of *psst* interrupted me.

I let it pass my ears, but then another one followed.

I raised my head from the book and looked to my left. Right at the end of the bookshelf, a small head was poking from behind it. A short, dark-haired boy.

"Come," he whispered, beckoning me closer.

I hesitated, checking around myself as I expected to spot his parents nearby, but I didn't detect or hear anything. Giving in, I returned the book and followed him.

I didn't focus on where we were heading, as my full attention was pinned on the boy. His trousers and tunic were tattered and so filthy that it was impossible to tell their original colour. His bare feet were muddy, but as he moved, he left no trace of dirt behind him.

"Who are you?" I inquired silently, with a tinge of wariness.

He halted and turned to me. His face was as white as bone. And his neck ... his neck was sliced, smeared with blood.

"Your neck ..."

He looked down at his bleeding neck. But it wasn't bleeding. No blood was seeping from the wound. It was as if it was stuck or ... painted. A deceiving image. "Oh, this is nothing."

"It isn't nothing. We should head to the infirmary, we—"

The realisation hit me like a bolt of lightning.

The boy wasn't a boy. Not quite. He used to be a boy, but he had died. It was his spirit I'd followed.

It was the first time I'd encountered a spirit. Teachers had informed me they only showed up two days prior to the Summer and Winter Solstice. But what baffled me was that it was precisely two days, not five like it was now, unless teachers had made a mistake and spirits emerged whenever they liked.

The boy's spirit was no older than ten, and I couldn't help but wonder what kind of monster would kill the kid by slashing his neck this cruelly.

"You're a spirit, right?" I inquired, only to make sure.

The boy nodded his head, smiling widely. "Right in the bull's ... eye." His smile fell quickly, and he cast his eyes down, starting to fiddle with his fingers. "You're the first one from the living to see me in forty years."

"How old are you?"

"Ten," he answered. "Well, I died at ten," he amended with a smile, but it soon faded as though he'd realised something.

"Who cut your throat?"

Only after such an inquiry had left my mouth, I acknowledged how insensitive it'd sounded. I didn't understand how I had the nerve to be curious. I might hurt the soul talking about his death, but the boy lifted his head, brown eyes flickering instead of being pricked by my blunt question. Perhaps the boy was excited that somebody from the living was talking to him. He'd mentioned that nobody had seen him for four decades. He was alone, roving as a spirit wherever spirits resided. Perhaps someone talking to him, even if the topic was about his own death, brought a beam of joy to the boy's ghostlike heart.

"I ..." He pursed his lips, eyes afar as if thinking. "I don't know. I'd been sleeping when it all just ... went black."

"Did you feel any pain?"

He grimaced. "No."

My heart twinged for the boy—for dying this young. At least his death was painless, but that didn't compensate for the fact that he would never experience all the ups and downs of a human's life.

At last, I tore my gaze off the boy to observe my surroundings.

I'd inspected every part of the library, but I couldn't recall being here before. I'd never stumbled upon it, but how could it be possible?

The shelves were filled with old tomes I'd never seen before. I took one out of the shelf carefully. The book's pages were dusty, and I was tentative to touch them, for they seemed like they could crumble into dust at the merest brush of my hand. Gingerly, I opened the random page of the book. The font was old, written in the ancient hand.

"What is this place?" I asked.

His eyebrows drew together. "A library?"

I smiled softly. "I'm aware it's a library, but as long as I've been here, I haven't seen this aisle before. I'm sure it doesn't belong to the library."

He frowned. "Yes, it does."

"No, it doesn't."

"But it does."

"It doesn't."

The boy slapped his forehead with his palm and dragged it down his face. With a sigh, he raised his head and said in a precise, serene manner, "It's a part of the library, but only those who search can see it."

I raised my eyebrows in incredulity.

The boy smiled. "You've been searching for an answer for over a year. My ancestors were kind enough to give it to you."

I didn't question how he was aware of my research. He was a spirit. I supposed spirits had nothing else better to do than to pry into the lives of the living. "If you're talking about my research on how to save my sister, then you're wrong. I don't have an answer."

The spirit's smile turned smug. "Don't you?"

I looked at the ancient book in my hands. "I don't ..." But

when I raised my eyes, the boy wasn't here anymore. He had vanished.

I concentrated back on the book, a smile creeping across my face.

Could this spirit be the key to my sister's salvation?

As the answer might be right in front of me.

When I was back home, it took me a few days to prepare everything: make a plan, gather supplies, and invent reasons to avoid Chase's repellent company.

He invited me to his manor to practise fencing, but I avoided it by offering him a half-truth, claiming I needed to spend the remaining time with my sister. His frown indicated displeasure, but he let it go, sparing me from his lessons.

Alise and Irisa persisted in urging me to shop for a wedding gown, but I avoided them as well. If my plan succeeded, I wouldn't need excuses to avoid people I disliked.

The following week, I was ready with all the supplies but not emotionally. However, the night before the Summer Solstice, I was close to being psyched up. The most challenging task I'd saved for last: priming my mum. Before doing so, I lingered in the living room where the rest of my family was and played the piano. For one last time, if my precarious plan was going to succeed.

Mum, Gen, and Kris were silent as my fingers danced through the piano's keys. I closed my eyes, allowing the music to send me to a peaceful world and fill not only the room with caressing tunes but my soul.

For the first time in my life, it didn't feel as if my chest was sinking or that my mind disagreed with everything I forced it to take as a given. Perhaps this was how it should be. Perhaps I had found my true path.

Once I finished playing, I caught the whimpers coming from Mum. She had Gen engulfed in her arms, whispering soothing words. Mum had reduced Gen to tears, for her face was buried in her chest as she sobbed.

Kris stood up and exited the room without uttering a word. When the atmosphere became somber, it was hard for anyone, but for Kris, it was unbearable.

I didn't leave like Kris but didn't shed a tear, either. It served no purpose.

That same night, I faced Chase. I had no clue how he appeared when I was eluding him, but there he was, fuming with rage, flailing his Goldy like a madman.

He thrust it into my chest and pulled it out. Blood spurted out, splattering on the floor, his clothes, everywhere.

"Traitor," he hissed, eyes bloody. "Traitor of our kind."

I tried to utter something but couldn't. My mouth was sealed like a casket, preventing me from speaking up.

I collapsed on the floor, and he plunged the sword into my abdomen once more.

"Traitor."

The sound of what seemed to be quiet weeping woke me up. At first, I thought it was I who couldn't keep the tears suppressed anymore, but that wasn't it. I breathed covertly through my mouth to steady my laboured breathing and pounding heart. I collected my thoughts, telling myself it wasn't real. Merely a nightmare. I was alive and safe.

In my periphery, I saw Gen's chest rising erratically under the sheets, as if she was striving to stifle her whimpers and avoid waking us. I returned my gaze to the ceiling, wanting to tell her there was no reason to cry because it wasn't her going through that portal, but I couldn't.

Not yet.

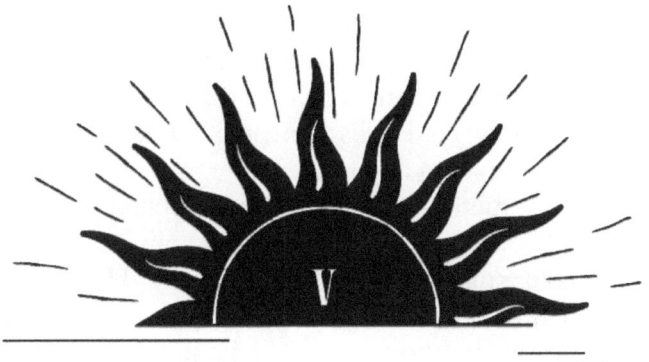

The summer solstice. The one day in a year when the sun bathed the grounds the longest. This day, all spirits could roam across the land until the next day, early in the morning, when they returned to their graves. This day, people mourned their youngest children while others watched them getting swallowed by the portal leading them to the unknown.

I'd witnessed every detail of the offering. I knew what to expect. But this year differed from the previous ones. Because, today, I wouldn't be one of the witnesses. Today, I would be one of the offered.

Gen was getting ready. Mum was combing her hair while Gen was sitting cross-legged on the floor before the mirror, staring blankly at her reflection. Every now and then, Mum glanced at me while I was brushing my own hair.

Yesterday, I had steeled myself for telling her my plan. As expected, Mum didn't look as if she was about to throw a party, but I left her no choice but to respect my decision and help me achieve it.

Gen was clueless about everything; confident today was the end of her life. She hadn't peeped a single word since yesterday—evidently lost in her head. Tired and hopeless, as if she'd already given up. I fought the urge to get ahead of myself and spill the beans to spare her from her misery, but then I would jeopardise my well-thought plan.

Kris was in the living room. He would go along. I hadn't primed him either, but I was positive he wouldn't object, given his tendency to embrace change faster than the rest of us.

"Did you know gold kills morphs?" I broke the gloomy silence, unable to bear it any longer.

"I've heard something about it," Mum replied.

When I'd been scheming my plan, I'd contemplated the idea of taking a gold knife from Chase's armoury. However, once I remembered how terrible I'd felt at the sight of his Goldy and shuddered just at the thought of it, I hadn't bothered creeping into his manor to steal one.

"Perhaps every townie should have a gold weapon in case morphs attack us one day."

Morphs could strike any day, after all. So far, they hadn't, but it would be foolish to disregard such a possibility. Who knew what was lurking in their beastly minds.

"Enchanters can be killed by iron," I added.

I assumed sharing information about everything I had learned from Chase about morphs and enchanters with my family was a must. It might be handy if other species attacked one day, and if I wasn't here to share my knowledge, they'd be prepared for it. Gods forbid, of course.

But no one had spotted any single creature, despite ordinary animals in the forest for a long time. Sometimes I doubted if morphs even existed and if we hadn't been told tales for our entire lives. In any case, I would be the one to find that out soon.

When I was done taming my waves into a plait and sharing everything I knew about the unfamiliar world, I glanced at the jewellery on my right hand, debating if I should keep them.

An emerald shone from the sunlight streaming through the window on the ring. I could take it off but opted to keep it for now. Additionally, I wore a bronze bracelet day and night. It was surrounded by stars, with the sun at the centre and a crescent on top. My parents had gifted it to me when I was merely a babe, and I had never taken it off. Why should I now?

"Lynn?"

I jerked my head up, meeting Gen's weary gaze in the mirror. "Yeah?"

"There's something under my pillow for you."

"Did you steal something?" My eyebrows rose. "Again?"

Mum winced but said nothing.

"Oh, no worries, Mum." Gen noted our mother's concerned expression. "I didn't steal anything from townies."

"So, you *did* steal something."

She smiled, and it was apparent that I was right. Shaking my head, I couldn't fight back a smile. I stood off the bed and went to hers. As she'd told me, when I raised the pillow, there was a folded piece of paper lying underneath it. I gave Gen a dubious look. She wasn't the only one watching me, though. Mum was interested, too.

"You stole a treasure map?"

She huffed out a laugh. "I wish," she said. "Come on. Open it."

Chuckling, I drew out the paper. In a slow, teasing way, I unfolded it to toy with their nerves. But as soon as I saw what was portrayed on the paper, my heart stuttered, and my muscles froze.

In no time, I snapped out of my stupor, folding the paper while keeping my emotions hidden from my family's curiosity.

"What was that?" Mum inquired.

"Nothing."

Gen huffed. "Not nothing," she said, earning a warning glance from me. "Just a man."

Mum's eyes widened in surprise as she stood up. "What man? What? Can I see it?"

I hesitated, my heartbeat quickening. Eventually, I extended the paper to her. It couldn't do any harm, right?

She looked down at the paper, then raised her eyes at me, reluctant. But as I was about to change my mind, she took it. She unfolded the paper, and I could have sworn I saw a fleeting sparkle that lasted only a second in her irises.

She looked up at me. "Did you draw this?"

"Yes, and Gen stole it." I shot a pointed look at my sister, who grinned, reminding me of a wicked witch.

I'd forgotten about the drawing, which I'd created out of sheer boredom. I hadn't encountered it for a while until now. When I hadn't found it one day, I'd made peace with its disappearance. There was a little pinch of my heart since I'd done my best to represent the glimpse of the black suit I had seen the mystery man wearing in my trance. A man who perhaps didn't exist.

But my heart whispered otherwise. And I silenced it.

"Is he real?" Mum resumed her inquiries.

I hadn't told her about my trance. Hadn't told anyone, for that matter.

"Of course he's not," Gen denied before I could. "I've never seen anything similar to him anywhere, and oh ... how I searched!"

I blinked, incredulously, at my sister. "You searched?"

"Of course."

I huffed.

"Is he truly not real?" Mum asked once again. She had never stopped staring at me.

"No," I assured her. "He's not real."

Mum pouted. "What a pity. You drew a very handsome man, honeybee."

Once she returned the sketch, I folded it before I could catch a glimpse of the representation of my wild imagination.

When I'd had the trance during piano play, all I'd seen was a man's broad and tanned hand as he'd been fixing a black cuff sticking out of a brocade jacket sleeve. But I'd felt him—the smoke—as well as heard him.

I feel you too, stranger, he'd said in a deep, soothing voice.

His voice had rung in my head for days, but over time, I'd forgotten its resonance. If I ever heard it again, I didn't think I would recognise it as much as I didn't believe I would ever meet this mysterious stranger in real life.

Mum was back to combing Gen's hair into a braid. Then my eyes locked with Mum's in the mirror, and she stealthily nodded her head. I returned to my bed and dropped the sketch, letting it fall. As I lifted a mattress, I pulled out the shackles I had bought from one vendor in town. With no pointless inquiries of why they had the single shackles lying on their stall, for I needn't know, I'd given them a shilling and paced away, hiding my purchase from prying eyes.

As I exchanged places with Mum, I caught Gen's stare. Slight lines formed on her sun-touched forehead. I sent her a brief smile, and before she could trace my movements, I seized her wrist and attached one shackle to it while another to the leg of Kris's bed.

"Lynn, what the ...?" Her perplexed look darted from her imprisoned wrist to me, then to our mother.

"I'm sorry, Gen."

She frowned. "What the hell is this?"

Mother handed me a strand of Gen's hair. Gen gave her a puzzled look. "Can someone tell me what is happening, for Gods' sake?!" She jerked her seized hand, intent on pulling it free. But she had no chance of escape when our mother had a key.

I took out a vial from my pocket, containing the liquid I had meticulously mixed the day before. As I uncorked it, I dropped the strand of Gen's hair into the potion.

I had discovered the so-called Conversion Potion in the first book I picked when the spirit of the boy led me to the invisible aisle in the library. I gathered all the necessary ingredients to make it, but the only missing piece was Gen's hair. According to the instructions, I had to drink it, and if the book was right, my appearance would become identical to Gen's for twenty-four hours.

"You're not going through that portal tonight." I shook the essence between my fingers. "I am."

"Elynn ..." Her blazing eyes shot up at me. "Release me!"

"Your sister is going to sacrifice herself to keep you safe, my little bird." Mother caressed her silky hair, and Gen instantly drew back from her touch as if revolted.

"Three hells, no!"

Gen's hair had dissolved in the murky brown liquid, and I swallowed hard. As I steeled myself for drinking what might be poison, I lifted a vial to my lips. Gen was watching me. She needn't voice what was in her mind as her withering expression had it covered.

Accepting her unsaid dare, I poured the liquid into my mouth, down to the last drop. With a swallow, all I felt was bitterness mixed with an acid taste, making me wince.

The room was in silence. Mother stared at me, waiting for an effect to manifest itself as I was. Meanwhile, Gen was throwing darts with her eyes, expecting one to hit me.

I didn't feel anything. It wasn't working. The boy's spirit had tricked me, or I'd done something wrong.

But I'd followed every step meticulously, reread it multiple times to make sure I'd been doing everything right.

"Nothing?"

Mum shook her head.

"Let me go," Gen grunted. "I need to face my fate, not you, Lynn."

Searing pain stung my wrist, and a yelp flew from my mouth. Gnashing my teeth, I looked at it. The skin under my bracelet mottled with red stains, which were only spreading with my stalling. Hastily, I removed the bracelet, and the burning ceased.

But it was the warning before the storm.

Something unfathomable twisted inside me, and my vision blurred. I couldn't maintain balance anymore. I dropped to my knees and clutched my head as if it could spare me from the tremendous pain dancing not only inside my head but in every single bone, nerve, and cell.

My whole body was aching, burning, as if I was set on blistering fire. Insides itching, bones seemed to measure down within inches. But it all had come to an end shortly.

And when the pain was over, the thud once some object hit the ground, caused me to wince. It was a hairbrush that must have slipped from Mum's grasp.

I raised my head and met Kristian hovering at the threshold.

He was staring wide-eyed at me. "What the ..." He trailed off, his stare shifting to Gen, who was gaping at me.

Mum's reaction was the same as her two children's.

"Did it work?" I asked.

Gen didn't say anything, but my mother said in awe, "I have twin daughters."

A joke but not one of us laughed. It was not a suitable situation for one to laugh. Not when my sister was glaring at me while I tried my best to convince myself I was doing the right thing.

As I was changing into Gen's clothes, she was cursing me the entire time. Mum scolded her for saying such cruel things to her sister, as cursing could bring bad luck upon me. At least that was what Mum said. Kris had been mystified at first, but Mum had filled him in on everything.

I stole a glance at the mirror to see if I looked like myself. And I didn't. Mind-blowing, let alone uncanny, it was to behold two lookalikes and see myself looking like someone else entirely.

The bracelet was back on my wrist. I wasn't going to leave the last piece that reminded me of my family behind. At least it wasn't burning my skin anymore.

"Think about positive things, Gen," I said, putting on her shoes. "You can decide your own fate now." I dared to flash her a smile.

She showed me a finger with her free hand.

"Genette Lucida Startel!" Mum exclaimed.

Gen acted as though Mum wasn't even here. "You shouldn't have done this. I was ready, prepared for what could happen to me in the empire," she said with strong tartness in her tone. "But no. You *had* to play a hero."

A weird feeling—close to guilt—passed through my chest, but to squash it, I assured myself yet again I was on the right track. I'd guessed it would be like that. In Gen's shoes, I would have been furious about the turn of events she hadn't seen coming, too.

"I heard you crying at night," I said, throwing a glance at the silent Kristian, but he didn't seem to notice it. Perhaps he was a heavy sleeper, but I believed he could have heard our sister's muffled sobs as well as I could. "It didn't look as if you were prepared for what was coming at all, Gen."

"It doesn't matter. You can't save me from everything. I'm not a child anymore."

As I finished putting on shoes, I leapt to my feet—which felt strange since I was shorter than usual—and walked over to her. I crouched before her and tucked the strand of her hair behind her ear.

"I know, but ..." I took a sharp breath. "It feels right. Doing this. I believe it's been my purpose all along. To be offered instead of you on the Summer Solstice."

Gen frowned. "You did this behind my back." Her ruthless eyes darted between Mum and me and even Kristian. "You all did this."

"Whoa, Whoa, Whoa." Kristian held his palms up in defence. "I had nothing to do with this. I'm still having a hard time processing what's happening. That Elynn looks like Gen, Gen looks like ... Oh, heavens ..." He pressed his hand against his forehead and breathed out a puff of air.

"This was all my idea, Gen," I said, causing Gen's blazing gaze to shoot back at me. "Kristian, as you see, had nothing to do with this, and Mum didn't have any choice but to go along with it. She would have lost either of us anyway. But she should lose me instead of you." Mum opened her mouth to object, but I hastened to continue before she could. "While I may have married Chase for the fortune we have never seen in our lives, I doubt he would have given me any without ..." I drew in a breath. "I'm not an eminent pianist; my playing wouldn't have granted our survival. I wouldn't have followed my mother's footsteps by sewing either, as it doesn't obtain much money. Unlike you, I don't know how to bake delicious cakes. You sustained our family during the crisis, and if needed, you can do it again."

Instead of flames, tears now bathed Gen's eyes. "I hate you so much."

I smiled at her, holding back the tears. "I love you, too, Gen."

As I embraced her, I'd assumed she wouldn't hug me back because of the pride, but she did, surprising me. When we let go of each other, I stood up and secretively wiped away the tears that had slipped through my shields.

Then I turned to my mother and Kris. "Let's go?"

As if there was a choice ...

Mum barely nodded, water running down her face. "Let's go."

"Kris?" I addressed my brother, who seemed to be somewhere else.

He flashed back to reality. "Yeah? Yeah, let's go."

I didn't forget to snatch the folded sketch and shove it in my pocket before I left.

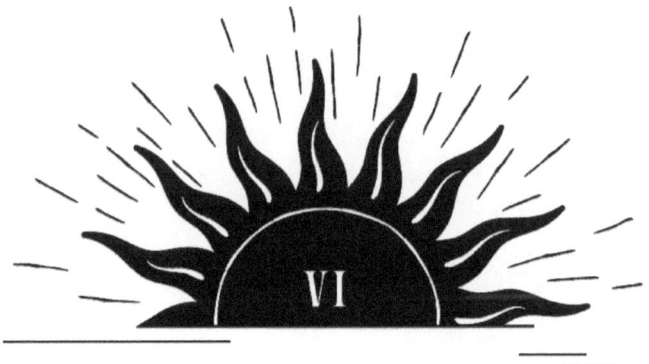

Hundreds of people thronged the town hall—more than last year. I wondered if they had come to offer emotional support to the offered or simply to watch the show.

Gen was at home, shackled to the bed. Remorse nibbled at me, but it had to be done or else she'd have exposed me. Kristian and Mum stood beside me. Both were quiet, but Mum's silence was unlike her. I figured she didn't feel like talking when she was about to see one of her daughters vanishing into nowhere forever.

The ceremony hadn't begun yet. Nobody was on the dais: no pledgers and no outlandish portal.

Sixteen-year-olds have been offered for over forty years, and yet it felt like the ceremony we all dreaded had been around forever. Before that, the Summer Solstice had been a traditional holiday when humans would assemble and celebrate. It'd been one of few days when murdered animals were offered to our Almighty Gods. Afterwards, there came drinking and dancing until feet hurt, as Dad once had told me. But the times had changed.

Now, instead of offering dead animals to the Gods, we offered minors to the Empire of Beasts, and it wasn't merriment that followed, but buckets and buckets of endless tears.

Or before, as some people were already crying.

At least Mum hadn't shed a tear since we'd left the house or else I would have fallen into the pieces I'd struggled so much to amass.

No one had ever returned from the empire—none of us dared to voice it, but we all knew—today was the last time they would see me.

"I thought about something ..." Mum inhaled deeply, as though she was about to cry. "When you told me what you were about to do."

"Don't cry, Mum." I placed a gentle hand on her shoulder and squeezed it lightly. "Please."

The corner of her lips quivered into a weak smile. "I'll be all right," she assured me, but I doubted it. "But I must tell you—"

"Mrs. Startel."

My whole body strained at the sound of a too familiar voice, whereas Mum looked in the direction where it'd come from. No muscle on her face twitched once she saw the man who was still my fiancé.

"Greetings to you, too, young man." He punched Kris's arm in greeting.

Kris rubbed the arm Chase had just touched as he composed a weak smile through a wince. "Yeah ... hello to you, too ... *man*."

"Chase," Mum greeted him coolly. I wasn't looking at him, nervous that he might recognise me even if I was a clone of Gen. "What are you doing here?"

"I came to support my fiancée," Chase declared. "Where is she, by the way?" He looked around, expecting to find me nearby.

No concern for my sister, nothing. As if he didn't care about Gen's offering. But I shouldn't be surprised. He had never shown any concern for Gen. Not once since we'd begun dating. He never cared to ask anything, being acutely aware she was going to be offered one day. As if she was no one, nothing. But what could I expect? Neither did he show any interest in me, not in the matters that didn't involve my body, at least.

"Away," Mum answered, her voice impassive, even cold.

"Why? She didn't come to give Genette a send-off?" My

mother shook her head in response. "Really? It isn't like her ..."

The unreadable mask Mum had donned was flawless. Chase, ignorant as he was, would never suspect a thing. "My daughter doesn't want to see her sister pushed into that portal. She has already said her farewell and decided to get away, to be *alone*."

I couldn't tell whether Chase believed her or not. I wasn't going to look at his face, the face I wanted to wreck with my fist that was clenching the material of Gen's sky-blue dress.

"If that's so," he said, "I'll also say my goodbye."

He smiled down at me. "Goodbye, Genette. It's unfortunate you won't be able to be Elynn's bridesmaid at our wedding."

A sense of resentment, as familiar as breath, surged through me. Still, I nodded, suppressing my true feelings for him one last time. Chase waved goodbye to us and strolled off. I heaved a sigh of relief.

"What a prick," Mum mumbled.

"I don't know," Kris said. "He seems decent to me."

Both of our eyes were on Kris now.

"He used violence against Elynn, Kristian."

Kris looked at me questionably, and I nodded, confirming my mother's statement. His jaw clenched and bluer than grey eyes glowed with fury as his head whipped in the direction where Chase had disappeared. He pushed his sleeves back, readying himself to go after him, but I seized his wrist before he did.

His angry eyes flicked to me.

"Don't."

"When someone hurts a family member, the family pays back, Lynn."

"You're better than that, Kris. Besides, you wouldn't take him down. He's a hunter, and you're better with your brainpower than throwing punches. You'll only get hurt."

He was pursing his lips hard, but as time passed, he let go of them along with his breath. "Fine, but I'm not going to—"

Loud trumpets slashed through all the noise. I whipped my head around to see the dais, releasing Kris's wrist. Three pledgers, who wore a shade of sun robes, emerged in the middle of the platform from the stairs. The hall and trumpets fell silent.

Pledgers smiled at us benevolently, but I couldn't tell if their smiles reflected their eyes. I was too far away.

The woman in the middle gestured at someone, and soon, the portal rose out of the floor behind them gradually. Some people gasped as if they beheld it for the first time. It used to inspire awe in me, too. Perhaps the portal was the most magical object in our region. It was made of a rectangular shape, the top forming an unstable oval. Its thick wooden edges had grown with moss, embellished with blossoms and leaves, whereas the inside of it was filled with pristine, mellow-yellow liquid. It was one stunning masterpiece with a deceiving image in mind. Its looks were harmless and spellbinding when, in reality, its purpose was to send minors to the deadly world for them to perish.

No one knew how the magical portal had appeared in our world, and nobody dared to question it. Even if somebody was curious enough to ask, I doubted the pledgers knew the answer. They were just following the rules, doing their job, raising no questions. Not to put themselves at risk, as they were the only ones who could communicate with the empire.

Even a simpleton could figure out that the portal always remained in our world and didn't come out of nowhere only for this particular day. Thus, it got me thinking. Could somebody besides the offered kids go through it out of curiosity? Couldn't someone have done it already?

"There's no easy way to say this," the woman standing in the middle spoke, her brown hands clasped before her. "The news hit us like thunder in the morning." She glanced at the white man next to her, as if pleading for help.

The man's hand grazed hers, and she gave him a weak smile. He then looked back at the utterly quiet crowd.

"A sixteen-year-old boy was found dead in his home this morning."

People remained silent. No gasps. No questioning. Nothing. No one was shocked.

At least once in five years, a suicide before the Summer Solstice took place. Perhaps the boy had assumed it was better to take his own life than to face whatever was waiting for him behind the portal. Perhaps it was grim death lurking there—a worse death than suicide.

We all fell under a minute of silence to pay respect to the loss of young life. After it, the woman in the middle cleared her throat, drawing everybody's attention back to her.

"This year, we have ten names of sixteen-year-olds. You may begin saying goodbye to your loved ones."

I looked at my mother, intertwining our hands. She slightly squeezed my hand and gave me a small, reassuring smile.

If I hadn't been scared before, now I was terrified.

I was about to go through the portal and never see my family again. I wasn't ready. I'd thought I was, but ...

No. I needed to pull myself together. Not show how I was afraid. Not in front of my mother, who would shatter if I exposed how frightened I actually was.

Pledgers began calling one minor by one in reverse alphabetical order. Families walked on the podium to say goodbye for the last time to their children, grandchildren, siblings.

I squeezed Mum's hand harder as slowly it was coming to my— Gen's—name.

My heart was pounding in my chest, skin running with cold sweat. To ignore the trepidation, I glanced at my hand, at the ring finger.

I slipped my hand from Mum's and pulled off the ring. As soon as it was gone, my finger weighed lighter. I took her hand, placed a ring in her palm, and closed it. Mum was tracking my every movement.

"Sell it," I said. "Don't return it to Chase. If he asks about the ring, tell him I have it."

Mum nodded, and I was glad that she didn't argue.

"Genette Lucida Startel!" the pledger called.

Here it goes ...

My legs began carrying me on their own through the crowd. I gripped the sleeve of my mother's dress, pulling her along with me towards the dais. I glanced over my shoulder to make sure Kris was following. Indeed he was. Then I looked back, where pledgers were already waiting. As we approached the guards, they showed us where to climb. While we were going together up the flight of steps, I thought I was about to faint here and now. I had no clue how I managed to mount the rest of the steps. Perhaps someone else was making me walk while I had an out-of-body experience.

My brain had a hard time fathoming that this was actually happening.

"Genette?"

Once I met the woman's stare, she summoned a serene smile that didn't touch her eyes. She was extending something.

It was a small leather bag. Did she hand bags like mine to everyone? I hadn't noticed. But I didn't stall long and took it as I didn't see why I shouldn't.

"What is in it?" I asked.

"An emergency kit. Things you might need, dear," she replied.

I issued a thank you and glanced at Mum, who, without hesitation, pulled me into a tight, loving embrace.

"I love you." She drew an uneven breath to add, "I will always love you and will never forget you."

"I know, Mum," I mumbled, trying not to break. "I love you, too."

I couldn't describe how painful it was to say the words meaning an everlasting goodbye. I had voiced them seldom. Perhaps if I had to, I could count on my fingers how many times I said the three words built of eight letters. This time, however, I'd said them the most sincerely throughout my entire existence.

For the very last time, I inhaled the scent of my mother. Roses and vanilla. A smell of home to remember until my last breath.

As we pulled away from each other, I met Kristian's gaze. Letting out a sigh, I invited him for a hug by spreading my hands.

"Come on," I prompted him with a cheeky smile. "You have to hug your sister for the last time, Kris."

He pressed his lips together, hesitating, but stepped towards me, and we embraced. For the first time, I learned what it was like to hug my brother, as neither of us could be described as huggers. Especially not him.

Since I was now shorter, he was towering over me when our height had been almost alike before taking the potion.

"It shouldn't be this way," he muttered, surprisingly not letting go of me.

"It should be this way."

He looked doubtful. "Should it?"

I nodded, somehow certain. "I feel it."

I didn't lie this time, which was new. It indeed felt right. Yes, I was afraid with every bit of my bones, which might shake soon, but if I had to pick, I'd rather go through the portal, discover whatever was behind it than stay and marry ... that man.

"If you feel it's right," Kris said, "then what brother would I be if I argued?"

I chuckled, and as I raised my head at him, I tousled his brown hair. He winced, but there was a shadow of a smile on his lips as he smoothed it back.

"It's time," the woman notified.

The warm aura between Kris and I vanished, along with our smiles. He backed away from me, and I glanced at Mum, who was staring with a broken gaze. Swallowing, I forced myself to look away before I changed my mind.

I couldn't change my mind, however. There were too many eyes. Even if there weren't, I wouldn't choose to bail. I couldn't.

I faced the portal. Innocent, even inviting, lucid portal. My feet were close to dragging *me* towards it. Every step taken was a challenge. The closer I got to the portal, the stronger I had to battle the urge to run back into my mother's arms and ask her to hold me and never let go.

But I didn't. My brain knew better. I listened to it, as my heart could only betray me.

As I halted a half-step away from the portal, I turned around to catch the last glimpse of my family. Kris was nowhere to be seen, but I didn't look around to find where he'd gone when I saw the tears washing Mum's face.

I hated that she saw Gen, not me right now. I could tell that she didn't like it either. But it had to be this way.

Unwillingly, I pictured her the way she was. A few wrinkles on her forehead and below her blue eyes. Dark-brown hair tied into a bun, revealing a grey hairline she didn't try to conceal. *My mother.* The last memory of her to treasure until my last heartbeat.

Again, I quelled the desire to run back into her arms and hold her.

She would be fine. Sooner or later. I hoped, at least.

At last, I stepped back, raising my hand to wave my farewell, but the portal swallowed me before I could. Everything that had been before me a mere second ago vanished, consumed by the dazzling yellow light.

Part II

Notes of Beasts & Bones

The portal spat me out like a disgusting drink. I tumbled, scraping my knees against the hard ground. Despite the searing pain, my ears rang, and all I could see was pitch-black darkness. For a brief moment, panic gripped me; I feared I had lost my eyesight. Yet, green dots began to replace the blackness, and the ringing gradually subsided.

My eyes had a hard time shaping the figures surrounding me. First, it was a chaos of green shades mixed with black, but as black disappeared, brown joined, and bit by bit, I found my bearings. It all reminded me of tree—yes, trees. I must be in the forest.

But not alone.

Minors, hurled out of the portal, writhed on the ground. Half of them wailed, some retched, and the rest threw up.

I searched for the portal, expecting to find a similar one I'd walked into on the dais not long ago, but it wasn't here. Only trees and sick adolescents.

At least I wasn't suffering from such a severe nausea that I'd need to spill all the undigested food on the grass. I was a trifle dizzy, but not as much as when the portal had expelled me, and my feet felt uncomfortable in Gen's shoes.

Grasping the leather bag—which miraculously I hadn't lost when I was thrown out of the portal—I managed to rise to my unsteady feet. The forest itself differed from the one I was accustomed to seeing behind the cottage's windows. I had to crane my head back to catch a glimpse of the sky veiled by thick branches and broad leaves.

"Fascinating, isn't it?"

I started, flicking my head to the speaker. A woman, no younger than thirty, was staring at me. She smiled, but her smile didn't reach her ocean blue eyes.

I was too distracted by the woman's attire to respond. She wore a white shirt with an embroidered paw on her chest, a long skirt of a similar shade to the portal, but it was more of a faded tint of yellow. If I was correct, she was wearing a uniform that belonged to *this* world, but I could be wrong.

"What is this place?" I asked.

"The Empire of Beasts." I opened my mouth to clarify myself, but she continued, "You're in Casidiarn's territory."

"Casidiarn?"

"Casidiarn is the capital of the Empire of Beasts."

I didn't even know what the Empire of Beasts looked like, so how could I know the name of the capital? Our town and the rest of the Mortal Region were against anything involving morphs, including their dwelling place. But if I was in the capital, it only screamed danger to me.

"What's your name?" she asked me before I could question her more about Casidiarn.

I didn't hesitate to reply. "Genette."

She looked at the leather notebook she had with her, which I had failed to notice before. "Genette Lucida Startel?"

I nodded curtly.

"It says here you're a good baker and a cook, is that correct?"

In my dreams. "Yes."

The woman stood on her tiptoes to look behind me at the rest of the adolescents, who were still puking in the grass. She grimaced.

"Who are you exactly?"

"I'm Holland."

"I didn't ask your name, *Holland.*"

"You're bold," she said. "That's bad."

"How is being bold bad?"

She was as expressionless as I, betraying nothing. "You'll find out sooner or later."

Her focus returned to the rest of the teenagers instead of answering my previous question. She tucked her notebook under her armpit and clapped her hands loudly to bring everybody to attention. "All right, enough with the crying," she addressed the rest. "It's time to stand up!"

I turned to them as well. Minors remained curled on the ground while incoherent sounds left their mouths. But only one peculiar girl snatched my full attention.

She was leaning against a tree, her arms folded across her chest, flawless coal-black curls falling on her shoulders. Her dark eyes were watching me as if she knew something I didn't.

I glanced down at my hands, as if I knew why. My skin had returned to its normal self—honey bronze. I was back to the body I was accustomed to—*my body.* And the girl knew that. Supposedly, she was the last one to enter the portal and saw me disappearing in it as another person. She wasn't affected by nausea, unlike the others. Not even a hint of sickness was visible in her ebony face.

I hoped the suspicious girl wouldn't be a problem.

"Stand up," Holland reiterated sternly, as nobody had risen to their feet.

"They are unwell," I noted.

She glanced at me, devoid of emotion. "Side effects are common. *They* won't care about them if we are late, kid."

"Are you talking about morphs?"

"Yes."

"What is our purpose here? What do humans do for morphs?"

Holland's face remained indecipherable. I couldn't discern any emotion. Nothing to provide a clue about what was in her mind.

"Our purpose here is to serve them," she stated, the words sounding rehearsed.

"How will we serve them?"

"Water," someone rasped behind me—a blonde, light-skinned boy, one of the few of his offered gender.

"You have water in your bag," Holland said with indifference.

"I can't see," he cried.

Pursing my lips, I opened my leather bag and searched for something to help the boy. I was relieved to find a canteen. The pledgers had proven they weren't cold-hearted by providing us with necessary supplies, for not only did the bag contain a canteen of water, but also a small sheathed golden knife.

As I was drawing a canteen from the bag, I tried my best not to brush my skin against the knife, even though its blade was sheathed—and I succeeded.

I squatted in front of the boy, flicking the lid off the canteen. I pushed his chin up and pressed the bottle's edge to his dry, desert-like lips.

"Drink," I said mildly.

I poured the water into his mouth as soon as it parted. He gulped it eagerly, as if he hadn't had a drop of water for days. In a matter of seconds, my water canteen was empty.

"Thank you," he mumbled.

Saying nothing, I shoved the empty canteen back into the bag and secured it. As I stood up, I glared unabashedly at Holland. "They can't stand on their own, and if you expect them to walk, you're insane."

"If they're not willing to fight the side effects, they are more likely to become their dinner."

I clenched my teeth. "They. Can't. Walk."

"Listen, girl." A cloud of exasperation passed through her. "Today is the Summer Solstice. Not only are humans offered to the Empire of Beasts, but it's *their* holiday. The lords and ladies, the queen and kings, the empress and emperor are feasting. They won't be pleased if something doesn't go according to plan. My task is to guide you to the lands where you are going to do the work *they* need you to do. You don't have to listen to me and go with me. But if you don't go, they will hunt you, and they will make a delicious meal out of you."

My knowledge about morphs and their world was lacking, but

when Holland mentioned the eating part, something told me she wasn't exaggerating. Morphs could do that. They could eat humans. If others remained here, they would be dead by night time.

I surveyed the wretched kids and clenched my jaw tight. I had many questions for Holland, but first and foremost, I needed to help her with these minors. They would not be morphs' dinner. Not today.

I crouched before the boy and placed my hands on his damp cheeks, forcing him to look at me. It didn't seem that he saw me. His focus was on nothing and no one.

"You've heard her," I told him, but he didn't react. "Focus on your other senses while you can't see. We need to get moving."

"I'll try," he mumbled.

"No, you'll do it." I removed my hands from his face and put them just above my knees. "You'll do it."

I stood up and took in the rest of the teenagers. Seven were left.

I sighed. "How much time do we have?"

"Lesser and lesser," Holland said.

I frowned, glancing at the tree where the suspicious girl had been the last time I saw her. But she was no longer there. Instead, she was helping another girl to stand. Our eyes met. She held my stare, but I looked away first to help the others walk and convince them to fight the side effects of the portal, or else this day would be their last.

Most managed to walk on their own, even aiding others among them. I helped the boy, Franz, who hadn't regained his vision after all.

The suspicious girl was helping another. Her presence kept me tense and vigilant. She could tell Holland I was an impostor, even if she said nothing so far. But it didn't mean she wouldn't.

The sun was hot today. Gen's tight dress clung to my sweaty back and my feet, confined in too-small shoes, cried in agony. Thirst gripped me like a vice, but my canteen was empty, and

Franz had lost his bag.

As we walked, no creatures stirred in the seemingly uninhabited rainforest—no bird chirps or panther eyes watching from the trees. Holland led the way. As her hair shifted, a nasty scar revealed itself on her tanned nape. The wound must have been deep, and I wondered how she had acquired it.

"I can see," Franz announced. "Just a little."

"Nobody gets blind permanently," Holland noted.

"It'd be nice if you explained our purpose here," I said, not hiding my irritation about her keeping us in the dark.

Holland barely glanced at me over her shoulder, somewhat interested. "I've got a list." She raised the leather notebook with a wave. "All your names are written here, along with your skills, and the kind of job you'll be doing and where."

Why wouldn't she just spell everything out? Why did I have to question her to extract something valuable?

"What job?" The question came not from me but from the suspicious girl who'd been a silent until now.

"You're all going to have a main job, but there will also be informal ones you'll have to do if you want to survive."

Still not an answer.

"What jobs, Holland?" I hissed, the bracelet on my wrist faintly heating my skin.

"I'm feeling sick," Franz mumbled, but I paid no attention to him.

"You're going to serve royals as maids, guards, or something else."

The suspicious girl scoffed. "You mean slaves."

Holland nodded, surprisingly not denying her words. "Those will be your main jobs, but you'll have others as well. Not as pleasant as the main ones." She drew in a long breath. "If some morph asks you to do something for them, you'll do it or else you'll get hurt."

I wasn't scared, but others exchanged wary glances.

"The scar on your neck," I said, softer this time. "Is it morphs' doing?"

She didn't respond. I took it as a positive answer.

Franz doubled over and vomited right next to me. I scowled,

coming to a halt and whipping my head away. But I held Franz firm by his arm, regardless.

"Disgusting," the suspicious girl said.

I shot her a glare. "Do you have a problem with something?"

She looked at me, unbothered by my biting tone. Saying nothing, she continued walking with the fatigued girl beside her.

I looked at Franz. "How are you?"

He straightened himself and looked directly at me. From the stable look in his azure eyes, I could tell he'd gained his eyesight back.

"Better."

"Can you walk on your own?"

"Faster, you two," Holland urged.

I ignored her.

"Yeah, I think so," he assured me.

I smiled a bit and let go of him. He began walking. Better than I'd expected. He'd do just fine on his own.

The further we went, the more it seemed like the rainforest was endless. Minors were gradually regaining their strength. Those who had been sick were now trudging like Franz. Left with my head as a companion, it was natural for resentment to start poking at me.

They were only sixteen, offered to the Empire of Beasts, where they were forced into slavery. How was this fair?

Holland's warnings didn't leave me peace of mind either. If a morph demanded them to do something, humans would do it if they didn't want to obtain a scar on their bodies or worse—get killed.

All I was sure of by now was that I'd done the right thing by coming here in Gen's place. Regardless of how strong my sister could be in all ways, how she could endure anything life threw at her, she was my family. I needed to protect her from anything at all costs. She was safer in the Mortal Region. I knew with all my heart that I hadn't made a mistake.

Nobody talked anymore. I didn't attack Holland with questions and neither did the suspicious girl. Holland was hard to interrogate. Besides, I had a feeling—which could be deceiving—she'd revealed everything she needed to.

Holland came to an abrupt halt, and we followed. She turned to us, drawing something out of her pocket. Then she cast the area around herself, as if afraid that something might be watching us. And perhaps we weren't alone after all. I scanned around myself but didn't spot anything lurking behind lush foliage.

"Take this, girl."

I looked back at Holland, then at what she was handing me. A pill lay in her palm—a green, innocent-looking pill from which I expected the worst.

"What is it for?"

There was no way I was taking the pill without being aware of its effects.

"Take it," she ordered, relentless.

But I hesitated. "What does it do?"

Her lips pressed tightly. Clearly, I was getting on her nerves with my defiance, but I didn't care.

She leaned closer and whispered, "I'm on the humans' side, Genette. I was in your place once. I advise you to take it for your own sake or else ..." She swallowed the unspoken word, and an emotion sparkled in her face. Genuine fear.

She wouldn't have whispered anything like that to me if we were the only ones here. She would have told everyone out loud. No doubt somebody was watching us, making sure we took the pills.

She pulled away, and her pleading eyes convinced me enough.

I glanced at the others. They all seemed mistrustful, except for the suspicious girl who stared at me as if she saw a fraud in me.

I took the pill. Holland didn't react or show anything that could mean relief or approval when proceeded to another person.

While I stared at the green pill, Holland handed out the same ones to everyone. They took them without hesitating and didn't argue as I had. I was surprised when the suspicious girl didn't refuse the pill either. I thought she would put up some fight.

As Holland stood in front of us, she ordered, "Swallow the pill."

Without lingering, I tossed the tiny pill into my mouth and swallowed it without taking the time to savour the taste.

The others swallowed theirs.

But nothing happened to my senses that would suggest the effect of the pill. I felt just the same as before, which included my physical health. Well.

In my periphery, someone fell—a girl. Then, one by one, they all began dropping like flies. My eyes widened.

They aren't dead, are they?

But before I could ask Holland, everything around me began spinning, and oblivion took over.

When I awoke, I stared at the ceiling for a while, and not a single thought passed through my mind, as if it was blank. Not until a reminder of what had happened before I dozed off threw me out of my haze.

Falling asleep, however, would be an understatement. A milder version of what had actually happened.

I'd been *drugged*.

Instantly, I shot into a sitting position, and my hands darted over my body to make sure I was real and safe and sound.

I felt myself.

I was alive.

But I didn't sigh from relief; the realisation didn't ease the pounding of my heart. As I barely shifted, the bed creaked underneath me. Only then did I acknowledge my surroundings.

The candle on the table issued just enough light to see the room. Besides the creaking bed and the dusty table in the corner, there was no other furniture in this claustrophobic bunker. Not like something else could fit in here anyway.

Where I was—I had no idea. How long I'd been unconscious, I couldn't tell either. If only the room had a window for me to at least have a clue of what time of day it was, but there was no window.

But there was a dark-wooden door across from me.

Once I crawled out of bed, my head began to spin. I blamed it on the pill Holland had made me and everybody else swallow if it wasn't because of the ridiculous smallness of the room. In a dizzy state, I managed to totter towards the door. As I planted my hand on the doorknob, I attempted to open it vainly, since it was locked.

As if I wasn't sure that I'd opened it right the first time, I twisted and pulled the knob until I was convinced that I was locked in here.

I tried not to get consumed by panic. *Inhale. Exhale. Inhale—*

"Let me out!" I screamed, rapping my fists against the door. I had no clue what could be lurking outside, but I didn't care about any other dangers at the moment. I needed to get out of here. My heart had reached the speed which could cause me to faint. I'd never been this terrified in my life. Terrified to be crushed by the room.

If I stayed here any longer, I'd go mad.

But the door didn't open.

I began to pray. And I prayed, prayed, and prayed like a madwoman to the Gods above to save me from this cruel torture.

I don't want to die. I don't want to die.

I'm not ready ...

The door opened, and I fell headlong. I cursed under my breath, then inhaled to fill my lungs with some air.

My heartbeat remained chaotic, but at least the walls weren't threatening to squeeze me into a pancake.

"A-are you all right?"

I'd forgotten there was a person here.

I raised my head and faced a brunette with fair skin clothed in a dirty-brown dress, which reminded me of what a maid would wear since a white apron was part of the attire. I managed to stand up on my unsteady legs, towering over the girl.

I narrowed my eyes at her. "Who are you?"

She lowered her gaze to a pair of dark brown shoes set on the neatly folded clothes she was holding. "I'm Thea."

Shyly, she tucked a loose strand of her hair behind her ear, her pinkie finger quivering. Presuming she didn't like to be stared at, I glanced over the slightly lit corridor instead.

"Where am I?"

"In the Realm of Bones mansion."

"In the Realm of what?"

She smiled. "Realm of Bones," she replied in a mild voice. "It's one of the five realms of the Empire of Beasts."

It irritated me that the Mortal Region had disposed of most sources about morphs' world, as knowing the map would really come in handy right now.

"How did I get here?"

"Well," she said, "like all of us. Through the portal."

"I meant how I got *here*, not in the empire, Thea."

She let out an awkward chuckle. "I-I don't know."

Perhaps it was not the best idea to question the girl, no younger than seventeen. Judging from her shyness, she hadn't been here for a long time, clearly serving in the mansion as a maid. A human, too, I figured. I wasn't sure what morphs looked like, but I doubted they would be shivering from me like Thea was.

I pointed at the clothes in her hands. "Do I need to wear this?" I couldn't disguise the repulsion in my inquiry.

Holland's warnings of morphs chimed in my mind. In other words: *disobey, and you'll get punished.* The ugly scar on her nape—which I could wager was cruel beasts' doing—was just an example of what I'd receive or what might happen to Thea for not succeeding at her task that must have been to come here and hand me this tasteless uniform.

She nodded.

I took the clothes along with shoes. "Am I a maid of this mansion?" I returned to a claustrophobic room and hid behind the door. I placed the shoes on the floor and threw the given clothes on the top of the door. Once I kicked off Gen's shoes, my toes curled with delight. My feet had been freed from suffocating in two-sizes-too-small shoes at last.

"Imogen told me you were assigned as one because Asenah was missing one maid."

I started wriggling out of Gen's tight dress. "Who's Imogen?"

It was a struggle to get out of the dress, but I did it. When I reached for the brown dress, I winced at it. But I couldn't expect to wear beautiful clothes while working for morphs to keep myself alive. This had to do. Not like I had a choice anyway.

There were some scratches on my knees. I must have gained them after the portal had spat me out. At least as I put on the dress, the long skirt concealed them.

"She's the chief cook here," Thea replied as I donned the unflattering white apron, doing my best to tie the straps into a presentable bow without having eyes on my back. "She's kind to good people. If they're not ... good, she could be ... a little bit mean."

Done with the apron, I remembered to retrieve the folded sketch from Gen's dress and slid it into the pocket. I slipped my feet into the shoes. They were a bit small, but after enduring a walk through the rainforest in Gen's shoes, I couldn't complain. I untied my hair, which I ended up swiping into a bun.

Since there was no mirror in the room, I couldn't see my final appearance. Whether the bun turned out to look appropriate or not. But then, why would it matter? I didn't need a mirror to know that the ugly uniform didn't suit me at all, especially when dirt brown almost blended with my skin tone. The messy hairstyle wouldn't ruin my appearance more than it already was.

Stepping out from behind the door, I scanned the room for the bag I had brought with me to this world, but it was nowhere to be seen.

Of course, *they* had confiscated it. It had a bloody golden knife inside!

I turned to Thea, who still lingered in the corridor, and smoothed out the creases on my uniform. "And who's Asenah?"

Something strange flashed in Thea's onyx eyes, perhaps fear. "S-she's ... She's the Queen of the Realm of Bones. A morph," she whispered the last word, "The mistress of the mansion."

My stomach dropped.

The queen of one of the realms. Not of the empire, thank the Gods, but she was still a *queen*. She had power. She could be formidable, which, of course, she must be.

"Is she bad?" I asked probably the dumbest question I could

come across.

Of course, morphs were *bad.* Dangerous species to any human. I'd read enough written tales about them to be aware of their barbarousness.

"Asenah is ... well, it's better not to disappoint her. But her twin cousins ..." She tucked the strand behind her ear once again. "It's better to avoid them if possible."

I scrawled a mental note.

"We should go," she said. "Imogen is about to finish making dinner. We're going to have to serve it to the morphs."

I shivered at the thought of seeing the morphs for the first time ever tonight. I hadn't braced myself for it.

"Dinner?" As we left the room, she closed the door. "How long was I unconscious?"

We walked side by side. I felt slightly uncomfortable being about a head taller than Thea. Like a mutant standing beside such a short and petite girl.

"Just two days," she answered.

"Just?"

Two days was a long time. I wondered what my family had been up to after I'd left. Gen must be all right. Hopefully Chase didn't unleash his anger on my family after discovering his fiancée was gone.

But I wasn't his fiancée anymore. I'd left the emerald ring to my mother to sell and receive a sufficient amount of money from it. I hadn't missed anything involving that ring. I despised the colour of it, as it reminded me of his hungry eyes every time he beheld me.

"Usually, when a person is brought here, they stay unconscious for about five days. The pill has that effect. But you were unconscious for only two days, which is surprising," she explained.

I didn't give it too much thought. "What about the other sixteen-year-olds?" My mind buzzed about one boy in particular. Franz. Was he here? "Are they all here?"

"No, they were sent to other realms to serve. All Asenah needed was one kitchen staff member, a maid, and someone who could take care of the garden since the previous gardener was—"

She left her sentence unfinished, lips pressed together as if holding back information. Without pressing further, we ascended the stairwell, and as we climbed, an arched window revealed the scenery outside, a lawn surrounded by pines.

The corridors here were grander than the ones at Chase's manor. However, it wasn't fair to compare the human's manor to a mansion of a morphs' *queen*. Of course, their world would outstrip ours in every way.

"In what animal can Asenah shapeshift?" I asked.

"A wolf."

"Oh, not the wolves."

Wolves and felines were deadly. Not as much as dragons, but they didn't exist anymore. There was no reason to fret about encountering one. Wolves, however ... a red zone.

Thea smiled a bit.

"How do morphs look exactly? Like us?"

"They have limbs and posture similar to ours, but their skin is furry or made of feathers or other types of skin. It depends on the animal. And well, Asenah and her cousins look like wolves."

I didn't want to meet them, but after Thea's description, I couldn't deny that I was also intrigued to see for myself what they actually looked like.

As we turned the corner, the other girls passed us, wearing the same attire as Thea and me. Thea waved almost imperceptibly at them.

Finally, we reached the kitchen. When I smelled food, my stomach growled in response to the divine smell, informing me I was hungry. For two days, I'd been unconscious and had no food in my belly. I *needed* something edible in my mouth. But something told me I wasn't going to receive a meal any time soon.

The kitchen itself was quite enormous. There was a mammoth dark-wood table in the centre where some people were chopping vegetables or stirring something in the bowls. Wooden counters had all sorts of tools placed on them. I recognised some of them as bowls, pans, and pots, but most of them were new to me.

I wasn't an expert when it came to kitchen matters. Not as Gen was. I bet she would have liked the assortment of kitchen gear, but she couldn't have this fate where she ended up as morphs' slave.

The people in the kitchen didn't notice us. Too preoccupied with the work in their hands. I counted six of them. One of them was a woman with ample hips wearing a white cap to prevent her auburn hair from dropping into the food, shouting orders to chop or taste something in a southeastern accent. No doubt she was the same Imogen Thea had told me about. The other five must be the kitchen staff who helped her to prepare food.

Not to hinder them, Thea and I stood by the door.

"Ten minutes left, and we have to carry the meal," Thea said quietly.

I nodded, continuing to observe people bustling around like workaholic bees until a bell rang.

My heart jumped at such an obnoxiously loud sound. I followed where it was coming from, and on the right, there were two rows of bells. The one that was ringing had *Dining Room* written below it.

"It's time," Thea said and began walking towards the wall.

I hurried after her.

The bell ceased ringing once we approached a counter where a stack of silver trays and covers were arranged neatly on the table. Thea explained how I was supposed to do my job, which was the same as hers.

In short, the dinner was made of an appetiser, the main meal, and dessert. First, we'd have to carry an appetiser to the dining room. We'd remain there until morphs were about to finish eating it. Then we would have to serve the main meal to them and stay there until it was time to carry the dessert. After bringing one, we'd vanish out of the morphs' sight. Nothing too tricky and complicated. I believed I'd do just fine.

When we got the food on our trays, the other maid helped us take an appetiser to the dining room. I paced behind her.

We reached double wooden doors guarded by two human-looking guards. Their eyes fell on us. Thea greeted them quietly, and both of them smiled at the girl. They must be humans.

I inhaled, trying to poise myself for what I was about to face within the dining room, but the guards put their hands on the door handles and opened the door before I was ready.

Since I was the last in the line, I couldn't see what the doors had revealed, regardless of my height. Thea stepped inside noiselessly with the other maid and me in tow.

And then I saw them.

A tray almost slipped from my hands, but thank the heavens it didn't.

When Thea had described morphs, I'd only roughly pictured their appearance. Thus, I hadn't expected them to be exactly how she'd characterised them—three wolves in the shape of humans.

The woman sitting at the head of the table had two wolf-like ears protruding from her long, jet-black hair. Her face matched a wolf apart from her eyes that could be compared to a human. Grey-blue. Just like my—no, not my sister's. *Definitely* not my sister's.

She must have been the infamous Asenah, the Queen of Bones, the mistress of this impressive mansion.

As uncanny as it was to see the wolf sitting at the dining table, she was also wearing a chestnut satin dress. The full grandeur of the attire was obscured by the table, yet I could tell the dress was expensive and well-designed one.

But a wolf in a gown! Could this world be taken seriously if it was full of bizarre creatures like in a carnival?

Two brown wolves that looked alike sat beside her, garbed in less formal attire: white shirts with brown suspenders. One of them had short black hair, another longer but secured in a lower bun.

I figured they were cousins of Asenah, the same ones Thea had warned me about.

Thea didn't linger to approach Asenah and set an appetiser covered by a shiny silver cover before her.

I followed her moves alongside the other maid and placed an appetiser before one of the brothers. I sensed their stares at me but ignored them along with the warning voice in the back of my mind yelling at me to flee.

But where would I go if I fled?

As I uncovered their appetiser, I stepped back with a tray and a cover in my hands. My inquiring glance shifted to Thea, not sure what to do next. She walked to stand by the double door, her back facing the wall, face emotionless. I stood next to her, mimicking the void look of hers without putting in much effort.

As Asenah reached for cutlery with her hands, I was surprised to find they weren't paws. Despite the fur, their shape was identical to mine. She ate her appetiser, wielding a fork and knife better than I would have, or most humans could. I tried not to appear marvelled, avoiding drawing unnecessary attention.

"How was your meeting with Amyas?" Asenah asked.

T-they could also speak?

She opened her wolf-like mouth and bit the cherry off the fork.

But didn't wolves prefer meat instead of berries or fruits? They were predators, after all.

"Boring," the short-haired male replied.

The long-haired nodded in agreement.

Asenah took a sip of the red wine. "I hope you two didn't embarrass our entire kin while being there."

If not for her wild exterior, I would say she was a well-mannered lady, but it was impossible to overlook the animal features outweighing human ones.

The wolves exchanged glances, their meaning known only to them. "No," the long-haired said.

Asenah didn't look at them as she took another delicate sip. "Did you get to know your future wife during the visit, Lupin, or their servants instead?"

The short-haired one covered his mouth, as if to suppress a smile, while Lupin winced.

"First of all, cousin," Lupin began, "I don't come on to servants, unlike Fillan." Fillan barked a laugh, and Asenah observed Lupin from the corner of her eye. "Second of all, dear Kayla was mostly away." He raised a glass to his mouth. "And finally, Amyas is having doubts about whether to let his precious sister marry someone like me or not."

Asenah's jaw tightened. "What?" she growled through her gritted teeth.

Now *that* was more like a wolf's behaviour.

"He might not have invited me for a little chat to explicitly tell me he doesn't want me to marry Kayla, but his attitude insinuated that he dislikes both me and Fillan." He took a sip of his wine and swallowed before speaking again. "I don't think the wedding is happening anytime soon, cousin."

"No." Her tone was unbending. "That's not happening. I'll talk with Amyas myself. Perhaps I'll coax him better than you two simpletons can."

"But why her?" Lupin asked, avoiding Asenah's challenging stare. "I mean, the princess is quite ... horrible-looking."

"Hideous," Fillan added.

"We all look hideous, you fools," Asenah said.

"But she was also unattractive at the Spring Equinox!" Lupin whined.

"Ugly or not, you're still marrying her," Asenah said. "We need an assured alliance. Only the Gods know when Drayard is going to snap."

Silence fell over the room.

Lupin and Fillan exchanged looks, a hint of fear passing through their identical faces as they swallowed hard.

Asenah's reaction was different. She seemed more lost in her thoughts than frightened, unlike her cousins.

I didn't understand why they'd fallen silent after mentioning someone named Drayard.

Fillan leaned closer to Asenah. "Careful with his name," he whispered so quietly that if not for the silent room, I wouldn't have heard him. "You might summon him by accident."

"Yes, only Gods know what *he* is capable of," Lupin agreed in a whisper, too.

"The Bloodsucker won't step into our lands," Asenah assured, and for a second, I'd forgotten how to breathe. I must have misheard the word she said because there was no way ... "He has more important things to do in his own realm than to stalk us. Besides, we haven't seen him in years. Summoning him is the last thing we need to concern ourselves with. However, that he's been too silent after his father's demise, that's something we ought to be taking seriously. He might be planning something unholy."

"Enchanters murdered his father, not us." Fillan sighed. "Why would he want to attack us?"

Asenah shook her head. "Not attack us, but force us into

helping avenge his father."

"It's been six years, and so far, nothing. We don't have to worry about the alliance with the Realm of Talons," Fillan protested. "Lupin doesn't need to marry an uncomely girl and spoil our family line with her horrible genes. The Bloodsucker won't do anything."

The Bloodsucker.

By now, I was sure I hadn't misheard *that* word.

But there was no way, no possibility, that they were talking about the same monster.

He didn't exist. He couldn't—

Thea nudged my arm, snapping me out of my frightening thoughts. I whipped my head to her, and she subtly gestured for me to fetch their main dish.

But before we left, my ears caught Asenah's following words. "Perhaps, but we still have to be prepared for anything that might befall us. The Bloodsucker or not."

IX

I was the only one stuck doing dishes in the scullery. Thea had left early without giving a hand to any of the staff. Imogen had sent her to sleep. One of her staff girls had whispered to me that Imogen always pampered Thea. I paid no heed to such a remark as my concerns were elsewhere.

Asenah and her cousins hadn't spoken much after the appetiser. Even if I was still processing everything I had learned about morphs in a single day, it wasn't my primary concern.

The Bloodsucker had occupied my thoughts ever since they mentioned him.

I couldn't believe they were discussing the same beast, the same monster my mother used to read tales about whenever I misbehaved. She assumed it would intimidate me enough to think twice about my tantrums, but she was wrong. I was more enchanted by the stories than scared.

The Bloodsucker was fictional. He couldn't be real, let alone be walking among us. And even if he *were* real, he couldn't be *alive*.

"Oh, heavens, you're scrubbin' like a crone."

Imogen snatched the scrub brush out of my grasp and gently pushed me away from the sink. She continued rinsing dishes herself, much faster than I. I hadn't even seen her enter.

"I'm sorry," I murmured.

She handed me a dripping plate. "You're lucky that I'm no morph or else you'd be mah dinner."

I took it, gripped a cloth, and dried the rest of the dishes as fast as I could, putting them in the cabinet. While in such a hurry, a bowl almost slipped from my hands. She observed me, expecting me to drop the bowl. I didn't. With a sheepish smile, I placed the unharmed bowl in the cabinet.

She did the scrubbing; I did the drying. The silence weighed down the atmosphere. Unable to bear it much longer, I blurted out, "Asenah talked with her cousins about someone during dinner."

"One rule of bein' the maid is that ye cannot listen to what morphs are talkin' about, lassie. Didn't Thea tell ye that?"

"No," I replied. "It's not possible to stand and not hear anything."

"Then act like you're not listening to them. If ye show any emotion that would betray your ears are catchin' every single word of thairs, they'll kill ye without a seicont thought."

I swallowed hard.

I didn't think anyone had noticed me listening. All three of them had been too immersed in their conversation and food to check if some new maid was eavesdropping or not.

"So, what were thay talking about?" Imogen whispered, intrigued.

"About someone called Drayard."

Imogen halted her movements, holding a wet glass above the sink. Then she resumed washing it as if nothing had happened.

"Is he ..." I dampened my lips. "Is he the same Bloodsucker from *A Tale of the Bloodsucker*?"

She neither confirmed nor denied it but started washing the same glass harder, even if it was already clean.

My heartbeat increased. Her silence had confirmed Asenah and her cousins were speaking about the same monster who might not have been fictional after all.

"Is he?" I persisted, despite my increasing pulse.

Silence.

"Imogen?"

"Yes," she blurted out. "He's the same. The one and only."

I had to lean against the counter, as I might have fainted. "But ... how?" I asked myself more than her but expected her to answer. "Since when are tales real?"

"You'd be surprised how many tales ye'v heard throughout yer life ur based on true stories, lassie."

She handed me the last glass, and I wiped it in an utter daze. It wasn't every day you learn that your favourite scary tale of all time was very much real.

"I don't understand how someone like him can exist, let alone have a *name*."

"Oh, he doesn't have only a name," she said with a raise of her auburn eyebrows. "He's also a king. *The* King o' kings an' queens and the King of Embers realm, too."

I blinked, astounded. "A monster is ... A monster is a royal?"

"Yes."

Oh, my ... "Have you seen him?"

"Dear Gods forbid something like that happening someday." She crossed herself. "No. I haven't seen him. Thank the Gods."

As I finished drying the last glass, I returned it to the counter. "I used to think that the Bloodsucker was a monster, not an actual person with a form. He's one of the species, right?"

She nodded. "He is." She dried her hands with a towel and pushed the loose strands away from her eyes. "A half-breed," she specified. "A half-breed of a bat an' a dragon."

My lips parted.

"Yes, dragons still exist," she confirmed my fears. "At least one o' them. His entire kind was assassinated by enchanters six years ago."

Chase had mentioned something about it.

"Why?"

"Dragons were a threat tae enchanters. Thay feared them. However, thay missed killing th' most dangerous o' them all." She drew in a breath. "The Bloodsucker, Drayard Emyur, and the bastard son of Arragon."

I'd heard about Arragon before. Again, I knew about him because of tales. In the war lasting for one hundred and five years, known as the Hundred Years' War, enchanters and humans had been fighting to liberate themselves from morphs. Arragon, being the King of kings, had led morphs into what wasn't an entirely triumphant victory.

But I had never heard of his son. At least not by his real name. "Arragon had a child with a bat morph?"

Imogen nodded. "Rumour has it she was a harlot bat. Drayard was conceived by accident, an' his mother left him behind his father's castle gates. He was called a bastard, but later on, he earned the Bloodsucker's nickname, an' no one has dared to call him Arragon's bastard ever since."

I wasn't familiar with that part of the story. All I knew was that during the Hundred Years' War, the same fearsome Bloodsucker—who apparently had an entire identity—sucked the blood from people, set on fire those who tried to stop him, and feasted on the offal of the fallen. After the war, stories of missing children ensued, suggesting that the Bloodsucker was also responsible for that.

And he was *real*, walking among us, terrifying not only human but also inhuman species, such as morphs.

"Try not tae question everything ye hear, lassie," she advised with a sigh. "Curiosity is what kills us humans. Be careful with that trait o' yers. It's not safe for one to possess it in this world."

I nodded but didn't take it seriously, considering the multitude of information I still had to process.

"It's late," Imogen mused. "Do ye know your way back tae your room?"

I winced at the reminder of the room that had almost left me unhinged. Preoccupied with other matters, I hadn't thought it would become my permanent bedroom.

"I can't go back into my room," I said, earning a quizzical look from Imogen. "I'm claustrophobic."

She appeared to be contemplating something. "Mah room's bigger," she said. "Ye can sleep in mine tonight."

A pebble among thousands rolled off my chest. Imogen wasn't bad; she might be a little strict, but she was a kind person, just as Thea had informed.

"Thank you," I uttered from the bottom of my heart.

Three days later, I was still sleeping in Imogen's bedroom, a space slightly more spacious than the one I had woken up in. Imogen's room lacked windows too, but at least its size didn't trigger claustrophobia. Imogen was kind enough to move into a smaller room, permanently relinquishing hers to me.

The staff kept addressing me by my sister's name. It was confusing, but I quickly grasped that they were referring to me, not Gen, believing I was her—a sixteen-year-old girl skilled in baking and cooking. Thank heavens no one had put my alleged skills to the test yet.

Homesickness had already set in, but I particularly missed the sound of the piano, which the mansion lacked. Even if there was one, I wouldn't be allowed to play it. At least I found a pencil and papers in Asenah's study room while cleaning yesterday.

My daily routine remained consistent: early morning wake-ups, preparing breakfast with Thea and the staff manager, Jill, and serving the wolves. Following that, cleaning the kitchen and helping to prepare lunch with Imogen. Serve lunch, clean up, and assist again. Last but not least, serve dinner—a more complicated task compared to breakfast and lunch.

But today, as I stepped into the kitchen, a surprise awaited me. Imogen was explaining something to a boy whose presence I hadn't noticed before, with blonde hair—

"Franz," I whispered.

Imogen noticed my stare. "Guid mornin', lassie," she said. "Here, come." She gestured while walking to the cupboard. I followed, and she handed me a basket. "Go tae th' greenhouse and fetch me some tomatoes with brussels sprouts, and I don't want to hear any complaints or else you're having a raw potato fer dinner tonight."

She wasn't joking. The last time I resisted bringing flowers to Imogen from the garden, claiming that Thea would handle the task better than me since she wouldn't get lost, as I had once, Imogen served me bread with jam while others enjoyed cooked beef for dinner. I had learned my lesson.

I took the basket from her, saying, "Already on it."

"All right, where was I?" Imogen turned to Franz.

"I ... uh ..." Franz scratched his temple. "You talked about how this Asenah loves milk in her morning tea?"

"Aye. She also ..." She glanced at me from the corner of her eye. "And what are ye still doing 'ere? Those vegetables won't come here by themselves!"

Franz and I exchanged glances. I could tell he was feeling a bit out of place, but he would get used to Imogen's tough personality and everything else his work entailed. I offered him a reassuring smile before I left to carry on with my task.

The greenhouse was in the rear of the mansion, close to a forest. Many flower beds bloomed along the paths. One path diverged into the heart of the garden, which I hadn't got an opportunity to explore yet. I also skipped it this time, rushing towards the greenhouse where all the vegetables were.

"Elynn Startel."

My stomach dropped as I came to a halt at the sound of *my* name. I looked back, meeting a girl who had left my memory until now.

The suspicious girl.

She had a wry smile on her face. Instead of wearing clothes she'd worn the day we'd got through the portal, she was dressed in garb smudged with muddy brown as if she was rolling in the dirt with it.

Oh, she was that new gardener.

How lucky I am ...

I turned fully towards her and crossed my arms. "I'm not scared of you."

The girl huffed out a laugh. "Me neither. I just want to know how you changed into Genette."

"How do you know Genette?"

"I know everyone in the town. It's not that big, Elynn. If you paid more attention to people around you, perhaps you would have known who I was in the first place."

I glanced around, alarmed that someone might be in the garden, but nobody was there. However, it didn't make me less worried. "Don't call me by my name. Someone might hear you."

"Nobody will."

"How can you be so sure?"

The suspicious girl's smile turned lopsided. "You didn't answer *my* question."

I gritted my teeth, the bracelet on my wrist heating as a reminder to calm myself. And I did. "I don't see a reason why I should answer you."

"Which you should," she noted. "I could tell morphs your true identity, which would get you in trouble if you haven't figured out where I'm heading with all this."

Scoffing, I shook my head in disbelief. I'd supposed the suspicious girl would be a problem. "What good would it do for you if you had access to that information?"

"To feed my curiosity. I'm sure you're familiar with such an urge."

I clenched my jaw. Did I have another choice apart from telling her?

"All right," I breathed. "I learned about a potion in the library and gave it a try."

"There's no book about potions in the library. You ain't fooling me."

"I was in the city's library."

"The city doesn't have such books either."

Yes, it did. She didn't know there was a mysterious aisle in the library meant only to be seen by the ones who searched, as the boy's spirit had claimed. Of course, the girl wouldn't buy a vague version of the story.

"You won't believe me if I tell you more."

"But I will," she assured me.

A moment of silence sank between us, but eventually, I spilled the beans about the boy's spirit to her. I told her he'd shown me the invisible shelves, leading me to the book that had saved my sister from her fate. But I said nothing about the boy's death. If she didn't ask how he'd died or who he was, there was no need to tell her that.

"Seems plausible," she acknowledged.

"What's your name, blackmailer?"

She clicked her tongue. "Clare."

With no goodbye, I pivoted on my heel, intent on resuming the task when she said, "Chase Holter will be looking for you."

My guts twisted. I didn't want to dwell on anything associated with him when it evoked the worst memories I wished I could erase from my mind entirely.

I glanced at her over my shoulder. "He won't."

I stepped forward, but apparently, she wasn't finished.

"But anything's possible. Chase had been a bachelor for quite a while and didn't look at a single girl until he saw you and became obsessed with you. He's a hunter, and he wouldn't miss a chance to hunt down some morph to save his fiancée."

"I am not his fiancée," I almost hissed but collected myself hastily. "Besides, he's not stupid enough to step into morphs' lands."

"Isn't he?"

I didn't respond. I was aware of Chase's obsession with me, but he wouldn't risk his life to come here. He was not that dedicated to our relationship. He might have already found another girl to wed. Alise perhaps. She was an inferior version of me and would have *loved* to live my life.

Pushing away the thoughts about my past, I walked off to find a greenhouse, gather the vegetables Imogen had asked me to bring, and not think about Chase who remained in the Mortal Region.

I *tried* my best to chase thoughts about him away, but that night I had a nightmare where he conquered the place of a monster. And there was no hero to protect me. Only me. An actress in my own play.

X

Nightmares about Chase hadn't ceased haunting my nights ever since Clare had mentioned the possibility of him coming here. Despite these incessant nightmares, being a morphs' maid wasn't as terrible as I'd anticipated after Holland's warnings. I'd choose to serve them over being Chase's wife for the rest of my life if I had to make the choice again.

However, I remained vigilant. Though Asenah and her cousins paid little attention to a mere servant, I still had to be prepared for anything. After all, something had happened to the former gardener whose disappearance everybody was silent about. When I'd separately asked Thea and Imogen about the former gardener, they had both dodged the question. All Imogen said was that curiosity could bring me death. Again.

Unable to face another nightmare, I refused to sleep one night. Instead, I found myself wandering around the mansion while everybody else slept. Aware of the morphs' heightened senses, especially their sensitive hearing, I avoided going anywhere near their chambers.

I padded outside, inhaling the calming scent of pine air, which sometimes chased away my nightmares.

Moving at a snail's pace, I neared the end of the garden and stepped into the moonlit forest. I made sure not to go too far, as getting lost or being spotted by any morph and getting myself murdered wasn't in my interest. Except for the flitting bat, I spotted no other creatures in the wild.

I paused, knowing I shouldn't venture any deeper. But as I was on the point of turning back, a golden light gleamed in my periphery.

I watched it as if hoping it would disappear, but it remained there, tempting me to investigate.

I had to head back. Even if the strange light was like a magnet drawing me in, calling me to proceed forward, I had to head back. I *must.*

But I didn't move.

Drawing in a breath, I surrendered to curiosity.

The light grew brighter the closer I got to it, and the night's light breeze brushed against my skin. I wrapped my arms around myself, but it didn't warm me when I was wearing a short-sleeved nightgown that wasn't made for night-time adventures.

As I halted before the hovering light, it didn't dazzle me as I would have expected.

I had seen nothing like it before: a melon-sized yellow orb streaming soft light as it levitated above the ground. What kind of creature was it?

"*Shapeshifters of the empire turn into beasts ...*" The chorus of voices shifted from within the light in a fluid echo.

Entirely spellbound, I took another step forward, looking for a source from where those words had come from, but there was only light.

"*... but shall return to their true form when days last as long as nights.*"

Was the light the one who talked? How was it possible?

But I worked for a queen who looked like a half-beast and half-human. Anything was possible. Something like a talking light orb should be the least staggering thing in these cursed lands.

"*The meant to be, yet doomed to fall, shall bear them lost and found whose creation's blood shall be spilled once the longest night falls.*"

The voices swelled into a clamour, sending a gazillion invisible, minuscule spiders crawling over my back.

By now, I believed I was dreaming or hallucinating. The latter seemed more plausible since I hadn't experienced a decent dream before. My nights were usually dreamless. Only recently had nightmares signed a deal to trouble me.

"*Only then, humanity may take over their shapes for life!*"

The light orb vanished along with the voices, and deadly silence returned, leaving me flummoxed.

The meant to be, yet doomed to fall? Some creation's blood shall be spilled once the longest night falls? What was the purpose of all this? A trick to addle my already tired brain?

I needed to return to the mansion. That was all I was currently sure of.

But once I turned around, a wolf stood in front of me. A real dark-brown wolf. Not the ones I was familiar with, in the shape of a human. No.

A *wild* wolf.

The beast bared its teeth, polished fangs glinting in the moonlight.

I tried not to show fear. "Good boy," I stammered, instantly regretting my choice of words.

Good boy? Wasn't there anything dumber you could have thought of to say, Elynn? I chided myself.

The wolf advanced, and I retreated a step. He snarled, advancing again.

My pounding heart was about to crawl out of my parched throat. I made to scream for help, but then I remembered I was in the Empire of Beasts. No one would come to my rescue; I would get slaughtered instead.

Run, a voice commanded.

I spun around and began running without throwing a single glance back.

I didn't need to assure myself if he was behind me as I could hear his steps threatening to reach me.

Turn right!

What?

Turn right!

The voice did not belong to me. Not sure why, but whoever had sent me the command, I complied. As I veered right, I was close to tripping over a branch, but I overleaped it just in time. The rush of adrenaline pushed me to keep going.

But I couldn't run forever. I wasn't in the right physical shape for it. I was already panting, my heart flying, and cold air stinging my lungs. The wolf would catch me at some point. I had to hide. Climb a tree ...

A wave of panic coursed through me. It was impossible to detect a tree that wasn't a pine. They weren't climbable.

I was doomed.

Keep running forward.

Here was that unrecognisable, urgent voice again.

Who are you?

No answer.

I must be having a bad dream. It all felt too surreal, like a nightmare. But, in nightmares, I couldn't stir, was rooted to the spot, and running was out of the question—the opposite of what I was doing now.

As I thought my minutes were counted—seconds—the voice in my head thought otherwise.

As if a miracle had fallen right from the heavens, the lone oak tree shone in a circle of pines.

I believed my eyes were deceiving me. There was no way ... But, after concentrating on one spot in the distance, the more real the oak seemed to be.

I exerted myself to increase all my remaining speed, and with a heart slamming against my ribs, I lurched to a halt for a mere second to grab at the branch and climb onto it.

When I was little and fond of climbing trees, Mum used to warn me I would fall and break a bone someday, but I never had. Hopefully, tonight wouldn't be the exception, considering it had been a while since I dared to claw my way to a tree's top.

My elbows were already on the branch when something sharp dug into my ankle. Clenching my teeth and perhaps committing a mistake of the Universe, I glanced back.

The wolf had clamped onto my ankle with his teeth.

This bloody wolf was about to eat me alive!

With each tug, he aimed to pull me down. I clung to the branch desperately, even though the death was already breathing down my neck. Just as I resigned myself to becoming the wolf's late-night feast, an unexpected yelp pierced the air. I didn't feel anything on my ankle anymore except for the pain. Curious, I stole a glance downward to find the wolf rolling on the grass, seemingly trying to rid itself of something clinging to its fur.

What the ...

But I couldn't gape like an owl to figure out what was wrong with my predator. I looked away, pulling myself up despite the pain gnawing at my muscles while clenching my teeth. I heaved my other leg on the branch and hoisted myself up, wasting no more than a second before getting onto a higher branch. The smell of my blood dripping down my ankle might already be luring more beasts, but I couldn't concern myself with that now. A retching sound below me reached my ears, but I didn't sate my curiosity by looking down this time.

I reached for a higher branch to lessen the chances of him catching me, but my foot slipped. With my legs dangling in the air, I managed to hold on to the wood. The wolf would tear me into ribbons if I didn't push myself to move, despite my aching muscles.

Not letting panic overwhelm me and refusing to give up, I hauled myself up, reaching another branch.

As I ensconced myself in the tree, I pulled the hems of my nightgown up to my shins. As expected, blood seeped through the bitten area.

I glanced down at my assailant, finding the wolf already staring at me, his copper eyes shimmering with wrath and disgust. I recognised those eyes. They used to glance at me during dinner, lunch, or breakfast once in a while.

I swallowed my fear and sucked in the air, releasing it with a shudder. The wolf turned around. Was he going to leave? Impossible.

But he *did* leave, and yet I wasn't relieved, not even when he disappeared from my sight. He might have gone to fetch his brother or the whole pack and wait for their meal to descend and finish me off if I didn't die from the blood loss or infection first.

I noticed blood on the grass. Had he been retching because of it?

The blood glistened.

I winced.

It began to change.

I blinked twice. Three times. Mystified. This couldn't be possible. Hallucinations blinded my perception. Wasn't that what happened from the loss of blood? What I was witnessing now couldn't be genuine.

Crimson transformed into yellow.

Once again, believing my eyes were playing tricks on me, I blinked, but nothing changed. My blood was yellow. Sparkling yellow. *Golden.*

The moonlight must be playing with lights and shadows, but I doubted that theory.

It *was* golden. It turned from crimson into *golden.*

Bubbles popped atop the liquid until it flamed up. My heart skipped a beat. I was going to die in the fire, which would spread across the forest ...

But I didn't need to worry, as the flame vanished together with the blood, leaving only a scorched patch of grass.

I looked down at my bleeding ankle, anticipating golden blood, but it was dark red as it should be.

I placed my palms on the ankle to stem the bleeding, but it didn't stop, painting my hands with crimson instead.

Chase had once talked about surviving. I hadn't listened much, but the information must have been at the back of my mind, surfacing in moments like these.

I ripped off the hem of my nightdress and wrapped it around my injured ankle. After tying into a knot, I clasped my wound tightly, whispering prayers for surviving until another day.

It wasn't safe to return to the mansion. The wolf might return any minute. I had to wait until I was sure it was safe to go back. *If* I would ever be safe if I returned.

I shouldn't have gone into the forest.

Curiosity is what kills us humans, Imogen's wise words smacked me as an ironic reminder.

I had been too caught up in figuring out who the source of

light in the forest was. Yet, I hadn't learned who or what it was. All I had heard were voices reciting words that now lingered in my mind.

I pressed my forehead to my knees, sobbing.

I had handed myself to the hands of death, all thanks to my curious nature.

I didn't die. I was merely overreacting.

At dawn, I hobbled back to the mansion unnoticed. My leg throbbed with pain, blood soaking the fabric wrapped around my ankle.

As I entered the kitchen, I thanked my lucky stars that it was empty. I poured water and drank it eagerly to soothe my parched throat, and I filled another vessel to take downstairs.

I descended into the servant quarters, leaning against the wall for support, and slipped into the tiny bathroom. I didn't close the door, which was a risk, but I'd rather be walked in on fixing a wound than being caved in. As I placed a glass on the edge of the cracked bathtub, I lifted my injured leg, unwrapping the blood-stained fabric. Once I poured cold water on my ankle, a sigh of satisfaction escaped me, and I closed my eyes, savouring the temporary relief.

I washed away the dried blood, uncovering four deep fang marks. Given their depth, they would take a while to heal.

For the first time, I appreciated the maid's floor-length dress concealing the wound. I had a sleepless night but taking a nap seemed pointless after what had happened. I doubted I would be able to fall asleep at all.

The wolf was either Fillan or Lupin. The dark-brown fur and copper eyes betrayed them. And if they had recognised me ... I didn't want to dwell on what might befall me. Would they finish their meal, or ...?

Walking around as if the wolf hadn't dug his fangs into my ankle a few hours ago was challenging. My heart raced once the time to serve breakfast arrived.

I breathed in, breathed out. I refrained from uttering a single word to anyone, only exchanging hellos. Whether Thea noticed my uncharacteristic behaviour or not, she chose to remain silent. Better for me. Nobody needed to be aware of my latest venture.

As the guards opened the double doors, I stepped behind Thea. Curious, I surveyed the table, finding one wolf absent. Fillan.

"Is your brother hungover again?" Asenah asked, her tone devoid of interest.

I placed a plate with a silver cover before Lupin and uncovered it before I made my way to the door, eyes downcast.

"I don't know," Lupin replied with a hoarse voice. "I haven't seen him since we left the bar."

"Perchance, he mistook the beds again?"

"Perhaps." But a flavour of doubt shaded his tone.

"What happened to your leg?"

I went still. As I turned my head, Franz stared at me, waiting for my answer. It was almost dinner time. I had been growing confident that nobody would question my odd gait, and my nocturnal adventures would remain my secret. But Franz destroyed my hopes.

As I opened my mouth to lie, Imogen emerged out of the blue and shoved a tray with a covered plate into my hands. Stumbling back, I almost dropped it but quickly regained my balance.

"Carry this tae Fillan's chamber," she ordered.

My eyes widened. "W-what? N-no."

Was Fillan back already? I'd hoped he was gone forever.

Oh, who was I trying to fool? My wishes never came true. Of course, he was back. And he was back to finish what he had started.

"What do ye mean, no?" Her eyebrows knitted. "Do yer job, lassie." She walked away.

I scanned the kitchen in search of Thea.

"Thea's helping in th' greenhouse," Imogen informed me.

With a frown, I pivoted on my heel and left the kitchen. But before I ascended the stairs, I rested my head against the wall and focused on breathing, trying to calm my pounding heart.

I would only have to step into his bedroom, place the tray on his bedside table, and depart. I would be all right. But after the night's events, I doubted I would walk out of his room unscathed.

I headed to the third floor and reached his chamber. The doors were already ajar, and voices came from the room.

"He came back feeling like this?" an unfamiliar man's voice spoke.

"Yes," Asenah answered.

I slipped into the room, keeping my gaze low to my feet. I was invisible after Thea had taught me the wonders of walking like a mouse. Covertly, I took a peek at the morphs. Asenah and Lupin stood at the foot of Fillan's bed. Next to the bed was another morph in a sparrow's form, and Fillan was lying under the covers. For a split second, I thought he wasn't breathing, but the sheets were barely rising. Fillan seemed ... half-dead.

I set down the tray on the nearest bedside table, shooting a furtive glance at the sparrow, who seemed to play the physician's role. Swiftly, I exited the room but lingered in the hallway.

I hid behind the partially open door, pressing against the wall where no one could spot the eavesdropping maid.

"Alcohol poisoning isn't the case here. Morphs can handle alcohol overdose extremely well," the physician informed.

Retching sounds followed.

"Do you recall trying something you aren't likely to eat, my lord?" the physician asked.

"No," Fillan mumbled.

"Not another creature, by any chance?"

"I said"—another sound of throwing up—"no."

"Hmm," the physician hummed. "In most cases, dryads, Ascended Sorceresses, and enchanters cause poisoning. This appears like poisoning, my lord."

"He might have eaten a dryad," Asenah intervened. "Those troublesome creatures are all over the forest. When my cousin's strong suit isn't wisdom, precisely when he is intoxicated, he might have eaten one, Mr. Willbourn."

"If that's what it is, the poison will come out of his body in a matter of days. It depends on how much of the dryad he consumed," Mr. Willbourn said. "But we can't disregard the possibility of enchanter's blood, which could cause much worse—"

"Enchanters can't get into this land unnoticed," Asenah interrupted. "Ascended Sorceresses are also out of the question. They all have sacrificed themselves for the Spell, and the unascended ones are in Casidiarn. I'm confident he ate a dryad."

I had heard of Ascended Witches but not Sorceresses. Weren't they the same, just called differently? Ascended Witches were full of wickedness in their hearts, unlike normal witches. To become Ascended was a complicated ritual of which there was no further information.

But the sacrifice for some unknown Spell was something brand new to me. What Spell, and why was I hearing it for the first time?

"Our birthday is in two weeks. He'll be fine by then, right, Mr. Willbourn?" Lupin inquired, concerned.

"I'm certain he will be."

As the physician proceeded to explain how to treat Fillan, I left.

It wasn't a dryad, however, who had made him vomit.

A hunch whispered that my blood had played a significant part. I hadn't been dreaming or hallucinating when I'd witnessed my blood turning golden, flaring up, and then disappearing. I couldn't comprehend what had caused my blood to do the impossible, but as the light reflected off my bracelet, a theory came to mind.

The same bracelet had burned me while I turned into Gen's lookalike. I had to remove it, as the pain was unbearable. It burned me later in the empire, but never before the Summer Solstice. Perhaps the bracelet was more than just an accessory.

I had no inkling of the powers held within the bracelet, but something was definitely up with it.

The dinner time passed, and as always, I found myself alone with Imogen in the kitchen. I had many questions for her, but none of them found their way out of my mouth.

"Why have ye been dragging yer shank all day?" Imogen asked.

Bloody hells.

I expected this question now. I had been lucky to evade it with Franz, but it might be impossible with Imogen.

Summoning my acting skills, I replied, "What happened to my leg? Did I hear it right?"

"Yes," she said, deadly serious, "ye did."

I winced. "Nothing happened."

My tone of voice was on the spot. There was no way she was—

"Don't lie, lassie," she said. "A've seen ye limping th' whole day."

"I fell off the stairs. Now it hurts."

Imogen stared at me, probably deliberating whether I was telling the truth, reminding me of Mum. My heart twisted.

At last, Imogen focused on the sink, resuming to scrub the dishes without questioning me.

Either she believed me or saw no purpose in extracting the truth.

"What do you know about Ascended Sorceresses and Witches?" I inquired, since I'd figured she wouldn't lecture me on this question. "Or are they one and the same?"

"Why do ye ask?"

I shrugged carelessly, attempting not to expose that I'd once again eavesdropped on something I shouldn't have. "There's not much written about them back home."

"That's because such information is transmitted from generation tae generation o' witches an' sorceresses, which, by the by, are not one an' th' same."

"So you don't know anything?"

"Weel." She dragged in a breath. "Sorceresses ur followers of th' Universe while witches serve the Gods. Once they're born, thay don't serve anybody, unless they choose to ascend tae gain all th' immeasurable power. Ascended Sorcerers, especially if thay come from th' powerful bloodline, with the Universe's blessing are Gods compared tae morphs' abilities."

"And Ascended Witches are blessed by Gods?"

She nodded. "That's right."

I dried a glass. "For what spell did Ascended Sorceresses sacrifice themselves?"

I placed the glass back into its place while Imogen remained silent. Another sigh left her as she handed me a clean glass to dry. "I see human lands still haven't figured it out."

I glanced at her quizzically. "Haven't figured out what?"

"Before th' sixteen-year-olds' offering started, the Ascended Sorceresses' coven had sacrificed themselves tae create the Spell that now protects the Mortal Region from unwanted visitors. No magic has been working there ever since. This way, morphs cannot step in th' Mortal Region without getting harmed."

I halted my movements, perplexity skidding through me. "If no morph can step into the Mortal Region, then sixteen-year-olds at the Summer Solstice are offered for no reason at all," I thought aloud. "The threat that if there's no offering, morphs will come and kill us is an absolute lie."

Imogen nodded.

I was close to crushing the glass. If not for Imogen taking it from my hand, I would have broken it. The bracelet was already heating my skin as I curled my hands into fists.

They had tricked us.

"Ye all right, lassie?"

I didn't reply but exhaled the heat of rage swimming through my blood and unclenched my fists. When the burning on my wrist lessened, I looked at a concerned Imogen. "But how is it possible for humans to forget about the sacrifice?"

"They can't forget what they don't know." Imogen put the glass away and closed the doors. She snatched a fresh towel and leaned against the counter, wiping her hands. "It was the sorceresses' mistake. Thay didn't tell anyone about this. Sorceresses are ... secretive and unlikely tae cooperate with humans. Most of thair families were mutilated by morphs. I assume thay thought it was wiser not tae tell a living soul about it tae protect thair other generations."

"But how did morphs learn about the sacrifice?"

"How do *ye* know thay know about the sacrifice?"

Her suspicious gaze bore into mine as I answered in a steady voice, "It's not hard to guess. They must be aware of it since no morph has ever stepped into our lands. At least it isn't noted in the records."

She observed me with a sceptical eye. I didn't betray anything. Her expression softened. "I believe ye already know the answer. Morphs actually travelled tae the Mortal Region, but when they didn't return, it wasn't hard fer th' rest tae realise that something was wrong. Morphs had thair own human witches—traitors," she spat the last word in revulsion. "While being there, thay found out about th' sacrifice, an' that magic doesn't work in human lands. Then thay reported it tae morphs."

My jaw clenched.

"Moreover, morphs decided to pay back the sorceresses an' invented the offering. Of course, their witches helped to implement it. Only human witches an' sorceresses can step into th' Mortal Region despite thair non-functional powers. But they've learned how tae create a portal, and the rest ye know."

I frowned. "That's why morphs need humans? To pay back the dead sorceresses because they can't get into the Mortal Region anymore? When they have already slaughtered their families?"

"Yes, and no," Imogen answered. "Four decades ago, morphs weren't th' wey they're now. They were like us, humans, but only with a power o' shapeshifting, more acute senses an' a longer lifespan."

"They weren't animals?"

"Thay *could* turn in tae animals, but they could also be in their human form if thay preferred it that way."

I couldn't believe my ears. Had I been living under a rock this whole time? I didn't know what morphs looked like before coming here. I didn't know about the sorceresses' sacrifice either. What other things had I absolutely no idea about? That *no* human knew?

"What happened that made them the way they are now, then?"

Imogen inhaled and let out a fatiguing sigh. Slight remorse gnawed at my chest for keeping her here when she was tired, but I needed to know. Besides, she didn't complain. "After feline morphs attacked a sorceresses' village and burned it, sorceresses decided tae do something about it. A curse was what they thought of.

"The curse's terms are that morphs stay as beasts forever, only at the Spring an' Autumn Equinoxes thay can turn back intae thair true form, but th' rest of the year they stay as beasts."

Shapeshifters of the empire turn into beasts but shall return to their true form when days last as long as nights ...

It wasn't some nonsense coming from the strange light bulb creature. It was the curse.

Now I understood everything since my first experience at a morphs' dinner. Asenah had pointed out that they all looked horrible when Lupin claimed Kayla had appeared unappealing at the Spring Equinox as well—one of the two days in a year when all the morphs could shapeshift back into their real forms.

"But why did morphs attack the village? Was there a reason behind their attack?"

"A don't know. For centuries there's been hostility between sorceresses an' morphs. That must have been the reason."

Morphs were brutal creatures. There had been no doubts before, but now, after learning this ...

They'd killed innocent people; they—

The boy's spirit from the library ... He mentioned not remembering how he died, only telling me that no one had seen him for forty years. His throat was slashed. Perhaps he was one of the village's victims. All the pieces connected, after all. If that were the case, morphs had slaughtered an innocent boy, and not just him. Morphs were monsters. They didn't deserve the curse. The curse was a sign of mercy. Instead, the sorceresses should have obliterated morphs for massacring their kin.

If only I had a golden knife—no matter that I shivered being close to a weapon made of gold—I would go upstairs and kill them in their sleep. Starting with Fillan, and then the rest.

"But how do you know any of this, Imogen?"

The end of her mouth curled into a knowing smile. "A've been servin' morphs for over a decade now. I've heard a lot since then."

If only I could somehow warn humans about this, how many lives would be saved! But there was nothing I could do. I was stuck here. Even if I tried to flee, I wouldn't survive a day in the wilderness without the necessary survival skills.

But I could always pour my blood into their glasses of wine ...

That night, I schemed on how to make morphs suffer, but drowsiness overtook me, and I slipped into a deep, tranquil slumber.

XII

Thea and I weeded the greenhouse, working like horses. Well, Thea was, while I cursed under my breath because of the dirt stuck under my nails. Thea seemed content with it, humming a tune I could easily play on the piano if I had one.

Her speed was incomparable to mine. In less than an hour, half of the greenhouse had been weeded. Thea was already watering the plants while I was still uprooting weeds from my side of the greenhouse.

I didn't have a green thumb. I wasn't capable of doing any labour. I could hardly, however, trouble myself with my lack of skills at the moment. I'd become irritated only because I had to do gardening. It was Clare's job, not ours. Perhaps I shouldn't be complaining when the garden was massive, and Clare was the only one taking care of it, but such a thought didn't end my vexation.

"Do you miss your family?" I asked since it had been silent long enough apart from Thea's humming, of course.

Thea ceased to hum and tilted her head in my direction. She put a loose strand behind her ear. "I try not to think about them too often."

I stopped pulling the weeds. "Me, too." I rose to my feet and walked to get some water. Lifting the canteen, I opened the cork and took a few thirsty gulps. "I have two young—older siblings. I miss them every day."

"I have five older brothers."

"That's a lot of brothers."

She nodded. "They took care of Mother and me while Father liked to have a bottle or two." Thea's chin dipped as she sighed, resuming watering the plants. "He used to abuse Mother, and one day my eldest brother, Drake, tried to stop our father from hitting her once again and ... accidentally killed him."

My eyebrows rose in astonishment.

She drew in a breath, as if to compose herself. "I miss my brothers and mother dearly, but not my father. He shall burn in three hells," she muttered in slight hatred. "What about your family?" She raised her head. A weak smile, just like her voice, was plastered on her face.

I debated whether to lie that my family was just as flawed as hers or not. But in the end, I knew I couldn't. She was honest with me, and I felt prompted to be honest, too, regardless of my family being perfect compared to hers.

"My parents fell in love at a young age," I began. "They knew they'd spend the rest of their lives with each other all along. Once they got married, they wanted to have a child, but they tried, and every attempt was unfortunate."

Thea stared at me with curiosity, and I almost felt guilty for having to alter the story.

"But after years of trying, my sister, Elynn, was born. My parents couldn't have been happier, couldn't have asked for another miracle, but then my brother made an entrance into this world, me following him a year later.

"They called us three the best miracles that had ever happened to them." I took another sip of water. "My parents weren't very pious, but after all those miracles, they celebrated the Spring Equinox for the first time. They travelled to the town hall to offer a dead doe to the Gods as gratitude for their kindness.

"My dad worked as a fisherman. Five years ago, he didn't return from his daily fishing. He'd died somewhere in the ocean."

I pressed my lips into a thin line as the shadows of the memory slid through me. "Since then, it's been my mother, my sister, my brother, and me."

"I'm so sorry," Thea said.

"It's all right." I managed an assuring smile. "I made peace with it a long time ago."

In fact, I had not only made peace with my father's death but had also come to terms with the fact that I would be serving morphs for the rest of my life. Sometimes, when I thought deeper, I couldn't help but wonder how I managed to stay this strong.

"Once, my mother told me that what was dead never truly dies," Thea declared. "All the dead return as spirits two days before the Summer Solstice."

"I've heard about that, too."

Yet, I stayed silent about seeing one before I was offered to the Empire of Beasts.

"I think I saw one once," she said. "It was the spirit of my father."

She placed an empty watering can by the entrance. "He tried to apologise for what he'd done. I thought I was dreaming, but it was real. He asked for my forgiveness, but I didn't give it to him. I ... I couldn't."

"It's understandable."

She looked down at her toes and then tilted her head to the left side of the greenhouse. More than half of the ground was full of weeds, waiting to be uprooted by me. "You should finish this." She gestured with her hand at the weedy side.

I sighed. "Well, I'm trying."

As she sent me a half-smile, she walked off, leaving me here to finish the work I was tasked to complete today by Jill. So far, I didn't see the end of it.

I got back to pulling out the troublesome weeds, working what seemed like hours, grunting occasionally.

"Didn't your fisherman father teach you how to work faster?"

Perfect. The last thing I needed right now was her.

"It's your job, not mine," I retorted, not bothering to even glance at her.

"But don't you remember what the wise woman Holland said?" Her voice was dripping with sarcasm. "That we won't be doing the main work all the time? We'll have other labour to do as well?"

If she'd come to spar with me verbally, she was wasting her time.

"Mind your own business, Clare."

Silence enveloped the greenhouse, and I thought she'd left, but I couldn't have been more wrong.

"It's truly bizarre to see a girl who had been living in the forest for most of her life turning out to be a snail at chores."

Clenching my jaw, I propped my forearms on my knees and cast a glance over my shoulder at Clare, who was leaning against the glass and picking the dirt from under her nails.

"Don't you have work to do other than aggravate me?"

"My work is being done by you. I came to watch," she revealed. "Troubling you is the most fun I've got here."

At least she was honest.

"Do you have any friends, Clare?"

"No."

I imitated one of her many wry grins. "Hmm. Shocking."

Clare frowned at me but then huffed, focusing on her nails. "I don't waste my time on people who don't deserve it, unlike you, Startel."

I knew what she had in mind, and it didn't bring the best feelings. I hadn't thought about Alise and Irisa for a long time. Why should I when they weren't my real friends? Gossiping behind my back? Spreading lies I had no idea about?

Pretending as if Clare didn't exist, I resumed working, or otherwise, I would never leave this greenhouse.

"Your ankle seems to be healing pretty fast."

I went stiff.

How was she acquainted with the state of my ankle? I hadn't run into her while I was limping.

My head whipped over my shoulder. "How do you know?"

Clare didn't even deign to glance at me as she said, "Just a lucky guess."

"You couldn't have possibly guessed that."

"Perhaps I could; perhaps I couldn't, but does it matter?" Her notorious wry smile graced her full lips. "You won't find out how I learned about Fillan's bite and that your blood poisoned him either."

I studied her without bothering to mask suspicion. By now, I was one hundred percent sure I wasn't the only one hiding something.

"My blood didn't poison him." I attempted to lie, even if she and I knew better. My blood had poisoned him, thanks to the bracelet.

She scoffed. "Save your lies for others. You'll need to try harder than that to convince me."

"All right. I won't try, but at least be less loud while you're spilling out things the ear of a morph shouldn't catch," I snapped quietly.

"Don't worry. Nobody's listening. Fillan has been in an agonizing state for the past five days, his brother Lupin somewhere in the city, and Asenah has gone on a trip. Only we, humans, are left here." I didn't ask how she knew all of this, as she wouldn't bother to answer me anyway. "If you want to get out tonight for a while, it will be the best time to do so. No wolf will bite you this time."

She pushed off the glass, turned proudly on her heel, and left.

With a shake of my head, I carried on with rooting out those pesky weeds.

The half-moon swapped places with the sun, reigning over the starry sky in all its magnificence. It cast only a faint light upon the ground, unlike the full moon that had illuminated the darkest nooks of the forest the night I was attacked.

However, the lack of light didn't deter me from taking a stroll through the garden.

I carried a sketchbook I'd made by tying parchments together and a pencil with an eraser I'd borrowed from the study room with the intention never to return them. I figured nobody would miss them as morphs' rooms were abundant with stuff they couldn't care less about. Weeks had already passed, and nobody noticed. Only to me, those three objects were my prized possessions, my only escape in this beastly place. Although I experienced a great disappointment that I couldn't find anything to colour my designs with.

My ankle had healed. I could walk as well as before the bite, but the marks of the wolf's fangs remained as a permanent reminder of my encounter with Fillan. Scars which would always remind me of the night's adventure I was reckless to take.

I didn't go further than the beginning of the forest. I'd learned my lesson. Although Fillan was still confined to his bed, and the other two were gone, the forest wasn't safe for humans.

I settled onto the bench, drawing up my legs and placing the sketchbook on my knees. As I opened a blank page, I outlined a woman's body before I surrendered to my imagination, sketching a new design for one of the many dresses and gowns I had drawn over my lifetime.

Dresses and gowns I would never be able to sew, let alone wear.

No matter how absorbed I was in sketching, the odd silence, apart from the sound of graphite against the paper, unsettled me. I had noticed it before at the rainforest but had never truly acknowledged how quiet it was in the Realm of Bones as well.

In the Mortal Region, the forest was always full of noises. Owls hooting, cicadas caterwauling, crickets chirping in harmony once the sun went down every night. The silence here was almost ominous. No animal, no insect, no bird in sight. I hadn't paid attention to such a minor detail the night I was attacked since all my focus was drawn to the light orb creature reciting the words of the four-decade curse. Now, when I did pay attention, I was tempted to go back to the mansion.

Someone wept behind me.

Startled, I didn't dare look to see who it was. The last time I allowed curiosity to get the better of me, I almost became a wolf's late-night snack but got away with a scar on my ankle instead. I wouldn't repeat the same mistake twice.

Choosing to ignore it, I resumed sketching, but then another, louder cry accompanied the previous one seconds later, tearing my focus off my work. Sighing, I set the materials down on the bench, rose to my knees, and squinted into the dark. Something twitched at the end of the garden by the neatly cut shrub.

A short figure that didn't seem either human or morph. Dissimilar size of leafy branches protruded from his head, and his ears were pointy. The entire body of the strange creature reminded me of a tree. A tree clad in a tunic of leaves.

I recognised the creature from the drawings and descriptions in the fairy tales. A forest nymph, or more specifically, a dryad.

As I stood up, I walked about the bench, interested in taking a closer look at the little weeping dryad.

Dryads weren't something one ought to be afraid of. They weren't dangerous. I needn't fear them, especially not a dryad who was merely a child.

As I took another step forward, the dryad stifled his cries, his wooden bottom lip quivering as his eyes shifted up at me. White-blue, as radiant as a comet.

"P-please don't h-hurt me," he stumbled on his words, striking like a bunny cornered by a fox.

I nearly laughed. A dryad scared of me. Me! But I restrained myself, for it would be unsuitable, let alone rude, to laugh.

"I'm not going to hurt you," I said gently, not to scare him away.

But he trembled while backing a step away. "I-I don't believe you."

I didn't move any closer, confident that it would only scare him more than he was already.

What was a dryad doing in such a dangerous zone anyway? Perhaps I should leave him be, but even if curiosity could doom me someday, it wasn't possible to put it on a leash. Being curious was a vital part of me.

"I swear by all the six Gods that I won't hurt you," I tried again.

As expected, he was hesitant. "Promise?"

"Promise."

He looked away, wrapping his hands around his tiny frame.

"What are you doing here?" I took a half-step towards him, and he didn't back away. I assumed he trusted me by now or didn't notice decreased space between us. "It's not safe for you here."

The dryad sobbed aloud, making me glance at the mansion. The wolf with sensitive hearing was sleeping there. I didn't know Fillan's health state, but he must have gotten better. If he decided to get out of his cosy chambers and come into the garden—

"I'm lost," he cried.

I turned my head back to him. "Lost?"

He nodded. "I ... I don't know where to go. My p-parents are somewhere in the forest." He looked down. "I don't know where." He exploded into another set of tears.

I took two full steps towards him. The dryad was smaller than me. His height barely reached my chest. I extended my hand to comfort him, but my hand stopped short in mid-air before my fingers touched him. He was like an animated tree. Did I truly want to touch that?

I pressed the hanging hand to my thigh. "How did you get lost?"

"T-there w-was a light," he stammered through the snivels. "I-I wanted to catch it, but I went too far."

Was he talking about the same light orb I'd had an encounter with recently? The same one that had almost sentenced me to death?

"You'll die if you stay here."

Perhaps he wouldn't, but if someone from morphs detected another creature in their land, the last thing they would do was to invite him for some harmless cup of tea.

"I... I don't know where to go." A sob left him. Quite louder than I would have preferred.

"There's a morph in the mansion," I warned him. "You can't stay here. Crying."

The dryad gazed at me hopelessly. His bottom lip stopped trembling, and something else shone in those unearthly eyes. Not desperation, not misery, but as if a realisation. "You understand me."

"Of course I understand you."

A faint smile appeared on his face. "You understand *our* language."

"What?"

"You can help me." I frowned, and he specified. "Help find my parents."

"How am I supposed to do that?"

His smile faded, as if it had never been there before. His eyes returned to the watery state, and he let out another sob. "I-I don't know."

He covered his face with his wooden palms—fingers like sticks with tiny leaves replacing nails—and burst into tears again. At least he was quiet this time.

I should go back to the mansion. It was pretty late. But another voice within me whispered otherwise, telling me not to leave the poor dryads' youngling all by himself for morphs to find and do Gods knew what to him.

My inner voice was a fool. He had gotten lost. I could do nothing to help him.

Yet, I stayed, observing the tearful, pitiful dryad. His tiny shoulders shook with each sob as his fingers masked his face.

Oh, bloody hell. I'm so going to regret this. "You couldn't have gone too far from them."

The dryad peeped through the gaps of his fingers.

"I'll try to help you find them," I said.

Despite my unfaltering voice and assuring smile, I felt anything but confident in my decision, which could only put me in another danger. One I might not be lucky to survive this time.

The deeper we ventured into the forest, the more my brain nagged at me to turn back and return to the mansion. But my body moved regardless.

I must find dryads. Any dryads except for the one who was dragging his feet beside me.

At least he had stopped crying.

But how was I supposed to find a dryad? It wasn't that encounters with them were seldom; they were just elusive, timid creatures. I assumed that their lost child would make them emerge eventually. However, as time passed, only the dryad's and my footsteps shuffled through the silent forest.

He craned his head at me. "What's your name?"

"Elynn."

After a sound left my mouth, it dawned on me that I had told him my real name. Panic hooded my nerves, but it faded in a fraction of time. No point in being apprehensive. A dryad wouldn't spill my secrets.

"It's an honour to meet you, Elynn." He smiled tentatively. "I'm Juniper."

We continued to stroll through the forest in silence until I succumbed to my swelling curiosity. "You said I understand you as if I shouldn't. How is it possible?"

"I don't know."

"What *do* you know?"

Juniper stopped, recoiling slightly at the harshness of my tone as fear entered his face.

"I'm sorry," I said, softening my expression.

His gaze shifted down. No word left his mouth or mine again as we resumed walking.

This was pointless. We would never find his parents. Juniper would have to cope with the fact he'd forever be a lost child.

He halted, and I gave him a puzzled look. "Why did you—"

Something slimy seized my uninjured ankle and yanked me down from behind before I saw what it was. I dropped flat, banging my forehead on the solid ground.

"*O-ow ...*"

The pain robbed me of my senses. I might have cracked my skull. Despite being in one hell of a lot of pain, I forced myself to lift my chin. Tears made it difficult to make out anything in the semi-dark forest. I tried to stand up, but something holding me by my ankle didn't let me. Roots ... Yes, *roots* slithered around my wrists like thin, endless snakes, impeding any further movements.

I had no power to help myself when roots held me captive. I could already hear a bell of grim death chiming above me. I knew it would be a terrible idea to pose as a hero, as all that I'd earned from it was nothing but pain, a possible concussion, and then death. I wasn't sure if I was ready to face it.

No, I was sure. I was *sure* I wasn't ready to *die*.

Then why did you go into the forest, Elynn? My inner voice mocked.

I knew the answer, and if I could, I would spit on my kind heart and beg my brain for forgiveness.

Probably another root wrapped around my scarred ankle, lifting me off the ground. In a sharp motion, the roots jerked me back and tied me to something rigid. As I glanced over my shoulder, I faced the tree's trunk.

Only then it occurred to me that someone was speaking to me.

"You kidnapped our child," they hissed from somewhere

close to me.

I searched for the source of the voice but didn't see anything. The forest was empty. Only pines tottered lightly as a crisp breeze brushed against my skin, now broken out in beads of sweat.

"You're going to suffer by attempting to end our child's life," another hissed, but the voice was much deeper than the previous one. "You shall be torn limb from limb."

Are those creatures who are threatening me invisible? I squinted. *Is that a little whirl of pine needles in the distance?*

Roots on both my wrists and ankles tightened, and little by little, they began pulling them off my body. More tears slid down my cheeks. I was about to beg for my life when a pleading voice beat me. "Mom, Dad, stop!"

"You shall become a cripple, and may morphs eat you alive," the male growled.

"Dad, please," Juniper's voice begged. "S-she helped me. S-she helped me f-find you."

The wind intensified, and in front of me materialised a male whose appearance was almost the same as Juniper's, but he was taller, more muscular, and more ancient. Behind him, a few steps away, a female was holding a little boy. A two-part dress of leaves adorned with flowers glided down her wooden legs. Her husband, or whoever he was to her in the nymphs' world, was also leaf-clad.

"Dad!" Juniper screamed at the top of his lungs.

At last, I didn't feel the tearing pain anymore, apart from the itchiness where my appendages connected to my body. However, roots seemed to refuse to leave, lingering on my wrists and ankles.

The male dryad looked at his son, whose eyes were covered in tears. "S-she did nothing wrong. S-she saved me. Without her, I wouldn't have come here and f-found you."

"You don't know what you're talking about, sweetie." The female dryad caressed his wooden cheek. "Their kind is a foe to us."

"N-no." He shook his head vehemently. "I saw a glosse and went after it. That's how I got lost. Nobody kidnapped me. I came across some garden, and she saw me. She understood me and went into the forest to help me find you. Elynn did nothing wrong. She *helped* me."

The female dryad's green, shiny eyes shot to me. They burned for a second but calmed down incredibly fast, wandering to her male. "She isn't a villain."

The male dryad was hesitant. He turned to me, his countenance unreadable as the roots carefully set me on the ground. They slipped off my ankles and wrists, disappearing deep into the soil. I watched in awe.

Dryads could manipulate plants. They were like one. I knew that but had forgotten about their powerful ability when being near death had blinded my thoughts.

Abruptly, weakness struck me, making my knees buckle. I was about to collapse when a male dryad's wooden hand clutched my arm, keeping me steady on my feet. His skin felt strange. Not only was it firm as it should be, but warm, unlike a tree.

He stared at me with the same eyes as the little dryad's. Blinding white-blue. "You saved my son's life." His voice came out genuinely soft and reflected his eyes that had been cruel only a few seconds ago.

I didn't manage to utter a word or make any sound, for that matter. I continued to be wary and stupefied by everything.

"She doesn't understand you, Nash," the female dryad said.

I opened my mouth to object, but the boy was faster than me. "She understands," he assured, rubbing the tears off his eyes.

The female looked at him, astounded. Juniper shrugged and gripped into her skirt.

"Whether you comprehend us or not," Nash addressed me. "We are in debt to you for bringing back our son and hurting you. Forever."

All I did was stare at him, unable to produce a single sound. I might have lost my voice.

"Thank you," he said sincerely, and let go of me. I leaned against the tree so I wouldn't fall.

The male dryad went over to Juniper, while a female approached me with an elegant gait, as if the wind carried her towards me. She studied me, and as she was about to stroke my most likely injured face, I pulled away. While her hand was hovering, a benevolent smile touched her lips. "You have the right to be afraid," she noted unsuccessfully, for I felt as alert as before. "But your face must be treated unless you want to walk with scars?"

I had figured my face obtained some nicks from being kicked to the rock-hard ground covered with pine needles. It was a miracle I hadn't lost consciousness and could still think with clarity, but would that last when the headache was getting worse?

However, I didn't want scars. I didn't want any pain in the first place. Was this female dryad going to help me with it? Doubtful. Still, I shook my head.

"So I supposed," she breathed out before she started to sing.

My body relaxed gradually. I couldn't determine if it was her voice that turned angel-like all of a sudden or something else, making me less tense and dazed.

"Can I touch your face?"

I nodded.

Her gentle fingers brushed against my cheek, and in an instant, the pain vanished before I could note the healing process. The headache lifted, leaving me feeling whole and unharmed. I became aware of a subtle breeze, carrying the scent of pine, swirling around us. As she gracefully withdrew her touch, the warm embrace of the wind dissipated, leaving me standing there, fully restored.

"Please, accept our apologies." She bowed her head, the gesture almost reverent. "For the damage." She looked at me one last time before gracefully turning to her family. The male dryad rested his hand on the boy's shoulder as they all turned away at the same time.

"Wait!" I exclaimed.

Somehow, I had found my voice.

The family glanced at me over their shoulders.

"I don't know my way back."

The dryad lady gave me an amiable smile. "The trees will show you."

A cocoon of wind, intermingled with pine spikes, rose from the ground in a whirl. Once it vanished, the dryad family was gone too.

XIV

On my way to the kitchen, I almost slammed the door in a girl's face.

"Oh, sorry," I quickly apologized.

She mumbled something, but my attention was drawn to the bustling kitchen staff.

They were always working like bees, but today, their fussiness was at a brand-new level.

Thea walked in, and as if she read the hanging question, she answered without needing to ask. "Princesses from the Realms of Talons and Woods are visiting for a few days."

"How wonderful," I muttered. "More morphs to be aware of."

At least my sarcasm elicited a smile from Thea.

"Thea an' Gen, please stop chattering an' come tae help," Imogen commanded, standing by the stove and stirring a pot with a wooden spoon, other hand resting on her hip.

Thea and I exchanged glances—mine reflecting irritation, hers a softer, empathetic look. After giving me a small smile, she approached Imogen, politely asking how she could assist.

I followed suit, but before I could ask, Imogen pointed at a few vegetables on a counter with her pinkie.

I hadn't slept much after a long night helping the dryad boy find his parents, only to be accused and physically harmed. Despite the dryads' apology and the trees guiding me back to the mansion, the damage was done. I vowed never to set foot in those woods again. This time, I was certain with all my heart.

I was worn out and so over this—

"Chop, chop," Imogen urged.

I zoomed back to the present, faced with vegetables that seemed poised to expose me.

The problem was ... I didn't know how to chop.

My hesitation did not escape Imogen's already suspicious gaze. She extended a sharp knife to me, and I hesitated, my eyes fixed on the tool that could easily be turned into a weapon. "Ye know how tae cook an' bake. Show off yer chopping skills, lassie."

I wanted to protest, but I couldn't. I was taking Gen's place, and I couldn't risk anyone growing suspicious and digging deeper into my secret—except for Clare, who had seemingly figured me out with a single look.

Pressing my lips together, I took the sharp knife and moved to the counter, grabbing a cutting board. I picked up a tomato, placed it on the board, and stared at it intensely.

It couldn't be *that* hard to cut a tomato, right? *Just position the blade and press until it reaches the cutting board.*

I attempted it, realising it wasn't as challenging as I had anticipated. But I wasn't enjoying it. Every cut required effort, and beads of perspiration had formed on my eyebrow. The tomato slices had to be perfect—masterpieces. I wasn't sure how long it took me to chop a single tomato into neat slices, but it was certainly longer than it should have.

"Oh, dear heavens! What are ye doin'?" Imogen exclaimed, taking the knife from me.

I stepped back. "Slicing a tomato?"

She laughed. "A turtle could slice a tomato quicker than ye, lassie."

I didn't doubt her. I could wager a turtle would excel at anything related to labour and cooking compared to me.

"Move. I'll do it myself," she declared.

I stepped aside, giving her plenty of space.

"Go stir th' pot," she ordered.

I approached the stove, took a spoon, and stirred the sauce.

"Mix 'til it heats."

She sensed something was off, for she gave me a suspicious glance every now and then. Perhaps she was questioning if I was who I claimed to be, but she remained silent, not asking anything. Too many ears were in the kitchen.

After the food was prepared, Thea, Jill, two other maids, and I took our trays to the grand dining room.

Thea went in first as the double doors opened, and as usual, the rest followed behind.

"How's our abode, Fawne?" Asenah's voice reached me as soon as I walked in. "It's your first time here, isn't it?"

From the corner of my eye, I saw two new individuals sitting at the table.

One girl with a yellow beak appeared quite hideous to my eye. Her face was eagle-like, except for the pale-blue eyes and snowy hair. The hair almost matched her fur, fixed into a coronet. She was the first morph female whose animal features didn't get along with human ones. She was a great disaster.

The appearance of the other princess in her accursed form was also peculiar, though less ugly. Her chestnut-brown hair was combed into an elaborate updo, and large ears akin to a deer stuck out of her scalp.

"It is," the deer morph agreed. Asenah had mentioned her name. Fawne. "Your mansion is extraordinary, Your Grace."

Jill placed a plate before Asenah. Apart from Asenah and two princesses in the room, Lupin quietly sipped wine, and Fillan was nowhere to be seen.

I served the appetiser to Lupin and walked over to the wall. Jill and Thea joined me while the other two quietly left the room. An additional plate rested in front of the unoccupied chair—a seat where Fillan normally sat. The mere thought of him showing up sent a shiver down my spine, and my body tensed.

"Lupin and Fillan are going to show you around the mansion tomorrow." Asenah bit a raspberry off the fork. "Where's your brother, by the way?" Her inquisitive gaze shifted to Lupin.

"He must be—"

The double doors swung open, and the other brother sashayed inside. My jaw clenched, forgetting I shouldn't reveal any emotion towards morphs. But here I was, glaring with unmasked distaste at him.

Fillan looked remarkably better than the last time I had seen him. It was only a week ago that he was puking in his chamber. Back then, he appeared as if death was about to claim him for one of the hells. But now, his appearance was the same as the first time I saw him: full of life and brutality.

"Here I am, here I am." He sighed and came to a stop, observing his guests. Fillan bowed his head to each of the princesses, greeting them separately. "Kayla, Fawne."

The eagle-like girl acknowledged Fillan with apparent alertness.

I remembered hearing Kayla's name mentioned before. If my recollection of the earlier conversation at this very table was correct, she was Lupin's betrothed.

Thea prodded my arm with her elbow. I glanced at her sidelong to ask what she needed from me, but her concentration was onwards. It hit me then. She had caught me staring where I shouldn't be.

"Forgive my cousin for his lack of punctuality," Asenah said. "The poor boy ate a dryad and suffered from its poisoning for an entire week."

Fillan huffed, plopping down in the chair. Next to him, Kayla squirmed, trying to shift away from him without anyone's notice. But that didn't go past my eye.

"You ate a dryad?" Fawne inquired, her brows raised in amazement.

"Well, that's what they told me." He held up a glass, and Thea hurried to fill it with wine.

Fawne and Kayla exchanged puzzled glances.

"You don't know if you ate a dryad or not?" Fawne asked incredulously.

Fillan parted his mouth, but Asenah interrupted him before he could utter a word. "He was inebriated." She raised a glass of wine. "Too inebriated to remember it." She took a delicate sip.

Fillan didn't add anything else. Either he genuinely didn't

recall biting me and having my blood affect him, taking the theory of eating a dryad for granted, or he indeed remembered everything but chose silence for some incomprehensible reason. I could only hope that the former was true.

As they savoured the last bites of their appetiser, the girls and I hurried back to the kitchen to fetch a proper meal for them. Once we got back, I heard Lupin ask, "And when is the wedding?"

When I silently placed a plate of food in front of him, I caught Fillan's stare. In a heartbeat, I averted my gaze and returned to the wall. I felt his eyes on my back, but when I turned around, his attention was on his brother instead.

"What about the Autumn Equinox?" Asenah suggested. "I have no wish for the wedding to turn into a caravan of animals."

"It's so soon," Fawne mused quietly, jabbing the lamb with her fork.

"Why wait?" Asenah asked. "Autumn is precisely majestic in the Realm of Bones."

Lupin decided to interject, "Actually, it is much more beautiful in—"

But he didn't finish. Shrinking, he grimaced as if in pain and stole a glance at Asenah, who was savouring the wine as she watched Fawne.

"The Autumn Equinox is an *ideal* day for a wedding," Asenah boasted, keeping her intense gaze on Fawne. A trace of irritation showed, as though she didn't like that Fawne didn't reciprocate the same amount of attention.

"Yes, it is." She tilted her head to Asenah's side. "But it's my father who makes decisions, not me. You may have to discuss matters about my wedding with him, Your Grace."

So, who was marrying whom exactly? Wasn't Lupin going to wed Kayla?

Asenah's mouth formed a wolf-like smile. "Very well."

"You know," Fillan said, "I've been patiently waiting like the good boy I am for somebody to ask me about *my* wedding that I've learned about only *today*, but here I am ... still waiting."

All eyes were on him now.

Asenah's furry fingers tightened around her knife.

"Perchance, you would like to marry an enemy, Fillan? Just like Tatyana Haroun?"

"I wasn't—"

"Tatyana didn't marry *him*." Fawne frowned at Asenah.

"Who knows? Perhaps she did."

"No. She was in love with him but not married to him. Their bond would have brought the end to our world."

Who is Tatyana?

"Not the end of our world, but a threat to our empire, darling."

"And for it, let's thank the Gods Tatyana was exiled before she could bear Aytigin's child."

And who's Aytigin?

"Where was Tatyana exiled again?" Fillan inquired.

Asenah was cutting a lamb's shank. "Only the emperor and perhaps empress know where their traitor sister is." She put a bite into her mouth, chewing it without showing any sign of enjoyment of the well-prepared food.

Were they all this snobbish to show no respect to Imogen's and her staff's prepared meals, which were a blessing once my tongue touched it after a long, laborious day? Or was it *I* who had a peculiar taste?

"And what about Aytigin Cresenbar?" Fillan questioned, earning a pointed glance from his cousin. "What was his fate?"

"Haven't you heard the whispers?" Fawne asked Fillan.

"That he was flogged and then guillotined in front of his people?"

Fawne nodded. "That's what is rumoured."

Fillan snorted, lifting his chin contentedly. "That's what happens to traitors. Even degenerates know how to deal with them. I'm impressed."

That was the last interesting sentence spoken throughout dinner, as the rest of the conversation was about Fillan and Fawne's wedding. I had expected Lupin and Kayla to marry first as they'd been promised to each other longer than the former couple, but apparently, that wasn't the case.

I turned a deaf ear to the tedious discussion, but I couldn't ignore Fillan's eyes straying to me every once in a while. Eyes that perhaps guessed something but weren't entirely sure whether it was true or not.

XV

I was ready to retreat to my room, collapse into the bed and sleep like there was no tomorrow after another cleaning spree in the kitchen, but Imogen had different plans for me. She insisted I stay. I had a guess why, but she didn't speak to me until all the staff had left. Once alone, she didn't wait to ask, "Ye know that lying about yer skills won't bring ye any good, lassie?"

"I'm not lying."

The unbending look on her face made it evident that she didn't believe me. For the first time, apart from my mother, someone had seen through my facade. Imogen had clear evidence, and only an ignorant fool could overlook the lie.

"Really?" Her eyebrows lifted. "Ye didn't know how tae slice a tomato. If ye don't know how tae chop a vegetable, ye don't know how tae cook at all."

"I wasn't having a good day."

Imogen sighed. "Why did ye lie in yer biography?"

I analysed her face, wondering if she was unaware of my incognito status. Perhaps she only thought I was untruthful in the file Gen had to fill.

My acting skills kicked in, ready to deceive the woman who had been so generous to me. She had given away her room when

I couldn't stay in the one I woke up in. While I felt obliged to return the favour and at least be genuine, I couldn't trust her. Even after almost a month here, I wasn't naïve enough to spill my secrets, not even to Thea, whom I could consider a friend—certainly a better one than the other two in the Mortal Region.

"I'm sorry." I dropped my gaze as if drowning in guilt. "I-I didn't want to seem like an utter loser because ... because I had no useful skills. So I lied."

It wasn't entirely false. I didn't have useful skills. At least not the ones that could help me do the daily jobs quicker.

"Useful skills?" Imogen asked. "What do ye count as useful skills, lassie?"

I took a sharp breath. "Cooking, baking, gardening, hunting, fishing ..."

Imogen's intense stare made it surprising that I wasn't sweating yet. "An' what skills do ye have? The ones ye stayed silent about in your biography?"

"None."

"That's impossible," she said. "Ye must have at least one skill, lassie."

I pursed my lips.

Perhaps it wouldn't hurt to tell her about my real skills. I couldn't foresee how revealing them would affect me, let alone if it would put me in danger.

At last, I confessed, "I can play the piano."

Imogen's lips curled into a smile. Was that a sheen of admiration in her eyes? "That's wonderful."

I half-smiled. "And I can sketch clothes," I added, my chest easing off. "Mostly dresses. Also, I know how to sew."

"And do ye think playing th' piano an' creatin clothes are useless?"

"Perhaps they are not entirely useless. I played the piano back in the Mortal Region and sometimes got paid for performing in townies' parties. But"—I released a heavy sigh—"skills like that can't be helpful *here*."

"Offered people were sorted by thair skills," she said. "If ye hadn't lied, perhaps ye would have been in some other realm, servin' lesser morphs who couldn't hurt you as much as Asenah with her cousins can."

"They've done nothing bad to me so far."

Yet another lie slid off my tongue with zero effort. Fillan would have killed me, but miraculously I had eluded death. But Imogen needn't know any of it.

"Weel, let's hope nothing will." With a faint smile, she redid her bun. "Now, let's teach ye the basics of th' cooking."

My eyes widened. "No."

"Yes."

"I can't."

"This *I can't* of yours isn't in my vocabulary. And it shouldn't be in yours. You can, and you will." She handed me a pan. I grimaced at it. "Come on. Ye never know when cooking can come in handy for ye."

"Imogen, if I try to cook anything, this kitchen will burst into flames."

"Not on mah watch."

But I remained resistant. "I'm not putting my hands of failure on any of these pots."

From the unyielding look in her eyes, I knew she wouldn't let this go easily.

"I'm not kidding, Imogen. This could end in a lot of worse ways."

"Then how ye'll make a guy fall for ye if you don't learn how to reach his heart through th' best way of them all?"

I rolled my eyes. "Ha. Ha. How hilarious." Despite my misgivings, I gave in quite quickly, taking the pan, mostly because I was interested in learning something new. "What are we cooking?"

"For starters, scrambled eggs."

I placed the pan on the stove.

"Now, now, is that really how ye start?"

I glanced at her quizzically.

Right.

"Of course, I'm mixing the eggs first, just *after* heating the pan," I said, acting as if I knew it all along. "How stupid you think I am, Imogen? You hurt my feelings."

She scoffed while I headed towards the icebox from where I

picked up some butter. I deposited it near the stove, which I turned on. Imogen was watching my every move like a mentor watching their student.

"Knowing yer unhurried pace, the end o' the world will come before ye cook the eggs."

Ignoring her snarky comment, I returned to the icebox. "How many eggs should I take?"

"Four," she answered. "And don't forget tae wash them with water."

I took four eggs and closed the icebox door with the push of my elbow. As I walked carefully to the sink, I tried my luck. "At dinner, they mentioned some Tatyana and Aytigin."

She frowned. "You cannot listen to thair conversations. It's risky."

I dared to roll my eyes again.

"I'm serious, lassie."

"I know that." I placed the eggs near the sink. "But who are they? Have you heard of them?"

"What did I tell you about curiosity, eh?"

I let out an annoyed sigh while cleaning the eggs one by one, making sure not to crack them by accident. "Curiosity is what kills us humans."

Even if curiosity could kill humans, so far, I was alive. With a scarred ankle but breathing, heart beating.

"You sound like ye don't believe it," she mumbled, as if offended. "I know it doesn't sound believable, but it's true." I picked up a bowl and began cracking eggs. "I knew people like you who were curious about everything they heard comin' from morphs' mouths. None of them lived long."

I searched her face for a sign of a lie, but I didn't find one.

"Don't forget to season the mixture with salt an' pepper."

I did just that. "What happened to the people you knew?"

"If I answer ye, do you promise to never question anything that goes on in morphs' lives anymore?"

That was surely not happening. I was always going to question everything. Perhaps I wouldn't ask Imogen, as she was hardly willing to answer my questions. She had been kind enough to tell me about the Bloodsucker, the curse, and the Spell, but she wasn't going to respond to anything I eavesdropped on anymore.

It was natural for me to lie again. "All right."

I couldn't tell if she believed me or not, as her face betrayed nothing. I put a bit of butter in the already heated pan and whisked the mixture.

"Once Asenah caught a maid eavesdropping on her conversation with a noble morph," she began. "The lassie disappeared that day. Two years later, a guard was caught by Asenah wandering in th' library, searching for Gods knew what at late hours. He was deliciously eaten at th' Spring Equinox."

My lips parted. Imogen only nodded, assuring me that every word of hers was real.

"Remember th' previous gardener ye asked about at first?" she asked.

"Yes." I poured the mixed eggs into the pan. "What happened to him?"

There was no way she was going to tell me his fate now, was she?

"He was curious." Anger glinted in her eyes. "He communicated with a creature in th' forest called a glosse."

A glosse. That dryad kid had mentioned the creature to his parents when his father was about to tear off my limbs. If Juniper had described a glosse accurately, I had met one as well. The creature told me about the curse, but why?

Imogen continued. "Glosses know what one needs tae hear beforehand, n' gives them a cryptic message or a riddle. When he stumbled across one in th' forest, it told him a riddle, which he figured out. Lassie, focus on th' eggs."

Distracted by her narration, I had forgotten all about them.

"I don't know what else to do."

"Just gently pull th' eggs across the pan."

I grasped a spatula. "Like this?"

"Aye, just be gentle."

"Imogen, they're *eggs*."

"Be gentle."

I sighed and softened my movements.

"Then lift an' fold until no liquid remains. Don't stir it constantly. I'll tell ya when tae stop."

I did as I was told. "So, what was the answer to the riddle?"

"Ways tae kill a morph. Enchanter's blood an' a piece of a dryad's skin. But he didn't know that one of thaim was false. Glosses really like tae spread false information.

"Finn knew what he was doing when it came to hunting an' makin weapons. He captured a dryad an' took a piece of his skin with a knife. He made an arrow's head of it an' was ready tae aim. Poor Finn was sure it'd kill Asenah, but as soon as th' arrow hit her heart, it didn't do her any damage. The glosse had deceived Finn. Only gold an' enchanter's blood can be fatal tae morphs.

"Asenah retaliated by chopping off Finn's head in front of the audience of servants afterwards. That's why no one has dared to speak about him ever since."

Imogen lowered her eyes. She inhaled, but it sounded like a stifled sob.

This Finn couldn't have been just a gardener to her, but most likely a friend she'd lost to his attempt to kill Asenah.

"I'm sorry for your loss," I said, but the words felt inadequate.

She took a deep breath and wiped a tear off her cheek. It was strange to witness Imogen cry, and the intimate moment made me uncomfortable. "Don't ask me or try to seek answers elsewhere." She looked at me, her eyes as serious as always, but glistening. "For your own sake, lassie."

All I could do was give her a nod, but no verbal promise that I would heed her advice.

"All right, stop with th' stir," she ordered.

I pulled away from the stove. "Who was he to you?" I asked. "Finn?"

A shadow of a painful memory briefly crossed her face.

Not a friend. It could not be just a friend. She'd been acquainted with every detail of his plan. Perhaps a lover?

"Eggs are done now. Remove pan from th' heat and don't forget to turn off the stove," she instructed. "Have sweet dreams."

She pivoted on her heel and made her way towards the exit.

"Imogen?"

She halted at the threshold, hesitating. "Finn was mah twin," she said in a whisper, but I heard her nonetheless. "He was my twin brother."

I opened my mouth to ask how it was possible as only one of the youngest siblings had to be offered to the Empire of Beasts, not two. However, Imogen left before I could, positively conscious of what my inquiry would be, a question she might not have answered anyway, much like the one about Tatyana and Aytigin. It was left as a mystery to solve on my own.

The princesses left a few days later. Before leaving, they gave the impression that they were about to flee far from the mansion and never return. Well, Kayla did while Fawne took her time to share a courteous farewell with the falsest smile ever. Asenah was smiling the same.

Surely, those girls were not Asenah's friends, only allies. The arranged marriage served as nothing more than a reliable bond against the Bloodsucker, who might seek vengeance against enchanters. Neither Asenah nor two other realms wanted to join him once he would. She had made it seem as if it would be a suicide.

After all, the Hundred Years' War hadn't unfolded smoothly. If enchanters hadn't initiated a truce, the war would have persisted, claiming more lives of soldiers and innocent people.

If I understood correctly, this Drayard Emyur, the Bloodsucker, would be a fool to go against enchanters. But then again, he was the notorious Bloodsucker who murdered countless people in cruel ways. *Morphs* were terrified of him. Asenah*, too,* was cautious of him. And she struck as a tough, merciless female who had slaughtered many humans simply for their curiosity.

Gods forbid, my path would never cross with the Bloodsucker.

So far, I had been heeding Imogen's advice. Even if I overheard something intriguing in the dining room, I chose not to question it, opting to forget instead. If prying killed humans, I wasn't willing to risk my life over some silly questions. Despite being a slave, I had no desire to die.

Since I had made a vow to myself, I hadn't ventured into the woods since the dryads' attack. If I couldn't sleep, I lit a candle and sketched more designs. I continued this routine almost every night until I grew tired, and the sleep fairies took me to their kingdom.

At least I no longer dreamed about Chase. My former "lover" had finally left me for peace of mind.

Currently, I was organizing books in the library. It was one of the few tasks I could do without messing anything up. I felt quite accomplished. Besides, arranging books in alphabetical order wasn't difficult or irritating, but the opposite—quite relaxing.

The mansion's library wasn't as vast as the one in the humans' city, but it had newer versions of books that didn't seem prone to crumbling at the mere touch.

In the back of the library, a large map of all three worlds was nailed against the wall. I'd seen the Empire of Beasts map before in Asenah's study but never had the opportunity to examine it. The library itself wasn't used often, so I didn't have to worry someone might walk in on me doing what I wasn't supposed to. Therefore, I took my time to study the map.

The Empires of Beasts and Skies sprawled across more of the map than the Mortal Region, which was separated from the Empire of Beasts by the Blue River. The Empire of Beasts was divided into realms like the Realm of Bones, Woods, Talons, Wilds, and Embers and had a capital, while the Empire of Skies seemed to follow the same ruling principle—a land divided into realms and having a capital.

I had learned in school that all three different worlds had been created merely fifty years ago. Before that, all kinds had lived together, ruled by a morph emperor. Enchanters hadn't been particularly pleased with it as they didn't have equal rights, nor did humans.

Such injustice was one of the reasons that led to the enchanters' and humans' rebellion, which escalated into a war lasting for over a century. While none of them won, enchanters came closest to victory. Consequently, morphs had to cede more than half of their lands to enchanters and a small part to humans. Ever since, the three kinds had been separated from others, ruling their own worlds.

"You've never seen the map before?"

I almost leapt out of my skin.

As I whipped my head to one of the wolf brothers behind me, feeling my body tense. Lupin observed me as if he hadn't had water for days.

I curtsied to him, disgusted with myself. But if I hadn't done it, my head would have most likely been chopped off.

"My lord."

As I straightened my back, I was about to retire, but he shot me a daring look that rooted me to the floor.

"You didn't answer my question, human," he said playfully, like a cat toying with a mouse. As always, I was nothing more than a mouse.

"No, I haven't seen the map, my lord."

A half wolf-like grin, signalling danger, appeared on his mouth. "I believe every person, human or not, should know our world's map."

Uncertain of what to say, my only desire was to leave. Yet, instead, I found myself agreeing. "Yes, my lord."

Lupin's grin widened, his eyes glimmering with starvation and thirst.

Run. Run. Run! screamed every instinct of mine.

But I didn't move. I didn't have another choice but to stay here and wait for his dismissal.

"You're new." He took a step towards me. I clutched my maid's skirt. He didn't notice it. "What's your name?"

"Genette."

I could bet on my life that he could hear the pounding of my heart. His senses were more sensitive than mine. But he must have been used to it. Every human's heartbeat would be frantic while standing this close to a morph. The creature that could eat a human alive only because it could.

"Genette." He tasted my little sister's name as if it was the most delicious dessert. I suppressed my disgust. "You'll be at our service today, Genette."

Bewilderment struck me. "Pardon me, my lord, but I don't quite understand what you mean."

Miraculously, my voice sounded still, unlike my quivering fingers.

"What a clueless, pretty human."

He took another approach, closing the healthy distance we'd had. A reek of alcohol drifted from him, irritating my nostrils. I tried to step back, but he wrapped one hand around my waist and pulled me against him.

"Forgive me, my lord, but—"

His mouth interrupted me, crushing mine. I tried to push him off, but his furry hands seized my wrists as he continued attacking me with his unpleasant mouth. I tightly pursed my lips, and he growled, sending tremors rippling through my body.

He shoved me against the wall. I grimaced in pain, but Lupin didn't care. With his claws, he tore the maid's dress, leaving me in only my trimmed bloomers that barely covered a small part of my legs.

"No undergarments?" he inquired in disbelief. "What an interesting slave."

My hands instinctively rose to cover my bare chest from his ravenous stare, but he smacked them away. A sickening smile distorted his mouth as he eyed me from head to toe, flicking his tongue over his mouth. When his eyes met mine, I shivered.

"P-please don't."

He didn't listen.

He lifted me, tossing me over his shoulder, and carried me out of the library.

Tears welled up, and I could hardly see anything when the water was blurring my sight. "P-please, I beg you."

He didn't respond.

A dreadful reminder flashed in my mind—words Holland had spoken once.

Other jobs.

There would be other jobs for us to do if we wanted to survive. Not only cleaning and cooking but also serving as their playthings. I should have realised that sooner. But even if I had, there was nothing I could have done to avoid what was about to happen to me.

"Stop crying, or my brother and I won't go easy on you, human," he snarled.

I pursed my lips, holding back another sob.

"Good human."

The door opened, but as I was turned towards the hallway, I could only guess where we were. It had to be one of their bedrooms.

"It's about time," another male voice said.

Fillan.

Lupin threw me onto the bed. Instantly, I shielded my chest, and the two brothers erupted in laughter.

"She's shy," Lupin crooned, casting a crooked, nasty smile at his brother.

"They're all shy, brother." Fillan's wolf-like face hovered over me. "Don't be afraid, *human*." His furry thumb brushed across my bottom lip. "You'll enjoy it."

"P-please. I beg you ... Don't."

He laughed at that.

I couldn't do anything. I was nothing here. Nothing but a slave. They could do whatever they desired to do with me. Whether with my permission or not. They were lords, and I was nothing but a weak girl at their disposal.

I didn't cry. Lupin had ordered me not to. I held tears under my shut eyelids, demanding them to remain there as long as possible.

"Open. Your. Eyes," Fillan commanded.

I forced myself to look, and Fillan showed his maws along with a broad, repulsing smile.

Both had their hands on me, and not only that. Moving me as they liked. Positioning me however they pleased ...

Help, I beseeched inwardly.

No pleas for them to stop escaped my mouth ever again. It

was pointless. They were famished animals that didn't care about asking or listening to any objections. If they wanted it, they made sure they had it.

Help, I attempted once again, as if some almighty power might hear me and save me. But of course, it didn't, and I found myself holding onto the last straw.

When I was with Chase, my mind was always on the stranger I felt in my trance, trying to sense him, to forget where I was and what my body was going through.

And this time wasn't an exception.

Once the twins finished with me, they shoved me in the hallway like some used rag. But I felt worse than that.

I wrapped my hands around my bare chest and finally released the tears I'd been containing this entire time. My body ached, bruised by their claws they liked to use so often. But I didn't care about it too much. I couldn't. I couldn't dwell on what had happened. I needed to get out of here so nothing like it would happen again.

I approached the stairs with wobbly legs. I could barely see anything when water flooded my eyes, streaming down my cheeks and touching my quivering lips.

With each step, it was harder and harder to move. All I wished to do was to find some safe spot, curl into a ball, and weep.

But I did not slow down my pace. I could not stay here. I had to go as far as I could from Lupin's and Fillan's chambers, because if they changed their minds ...

The likelihood of it happening again made me shudder even more.

I prayed no one would catch me walking like this. At least one thing could actually come true. The help I'd waited for while they were ruining me hadn't come. But I was begging for what didn't exist. Even if, sometimes, I could hear somebody's voice apart from mine in my head during perilous situations, I was inclined to believe it could be explained logically.

I imagined things just to ignore this brutal reality—the crystal-clear truth that I was all on my own here.

When it seemed like an eternity had passed, I reached the underground. Everyone was already asleep. I didn't want to go to bed like this, coated in their repulsive smell. But I couldn't risk fetching water to clean myself from upstairs either.

"Gen?"

I raised my chin, meeting a startled Thea who held a candleholder. I could only imagine the scene she witnessed—a girl, tears washing her face, body trembling, and exposed.

In the candlelight, I watched her cheeks paint red. She averted her gaze, causing more tears to flood my eyes.

"Were you ..."—she swallowed—"... by them?"

All I managed to do was nod when the sob was constricting my throat.

"Do you want to ... talk?"

I shook my head without hesitation.

Thea looked down. "I ... I can draw you a bath. If you're okay with it."

I nodded.

When Thea passed me to bring me what she'd promised without glancing at my side, I slid into the bathroom and curled up in the corner as I had wanted. As soon as I clamped a hand over my mouth, a sob broke out of its cage.

I knew what had happened. I was utterly aware. But still, a part of me hoped it was just a terrible, *horrible* nightmare from which I was going to wake up any minute now.

But I did not.

As I composed myself, I allowed the sickness to escape my guts into the nearby bucket. Then I turned away, taking a sharp breath.

But nausea had never truly left me. It lingered. Perhaps it would never leave me. It would always stay, reminding me of this day forever.

As Thea prepared a bath, I rubbed my skin countless times but the sensations from their fingers and tongues and teeth never disappeared.

All red from scouring my skin, I got out of the tub and wrapped Thea's brought towel around my body.

Marks of their claws and teeth stained my chest, neck, and arms. Another bucket of tears filled my cried-out eyes, not because I was sorry it had happened to me, but because I was livid. However, not enough to return to their chambers and kill them in their sleep. I would die if I tried that, and I couldn't perish until I exacted my sweet revenge on them for doing this to me.

Thea patiently waited behind the door, my nightwear in her hands. I took it from her, not forgetting to thank her, and dressed up inside the bathroom. As I left, I encountered Thea's moistened eyes.

"Have you been crying?" The question came out hoarse.

"No."

"Why did you cry?"

As she blinked, a traitorous teardrop rolled down her cheek, which she wiped away with the back of her hand.

"It's not right." She sniffled, looking up at the ceiling and blinking away the tears. "What they're doing to us ... what they ..." More and more tears ran down her face. She didn't wipe them off this time.

I didn't understand why she was acting this way. Perhaps she was just an empathic person. Or—

"They did it to you as well."

She stayed silent. Although she didn't say yes, she didn't deny it either.

I wasn't the only one. Of course, I wasn't.

The mocking words Asenah had said when I first served here hit me like a bolt of lightning. She noted her cousins were interested in servants. Of course, they had abused not only Thea and me but others, too. Gods knew how many sixteen-year-old girls were their victims.

I felt sicker than ever. And more determined to make Lupin and Fillan pay.

"When did it happen?"

My blood was already boiling and so was my bracelet. Could I strangle Lupin and Fillan in their sleep? I wished. They could only be killed by an enchanter's blood or a weapon made of gold, and I had neither. Besides, killing them would show mercy, and they needed to suffer for what they had done, not be killed. Their death would be nothing but a small price to pay for their unforgiving crimes.

Thea lowered her stare. "Not here," she muttered. "I can't speak about it here."

Taking a hint, I strode towards the room, which I could call my bedroom from now on, with Thea behind me. When I reached it, I opened the door for her to step inside first. Once she did, I also entered and shut the door.

I hadn't expected to feel safer here, and I didn't. They lived in the same building. What if they came here and—

No, I couldn't fret over it. They were not coming back. At least not tonight.

"It happened three days after I woke up here."

I turned to Thea. Her arms were folded across her chest as she stared at her feet.

Three days ... Only three days after she began working here. She was just a child. *Sixteen.*

Involuntarily, I pictured Gen in Thea's place. She was Gen's age when they had done that to her, after all. Fortunately, the victim was me instead of my sister.

I contemplated how the fire would affect morphs. It could be one of the many torturous methods I would use against those sick brothers.

"Were other girls abused as well?"

She nodded.

"How many?"

"Too many."

My hands clenched into fists, teeth gritted. The bracelet burned my skin, but the pain meant nothing after what I had experienced tonight.

As I took a step towards Thea, my rage ebbed. I placed my hands on her shoulders, making her look up at me.

"I'll make them pay," I said resolutely but quietly, in case the wrong ears listened.

"How?"

"I'll make them pay," I repeated assuredly.

She cracked a weak smile. A smile forced through the pain we had experienced together but at different times.

She embraced me, and I didn't hesitate to do the same. We stayed in each other's arms for a while in peaceful silence. I closed my eyes, and for a moment, I forgot about all the terrible things I had gone through lately.

But that didn't last for long. Those memories would always be a reminder etched in my mind to arise at the most unexpected times.

"Can you stay with me tonight?" I asked.

"Yeah."

My chest fell into ease.

Tonight, I wouldn't be able to sleep alone. I needed someone to hold me if I had another nightmare. Most likely worse than the other ones.

I had come to realise no decent men existed in this unfortunate world. I hadn't met many of them, but those I had encountered were all awful people in their own ways. However, there was no point in wishing for someone decent, as I would never experience romance in my life anyway.

I was destined to be a slave.

Thea's breathing evened out. We had to squeeze up to fit on the single bed. I couldn't fall asleep, but it wasn't because of the person pressed so close next to me.

I slipped my hand under the mattress and pulled out the folded sketch. Once I unfolded it, I was met with the imaginary man I had drawn a few years ago.

I traced my finger against his imaginary face. "You're not real, are you, stranger?" I whispered, as if my own creation would answer.

I stared at the sketch for so long, I wished that alone would summon the man.

But he did not appear.

Frustrated, I crumpled the sketch up into a ball and threw it into the corner of the room. It ricocheted off the wall, dropping to the floor. I stared at it, lying like trash, unable to shut my eyelids and drift into a slumber. Guilt pricked my conscience, which was ridiculous.

He was fiction.

I had invented him.

But there I was, quietly approaching the ball. As I lifted and unfurled it, I looked at it one more but not for the last time.

I fell asleep with the drawing pressed against my still-beating heart.

XVII

Today was *their* birthday.

Morphs had been invited from all over the empire to celebrate it. All guests were of noble blood, clad in the most elegant gowns and suits. On some of them, such attire looked comical. After all, they were animals walking on two limbs, wearing luxurious clothes. Only twins, Asenah, Fawne, and a few others nailed their looks.

Kayla, Lupin's fiancée, wasn't as nice-looking as her friend Fawne standing beside her. The poor eagle was too bird-looking to appear at least decent in any of the gowns, really.

Asenah was sitting on the elaborate throne, conversing with other noble, haughty "ladies". I was shocked that the throne was carved of wood and not of bones.

I was serving with other servants in the garden. Its decorations were all thanks to Thea, Clare, and me. Thea and I had brought the tables and chairs to accommodate as many morphs as possible without making it look overcrowded, while Clare had done a splendid job cutting the bushes into lovely, diverse shapes. I couldn't argue. She was a gifted gardener.

But the garden was this beautifully decorated for *them*. Though it was not like we'd had a choice. If it were my will, I'd have destroyed it without a blink.

As I carried the drinks, I caught snatches of morphs' conversations with one ear and listened to a quartet of musicians performing mild tunes with another. I kept my distance from the twins, not even glancing once at their side, afraid that if I did, a malicious idea would pop into their sick minds.

Ever since that ... that night, I'd been strained around the clock, wary of one of them approaching me and catching me off guard and ...

A shudder ran through me, and glasses shook on the tray.

Drawing in a deep breath, I resumed my job.

As expected, nightmares had only become worse. I was scared to close my eyes and drift into a slumber where Lupin, Fillan, and Chase would be waiting for me, leering at me with their hungry eyes and drooling mouths. Instead of experiencing something like that in my own head, I chose not to sleep at all.

Dark circles marred my eyes, but no morph looked at me to notice that. Even if they did, they wouldn't care. I was just a human. Their slave. Nothing. No one but dirt on their exposed feet.

Thea and Imogen were my rocks, but mostly Thea. She understood what I was going through as she had experienced something similar. Imogen wasn't abused, but she treated me as amiably as possible and had offered to lend an ear whenever I needed to talk. However, I had never taken her up on that sweet offer.

As I descended into reality, someone glancing at me from time to time snagged my attention.

A panther.

She wasn't part of any group, observing others, including me. I avoided looking at her. It was strange that a morph would be interested in observing a human at all.

I returned to the kitchen to refill the drinks.

"How is it out there?" Imogen asked while preparing delicate and ridiculously tiny sandwiches for the morphs.

Despite their efforts to masquerade as dignified and graceful creatures, they remained beasts more suited to the wilderness rather than in mansions, seated at the tables, devouring the most exquisite food while being served by actual human beings.

I stepped closer to the full pitcher of alcohol and began filling the glasses one by one.

"Disgusting," was all I could say without spitting the word out. Imogen huffed out a laugh. "How old are these imbeciles turning? Five hundred, six?"

"They're not that old. If they were, they wouldn't be Asenah's lap dogs."

I poured the last glass and raised the tray.

"Well, then." I pivoted on my heel. "I hope they get eaten by the Bloodsucker."

"Careful now," she drawled, a hint of tease in her voice, "ye don't want to summon the monster."

I glanced at her over my shoulder. "If it means the brothers get eaten, then the monster might as well be my guest."

Working like a bumblebee, I flitted from one circle to another. To my amazement, I didn't drop any of the drinks. I reckoned some of them would fall at some point, as I was holding one tray with ten full glasses. Walking quickly was a challenge, given the risk of tripping over small rocks, let alone trying to be invisible. Yet, I was actually doing a great job.

It didn't last long, however.

The wind picked up. Morphs voices rose an octave higher, and turmoil broke out throughout the garden.

I lurched to a halt, steadying the swinging tray in my hand.

Every single morph had their heads raised skyward, and I followed their stares. I wish I wouldn't have.

The silhouette of a dragon loomed above me, landing straight upon me.

XVIII

I was on the verge of dropping the drinks and fleeing wherever my legs could carry me, but I couldn't move. My legs refused to obey me, as if frozen.

No, the dragon wasn't landing on me. It had seemed like it was, but it wasn't. It landed approximately ten steps away from me instead.

A dragon. A bloody dragon.

It was bigger than I had imagined. When I listened to bedtime stories, I visualised dragons as the size of my cottage, just slightly bigger. But I was wrong. So, so wrong. It was almost as big as Asenah's mansion.

His massive wings flapped, dishevelling the girls' hair that their handmaidens had carefully styled, and blowing off the hats of those who wore them. His scales were dipped in burgundy, eyes bigger than rocks, the colour of gold and sprinkled with red. And two bats, I noticed only now, were flanking him.

In a flash, a claret-red cloud replaced the dragon, dispersing bit by bit. First, the shape of horns appeared, then wings, and at last, a whole figure standing on its two legs instead of four and dressed up.

With his hands in his black trousers, he slightly tipped his chin up.

The air in the garden hung heavy with silence.

Drayard was here.

The Bloodsucker.

Could it be? Could it be that I had summoned the monster? The main character from *A Tale of the Bloodsucker?* Drayard Emyur, the King of kings and queens?

Impossible.

I blinked, but he remained there. *Real.*

Once again, my imagination had deceived me. Despite the dragon tail, wings, ears, horns, and a face, Drayard didn't embody the monstrous beast I had envisioned—with no self-control, thirsty for blood and eager to feast on the organs of his prey. Instead, he turned out to be yet another morph, draped in finery that suited him more than most. I caught myself admiring his style. Clad in a white undershirt and a black tailcoat, intricately embroidered with gold, the rest of his attire—including a waistcoat, tie, and trousers—was all black. I couldn't help but speculate on how he endured the blistering heat.

Yet there was something ineffable about him that made him stand out—like a peacock's tail drawing attention. I doubted it was solely because of his striking sense of style or the fact that he'd interrupted the celebration by landing in the middle of the garden.

I was brought out of my audacious observation when, one after another, morphs dropped to their knees, pressing their foreheads against the ground as if he were a holy statue of one of the Gods in a temple. This time, my legs agreed to listen to me, and I followed suit, carefully kneeling before him, making sure not to spill any of the drinks.

It was a miracle that my heart stayed within my rib cage ever since his landing.

"Rise," he commanded in a baritone after a pregnant pause. The cold demand carried an air of extreme confidence, making it impossible to mistake him for anyone but a king—*the* King, with immeasurable power.

One by one, they rose, and I stood up as well, the tray quivering in my hands.

Drayard was no mere accursed morph. The ubiquitous power emanating from him was unparalleled, a force I had never witnessed before. He was not a God but as close to a God as one could ascend.

"Drayard Emyur," Asenah addressed him with a hint of wariness.

Drayard acknowledged her and the twins, who took a step back, hiding behind their cousin like frightened children.

Cowards.

"Asenah Louvel." The Bloodsucker dipped his chin in greeting.

"W-what ..." She rolled back her shoulders, evidently trying to regain composure despite her fear. "What are you doing here?"

I was certain Drayard could sense her fear. Not entirely sure why. Although he didn't show it, I knew he was revelling in it. In his place, feared as he was, I wouldn't only relish their fear but take advantage of it.

"Ah, well." He drew his gloved hand from his pocket. "The rumour of your beloved cousins' celebration spread throughout my land. I was exceedingly pained to learn I wasn't invited."

"But you never attend birthday celebrations, Drayard," Asenah noted in a cautious and reasonable tone, playing it safe. "Especially lords' birthdays."

"Correct, Asenah. You are acquainted with me quite well." As he stepped forward, a wave of tension rippled through an already strained crowd. The corner of his mouth barely twitched, attesting to his awareness of the effect he caused. "However, to not be invited whether I come or not is quite a stab in the heart," he said dramatically, a masked threat underlying his words.

Asenah joined her hands together, transforming back into the queen I'd seen many times in the dining room. "Is it the real reason you're here? To show that you're upset for not being invited, or is there a bigger, more rational reason? We all know you don't waste your precious time on insignificant celebrations like this, Drayard."

"Is it truly impossible to believe I came here to celebrate?"

"Yes," Asenah replied carefully, "it is."

A tense silence stretched out between them, affecting

everyone else. Drayard's expression didn't alter, and neither did Asenah's.

He put his hand back in his pocket. "You do not need to worry, Asenah. I'm harmless."

But it didn't take a genius to understand that his tone meant the opposite.

Asenah was right. There had to be a reason why he was here, and it couldn't be that he wanted to celebrate the twins' birthday. Was he going to burn this mansion with other morphs? But no, that would—

Oh, who was I kidding? The man was dangerous. A red zone. He might spit fire if he wished. He might suck every guest's blood if he desired. He might feast on everybody, and nobody would be able to stop him because *he* was the frigging Bloodsucker. He could do whatever he wanted without getting punished since he was also the *King*.

Drayard's eyes moved to the twins, who were still hiding behind their cousin's skirt. "Turning seventy, right?"

All the twins could do while being petrified was shift their heads in almost imperceptible nods.

Drayard's mouth curved into one devilish smile. It didn't reach his eyes, but no one expected the Bloodsucker to be a warm-hearted bastard.

He must retaliate. The Bloodsucker hadn't been invited. He was going to—

"I've brought presents for you," he said.

I winced.

Is this some kind of joke?

"Sweethearts," he addressed no one.

Or so I'd thought.

The bats, fluttering around him like his pets, transformed into female bats, landing two steps behind their master.

Of course, those bats were morphs. Why hadn't I realised it sooner?

Right. The Bloodsucker's entrance had me transfixed.

Dressed in crimson dresses that revealed more of their fur skin than the other females in the garden, both girls struck as walking threats with cunning looks in their eyes and faces that ...

were not much to look at.

"Come here, Your Lordships," Drayard said.

The twins hesitated. Asenah grabbed their jacket collars and flung them towards the creature that screamed danger, most likely their worst nightmare.

"Closer," Drayard urged.

The twins obeyed.

As they stood right before the Bloodsucker and his two bat girls, Drayard towered over them both. But it wasn't the apparent height difference that made the twins look like little puppies in front of the powerful fire-spitting, bloodsucking dragon. It was the latter's vast and palpable power.

"Kneel," Drayard ordered.

In no time, the twins dropped to their knees, lowering their heads. The two wolves who had acted tough and dominating a few days ago were now shivering with fear in the presence of the half-breed.

I hadn't realised I was smiling. Quickly, I dropped the smile, hoping no morph had noticed. But no one had. Drayard had their full attention, not some worthless human.

"Would you like me to burn your home?" Drayard inquired.

The twins shook their heads vigorously.

"I don't hear you."

"No, Your Highness," they both uttered.

"Very well. You will accept my present, then?"

"Yes, Your Highness."

"Sweethearts." Drayard waved his black-gloved hand. "You have my permission."

Lupin and Fillan looked uncertain, as if doubting whether it was a trick or not. I hoped it was, because if Drayard was giving the bats as entertainment for them after they had had enough fun with my body, it would make my blood boil.

"You two can arise now," the Bloodsucker said.

The twins rose to their unsteady feet, and the bats approached them. Batting their absurdly long eyelashes, the bats caressed the twins' faces with their claws.

I glanced at Fawne and Kayla, who didn't seem jealous of the bats touching their fiancés. Both of them were as aghast as anyone else.

I spotted Thea by the quartet. Her fair skin was blanched, and I worried she might faint. But I couldn't rush to her when the Bloodsucker was the centre of attention, and nobody else was moving. I expected to see Clare nearby, but she was nowhere to be seen.

"You have an hour with them," Drayard informed, but the twins didn't budge. "What? You have an hour to enjoy the company of my two best girls. I'm certain you have heard of how professional the bats are in that field."

I certainly hadn't. Wasn't his mother a bat?

Still, the twins balked.

Drayard did not appreciate it. "If you don't want my birthday present, I am willing to take it back and turn your birthday celebration into hell."

"No," both said simultaneously, not hesitating anymore.

A pleased smile appeared on the Bloodsucker's face. "Wise choice, Your Lordships."

In a heartbeat, the twins disappeared with the bats within the mansion.

Drayard shoved his hands into his pockets and scanned the guests, causing them to tense more than they already were. To my relief, his eyes passed over me. The last individual he fixed his gaze upon was Asenah.

"May I take a seat on the throne?"

Did he really have to ask that?

Asenah wasn't thrilled, but without saying anything, she stepped aside from the throne, allowing the Bloodsucker to take it over. While everybody was gaping, he approached the throne, turned around, and took a seat without harming his wings.

"Don't mind me for interrupting," Drayard said nonchalantly. "You can now resume your festivities."

As simple as it sounded, morphs couldn't do that. They were all too aware of Drayard's presence, cautious that he might strike and burn them at any moment. But he didn't give an impression as if he was about to do that. Or it was all just a perfect act.

Even as people slid into conversations and the music resumed, it wasn't the same as before. Unease hung over the garden like a cloud.

I couldn't tear my gaze off the Bloodsucker, who observed the guests instead of joining any activity. I knew I shouldn't do anything to attract his attention, but I couldn't help but follow his every movement, like a feline before it pounced on its prey.

He propped his elbow on the throne's arm. "Where's my drink?" he voiced loud enough for everyone to hear.

I scanned the area for the other maids who had trays with drinks, but they were nowhere to be found. I was the sole remaining servant.

Swallowing my fear, I took a hesitant step towards the throne.

I had heard and read his tale countless times. I had it all memorised in my head. I knew what he could do. *How* he could—

When I was only three steps away from him, I stumbled over something. I landed on my knees, dropping the whole tray to the ground. The drinks spilled, and some glasses shattered, but that was the least of my worries as everyone burst into laughter.

I did not dare to lift my gaze, continuing to stare at the grass, wishing to dig a hole underground and never surface again.

I clenched the grass tightly in my fists.

Pull yourself together.

Be strong.

And be brave.

I threw a glance at the girl who had been staring at me before Drayard emerged. She was sneering at me, malevolence glowing in her greenish eyes.

A panther. A sneaky panther who had made me stumble and fall, turning me into a mockery before the audience of beasts.

My blood flamed, and the bracelet heated against my wrist. I resisted the urge to lash out, opting instead for blowing strands of my honey-blonde hair from my eyes as I locked eyes with the panther.

"Stupid human," some morphs barked through their laughs.

I brought the tray closer and began collecting both unharmed and broken glasses.

Laughter echoed around me, but I ignored them, repressing my tears. Eventually, the laughter subsided as morphs returned to their conversations.

I sensed a new pair of eyes on me, but as I looked up, I caught no gaze.

As I returned to the garden with refilled glasses, I approached the Bloodsucker and extended a tray of drinks to him. He didn't look in my direction, taking a glass without ceasing to observe the guests.

Asenah had her blazing eyes on him ever since he had sat on her throne. I was confident he was aware of her glare, which he didn't care about. She wouldn't dare raise a hand against the bloody dragon king.

The sunset had already dyed the sky in orange and yellow hues, signalling to guests that it was time to disperse. But the celebration continued, although not as lively as before the Bloodsucker's entrance.

I was so over this birthday. I wanted it to end, but I couldn't determine when it would be over as I had no clue about the typical duration of morphs' celebrations.

A high-pitched scream echoed from within the mansion, abruptly silencing the guests and musicians.

Everyone exchanged confused glances with the morphs nearby, bewildered as to whom that piercing scream could have belonged. Shortly after, Fillan came running as though he'd seen a ghost. His shirt was half unbuttoned, as were his trousers.

It didn't take long for another disarranged brother to show up, running just behind Fillan.

Both were visibly terrified, their eyes frantic as they halted, slightly bent over, propping hands on their knees, trying to catch their uneven breaths.

As the twins looked at Drayard in unison, they stepped back in unison, as if they'd rehearsed it.

The bat girls also returned from the mansion, approaching their master with graceful movements. They turned around and settled elegantly in front of the throne, coy smiles dancing on their appalling faces.

Asenah arose from her seat. "What happened?" she asked.

"T-they ..." Lupin raised his quivering forefinger, pointing at the bats.

Asenah turned to Drayard. "Drayard?" she addressed him politely.

He lifted his head to look at Asenah. "Yes?"

What an innocent tone he had released! It vividly suggested that whatever had transpired, he played a significant role in it.

"What have your bat whores done to my cousins?" Asenah demanded.

Drayard shifted his gaze to the bats. "What did you do, sweethearts?"

The bats tilted their heads back, fluttering their eyelids innocently.

"We played with their prized possessions and, accidentally, sent them into a deep, deep slumber," the bat to Drayard's right crooned. "Unfortunately, they don't work anymore." She issued a theatrical sigh and pouted.

"It was a complete accident," the other bat assured. A smile attempted to creep on her lips, but it never did. "Our apologies, Your Highness." She lowered her head remorsefully.

I frowned, confused at first, but gradually a realisation began to unravel. *Did they—*

"I lost my manhood!" Lupin cried.

"Our manhood!" Fillan whined.

I had the urge to laugh. *Maniacally.* However, I battled the urge with some effort, saving it for later.

"You did this," Fillan growled at Drayard.

I was certain he had made a colossal mistake by displaying his wolf-like instincts to the Bloodsucker. I was proven right when Drayard cast him a bone-chilling look. Fillan instantly shrank and recoiled, realising he shouldn't have spoken to the infamous Bloodsucker in such a manner.

"To your knowledge, my bats can do whatever they please once they're out of my sight," Drayard remarked, pressing one of his talons to his mouth. "In this matter, if they don't want your *manhood* to work, they do as they desire."

"Tell them to undo whatever they did," Asenah commanded.

Her silent fury didn't seem to affect Drayard, not even one bit. "Ah, but it's impossible. How long does it take for the sting to go away?" he addressed the bat girls.

"Usually a month," the right one said.

"Or two," the other added.

"Sometimes half a year," both chirped in harmony.

Asenah continued glaring at him, but shortly, she diverted her ire to her cousins, who looked like kicked dogs. "It's your problem that you accepted Drayard's present," she snarled at them. "Now you deal with it."

The wolves lowered their eyes, avoiding Asenah's glare like two misbehaved kids, while Drayard and the bats were relishing the whole scene.

The celebration resumed, and I continued to serve.

I knew the Bloodsucker was lying. He was the one who had ordered his bat girls to incapacitate the brothers' parts. It hadn't been an accident, as his bats had claimed. Drayard wasn't even trying to hide it. There was no purpose, as nobody would dare to blame him, only to be sent straight to hell for trying.

But I didn't understand why he had done such a thing. To entertain himself? To pay Asenah back for not inviting him to the twins' birthday celebration?

Whatever his reasons were, they didn't matter. I wasn't going to find them out anyway.

As the celebration finally came to an end, servants were left in the garden to clean up the morphs' mess.

Most of the guests departed, but the most privileged morphs remained, and Drayard was among them.

Obviously, we humans were afraid to go back to the mansion with the most dangerous creature. It wasn't surprising that everyone took their time to tidy the garden.

"He has shown up here before, right?" I asked Thea.

I needn't mention his name for her to understand who I was talking about.

She shook her head. "Not while I've been serving here."

I placed another empty glass I had found shoved in a bush on the tray. Those morphs, even with blue blood streaming through their veins, were slobs. There were tables where they could have put empty glasses, but they must have cluttered the garden instead. Perhaps they had done it on purpose so that humans would have more work after the celebration, which wouldn't shock me.

"Why do you think he's here?"

"I believe for a far more important reason than to harm Asenah's cousins' sensitive parts," she said with a faint smile.

I chuckled. "At least we are safe for a month."

"Or two," she added.

"Or half a year," we both said at once and exchanged crooked grins.

We cracked up, giggling like two madwomen. Some servants smiled at the sight of us because seldom did somebody produce an honest laugh. I had learned to cherish those moments as they helped me preserve my sense of self and maintain my sanity.

That very night, sleep eluded me due to my growling stomach. No wonder it was playing a march. I had only managed to have breakfast as I was preoccupied with decorating the garden and later serving morphs.

Since it was pointless to fight the hunger, hoping I would fall asleep sooner or later, I lit a candle and proceeded to the pantry upstairs.

I still couldn't believe I had met the Bloodsucker a few hours ago. The same one I had heard stories about since I was three. First, sweeter versions, and only as I grew older, my mother introduced me to the entire tale.

As I opened the pantry doors, someone giggled. Frowning, I moved the candle to identify the source and froze.

Franz was whispering something to Thea, who had her back against the wall. I blinked in confusion. They noticed me, and the whispers and giggles faded into silence. They stared at me wide-eyed, as if caught doing something they shouldn't.

But I had indeed caught them doing something.

Franz opened his mouth to say something, but I beat him to it. "I wasn't here. I saw nothing." I moved back, but before I closed the door, I winked at Thea. Even though I couldn't witness it, I could swear she blushed.

Unable to contain a smile, I sneaked into the kitchen. Franz and Thea? Who would have thought? Although, when I thought more about it, it wasn't that surprising.

Rummaging through the counters, I looked for something that wouldn't need to be prepared but would satiate my hunger.

But I halted in the middle of my search, feeling that I wasn't alone.

Someone was in the kitchen with me, swallowed by the shadows, *watching* me.

I snatched the first thing my eyes spotted—which happened to be just an apple—and scurried out of the kitchen, praying that whoever was there wasn't following me.

As I glanced over my shoulder, nobody was at my heels. I sighed in relief and returned to the bedroom.

I chewed on an apple while sketching a suit for a man, but I drifted off before I could finish it.

XIX

The next day, the grand dining room was more crowded than usual, enveloped in an eerie silence. Fear lingered, stifling any attempt at conversation, as the Bloodsucker sat among them, but without his bats. With or without them, his presence unsettled them regardless.

I recognised all the faces and was familiar with their names, except for one. Among them sat the same female who had tripped me the day before, causing me to fall in front of all the morphs.

The panther dominated the centre of the table. No one dared to sit next to her, as her mischievous gaze insinuated one could expect anything from her. By now, I was sure she was the one lurking in the shadows when I had gone for a midnight snack in the kitchen. Panthers were sneaky animals, after all.

Asenah and Drayard had taken seats at opposite ends of the table, while Asenah's cousins, along with their fiancées, occupied their usual places on either side of her.

After a prolonged, unwelcoming silence, Asenah finally asked, "How long do you plan to stay here, Drayard?"

The Bloodsucker took a sip of wine. "Not long."

To avoid displaying any interest in the conversation, I concentrated on Drayard's wings, noticing small cuts and imperfections. Only the claws atop his wings remained unharmed. Despite the flaws, his wings were still magnificent, blending wine-red seamlessly with a shade of black at their ends.

"Why are you here at all?" Asenah continued questioning, staring at him keenly.

"Are you allowed to question your king's motives, Asenah?" Drayard retorted.

Displeasure crossed Asenah's face, but no other word left her mouth as she resumed eating while keeping a wary eye on Drayard.

"How are things in Casidiarn, Dara?" Drayard addressed the panther female while taking a bite of roast mutton.

"Nayden and the council are still trying to solve the curse," Dara said blandly.

"Isn't it strange how forty years have passed since the curse, and nobody has figured out how to solve it yet?"

Kayla, Fawne, and the twins nodded in agreement, their gazes fixed on their plates, while Dara with Asenah remained motionless.

"They don't understand what *lost and found* might be," Dara admitted while cutting roast mutton.

"I believe their sorceresses aren't particularly helpful either."

Dara winced. "Witches can't be trusted."

"They can't be, indeed," the dragon agreed. "But the curse is four decades old. It's the main problem of our lands, and the emperor isn't determined to vanquish it, nor is his council, nor is the empress."

Despite blaming the rulers, his tone was impassive.

Confusion clouded Dara's face. "They want to get rid of the curse as much as any morph. Why wouldn't they make it a priority?"

"Let's see ..." he began. "They did nothing when enchanters massacred a part of my kind, leaving it as my problem to deal with. They are throwing parties for no specific reason instead of focusing on the curse. Then they punish sorceresses for their ancestors' crimes instead of communicating with them to extract valuable information." He tilted his head. "Should I continue?"

"Are you accusing my family of being bad monarchs?" Dara asked.

"The Haroun family has ruled since the beginning of morphs. Some ruled better than others. Some almost led morphs to their downfall." He stated the facts I didn't know about and certainly didn't care to learn, despite my ears listening attentively to this conversation. "I have nothing against lion morphs and your family, Dara. But Nayden needs to rethink his reign's purpose or pass it on to someone else more suited for the duty."

"Is that someone else you, Drayard?" Asenah asked with a shade of bite in her voice.

I heard his faint smile in his words as he replied, "I'm a warrior, not a ruler, Asenah."

"If being the emperor of the Empire of Beasts is too extreme for you, then you have someone else in mind. Someone you picture as a great monarch," Dara surmised. "Who is he?"

Drayard toyed with silence while he sipped his wine, tasting and savouring it. Although neither of the twins with their betrothed showed it, I could wager they were as intrigued by the words exchanged in the room as I was.

Eventually, the Bloodsucker swallowed, ending this tormenting silence. "Who was talking about him, Daraine?"

He caught her off guard, for she seemed a bit bemused. I could have sworn her emotions changed because of the way he'd called her *Daraine*. But her bemusement shifted to gravity a matter of a heartbeat. "A woman can never rule the empire on her own. You should know that, *Drayard*."

"Why, yes, but you see, it's been like that for over a thousand years. Only males have been allowed to rule the Empire of Beasts and its realms."

Asenah harrumphed.

"Yes, Asenah, I am well acquainted with the fact that you're a queen," Drayard remarked. "But I'm sure you are also aware most rulers don't take you seriously."

Her jaw clenched, and she took a hefty gulp of wine, voicing nothing.

"As I was saying," he continued, "we are underestimating the female kind, burdening them with obligations before birth, such as forcing them into arranged marriages and childbearing. For lower families, there goes whoring, entertainment for men. Merely a few are regarded as higher, but with exceptions nonetheless. But what about ruling the nation? Perhaps they could do better than a man? How can we claim a woman can't rule if none of them has been given a chance to try? Haroun males have been ruling for over a millennium, and not much has improved since Macegan claimed the throne. We are one of the few nations falling behind the world, and we will not improve without trying new things, which means stepping out of our system's established boundaries."

Silence fell over everyone, broken only by the loud chewing of Lupin, audible even to human ears. As soon as he realised he was the sole source of noise, he stopped eating and quickly gulped down his wine.

Asenah then spoke. "You're a man. How can you say that?"

"I keep an open mind," he said half-heartedly. "I'm not saying all men are terrible rulers. I, myself, can tell from experience my ruling in my realm is splendid." Dara slightly shook her head. "But we haven't given women a chance to prove they could also reign, perhaps be even better at it. They do have a nature to manipulate to get what they need."

Dara arched her brow. "Are you saying manipulating is a required trait for a ruler?"

I was on her side with this one. Being manipulative was a negative trait, and no ruler should possess or use it unless they had no other choice.

"How else are you going to trick your enemies?" Drayard asked.

Silence.

As no one spoke, Drayard went on. "Men can also master the skill of manipulating, but they could never manipulate the way a woman can. They're the gender that not only has power with their minds and voices but also their bodies."

I gritted my teeth, my nails digging into the tray, resisting the urge to smash it against Drayard's skull.

"However, it's not what gender rules the nation that matters," he said. "It's the needs of the people we should address so they would appreciate the empire, instead of cursing it every day. And not much is focused on them, is it?"

Nobody answered, but I didn't think it was needed when he was stating undeniable facts. Instead, they exchanged wary looks with one another, except for Drayard, Dara, and Asenah. Asenah and Dara were observing him with suspicion while the Bloodsucker was savouring his meal. He didn't voice another assertion during the rest of the dinner, despite dissimilar looks towards his side.

The temperature outside was hot as I gathered vegetables, enduring the scorching heat in the greenhouse. Loose strands of my hair clung to my clammy forehead and neck. The uniform felt uncomfortable against my sweaty body. I tried to collect all the required vegetables into the basket as quickly as possible so I could hurry out, open the freezer, and duck my head inside to cool down.

"Your gardener is doing a great job."

My muscles stiffened as I heard the masculine voice that could only belong to one creature.

"Don't you have gardens back in your realm?" Asenah asked.

I could make out their blurred bodies through the greenhouse's glass walls. Desperate for cover, I scanned the area, but the greenhouse was all exposed, nothing designed for hiding.

I dropped to the ground, concealing my head behind the basket. This was my only way to avoid being seen. Even if they did notice, perhaps they would ignore the basket lying randomly amidst the greenhouse.

"I do, but they're different." Drayard's voice sounded distant, as if he were elsewhere, not with Asenah.

They continued their amble. I prayed to the Gods that they wouldn't step in here. It would be foolish if they did, for it was impossible to breathe in here. I had to get out, or I risked fainting. But I couldn't. Not with morphs around.

"Have you found a woman to adore, Dray?"

I wouldn't mind beholding Drayard's reaction, but all I could discern was their blurred bodies.

"I'm not in a rush," he murmured, his voice dismissive.

Asenah didn't take his tone of voice as a hint not to touch that topic. "Shouldn't you be? You should have had an heir by now."

I was certain Asenah was playing with fire. Literally.

"The same applies to you, Asenah," he noted.

Asenah giggled.

She *giggled*.

I hadn't realised she could be capable of such an innocent, girly sound that did not suit her one bit.

"I haven't found anyone worthy of me yet," she said.

"You haven't, or they just don't like you?"

A deathlike silence descended between them. Asenah, however, took his rhetorical question as a joke, and her strained titter echoed throughout the garden a moment too late. She took a step closer to him. "Perhaps together we could ... fix our little problem?"

What was Asenah playing? I had lived here long enough to know she loathed Drayard, arranged weddings with other realms to have an alliance against him if one day he snapped. But now she was trying to seduce him into sleeping with her and marrying her? It didn't make any sense. What was she striving to achieve now?

"Perhaps," he answered coolly.

Even if Drayard was the most feared morph in the world, he wasn't the wisest one.

"Our offspring could be the rulers not only of two different realms but the entire empire. Our son, the King of kings and queens as you are, and our daughter ... an empress." Her voice was just as poisonous as the snake's venom but somehow alluring at the same time. "Just as you covet."

I did not want to hear this conversation. It made me want to vomit, acknowledging such odd circumstances.

"Perhaps." Another bland response came from his mouth.

He wasn't moving but standing still while Asenah was tracing lines on his chest covered by a dark shirt.

"They would be so powerful," she continued. "With the

dragon's, bat's and wolf's abilities ... if we get lucky."

It must be the most disgusting way to lure someone to bed I had ever heard.

"Perhaps," he said impassively once more.

Was he enjoying this? Was he bored, or was he waiting for something more from Asenah to break the ice?

I begged the Gods that if they were on the verge of tearing their clothes off and engaging in the Sinner's Tango, they wouldn't do it in the garden while I was here, wilting in the torturous heat.

"You'd be my King. I'm your Queen ..."

"I'm your King already, Asenah."

"I know, but you know what I mean." She leaned closer to his face. He didn't move. "Imagine the wild sex we would have together ..."

Disgusting. Disgusting. Disgusting.

A laugh left Drayard's mouth. Humourless and hollow.

"Your acting skills need to be rechecked, Asenah." He pulled away from her touch and turned towards the bushes. "What happened to your love for the Princess of Beasts? Would you truly go for a man rather than a woman?"

"I don't understand what you're talking about."

"But you do," he assured. "You seem to have forgotten how old I am and how much I've gone through in my life. I'm not a gullible boy anymore. The world fears me not only for my powers but also for my wisdom, Asenah. Do you think I'm unaware that you marry off your cousins to princesses from other realms to strengthen alliances in case I declare war against the Empire of Skies? Do you think I don't know about your unrequited love for Tatyana Haroun?"

Oh, how I would love to see her reaction!

"H-how did you know?" Asenah inquired, unbelievably.

"You're going to need to try harder to hide something from me. I'm not the King of kings and queens just because that title was given to my ancestors to prevent them from taking over Haroun's dynasty. I didn't only inherit the title; I earned it." His wings spread behind him in one swift, spellbinding motion. "I am your King, and there's nothing you can do to change it."

With a flick of his striking wings, he sprang into the sky, leaving not only Asenah speechless and unmoving, but also me.

The Bloodsucker didn't show up for dinner. I was relieved. Being in the same residence as the fire-breathing dragon, who could also suck blood at any moment, wasn't tremendously relaxing.

Nobody talked about him. He never came back after disappearing into the sky this morning. He had left for good.

Once I served the last meal, I returned to the kitchen, where Imogen was waiting for me with a tray.

I placed mine on the cabinet before looking at her.

Her face was pallid.

"Imogen, are you all right?" I asked worriedly.

"I'm fine, but ..." With a deep inhale, she issued a breath. "Drayard returned and asked for dinner to his temporary chamber, making a request for it to be *you* who serves it."

I couldn't follow the emotions that struck me immediately after she said those fatal words, indicating something I didn't even want to contemplate. I reckoned my heart was about to leap out of my chest from its wild throb.

"I'm so sorry," she whispered.

Sudden panic constricted my throat. I swallowed it with effort.

"No." I shook my head as tears burned my eyes.

Not this again. First the twins, now ...

"You have to go there," she said. "You have no choice."

"No." I stepped back. My knees felt like jelly.

"I'm so sorry, lassie."

It wasn't her fault. It wasn't anyone's fault but morphs, and they didn't care.

I took the tray and glanced at Imogen one more time in search of strength, which I hardly found, before leaving the kitchen without another word.

My first maid's outfit was torn in the library. Thea had given me a new one. Would this one be ripped in the room where the Bloodsucker was staying?

My legs trembled, but I did not stop mounting the stairs. I had no choice, and I abhorred that. I wanted to scream again, plead for some non-existent help. But then again, if I screamed, my cries for help would change nothing.

As I reached his door, I drew in a calming breath and exhaled through my mouth to ease my jittery nerves, but it was no help. At last, I plucked up the courage to knock.

"It's open," a deep voice came from within the room.

My hand was tense and sweaty as I placed it on the door handle to open the door. Once I stepped inside, I discovered *him* standing before the arched window with his back to me. His breath-taking wings tucked and gloved hands clasped behind his back.

"Close the door, please."

I swallowed.

He did not tell me to leave the food. He did not dismiss me, either. I had no other choice but to deal with my fear and obey. As he had ordered, I shut the door behind me with a quivering hand.

I turned to him, only to discover that he had fully turned to me. The tray almost slipped from my hands, but I grasped it tighter before it did. He watched me with his curious golden eyes, tinged with flecks of red, like a hawk. It horrified me more than any ravenous stare. Although I was sure I was standing with my clothes on, I felt more naked than the time when the twins—

Drayard's expression changed for a fleeting moment, but it quickly swept back to its previous state, confusing me.

With unwavering confidence and a palpable air of authority, he approached me, stopping just a step away. I had to crane my neck to meet his gaze as he towered over me by a head. His imposing height and apparent dominance should have unnerved me, but they didn't. He took the tray from my hands without grazing my skin and headed for the bed, where he took a seat, placing the tray beside him.

As his eyes returned to me, I instinctively took a cautious step back.

"I'm not going to hurt you," he assured me, noting my fear, but then added with a smirk, "Not now at least."

I didn't expect anything different.

"They can't hear us as they don't know I'm here," he went on, and a wave of nausea twisted my insides. "Well? I'm sure you have questions unless you intend to keep staring at me as though I'm about to attack you?"

I tried to swallow a knot of fear, feigning strength. "What do you want?" To my surprise, my voice came out steady and even polite.

He leaned back on his gloved hand, seeming thoughtful. "Oh, I don't want a lot, Honeylove." He looked down, furrowing his brows, but then his expression softened as he lifted the cover, revealing a steaming roast chicken. "That's nice."

"What do you want from *me*?" I clarified my question. "If you want my body, then go on with it already."

His head flicked to my side; his eyebrows furrowed again. "I don't fool around with humans."

A relief blessed my body. Just a bit, but not nearly enough. Even if I wasn't here for *that,* he had requested *me* to bring him food for another unknown reason. Perhaps much worse than being assaulted again.

"Then what do you want from me?" I pressed.

Drayard took his precious time to answer, playing with my nerves as if I were yet another puppet in his spectacle. At least his devouring gaze was on the chicken and not me.

He pulled off his gloves, baring his scaled red hands. He

peeled the leg from the chicken, and once he tasted it, his eyes closed as he ... moaned.

It was muffled, but still a moan. I didn't want to be a part of this, yet here I was, the witness of the Bloodsucker being turned on by the mere bite of roast chicken.

Drayard snorted as his eyelids snapped open, eyes on me. I didn't budge.

He was *mad*. Laughing out of the blue was a mad-like thing to do.

"What's your name?" he inquired.

What's your name? the other voice with predatory aftertaste echoed, and the snippets of the revolting memory flashed before me.

The library. The wall. Lupin's wolf-like face. Fillan—
"Are you all right?"

I came back, meeting the Bloodsucker's concerned stare. Wait ... concerned? No, that couldn't be right. Folding my arms about myself, I released a calming breath, and the vestiges of the memory diffused until it belonged in the past again.

"Yes," I lied. Not like he cared anyway.

He stared for a little longer until he resumed savouring his chicken. Without any sounds of pleasure this time, thank heavens.

"You didn't answer my former question," he reminded me between bites.

Silly me for thinking I could get away without telling him my name. For a minute, I debated challenging him. Since he had ignored my question, I should reciprocate, but who was I compared to him? Right ... *No one.*

"Genette," I said and immediately regretted telling him my sister's name, even if telling him my name was out of the question.

"I was asking for your *real* name," he said. "Not your sister's you're pretending to be."

My eyes bulged.

How does he know about my sister? How—

On the other hand, how did he come to know about Asenah's plans? Could it be only because of his wisdom or superiority over others?

"Are you going to tell me your real name or not?"

He brought me back from my musings, and utter shock and puzzlement evaporated to anger. My bracelet stung my skin, and his gaze lowered to it. Quickly, I covered my hand behind my back.

"If I tell you my name, you tell me why I'm here." I tried to negotiate.

He looked up and half-smiled, but other than that, he said nothing.

His unresponsiveness was really starting to grate on me. "If there's no use of me, then dismiss me."

"No, you're staying."

I scowled, crossing my arms. "I've heard stories about you."

"Ah, my heroic deeds?"

"No."

Did he even have those, or was he fooling me?

He sighed. "What a pity."

Yes, he was indeed fooling me. "I know *A Tale of the Bloodsucker*. I have it all memorised."

A teasing smile tugged at the corner of his mouth. "Are you fond of me, Honeylove?"

"The point is," I said steely, "I'm not a clueless or foolish girl. There's something you need from me. Given your appalling past, I believe the roast chicken is only an appetiser when the whole meal is me."

He showed no reaction. Not even the slightest indication of whether I was right. All he did was say in wonder, "The Mortal Region has stories written about me?"

"Not only about you."

His eyebrows went up. "Am I painted as a villain?"

"More like a monster."

"Such flattery."

Silence settled between us. I needed to leave this room and keep my distance from him, but I couldn't do it without his dismissal. I must remain here.

What an insufferable scoundrel.

Now, now, you're not a saint either. His voice emerged in my head like thunder in a clear sky, causing the hair on my arms to rise. *Didn't your parents teach you eavesdropping might get you decapitated?*

"You can read thoughts."

Now everything made sense. *Why* his snort had been out of the blue earlier. *How* he was aware of Asenah's plans just as much as he knew I'd been in the greenhouse earlier this morning. He knew those things because he was a telepath. But it was strange. Morphs couldn't read anyone's thoughts. They didn't possess such ability, unlike enchanters. The only way to explain his mysterious power would be that he wasn't who he claimed to be.

"But how can you read thoughts?"

"I'm still trying to figure it out," he mumbled and sank his teeth into the chicken's leg.

I frowned at his silly answer and did the algebra in no time. "Aren't you, like, one hundred years old?"

"One hundred eighty-one years old, Honeylove," he corrected.

"Don't call me that."

"Why don't you tell me your name, then?"

I let out a sigh. "My name's Elynn," I said, giving in. "Happy now, *Your Highness?*"

He cracked a smile. "Delighted." Although it was obvious sarcasm, his tone carried a faint amusement. "I'm Drayard, in case you didn't know."

I dared to roll my eyes. "So, are you going to tell Asenah I was eavesdropping? Get me beheaded?"

"No, but you should be more prudent next time."

"Oh, how considerate of you!" I exclaimed. He didn't react. "Does it mean she isn't aware of it?"

"I can assure you that she's not."

Why I believed him, I couldn't tell. He seemed genuine, even if, from what I had seen, he was fond of wearing invisible masks. But why would he lie about it?

"So, is this a dismissal?"

"No."

I curled my lip in annoyance as I watched Drayard continue to eat with a smile, frustrating me even more. However, despite its wicked purpose, his smile was not like the ones I'd seen him plastering on in front of others, but reflected in his eyes.

"Are *you* going to kill me?" I asked.

"Not if you answer me one question."

"Can't you just get your desired answers from reading my thoughts?"

"Answer my question, and you're free to go." He dodged my question. Just. Like. That.

"Am I your prisoner now?" I asked scornfully. "The last time I checked, I was Asenah's slave, not yours, *Your Highness.*"

"You have a sharp tongue, I see."

"Yes, my only weapon."

He tilted his head to the side. "A weapon if you know how to use it; otherwise, it can put you in extreme danger."

I gritted my teeth. "Eat your bloody chicken."

He huffed out a laugh, placing a bone on the plate. "I see you've forgotten who I am, Elynn." He arose, his wings extending behind his back in a sharp motion.

I flinched, not expecting that, but he must have misinterpreted my reaction because he said with a sinful smirk, "You're back to being afraid of me." He locked his shoulders, presenting himself more menacingly as he stood at his full height, his wings conquering most of the room's space. "Good."

But I was not afraid. I felt disgusted, in awe, and curious, but not afraid, regardless of my palpitating heart. He was like his tale. While designed to evoke fear, it stirred intrigue within me. Yes, he was scary, but his frightening demeanour carried a charm that kindled my interest, making me forget all about the menace he truly was.

Instead of correcting him, I sneered. "What sick game are you playing?"

"I'm playing not only one sick game," he said, and the candlelight dampened, the entire room switching darker, colder, "but many of them."

Just kill me already, you psycho.

I've been called worse, he said, unaffected.

Get out of my head.

It's not my fault you're sending your thoughts to me.

What?

What?

"Answer my question, and you may go," he said in earnest.

"Promise?"

He nodded. "Promise."

I inspected him suspiciously.

Right then, I was certain of one thing—I couldn't trust him. As clear as it was. But did I have another choice? The answer was one and only. I. Did. Not.

I jerked my chin up. "Go on, then."

He gathered his hands behind his back, pausing a moment before voicing, "If your human mother couldn't bear children, how were your siblings born?"

My jaw dropped.

What the ...

"H-how ... How do you—"

"Answer my question, Elynn."

I stared at him in disbelief and absolute shock.

How did he even know I also had a brother? Or that my mother couldn't have children for a while? He couldn't have read my mind *that* far. But then again, I had no clue how his telepathy worked precisely. Perhaps from a single glance, he could read every detail about me, *see* my every memory.

But then why would he ask me if he had the power to tell everything about a person from a mere glance?

I must get out of here as fast as possible. Away from him and his abilities, but the only way to do it was to answer his inquiry.

"The same as I was," I replied gravely. "By the Gods' miracle."

"No, but how—"

"You promised if I answered your *one* question, you'd let me go."

Perhaps it was a bad idea to challenge the most lethal creature alive, but I couldn't help myself. I didn't understand what had come over me, where I had found such boldness that could easily turn me into ashes.

Drayard stared at me with such intensity that I half-expected him to open his mouth and spit fire for opposing him, but it didn't happen. Instead, he put back on his expressionless mask. "Then, you shall go." He turned away, finally dismissing me.

Without hesitation, I left the room, but just as I thought I was free from him, his voice echoed in my head.

Never remove your bracelet, Elynn.

Throughout the night, I tried to unravel the meaning behind the Bloodsucker's words, my gaze fixed on the bracelet as if it held the key to my answers. It always burned for some mysterious reason, but I never understood why.

Undoubtedly, the bracelet had saved me in some magical way from Fillan's fatal maws. But how and why?

Drayard might know. But as I asked him in my mind, naively hoping he would shed light on his cryptic words, no response came.

Because he wasn't in the mansion anymore. He could be gone for real this time.

And I didn't know whether I should be worried about his possible return someday or not.

"**G**en," someone said while shaking my shoulder. As I cracked one eye open, Thea's face, lit by the candle in her hand, came into view.

"Wake up," she said. "We must go."

I sat up, staring at her drowsily. "Go where?"

"Upstairs. Everyone is going."

Being abruptly awakened, presumably in the middle of the night, made it harder for me to process information, but I didn't need much time to realise that something was far from being all right.

"Thea ... what's going on?"

"I don't know." I stood up and took her hand. "But I'm scared. I'm really scared."

I couldn't help but feel the same.

We crossed the hallway, ascended the stairs, and entered the room we seldom visited—the antechamber. I had cleaned it a few times. On the opposite wall, two double doors stood between cream chairs with brown edges, matching the cream wallpaper trimmed with wood. Dozens of servants, including guards and Clare, were already present. Clare didn't seem to notice me, or perhaps she avoided looking at me on purpose.

There were no whispers, no sounds except feet padding against the floor. I looked at Imogen standing by the doors. She shrugged as if to say she didn't know why we were here either.

The other doors swung open, and Asenah entered like a storm. She stood in the middle, fixing us with a bone-chilling gaze.

"I won't waste my time with a preamble." Her voice had never been this cold and strict. "There is a snitch among you."

A snitch? Involuntarily, I stole a glance at Clare. Her face betrayed nothing. I shouldn't throw accusations, but the girl was the only one suspicious and mysterious among us. I wouldn't be surprised if she turned out to be a snitch.

"This *snitch*," Asenah said with disgust, going from person to person, looking directly into our eyes for a lie, "told all my plans with other realms to the Bloodsucker. I'm giving them a chance to step forward and give themselves away or else you will all regret being born as humans."

I clenched my teeth. My bracelet began stinging my flesh again, but I couldn't cover it as I had given my right hand to Thea. Drayard had noticed something was off with it. There was a chance Asenah might see that too once she got near me.

"Well?" She was getting closer. "Which one of you did it?"

It might as well be me. Drayard had known I was hiding in the greenhouse while he and Asenah were in the garden. He might have read my mind. Even if it technically wasn't my fault, it had to be me, this supposed snitch, because who else could it be?

She reached me at last. While most people avoided her cutting stare, I held it strong. She observed me longer than the rest. I wished to spit at her ugly wolf's face for taking the lives of innocent people, but, of course, I didn't. Just as she opened her mouth, as if about to accuse me, another voice sounded.

"It was me."

All eyes turned towards Jill, the staff manager, responsible for keeping Asenah flawless, managing our work, and assisting with dinner.

She took a step further, avoiding the stares. "I'm sorry. I ... I had no choice. He cornered me, and I got scared and ... and he asked me if there was something he needed to know. At first, I denied it, but he didn't believe me. I didn't have a choice. I knew what he could—"

"Enough." Asenah crossed over to her, gripping her neck. Thea gasped, and I tightened my hold on her hand as Asenah lifted Jill, her toes barely touching the floor. Jill struggled against Asenah's grasp, trying in vain to pry her fingers off her neck while gasping for air, tears streaming down her face. "You know what happens to traitors." She squeezed her neck harder. I had to restrain myself from doing anything rash. "You all must witness what happens to those who disobey."

Asenah's claws dug into Jill's flesh. Blood oozed out, sliding down Jill's pale neck. She never stopped wriggling and begging. "M-mercy."

We could do nothing—only watch, even though not all of us did. Thea refused to look, but I did not, watching with undisguised hatred. I didn't let myself blink until Jill stopped stirring and Asenah let go of her. Her lifeless body crumpled to the floor, her long brown hair covering the mess. Eventually, the puddle of blood seeped through.

Asenah turned to us, her fingers dripping with blood, droplets landing on the shiny floor, yet she seemed unperturbed. I could discern no sign of guilt in her features, but what else was I expecting? To her, Jill was just another inconsequential life. "I need a new personal maid now—one who can also oversee your responsibilities," she declared, her voice devoid of emotion.

She wasted no time in choosing a replacement. Her decision was swift, as if she had known her next victim before killing Jill, for her chilly eyes fixed right on me. "You will do."

That was all she said before striding off, disregarding Jill's body as if it were nothing more than trash.

As soon as she was gone, Thea and some others broke into tears. I pulled her into a hug, letting her cry on my chest.

"She needs to be burned," Imogen announced to everyone, her voice on the verge of tears, but she controlled herself well. "We all should say our goodbyes, but those who can't bear to see her body burn should stay here and wipe the blood off the floor."

Most chose to go.

Imogen led the way while guards carried the body behind her, and I comforted Thea.

"It's the full moon," Thea murmured, barely audible. "Morphs become more brutal during the first full moon. It rattles the looming beast inside them."

Although her words explained Fillan's aggressiveness the night he'd bitten me, they didn't justify Asenah's actions. "Thea, what Asenah did is unforgiving. Whether it's a full moon or not, it doesn't excuse them from what they do. They all have no humanity, and we shouldn't search for reasons to explain why they are the way they are."

They found a spot to burn her body not far from the mansion. It was all done to honour the tradition in the Mortal Region, rooted in an archaic belief that burning a body increased the likelihood of the Gods above opening their hearts to welcome a soul into their world.

I didn't mourn Jill, unlike Thea. I hadn't known her well. We hardly exchanged any words since the day I had awakened in the mansion. Instead, I served as Thea's emotional crutch while the skin under my bracelet burned as I watched Jill's body envelop in flames in the forest's depths. I never looked away. Not until the wind blew away her ashes.

My who-make-to-pay-first list altered. Instead of Fillan and Lupin occupying the top positions, Asenah claimed the leading spot.

Ever since that night, I endured a considerable and tormenting amount of time with her. While my hands were busy fixing her healthy, long onyx hair into the hairstyle she wanted, I found comfort in channelling my thoughts towards inventing plans for her retribution, rather than yielding to the urge to slide my hands around her throat and squeeze tighter and tighter.

At least she wasn't a telepath.

Much to my relief, Asenah never tried to talk to me. Had she attempted to engage in conversation, I doubted I would have kept my voice polite and unbothered.

When it came to my responsibilities as a staff manager, I didn't hate it as much as I would have assumed. Organizing the work and giving orders didn't bother me. I even found some pleasure in instructing Clare on her weekly tasks for the garden. At least I didn't have to do any kitchen work anymore. Although I still carried dishes to the dining room when there were guests, but Jill also used to handle that.

I almost missed my twentieth birthday. Nobody was conscious of it, but I didn't expect them to be. They still took me as my little sister.

Autumn arrived, and with it, the Autumn Equinox—the time when day and night were not only equal in length but also when morphs could turn into their real form. It marked one of the two days in a year when they resembled us, humans, but were far more powerful and brutal creatures. When the day came, I would be in the Empire of Beasts for three months. Time had passed by quicker than I had expected.

On the same day, Fillan was marrying Fawne. Apparently, Asenah didn't call off the wedding even after learning that Drayard had known about her plans all along. I assumed that her goal of having allies against the Bloodsucker wasn't the sole reason for forcing her cousins into undesirable matrimony. But I couldn't care less about her actual intentions.

The only positive outcome of this chaotic month was that Fillan and Lupin weren't functioning enough to assault other servants. At least, I hadn't heard of it. The bat girls had done a noble job. Pity that it wasn't permanent.

Thea brewed tea while I gazed at the forest beyond the window, trying to spot any hint of autumn. But there was none. Pines lacked the magical ability to change into multiple colours and shake off the leaves, unlike deciduous trees during this season, reminding me of how much I missed home, and it stung my heart, for I would never see it again.

At this hour, the staff, including Imogen, was taking a break from the kitchen. I could only imagine how sick they must feel after spending most of their day in the same environment.

"How could Imogen and her brother be offered together?" I asked Thea while she poured boiling water into my cup with herbs.

Thea was looking better after the incident, and considering

that Jill used to be her friend, she was coping with her murder pretty well.

"She told you about Finn?" she asked, amazed, while filling her cup with water. I nodded. "They both were sixteen and had to be offered together." She rested a kettle on the stove and slid into a chair across from me.

"But only one could be offered," I noted. "The youngest child of the family, not two."

"I don't know, Gen," she mumbled, her eyes fixed on the cup.

"Liar."

Thea wasn't difficult to read. She was like an open book of emotions. I could easily tell when she was lying. Thea betrayed not only her eyes, which were focused on anything but me, but her tone of voice. Her tone always dropped lower when she lied.

Apart from reading Thea, I had also learned to understand others over these past three months. I could discern who was telling falsehoods or didn't like someone from their feigned expressions, a skill that mainly applied to morphs as they were creatures who always wore invisible masks on their faces.

"I truly don't know."

"You *do* know, Thea. Don't lie to me."

"It's not my story to tell." At last, she raised her eyes. "I'm sorry."

"She won't tell me."

"I can't tell you, Gen. I'm sorry."

"Thea, please," I pleaded, but she had her lips pursed reluctantly. "Please? Please. Please. Please—"

"Fine," she relented, and a satisfied smile pulled at my mouth. "But don't tell her I told you."

I nodded, my smile kicking up a notch. "Never."

"Do you promise?" she asked unsurely.

"Promises don't do any good. They could be broken very easily."

A faint smile welcomed her face. "*They* take promises here very seriously. Sometimes they use magic to guarantee one of them will keep it."

"For real?"

Thea nodded.

"How do you know?"

"I saw it once."

Now it was clear why, before Drayard left, he had promised to let me go if I answered his question. He could have made me answer another one if he wanted, but he didn't because he was a morph and took promises seriously.

A promise could be morphs' undoing.

I made another mental note that might come in handy sometime.

"All right." I set a hand on the left side of my chest. "I promise not to tell her or anybody else."

She chuckled, tucking a loose strand behind her ear before she began, "About fifteen years ago, back in the Mortal Region, Imogen and Finn were creating a plan to protect their youngest brother from the annual offering."

"They weren't the youngest?"

She shook her head. "No, Imogen and Finn were about twenty years old. They were at the start of creating their own lives, but the threat of their little brother being offered to this world made them rethink the purpose of their life." She took a sip of still-hot tea and winced a little. The heat must have singed her tongue. "When they came up with a solution, they went to pledgers and made a bargain. Instead of their brother getting offered, they offered themselves. Imogen and Finn thought that having more wisdom would be better than throwing an inexperienced sixteen-year-old into this world. Besides, they had been trained to hunt ever since their childhood. They come from a family of hunters." She spoke the last two sentences in a pitched voice to ensure they wouldn't reach morphs' ears.

Imogen's situation reminded me of my own. Guided by the boy's spirit and the book, I got the idea to offer myself instead of my sister. Except that I didn't go to the pledgers to seek permission. Instead, I tricked them into believing I was Gen with the help of the potion.

"But how did morphs not realise they weren't sixteen?"

"Morphs don't recognise the age difference. They believe whatever pledgers write in the sent lists. They don't age as fast as we do. Most of them look like they are in their early twenties in their human form. How can they tell a human's age if they don't know what sixteen-year-olds are supposed to look like?"

I noticed that both morphs and humans didn't grasp that I was older. Or it was because I looked younger than nineteen, now twenty.

"Flaws of a long life." I took a sip. Hot liquid skidded down my throat, warming me even if it wasn't cold. As if it warmed more of my soul than my body.

"I wish I could live longer," Thea admitted.

I stared at her unbelievingly. "Really? You'd rather live this accursed life?"

"Not this life," she muttered. "If I were a morph or enchantress, I'd run away from here, find someone to love, and create a family with them. I'd spend my thousand years with people I love."

"That's ... adorable."

And naïve. But I did not share my negativity with Thea.

Her giggle got me smiling, which reminded me ... "What's going on between you and Franz? Are you two lovers?"

She sipped her tea, but not even the rim of the cup could hide her rosy cheeks.

"Thea," I teased.

She pursed her lips, looking down at her cup.

"Even if I said I saw nothing, I didn't say anything about the hearing part," I whispered.

The colour in her cheeks enhanced. I couldn't help but think it was adorable. A young love was a remarkable thing. Besides, Thea deserved it, despite the circumstances surrounding Franz and her.

"Maybe," she said, acting all secretive, but her behaviour gave her away. She didn't have to pretend.

"Well, be careful," I warned, but then I realised it was something Imogen would say, so I was quick to amend myself. "I mean, other maids can spread a rumour, and you know, jealous people are capable of all kinds of mischief."

She nodded, resting her cup down. "What would *you* do if you were one of *them*?"

I frowned. "I wouldn't like to be any of them at all." I slid my palms around my cup. "But if I was ..." Thea was staring at me like a little girl who was about to hear a night-time story. "If I was one of them, I'd make them all pay for their crimes."

Disappointment washed over her face. "That could be a long list."

"I promised I'd make them pay, Thea. I intend to keep my promise."

I meant my words the night I came downstairs with no fabric on my body and learned the twins had also abused her. I would make them pay for what they had done to us, to other human girls, despite the cost.

"I know." She released a resigned sigh. "But I asked what you would do if you were one of *them*."

"I don't know," I said gravely.

"Come on." Her lips turned up in a soft smile. "Dream about it."

"I don't dream, Thea."

I have nightmares.

Her smile wavered. "Imagine, then?"

I mustered a feeble smile. "I don't allow myself to imagine either."

"Why?"

My smile vanished, and my palms tightened around the cup as if it were holding me away from a breaking point.

"There's no point in imagining. Nothing we could ever imagine would come true, and we should make peace with the reality ahead of us." I fought back the tears as shadows of what my life had become passed through my mind. "Imogen will never leave further than this kitchen. Finn and Jill will never be resurrected. They are *dead*. You will never have your desired loving family, and I ..."

I never allowed myself to imagine or dream about anything my heart craved for. If there was a point of dreaming earlier, now it was absolutely pointless.

I feel you too, stranger.

All right, I might have been a hypocrite by saying I never imagined anything, for I forced myself to picture the stranger from my trance when I was in the hands of other men. At those moments, the vision of him dispatched me to a better place, protecting me from all the horrors. But he could also be a mirage my mind had created to shield itself from awful things encompassing me, despite my heart being against the belief.

"And you ...?"

Thea's voice pulled me back to the present. My mouth had gone dry, and tears stung my eyes. I refrained from raising my cup to dampen my throat or bringing my hands to rub away the tears. I couldn't allow Thea to know I was on the edge of crying, as it would lead to her asking questions.

"And I ..." I swallowed the lump in my throat, endeavouring to sound steady. "And I will never learn what true love feels like."

XXII

I found myself surrounded by people dressed in attire fancier than I had ever seen. Men sported suits with bow ties or vests that matched their ladies' autumn-inspired gowns. The music, played by various instruments, blessed my ears and warmed my heart while a dozen couples were engaged in a lively gallop in what appeared to be a ballroom.

But why would I be in a ballroom?

The mixture of perfumes irritated my nostrils. Regardless of the cloying scents, my nose strangely didn't wrinkle.

Sighing, I looked down at my hands—unusually broad and encased in black leather gloves.

Perplexity gripped me.

These hands weren't mine.

These hands belonged to a *man*.

I wasn't dreaming, was I?

I tucked my hands into my pockets. No. *He* tucked *his* hands, not me. Or was it me dreaming from a man's perspective? I had heard dreams could be uncanny, but if I was dreaming, I wouldn't be conscious of it, right?

Whether I was dreaming or not, I, in the body of a man, turned around and slipped into a deserted hallway through double wide-open doors.

The interior swept my breath away. Everything seemed constructed of marble and gold. Crystal chandeliers dangled from arched ceilings, casting a cosy light—perfect for wandering when the outside was swallowed by darkness. My—his—barely audible footsteps bounced off the walls, dying away in the distance. The smell had a peculiar quality, refreshing yet heady.

"Is that the King of Embers exploring the forbidden area without permission?"

I startled.

The King of Embers? Wasn't that the Bloodsucker himself? But how?

Halting, he glanced over his shoulder, and I caught a glimpse of wings I had seen before.

Indeed. It was the same ill-famed Drayard. But why would I dream from his perspective?

A short and petite woman leaned against the wall, garbed in yet another shade of autumn ball gown, almost drowning in it. Grey-green embroidered with bronze complemented her brown complexion, bringing out the olive in her eyes. Dark-brown hair done in two knots, the rest left flowing down her shoulders in smooth curls.

Her looks were lovely, but I had a strange feeling about her.

"What is it you want now, Dara?" he asked.

Of course ... it's that sneaky panther!

"It's been a while since I saw you here." Familiar mischief highlighted her words, tinged with suggestiveness.

Drayard resumed strolling through the hallway, but Dara didn't let him go that easily.

"I know you're not here to party, Drayard."

He quickened his pace.

"Should I tell Nayden about you wandering around his castle without his knowledge?"

Drayard halted, hesitating before turning to the panther.

A satisfied smile tugged at the side of her violet-painted lips.

"Is there something you want?"

"I do want something, yes." She pushed herself off the wall. "I want to know the real reason you attended the Autumn Equinox's celebration."

"The same as any other guest. To have a good time."

"No, that's not it." She pouted, looking slightly up at the ceiling before her naughty eyes returned to him. "You don't know what a good time means, Drayard. So don't waste our time and tell me exactly why you're here, and I'll leave you to it."

Drayard stared at her with unyielding intensity, as if trying to read her thoughts, which were unexpectedly hard to reach.

How was I aware of—

It clicked then. This was not a dream. This was *real*.

How was it possible?

Dara huffed. "You know I was trained to keep my thoughts to myself, right?" she said. "Try as much as you like, but your endeavours will remain pointless."

I could feel the annoyance emitting from Drayard. The panther had detained him from whatever his mission was, and he couldn't confide in her with his plans. He didn't trust a single soul apart from himself.

It was insane how I could hear his every thought as well as I could hear mine.

"I'm not in the mood for games, Dara." He took a formidable step towards her. "If you say even a word about my doings to Nayden, I will have something to say to whoever you might be betrothed to someday. Something that would strip you of your title, princess of the Realm of Wilds, daughter of Ariel Fahedos, who is the most revered advisor of the emperor."

Dara's eyes narrowed, a gleam of anger sparking in them. "No one will believe you."

"Do you intend to risk it?"

She was silent.

Whatever Drayard was holding over her, it was working.

With undisguised dissatisfaction, she turned on her heel and, after several steps, disappeared around the corner.

He tarried for a bit longer after Dara left. But eventually, he continued venturing through the enormous and complex castle, passing different hallways, mounting stairwells, entering various grand and regal rooms, clearly searching for something.

What was he so eager to find?

He halted at the sounds emanating from somewhere behind a wall.

Moans.

He grimaced and was made to go but froze as if he realised something.

As he tilted his head to the right, the gap between the doors snagging his attention. One door was opened just a crack.

No ...

It's Nayden's chamber. His voice, full of acknowledgement, echoed in his mind as if he was talking to me, but I wasn't sure about that.

He crept towards the doors and leaned his back against one that was shut, peering into the room through a small opening.

A blonde man had his lips locked with a woman who shared his hair colour. His hands rested on her hips, and their kissing intensified. He guided her to the bed positioned at the perfect angle for Drayard to observe almost every detail.

Drayard smirked.

He *smirked.*

How perverted was the Bloodsucker?

He turned his head away from the sight and propped it against the door, smiling as if he had discovered gold at the end of the rainbow.

That's disgusting.

Hello, Honeylove. The deep voice rang in my head, as caressing as the cloud must be, but it spooked me regardless. *What are you doing in my head?*

I couldn't care less about him sniffing me out in his mind when dissimilar, pleasure-laden voices wafted their way to Drayard's ears, and then to mine.

Get away from the door, you pervert! I snapped at him.

Why should I? His smile grew bigger. *Two siblings having sex might be my quirk.*

Two siblings?

Yes, their names are Nadira and Nayden. You may know them as the emperor and empress of the Empire of Beasts.

Ew ew ew ew.

Ew, indeed.

Then why are you listening to ... that? I asked, beyond confused.

Get out of my head if you're not fond of it.

And you're telling me you are fond of it?

Listen, you've been in my head long enough. It's time for you to leave.

So he'd been aware of me all along.

If I knew how to get out of your head, I'd have long since gone, pervert!

If you don't know how, how the hell did you get into my head in the first place? His voice wasn't as mellow as before but rather vexed.

Oh, he didn't like it when somebody *else* was in his head, but he felt free to roam in other minds. How the tables had turned!

I don't know. I'm currently sleeping, Drayard.

At least I supposed I was while my consciousness was with him.

Naked?

His question took me by surprise, even though it shouldn't have.

I thought you don't fool around with humans?

Sleeping with and seeing a naked woman are two different things, Honeylove, he drawled, his voice again coming back to the sweet state, which made me want to gag and feel an unsettling thrill at the same time.

Another one of Nadira's moans arrived.

Seal your sensitive senses, at least! I exclaimed.

Get out of my head first! he insisted.

I don't know how to!

Then try!

He was growing increasingly annoyed with me. So was I with him. I hesitated, not to attempt escaping his mind, but to understand it—which was mostly an impenetrable void. I wanted to know how he knew I was an impostor and was aware of my mother's unlucky attempts to have a baby ... I wanted to learn all his secrets.

The atmosphere shifted abruptly. A sudden coldness enveloped me, and an inexplicable sense of dread began seeping through. A voice echoed from afar. A voice like—

Panting and moaning snapped me out, forcing me face the wall again.

I wished to seal my ears under as many locks as possible, but his senses remained open, and I could do nothing to get those siblings muted!

I can't get out of your head, you monster! Step away from the door and stop torturing us both, please!

The last time I checked, I was in a position to give demands, not you, Honeylove.

Oh, bloody hells!

If he was going to play like that, I might as well join the game instead of getting kicked off the chessboard.

You have a mind of a devil, I see.

My most prized weapon, he said, his voice a bit unsteady, as if he was trying to conceal another emotion urging to peek through his tone.

I stifled a laugh, or at least I tried when it escaped anyway. I could sense his smile as much as I could feel mine. But I pulled myself together, quelling that ridiculous imaginative smile.

Drayard?

Yes, Elynn?

Get away from the door!

He sighed. *Elynn, you may have forgotten with whom you're talking. Again.*

Oh, I'm aware, Bloodsucker. *It's just impossible for you to kill me when you're so far away.*

Are you willing to try me?

My heart stuttered, escalating into an insane rhythm. I had gone too far.

No ...

Good. Now get out of my head. My virgin ears are suffering.

Virgin ears? Seriously?

Get out of my—

"Oh, yes!" the woman's satisfactory voice echoed behind the door. "Just like that!"

The man's panting intermingled with her moans, engulfing me with abomination. Drayard didn't move an inch from the door, making us go through this torturing tryst between *siblings*. What a brute!

Elynn, he warned me.

I'll try, was all I said.

I attempted to distance myself from him, to remember where my body was—lying underground in Asenah's mansion on the uncomfortable bed—

Faster, he urged. *My ears are bleeding.*

It's your fault you made such a ridiculous ultimatum.

He was silent.

I focused back on trying to shift back to my body.

My body is feminine. I'm Elynn Startel. A twenty-year-old woman sleeping in one of the servants' rooms in the Realm of Bones mansion. Get out of Drayard's head. Get out, I ordered myself.

My body—yes, my body—sat up. My chest heaved as if I had been pulled out of the ocean, and now I was recovering from it.

I looked around me to make sure I was where I had expected to be. Indeed, I was in the room where I had fallen asleep in the first place. Not leaning against the door and listening to two related people participating in the Sinner's Tango. A sigh of relief left my steadying lungs.

I didn't want to experience being in the Bloodsucker's head ever again. I had no clue how it had happened, but I prayed to the Gods that it would never repeat.

XXIII

Asenah looked gorgeous in her real form, with raven hair braided into an updo, freckles dotting her light cheeks and the bridge of her long but elegant nose. A mole just above her lip, which would have painted her as coquettish if not for the stern look overshadowing all the alluring, stark features on her face.

I had the task of helping the Queen of Bones prepare for her cousin's wedding. She personally chose a gown—one in the colour of cream, long-sleeved, with elegant simplicity, except for the chocolate-brown fur wrap that seemed to have once belonged to an animal. It suited her well as a queen.

I *loathed* her.

I spent three hours with her. Her hair and face took the most time. She had already been beautiful before cosmetics, but now she was breathtaking. Any man's mouth would fall open at the sight of her. Although, according to the Bloodsucker, Asenah wasn't interested in them. She wouldn't pay attention to any male morph who gave her heart eyes anyway.

The thought of the Bloodsucker didn't evoke positive emotions. I was still grappling with the fact that I had been in his head only twelve hours ago. I'd prayed this morning he wouldn't make an appearance at the wedding. It seemed like he might have important business to do with the new sickening information he had learned yesterday. Hopefully, whatever it was, it would preoccupy him.

When I left Asenah's chambers, I strode to the kitchen, where I felt the safest in the entire mansion. Imogen was a tough woman. Anyone could feel safe around her.

"When Fillan weds Fawne, will he be moving out?" I asked her while picking glasses out of the cabinet and sorting them onto the empty silver tray.

"I'm not sure." She placed a pitcher of red wine before me. "Fawne might move in 'ere."

"Why?" After I placed as many glasses as I could fit on the tray, I closed the cabinet doors and proceeded to pour wine into one glass after another.

"As I understand it, when morphs get married, a woman moves in tae live with her husband, not th' other way around."

"Even if Fawne's title is higher than Fillan's?"

After all, Fawne was a king's daughter, whereas Fillan was only a cousin of a queen. She was a princess; he was just a lord. Lesser than her.

"Even if Fawne's rank is higher than Fillan's," Imogen echoed.

"Does the King of Woods have an heir if he's giving up his daughter to the Realm of Bones?"

"He'll be here today. Why don't ye ask him yersel', lassie?" Imogen gave me a crooked smile.

I cast her a pointed look. "Hilarious."

As I put the pitcher back on the countertop and raised the tray, I strode out of the kitchen.

The wedding hadn't started yet. Guests had only begun to gather in the garden.

It felt odd to be around human-like morphs, having grown accustomed to their animal-like exteriors. Morphs, some more beautiful than others, cracked jokes, and their refined laughter resonated through the garden. As I moved from one group to another, they extended their not-furry hands to take glasses of wine. Regardless of their flawless manners, I refused to be deceived. They were monsters. Every single one of them.

The whole mingling-in-small-groups theme brought back the memories of the twins' birthday, only lacking Drayard's grand entrance and people kneeling before him.

"Don't you just *love* morphs' weddings?" Clare appeared out of nowhere.

"Long time no see," I said with plain bitterness, not bothering to disguise it in my tone.

I had been avoiding her like the plague, taking different paths to avoid running into her. I didn't like her and had a bad feeling about the girl ever since the day we'd been offered. I was sure she wasn't very fond of me either.

"But still alive," she noted. "Both of us."

I offered her a false smile.

"Where were you when the Bloodsucker emerged at the birthday celebration?" I whispered after a while, looking around to make sure that no one noticed the absence of the servant who was supposed to carry drinks. But they were all absorbed in their conversations.

"Where the fire couldn't reach me."

"He didn't attack."

"It doesn't mean he isn't going to today."

I frowned. "He won't show up here."

"Who says he's not already here? In his original form?"

Before I could formulate a response, she walked off, leaving me with traces of her last words hanging in the air.

They unsettled me. Clare might be right. If Drayard was already here, he would kill me without a blink. I was in *his* mind. He would make sure nothing like it would ever happen again, and the only way to ensure it was to end me.

As I served wine to morphs, every muscle in my body was beyond strained. I kept searching for the pair of golden-red eyes among each of them. Morphs' eyes were the only feature that didn't change when they shapeshifted. But as a half-breed with the ability to read thoughts, maybe he also had the power to alter eye colour.

Even if he was already here, he wouldn't pass unseen, right? Drayard wasn't the type of morph who preferred shadows. No. He relished the spotlight.

The symphony shifted into another tune, prompting guests to claim their seats on benches before the arch. It wasn't white and bedecked with flowers and leaves, as the tradition suggested, but brown and decorated with pine spikes. The aisle itself had wooden benches on either side of the brown carpet leading to the wedding arch.

I hadn't decorated the garden this time, but whoever had designed the wedding aisle had done a splendid job.

I spotted Thea and followed her beckoning gesture, moving closer.

The wedding was far different from the ones I was used to seeing in the Mortal Region. Not only did the colouring of the wedding aisle differ but also the ceremony.

Such music played in the Mortal Region when bridesmaids made their way to the altar, accompanied by flower children scattering petals along the path, not as a signal for guests to gather around.

When Asenah appeared, I thought she'd be the bridesmaid as she walked towards the altar and people arose, bowing their heads out of respect for their queen, but that wasn't it. As she halted below the arch, I understood she would play the role of a priest to unite the couple.

Once she turned to the gathered, a solemn smile was engraved on her face. She nodded to the quartet, signalling for them to play something different.

As the first notes of the cellos sounded, it reminded me of the wedding march played in human weddings, but some notes changed, making it sound more dramatic than the version I was used to hearing.

The "lovebirds" emerged, with Fillan leading the way. In his human form, he looked dashing, rendering me sick. There was no denying he had good genes. His fawn-brown suit seemingly represented his realm. His fiancée, Fawne, wore a ridiculous cake-like white wedding gown, concealing every inch of her skin except for her ivory face. Her brown hair was intricately braided into a coronet, adorned with pine needles. But most importantly, she walked *behind* her fiancé.

"What is this?" I asked under my breath, as if I didn't know the answer already.

It was simple—women could *not* be equal to their husbands. They could *not* stand higher than their men. The wedding must have been one of the ways to convey the message. I would have been in Fawne's place if I had stayed in the Mortal Region and married Chase.

The epiphany had shaken me more than I would have expected.

I had been prepared for it—to be lesser than him. I used to think that allowing him to use me however he liked was how it should be, that I deserved it, but I was wrong. So, so wrong. Only seeing an example of what my future would have looked like made me realise how mistaken and blinded I had been by forcing myself to believe I was lucky Chase had chosen me instead of another girl who was jealous of my "success".

Fillan halted before Asenah first. He didn't even glance at Fawne once she stood beside him.

"That's morphs' weddings." Thea sighed, telling me what I had already taken as given.

Dancing, drinking, mingling and even dallying with each other were the activities morphs engaged in after Fawne and Fillan had become wife and husband.

I studied Fawne's family she was standing next to, away from her husband, who was downing one glass after another.

Fawne's mother was an older version of her. Both had brown hair, russet eyes, and the same diamond face shape. Her father had such broad shoulders that every time I got near him, a ripple of tremors ran down my body. He was one of the cruel rulers. Mightiness streamed off his posture and stoic expression, but his power paled in comparison to that which I had witnessed someone else hold.

Fawne's hands were draped under a small girl's neck, hugging her from behind. I guessed her to be Fawne's little sister. Despite Fawne's lips forming a faint smile, she seemed more on the verge of tears than smiling.

I caught myself feeling a smidgen of condolence towards her, but I quickly reminded myself that she was just another morph who had killed innocents, and any sympathy I felt, vanished.

At least Drayard hadn't made his appearance. Clare had made me anxious for no reason at all.

Everything went smoothly, so far. I found myself lacking some drama. Serving drinks and catching bits of gossip and politics was like watching paint dry. I was starting to miss Drayard's outstanding entrance. And here, I'd never thought I could be so fond of drama.

As I returned to the kitchen to refill empty glasses, I glanced at the clock. Four hours until midnight. Then, morphs would turn back into beasts, and, as I figured, the celebration would cease.

I refilled the glasses. I was hurrying back to the garden when a hand clamped over my mouth. I froze.

A deep voice whispered into my ear, "Hello, Honeylove."

The tray slipped out of my hands and clattered to the floor. All the drinks shattered. The spilled liquid touched my shoes, but I didn't look to assess the damage as my blood ran cold, legs became light, and my heart raced with the terror settling in me.

His leather-covered hand was still pressed against my mouth, but it was pointless. Did he think I'd scream? Nobody would help me if I did.

Or perhaps, he kept it there as a precaution, not wanting me to alert others of his presence.

"Did you miss me?" he breathed in my ear.

I was tempted to turn my head and see his real form, but fear stopped me.

"P-please," I managed to get out against his palm, "don't hurt me. I won't invade your thoughts ever again. I promise."

I felt his smile as he whispered, "You can't be sure of it."

He was right. I couldn't. I was simply not aware when I had entered his mind and had no comprehension of how it had happened.

I was so dead.

"Are you going to kill me?"

I dreaded the answer, even if I already knew it.

A dramatic sigh sounded above me. At least his mouth wasn't near my ear anymore. "You think so low of me, Elynn."

I didn't buy it.

"Then what is it that you want?"

It felt like hours had passed instead of seconds until he whispered the answer against my ear. Emotionless, yet hair-raising.

"On the count of three, I want you to run and don't look back," he said. "One ... Two ..."

His hand left my mouth, and I didn't think twice before I bolted through the doorway, straight into the garden. Nobody paid heed to some maid as I ran into the forest, as far away from the Bloodsucker as I could.

And I didn't dare to look back.

I was, without a doubt, lost.

Only when I couldn't run any longer, I halted and planted my hands above my knees, taking some time to catch a breath.

My heart beat fast, not only because of the sudden and unprepared run, but because of the dread I felt with every fibre of my being. But I had no luxury to rest. I had to keep running.

I scanned the area for Drayard, but he wasn't here or just not within my sight.

Perhaps it wasn't his plan at all—to chase me into the forest and murder me. Maybe he had *tricked* me into thinking he was going to kill me. Or he had already doomed me by making me go to this disreputable forest so he wouldn't have to do the dirty job himself as another creature would take care of me for him. The King of kings and queens would never smear his hands with human blood. The Bloodsucker or not.

Just in case, I waited to test my speculation. I might be risking my life by tarrying in one place longer than I should, but I couldn't run anymore. Not for now, at least.

I sat before the trunk of a tree and propped my head against it, waiting for my heartbeat to return to its normal rhythm along with my heavy breathing. I waited and waited, but there was no sign of the dragon or the man in the soundless forest.

By now, I was sure I was right. He had intentionally made me get lost, acutely aware that a human wouldn't survive long in the forest located in the morphs' domain.

I had to go back. I had to find my way back to the mansion. It was safer there than here. But then, if Asenah didn't find me in her chambers to prepare her for sleep on time, she'd kill me. And if I stayed here, I wouldn't survive the night.

I stood after I felt energetic enough to continue my journey, but I didn't run without any limits this time. I wandered in slow, aimless steps. I had no purpose to rush them as, for now, I couldn't detect any danger lurking close by.

One significant problem with coniferous forests was the similarity of the pines, making it challenging to distinguish the tree I had already passed from the newly encountered one. I hadn't spotted any deciduous tree during my run or at present. I must have gotten lucky to come across one when fleeing from the wolf.

Oh, dear Gods above, I had no clue which way to go at all! I couldn't even guess which direction could lead to the mansion.

I stopped.

My hands curled into fists.

My teeth clenched.

My bracelet heated up.

The sudden outburst took control over me. With a sharp spin, I hurled my right fist straight into a trunk, but as the pain lanced through my knuckles, I jerked it back with a quiet yelp, giving it a shake.

As I surveyed my bruised knuckles, the flame of anger eased in me, smothered by the pain. The bracelet ceased to burn my skin as well.

My attention drifted to it.

Never remove your bracelet, Elynn.

What would happen if I did remove it? For just a minute ...

I found the clasp, ready to face the consequences of removing it. I was about to perish here. Might as well sate my curiosity before someone hiding in the forest's depths slaughtered me.

"Elynn?"

I stiffened, raising my eyes.

I'd heard her voice. I was sure I'd heard *her*.

Gen.

But I didn't whip my head back to make sure if I was right. I couldn't. The forest could have Gods knew what kind of creatures. There might be one that fooled people into thinking there was someone they loved. And if one looked at it, they'd be damned. It was definitely a trap, as there was no way my sister was here. It was just impossible.

"Lynn, is that you?"

Again, that soft voice which belonged to *her* but couldn't be *hers*.

I pursed my lips, telling myself not to look.

A trap. A trap. A trap.

I felt her hand on my shoulder, that familiar touch. It couldn't be false. It felt too real.

I risked a glance over my shoulder and met my sister's grey-blue eyes that appeared darker in the dim light. Grey-blue eyes that were nothing like the ones I'd grown accustomed to in the last three months. Grey-blue eyes that I was familiar with for over sixteen years.

"Gen?" I said unbelievingly, turning to her fully.

She nodded slowly and brought me into her warm arms, whispering, "I've found you. I've found you."

I wrapped my hands around her, a tear escaping my eye and trickling down my cheek, reaching my dry lips.

She was real.

Gen was *real*.

As we pulled away from each other, it was only then that I took notice of her appearance. I wasn't sure how I was supposed to react, let alone what to think.

Gen was armed. *Heavily armed.* A quiver of arrows protruded from behind her shoulder, a belt with golden knives encircled her hips, and she held a bow in her right hand. My sister resembled a huntress on a serious hunting spree.

"What ... What are you doing here?" I asked.

"I came to find you and bring you home, Lynn."

I frowned. "How did you know where to go?"

"It's been three months since you were gone. I had plenty of time to figure out where you might be."

I scrutinised her face. It didn't take a genius to realise she was hiding something.

"Is Kris with you?"

She hesitated before shaking her head.

"Did you come here alone or with someone?"

She pursed her lips into a guilty smile.

"Oh, no, Gen, what did you do this—"

"Netty, I thought I—"

My eyes flew to the one who interrupted me. When I saw who stood about five steps away from Gen, bile climbed up my throat. I thought I would vomit right here, right now, at the sight of him, but, shockingly, I didn't.

My former fiancé gripped a golden sword—his beloved Goldy—ready to fight anyone who crossed his path. Not only had his hair grown longer but a thick and bushy beard hung down his chin. *Someone must have missed their appointments with the local barber.*

His mouth pulled into a sick smile that evoked unpleasant memories. "Hello, Ely."

I grasped Gen's wrist and pulled her behind me. She yelped, letting me know I was harsher than intended. But it didn't matter as long as I stood before her, using my body as a shield because I would *not* let him near her.

"What are you doing here?"

My skin under my bracelet burned, but the pain was nothing compared to the emotions boiling inside me for the man standing before me.

Chase stepped forward.

"Stay away," I growled, matching the growl of a wolf.

He stopped. "Three months with morphs turned you into a beast as well?" He smiled even more widely. "I like it," he whispered and licked his lips.

"Burn in hell."

He looked genuinely taken aback by my words. "You've changed," he said thoughtfully and risked another step forward. I glared at him, daring him to advance more. I might not kill him, but I was sure I would put up a fight. "What have they done to you, Ely?"

My sister stayed behind me. Silent.

The wind whistled, and the words brushed against my ear. *Do you need help?*

A voice of a boy. A dryad. *Juniper.*

"Not yet," I responded.

The breeze disappeared, and Chase stared at me strangely. Gen stepped out of my shadow, eyeing me as weirdly as Chase. As if I were a stranger in the wild.

"What have they done to you?" Gen asked cautiously, dismayed by *me*.

I hadn't lost my mind yet, but from their perspective, I must have looked like a twitching madwoman talking with herself.

The unsettling look in my sister's eyes made me rethink my behaviour. Although she had come here with him, the man who'd tortured me without one iota of conscience, Gen was my sister. Despite my hatred towards this monster, I had to compose myself.

I possessed weapons capable of causing him severe harm. The dryads were in debt, after all. But for the sake of my sister and myself, I tried not to entertain murderous thoughts. I was a human, not a morph, and I would not stoop to their level.

For now, I managed to push aside the negative feelings towards Chase.

"I don't want to talk about it," I muttered to Gen, not looking away from Chase's emerald eyes that had haunted my sleep ever since Clare had—

Clare had warned me that he would come, but how she knew that was the least of my concerns now.

Gen's concerned expression melted into sympathy, and she stepped closer to hug me. I accepted her gesture but continued to shoot daggers at Chase with my eyes over Gen's shoulder.

He would pay for treating me wrong, but now was not the right time or place.

"I want to go home," I mumbled.

I didn't allow myself to falter, even if the thought of returning home to my family made me want to dissolve into tears.

"You will," she assured me.

Once we began our journey home, I kept at least five feet away from Chase. When night fell, and they went to sleep, I dared not close my eyes for more than a minute, afraid that Chase might invade my tent and force himself on me.

As midnight approached, he tried to slip into my tent. I threatened to gut him with the golden dagger Gen had given me for self-protection. Although I disliked carrying it, it could save my life if a morph leapt out of the shadows. It proved effective, as Chase became scared and fled. He never dared to come back or venture within five feet of me again.

Gen, too, was uneasy around me. There was a time when I envied the Bloodsucker who relished in the fear he instilled in others. I had even entertained thoughts of what it would feel like if I had powers like this. Now, I took it all back. My sister's apprehension towards me did not bring satisfaction, filling me with self-disgust instead.

The journey seemed to last forever. The forest was bigger than my initial estimate, yet still the same. A caressing breeze accompanied me, and Juniper occasionally reassured me of his presence, ready to help me if needed.

I had many things to tell Gen—things I had learned that could transform humans' lives drastically, but my mouth didn't part to speak. *Later.* I promised myself to tell her everything later.

The following night, as Chase hunted for non-existent food, Gen and I sat by the bonfire. She hugged herself as lately, the nights had turned colder. Although my maid's dress wasn't thick with layers to protect me from the cold, it didn't bother me when I was all tense and troubled about more important matters than the weather change.

"Why did you ask for his help?" I finally spoke.

"I didn't."

I looked at her, puzzled. "Then how did it happen that he's here?"

She sighed heavily. "Chase came into our cottage searching for you after you were offered. At first, Mum didn't tell him where you were, fearing he might rat us out to the pledgers, but then he saw me, not offered.

"Mum had no other choice but to tell him the truth. He didn't know you'd broken off the engagement when you'd given your ring to Mum. He still isn't aware of it." She held out her palms to the bonfire, occasionally rubbing them together. "When he found out, he was ready to find you, no matter what. I asked why because I didn't consider Chase a person who would fall in love so deeply as to risk his life for a woman. He blurted out something about you two belonging to each other, and that without you, he wouldn't survive." I rolled my eyes, and Gen's lips curved into a faint smile. "But before he went straight to the empire, I volunteered to help find you. After all, you locked me to the bed against my will," she grumbled, stating it more like a joke than a matter of fact. "So, we planned this together. Chase trained me to fight in case we ran into a morph. In my spare time, I examined Chase's map of the Empire of Beasts. It took me a month to plan out our journey. Thank Gods, no morph crossed our way."

"How long were you travelling until you found me?"

"A week or so."

"And no morph had emerged?"

She shook her head.

"That's impossible, Gen. I lived with morphs, got to know them. Two humans in their lands would have caught their attention. Their senses are far more sensitive than ours. They could smell food from miles away."

Either Chase and Gen were blessed by Gods, or something was off. There was a reason they were so lucky to not encounter any beasts.

"Miracles happen, Lynn. Can't you just believe that?" She said it so optimistically that it was unlike her.

"No, Gen. Reality is different."

"We found you. You'll be back home soon. That's what matters. It shows that miracles are real."

I looked at her weirdly. Yes, that was indeed my sister, but she acted out of character.

"What cult have you joined? A beaming sunshine one?" I asked with a tease.

Gen rolled her eyes. "No. It's just I've learned that looking at the bright side of life simplifies it more than seeing it darker than it is."

Now it was my turn to roll my eyes.

"What about Kris?" I inquired, remembering how he acted after our mother told him about what Chase was doing to me. "Did he allow you to train with Chase?"

She looked at the starlit sky, releasing a sigh. "Well ..." She trailed off.

"You didn't tell him."

She didn't say anything.

"Does he know you're here?"

Silence.

"Seriously, Gen?"

"He thinks I'm in the city. If I had told him where I was actually going, he would have followed."

I shook my head slightly. Yes, only Gen could do such a thing. She tended to act as a soldier on the battlefield, which was also my thing.

My gaze fixed on the dancing flames in front of me, and the tension in my shoulders eased. Since Chase was nowhere in sight—secretly, I hoped he would remain this way—I could let my perpetually vigilant senses relax and embrace the thought that I was truly going home.

No human had ever returned from the Empire of Beasts before. I might be the first one if the rest of our journey went smoothly.

"The Bloodsucker exists," I said after a long but comfortable silence punctuated by the crackling flames.

Gen's eyes opened wide, jaw dropping. Just as I'd expected her to react. "No way."

"He does, and he's far from a monster. At least, he doesn't look like one," I mumbled the last words before adding, "He's also a half-dragon."

She didn't blink. Stunned. "Dragons still exist?"

"No, only one does. He's a half-breed of a dragon and a bat. Drayard, Arragon's bastard son."

Gen had heard about Arragon before, as stories about him were created in the Mortal Region. But these stories weren't as popular as those about his son.

"Have you met him? The Bloodsucker?"

The memories struck my mind. When he had requested me

to bring him roast chicken, when I was in his mind, and when he ordered me to run and never look back.

"Unfortunately, yes."

"Is he as terrifying as in the tale?"

I hesitated, eyes on my dirty nails. "I don't know," I said. "He's ... strange. He didn't show his Bloodsucker's side. But every morph was intimidated by him, some more than others. He's not only someone who can tear your insides and feast on them but is also superior to the rest of *them*—the King with a capital K. Quite an important person in this world."

She said nothing, shocked by the information.

"But before you found me in the forest, I was running," I went on. "Running from him because he came back to kill me."

"What did you do to bring his disgrace upon yourself, Lynn?"

I hesitated. I didn't know how to explain how I'd been in his head once.

I clenched my hands to hide my dirty nails. "A good question, which I—"

As Gen noticed where my eyes were, she attempted to cover her hand, but I grasped it before she could, looking closer at the little accessory shining like a star on her ring finger.

An emerald ring.

Different from the one I remembered.

But still a *ring*.

An *engagement* ring.

How didn't I notice it sooner?

My eyes shot up at her. "What the hells, Gen?"

"Don't overreact," she muttered. "It's not what you think—"

"Don't you even try to convince me it's not what I think it is." As I raised my voice, only then I realised I shouldn't have as we were still in the morphs' area. I spoke quieter. "I can *see* it's—"

"It's not!" She jerked her hand away from mine. "And why should *I* explain my motives when *you* were silent about the real reason you were going to the empire instead of me?"

I frowned. "Don't change the—"

She scoffed. "Seriously, Lynn? Big sister acting like a hero, but *are* you one? Or are you just convincing yourself that you're doing good for others by sacrificing yourself when, in reality, you're running from the mistakes you made?" I must have been too slow to mask the incredulous look, for she said, "Yeah. Mum told me the ulterior motive behind your sacrifice. You did it to run away from your marriage."

"It's not—"

But I didn't finish, for Chase emerged from the woods with a dead bunny in his hand.

I didn't ask how he'd found an actual animal in the forest that wasn't a morph. The bunny might as well have been one, but the claws of guilt threatened to suffocate me. I couldn't focus on anything else, wishing I could explain everything to Gen.

But that would have to wait.

My thoughts drifted to the first friends I had made and left in the mansion. Imogen and Thea. Guilt struck me once again.

I was free from morphs' slavery, but they weren't. Even if it wasn't my fault, I still felt terrible.

At last, we reached the Blue River, separating the Mortal Region from the Empire of Beasts. Right across it must be the beginning of the invisible Spell Ascended Sorceresses had created to keep any magic away, including its creatures.

On the right lay the remnants of what had once been a bridge, destroyed in the aftermath of the war to segregate morphs from humans. Now, the Mortal Region celebrated a day known as *No Bridge Day*, commemorating the moment when our lands achieved official independence. The ruins of the bridge served as a symbol of our independence, marked by its brutal destruction carried out with hammers, axes, and other weapons available to humans at that time.

Chase and Gen were already floundering through the water, neither of them offering me help. I didn't care about Chase. He knew better than to utter a word to me. But Gen ... I was worried that our relationship had irrevocably changed. Regardless of whether I explained myself or not, we might never be the same again.

Today was warm and sunny, but as I dipped my feet into the water, its chilliness nipped at my skin.

Drawing in a breath, I pushed myself to move further.

With each step, the water grew deeper, and my heart rate quickened. It was already above my waist. I had never learned to swim, as there had been no need for such a skill back then. Now, I thought differently.

But I was halfway through the river. Surely, it wouldn't get any deeper than it was now?

As I took another step, I unexpectedly hit a deep hole, and water engulfed my entire body, including my face.

Everything within me ceased to function. I couldn't think properly; I couldn't move. All I was conscious of was that I was about to die.

No, no, no, no. I need to see my mum. This isn't how I'm going to die. Not by drowning. This is not—

My muscles relaxed, and I felt my consciousness slipping away until a pair of blood-red eyes flashed before me.

I needn't be a fish expert to know what was staring at me with sharp exposed teeth, prepared to devour me.

Piranha.

My father had once described them to me. Since then, I could recognize the fish anywhere, as red eyes and sharp teeth were their distinctive features. He also told me they could eat human meat if they were ravenous.

I let out a scream, releasing bubbles into the water. Somehow, I regained my ability to move and tried to reach the surface, confident it was just right there. But it seemed like more and more water swelled above me as the light I'd seen a moment ago turned into gloom.

But I wouldn't die from drowning. The piranha would eat me first.

Help. Me.

It charged at me and bit my wrist, shaking it with the razor-sharp teeth. I was sure it was about to rip my hand off when someone grasped my arm and hauled me out of the water.

Strong arms wrapped around my waist as I coughed, pressed against a masculine body. Must be Chase.

He gently placed me down. I got on all fours, coughing the water from my lungs. I rested my forehead on the ground, desperately trying to breathe, to quell the insane heart rate, and gather every ounce of oxygen I could provide my lungs with.

I was alive. I was actually *alive*.

I looked down at my wrist, the one the piranha had bitten. To my surprise, it was untouched. Frowning, I took a closer look, examining my wrist from all sides, but there was not a single mark. Perhaps it was another wrist. But as I inspected it, even moving my bracelet, I found no marks either.

Unbelievable.

Thank heavens, I hadn't lost my consciousness or else Chase would have—

I lifted my gaze at the one who'd saved me from death. It wasn't Chase.

My mouth opened to scream, but nothing came out of it.

Drayard was back in his dragon-human form, donned in one of his black suits despite the warmth of the day. His hands were casually stuffed in his pockets, and unearthly golden-red eyes fixed on me.

"At least for once, I've made you speechless, Honeylove."

I dropped to my bottom and crawled back to put as much distance between him and me as possible.

He sighed, as if disappointed, and appeared before me in a blink, crouching down. He was so close that I could smell the slight sweat coming from him. His gloved finger touched my jaw, pushing it up and snapping my teeth together.

He smiled contentedly. "I advise you to reconsider your return to the Mortal Region."

Despite his smile, his voice carried a warning. I should have asked him why, but the strangled words left my vocal cords instead, "P-please, don't hurt me."

His smile dropped, and he drew back. Standing erect, he fixed the wet sleeve of his splendid jacket.

I wasn't sure if I trembled more from fear or from cold, probably both. I felt powerless, and—

The dagger!

I had the golden dagger. Gold hurt morphs. He was a half-breed. I could—

I delved my hand into my pocket, only to find it empty. I was sure I had it before I went into the river. Positive. I must have lost it there.

"Looking for something?" he inquired, watching me with one eye.

I pulled my hand out of the pocket and drew my knees to my chest. "Why did you save me?"

"Your death isn't in my plans, Elynn."

I stared at him, puzzled. "Why did you tell me to run, then? For fun?"

"No."

"Then why?"

He remained silent, smoothing zero creases on his jacket.

He was surely hiding something major from me. I didn't want to consider it, but I did anyway. I might be somehow involved in whatever his schemes were. The Bloodsucker wouldn't ask about my mother's pregnancy, let alone bother to save a worthless human from drowning for no reason. But I had no idea why he would do such things, and I wouldn't figure out anything on my own unless he answered me, which he wouldn't.

"The piranha attacked me, and there are no marks on my wrist," I noted, hoping at least this question he would condescend to answer. "How's that so?"

"What you saw wasn't real," he said. "It was an illusion to ward off morphs."

"But I'm not a—"

"Your lover is looking for you."

I shot him a murderous look, forgetting that he could kindle me like a tinder. "He's not my lover."

"My apologies, Elynn. Your fiancé."

As I carefully arose, my hands formed into fists, the bracelet slightly burning my skin. I didn't bother asking how he knew that. "*Ex*-fiancé."

"Ah." He looked down. "That explains why you're not wearing any undergarments."

Confused, I followed his gaze to my chest. I was all drenched, and it was no surprise that the thin material almost exposed what was hidden beneath the dress. I promptly covered my chest with my hands and jerked my head up, locking my eyes with his. He *smirked.*

"Bastard," I gritted out.

"Elynn?!"

Drayard glanced over his shoulder at the sound of my sister's voice, his wings spreading wide behind his back, ready for flight. But before he took off, he looked at me. "Convey my regards to your mother. She did a great job raising you, Elynn."

He sprang into the sky and disappeared somewhere above the clouds, leaving me nonplussed.

Gen emerged with Chase behind her a moment later. Many unanswered questions I had for Drayard were already spinning in my tired head—questions he would refuse to answer if I ever met him again, which I hoped I wouldn't. Yet, the curious part of me wanted to see him again, just to extract the information from that mysterious creature.

"What happened?" Gen asked.

"I got scared of the water."

Gen stared at me dubiously, but she didn't question me either. Thank heavens, as I wouldn't have been able to explain how I was saved by the same creature who had scared me into running into the forest, where I had gotten lost in the first place.

XXVII

With gen's help, I crossed the river with no obstacles this time. As I walked deeper into the familiar forest, the weight on my head intensified.

I needed some sleep. Perhaps I had hallucinated, and Drayard hadn't been there to save me. I hadn't seen a piranha; I hadn't been drowning. I opted to believe it all had been a horrible hallucination induced by recent sleepless nights, regardless of my instincts rejecting the notion.

As we got closer to the cottage, I stirred with excitement despite the headache. When only half a mile was left until we reached the place I called home, Gen caught my wrist.

I met her weary eyes.

"Before we go further, there's something you must know."

The grave note in her voice worried me. "What is it?"

"Two weeks after your offering, Mum got sick. At first, we thought it was a common cold until she started coughing blood."

My heart sank. "Is she ... dying?"

Gen nodded, and I jerked my hand from her hold.

No, I refused to believe her. Mum couldn't be dying. She was a strong woman who could do multiple jobs at once. The death of my father hadn't broken her. Some stupid illness wouldn't break her either.

I spun on my heel and sprinted home, ignoring Gen's warning calls to put on safety equipment. I didn't care. Besides, where would I get it? This safety equipment?

I paused once I reached the cottage. It looked just as I had left it, but something about it made me feel like a foreigner, as if I no longer belonged here. Cold. Uninviting.

It was ridiculous. It was the place where I had grown up. It was *my home*, and I was *back*. Perhaps it was hard to believe I was standing here when no thought had crossed my mind that I would see this cottage in real life ever again.

Maybe it was all just a big lie, a dream.

But I didn't dream. It must be real, then. Or a nightmare.

As I stepped inside, I discerned the change in the atmosphere right away.

The cloud of gloom had settled upon the corridor, and the air, once filled with the mouth-watering scent of Mum's homemade meals wafting from the kitchen, now hung heavy, making it difficult to breathe.

I walked into the living room, where I opened the shutters and pushed up the windows to welcome the autumn air inside.

"Lynn?"

I turned my head to the man standing at the threshold. His dark brown hair was uncharacteristically disarranged, as if he had just woken up.

When Kris's bleary eyes parted wider, I couldn't contain my joy. I darted towards him and threw my arms around him. Surprisingly, he didn't resist and hugged me back.

"I missed you," I murmured, trying not to surrender to tears.

"Likewise," he said as we pulled away from each other. "But how is it possible that you're here?"

"I brought her back."

I looked at Gen, noting the absence of her weapons. I supposed she had to give them back to Chase. The bow, arrows, and knives were certainly not hers.

"How?" His tone of voice dropped lower.

"I went to the Empire of Beasts."

A tense silence settled in among us.

Kris's chuckle broke it. "Right. You went where, again?"

"I went to the Empire of Beasts," she repeated in a calm voice.

Kris gave his head an unbelievable shake before he turned his head to me. "How are *you* alive?"

"I'll tell you both about everything later, but first, where's Mum?"

Kris dropped his gaze at the mention of her, while Gen answered, "In her room, obviously. But before you go in, put on safety—"

Not listening to her, I proceeded towards Mum's bedroom. Quietly, I opened the door and paused, my gaze fixed on the figure lying beneath the sheets.

My mother.

Taking a deep breath, I stepped inside the dimly lit room. As I approached her sleeping figure, I knelt beside her bed and caressed her hollow cheek. Her skin had lost its colour, as pale as paper, but at least she was breathing.

"You should put on safety equipment," Gen whispered behind me.

I ignored her, my attention fixed on Mum, who appeared lifeless, resembling a corpse. But she was sleeping. *Just* sleeping. I had to keep reminding myself of that, or I might forget.

The air in this room carried an unpleasant smell as well. Standing up, I walked over to the closed window and opened the shutters. Pushing the window up slightly, I allowed fresh air to circulate, dispelling the suffocating odour.

I turned to Gen.

As I reached her, I grasped her arm and dragged her out of the room, moving farther away from the door.

"What are you—"

I let go of her and whispered, "Did you really leave Kris to take care of our ill mother?"

Judging from the one time when our father gave Kris a goldfish to take care of, and it almost died within days—our mother had to intervene to save it—my brother could never be trusted to take care of anything, let alone another human being. He was hardly even taking care of himself.

"No, of course not," she denied, matching my quiet tone.

"Chase paid for the help she could get. The physician, people who would look after her while I was gone. She wasn't left alone with him, Lynn."

"You asked Chase for help?" I took a step towards her. "Are you insane?" I hissed in a whisper, careful not to wake Mum. "He doesn't give things for free. What did—oh ..."

Unwillingly, I looked at the ring, but it wasn't there anymore. I raised my inquiring eyes at Gen, who was smiling—the same kind of smile I had seen before, as if she had stolen something valuable and gotten away with it.

"Bloody hells, Gen." I glanced around, but Kris wasn't nearby. I looked back at her. "Whatever you're planning, be careful."

"So, you believe I'm not planning to marry him?"

"Yes, just be ... careful. Chase is—"

"I know," she breathed. "I'm aware."

"If he does something—"

"Lynn, I know what I'm capable of, and that douchebag has absolutely no clue how he's being played."

I didn't want to feel it, but pride enveloped my chest nonetheless. Even though I wasn't acquainted with the whole situation, it didn't stop me from feeling proud of Gen. I would catch up with the details later.

"I'm back now," I said. "I can take care of her. Together, we can all look after her. You don't have to involve that man in this."

"We need money to afford the best physician, and, if you haven't noticed yet, we don't have the money."

"What happened to the engagement ring I gave her? Didn't it help?"

"Mum sold it to pay bills you had no idea about. She hid that from us. We were in a huge debt after Dad died."

My eyes widened. "What?"

"This was my reaction too. She told me if you had known, you'd have married Chase faster. She didn't tell Kris or me because we were considered too young. That is, until you offered yourself to the empire, leaving Kris and me to care for Mum." A note of indignation sharpened her last words.

"Are you implying that you would have liked to go to the empire, and now you're mad at me for taking that opportunity away from you?"

"It was *my* fate, Elynn. *I am sixteen*, not you. Yet you took it away, pretending to be some heroic figure who saves the day when you'd have been more useful if you'd stayed and married Chase instead."

Her words struck me like a slap to the face, but the pain was far deeper.

"I'm sorry, all right? I'm sorry for not sharing the other side of my motive. But back then, I was already weak, and I couldn't bear the thought of the look in your eyes if I had told you I was also doing this to escape Chase. When I learned about the Conversion Potion, I realised it could save you from the offering and me from an unhappy life. I had to take the chance, even if I didn't know what awaited me out there. But I'm glad I made that choice. I would do it again because you wouldn't have survived what I endured there, Gen."

"Then you don't know me at all if you believe that. Besides, you seem fine, so how can I be sure you aren't pretending to have faced something terrible to make me feel better about your decision to offer yourself? How can I know you're not overdramatising the situation?"

I almost laughed. Almost. "Let me tell you something, Gen. *Never* get tricked by the exterior of a person. Most of the time, it turns out to be false. My outside might seem fine, but you can't look inside of me to see how shattered into pieces I actually am."

Her look softened briefly, only to return to its relentless state. "As long as you're not telling me what happened to you there, I can't believe you."

"If I was ready to talk about it, I would have told you already. But I'm not, and I don't think I will be ready anytime soon. So, believe what you want to believe until I'm ready to share."

I spun on my heel and headed towards the kitchen, done arguing with her. Gen waited a bit before following suit.

The kitchen wasn't empty. To my amazement, Kris stood before the stove, heating a kettle. I halted at the unexpected sight.

Kris looked at us over his shoulder, and Gen snickered. He was wearing an apron. Mum's white apron with ruffles.

"What?" He grimaced. "Haven't you seen a man in the

kitchen before?"

"Not just any man, but *you*," I remarked in disbelief.

Once Gen and I exchanged glances, we both exploded into laughter, regardless of what had happened in the hallway seconds ago. Kris scowled, adopting the posture of an irritated housewife with his hand on his hip, making us roar even louder. I propped my hand against the wall, tears spurting. Gen slid into a chair, banging the table with a flat palm. Kris lost his scowl and rolled his eyes.

Although drained of energy and with the mounting headache becoming harder to ignore, I couldn't stop laughing. Not until the pain struck my belly, and the laughter disappeared as I clutched my aching stomach.

"Lynn, are you all right?" Gen inquired, concerned.

"Never been better." I straightened my back and went over to the table. Taking a seat, I watched Kris, who resumed making us tea. "So, darling *housewife*"—he shot me a pointed look—"I thought you'd be in the city by now, charging for a spot in the government."

"I was." He poured boiling water into the mugs. "But Mum got ill, and I was forced to pause my plans."

"Why forced? Chase's hired physician was taking care of Mum." I gave Gen a knowing look.

"Yes, which Kris was very against," Gen pointed out.

Kris remained silent as he served us tea in a delicate, careful, and slow manner, reminding me of myself. I smiled as he placed a mug before me and backed away, bowing to us with a flourish.

"Bon Appétit, annoying sisters."

"It's tea, you dork," Gen muttered, pulling her mug closer.

"The least you could do is thank me, dwarf," Kris retorted.

Gen smiled scornfully and showed him a finger.

Kris responded with a matching smile, reciprocating the gesture.

As I smiled, watching them, I couldn't help but wonder how the hells I'd survived this long without them.

"So," I said, drawing their attention to me. "I might have found a way to pay for Mum's care without including Chase."

"Here we go," Gen began as Kris took a seat with his own mug of tea. "You haven't even been here for an hour, and you're already starting with your solutions, Lynn."

Memories entered my mind, but I shooed them away, straightening my shoulders. "Come on. Our family can do better than depending on noblemen. We are Startels, for Gods' sake. We're going to save our mother. We're going to work so hard the whole Mortal Region will know our names."

Gen scoffed. "Yeah, good luck with that."

I smiled. "I knew the positivity in you was temporary."

She rolled her eyes, resuming to blow on her tea.

"What did you find that could help us, Lynn?" Kris inquired.

I told them everything they needed to know. All about the Spell protecting our lands from morphs' invasion, assuring them that the entire offering was nothing but a trick. The story of its creation, emphasising the absence of magic in our lands for four decades. I didn't forget to share information about the curse, mentioning that not only were golden weapons fatal to morphs but the blood of Ascended Witches, Sorceresses, and dryads poisoned them.

After listening to me, they needed time to process everything. I downed my tea, my mouth dry after incessant talking. Exhaustion crept over me, and I rubbed my eyes, feeling my body urging me to sleep.

"How come we didn't know about the sorceresses' sacrifice?" Kris asked into the silence. "How is it possible for every human not to be aware of it?"

"I don't know," I said. "Any more questions before I go to sleep?"

"Yes," Gen said. "What happened to you there?"

I jumped off the chair. "Good night!"

As I pivoted on my heel, I heard a sigh. I was about to depart when Gen asked, "Don't you want to take a bath first?"

"Too tired for that." I threw her a glance back. "Wake me up once our mother awakes, all right?"

"All right. Good night, good day sleep, then," Gen said.

Kris waved his hand. I reciprocated with a faint smile before dragging myself into our bedroom, falling onto the bed, and drifting off shortly.

XXVIII

I woke up with a stomachache when it was dark outside. The bile rising up my throat forced me out of bed, and I hastily pushed up the bottom window, leaning over to empty my stomach.

The remnants of another bunny that Chase had caught in the morning stared back at me with a disturbing redness. Worry rushed through me. I didn't know what to do. I closed the window, choosing to ignore the unsettling sight.

In the kitchen, I rinsed my mouth with water, hoping to erase the taste of vomit and blood, but it was no help. The coppery taste and the remnants of nausea lingered, and my headache hadn't eased after my nap. It had only become worse.

"Lynn?!" Gen called from the hallway.

I emerged from the kitchen, meeting Gen straight away. I forced a smile, concealing the fact that I had just vomited outside our bedroom minutes ago. "What's up?"

"Mum's awake."

Without hesitation, I bolted towards her bedroom, finding the door already ajar. Kris lounged on the chair in the corner, absorbed in a book he had already read, while my frail mother smiled at me as she attempted to sit up. I rushed to her, placing my hands on her arms.

"You're here ..." she whispered, her voice hoarse and weak.

"I'm here."

She raised her bony hand, but it failed to reach my face.

"I had a dream about you, honeybee," she said, and I knelt beside her bed, holding her raised hand. "Do you want to hear it?" she asked with a faint excitement that cracked my heart.

Gen adjusted our mum's pillows for comfort while I nodded, suppressing my tears.

Whatever illness she had, it was eating her alive. Her time was running out.

"You were here, wearing the most beautiful dress ever to exist, looking like you'd fallen from a painting." She smiled wistfully, and I pursed my lips to steady them. "You weren't alone. You were gazing at somebody in your hands, cooing at it. A baby." Her eyes sparkled. "You were happy. The entire aura around you was filled with happiness. It felt so, so real."

She took a deep breath. "I took a step closer to look at the baby, and it was the most beautiful baby I've ever seen. Your daughter ... she was something else, honeybee."

Although it was her dream, or more like a hallucination, and it would never come true, I kept silent because of the joy in her eyes. I didn't want to shatter her happiness, even if it was a false one.

"Meira," she breathed, and I thought she was mistaking me for herself, but she clarified, "You called her Meira. I might sound self-centred by telling you your daughter's name to be my name, but you chose that name yourself. It surprised me that you named her after me."

I wanted to ask why, but I refrained, knowing that any sound from my throat would result in me being unable to hold back the tears anymore.

"There's something I need to tell you before Gods take me, Elynn."

"D-don't say that." I stammered, and as I blinked, tears trickled down my cheeks.

"I'm dying, sweetheart." She caressed my cheek with her feverish hand. I leaned into her touch, savouring it as it might be the last.

"N-no, you're not."

"Hey, listen to me," she said. "I'll always be in my children's hearts. I'm not leaving you. My soul will forever stay with you."

"But you can't die. You're strong, Mum. You have to fight." I took her hands in mine, as if by holding her, I could shield her from the claws of the grim reaper. "You must fight."

Gen's eyes met mine, tears streaming down her face in sync with mine.

Mum, despite the gravity of the situation, wore a smile. "There's something you ought to know."

I inhaled shakily and pursed my lips, repressing the first sob.

"Twenty years ago, I visited a shaman for another once-a-week visit. She tried to help me have a baby. When I was coming from the town, Gerard ran to me like some madman. I can still remember that crazy look on his face." She chuckled, lifting the weight in the room. My lips curled at the corners, but the smile quickly faded. "He threw his hands around me and kept bubbling that a miracle had happened. At first, I didn't understand. I thought he'd gone nuts, but he beckoned me to come inside. As I stepped into our living room, I saw a basket. When I looked inside it ..." Mum paused. "It was you, Elynn."

I looked up, my heart racing after the revelation struck me like thunder in a clear sky.

"You beamed at me with that adorable baby smile, completely unaware of what was happening. Gerard and I fell in love with you immediately. It was impossible not to.

"Gerard said he found you on our porch in a basket with money that could have sustained us for eighteen years, but we donated most of it to the poor. The bracelet you're wearing was also in the basket, along with a letter." She stirred in bed, trying to sit up again, but Gen and I held her back. "Please, I need to show you the letter, Elynn."

"Lie down, Mum. I'll find it. Just tell me where it is."

Mum was hesitant, but she relented. "It's on top of the wardrobe."

I stood up and approached it, reaching for the top effortlessly. My hand searched for something letter-like, and once my fingers brushed against it, my heart sank. Steeling myself for whatever I might find, I drew out the letter—the envelope with no signature.

It must be a lie. Mum might have hallucinated—

"Go on," Mum encouraged. "Open it."

Because Mum wanted me to, and her time was counted, I pulled the letter out, reluctant to see if it was real. My fingers trembled while unfolding the letter, revealing graceful handwriting. I moistened my lips before reading it aloud.

"*Dear Meira and Gerard Startel,*

"*I've been watching you for over a week to make sure you are the best family my daughter could have. You gave an impression like you both were kind people, and my daughter would have a safe and loving life with you.*

"*Please do not regard me as a monster mother who left her child behind. I had no other choice. If she had stayed with me, evil people would have found out about her and made her suffer, which I couldn't let happen. I ought to leave her here in good and safe hands.*

"*You might notice she's not like the other babies you might be used to seeing. Please try to ignore that and never remove the bracelet from her wrist. Never. Raise her as you would raise your own child if you could have one. I beg you.*

"*I leave you money, enough to last you until she'd grow old enough to provide for herself.*

"*I know I am asking a lot from you already, but I have another request.*

"*When I held the baby in my hands, I beheld the light in her. I hope you will also be able to see it. One day she might do wonderful things, but evil people out there, people with powers, would want her dead. She should not enter mine or her father's birthplace.*

"*'My last request would be to name her Elynn. You probably already have a name picked out, but please, let her be Elynn. It means light and most beautiful woman. The name would suit her well.*

"*Thank you.*

"*P.S. she was born on August 20th, 1:25 a.m.*"

XXIX

Huddled together like bunnies in a burrow with my siblings and Mum, I stared blankly at the ceiling while my mother said something to Gen.

Not my mother.

I closed my eyes, trying to let everything I had learned sink in without any idle outbursts. Even if my entire life had been nothing but a lie.

The letter lay in the pocket of the apron I was still wearing. Although it was just a paper, it felt heavy, tempting me to unfold it once more and look at the delicate handwriting to make sure I understood it right. To make sure I wasn't imagining things. To make sure I wasn't a girl whose birth mother had left her on strangers' doorstep.

But I remained numb.

I shouldn't feel this shocked. A small part of me had always sensed that I couldn't be related to them by blood. My siblings and I were different, like the moon from the sun, and I didn't mean our personalities.

I had questioned it before, why we looked nothing alike. Mum reassured me I had inherited most of my genes from the grandmother Lucida, whom I'd never met. I would be lying if I said I believed her right away, but—

"Finally, I can die in peace," Mum said.

My eyelids shot open, and I turned my head to her. "You're not dying, Mum."

"But I'm not your mother, honeybee," she said. "You read the letter."

Frowning, I sat up. "You *are* my mother, and you will always be my mother. Gerard will always be my father. Gen will always be my sister, and Kris will always be my brother. I love you, and you're not going to die, Mum. I won't let you."

"Whoever you are, Elynn, it's not in your power to fight against death."

"You. Are. Not. Dying."

I wouldn't let her. I couldn't.

The corners of her lips twitched in an attempt to smile, but she failed. I didn't think she could smile anymore. She was slowly drifting into an eternal slumber, and I could feel it in my bones—the time ticking against our favour.

"I couldn't be more grateful for my life," she said. "Some woman gave me Elynn, the child Gerard and I had been praying for five years. Then, she gave me Gen and Kris."

"What?" The question left not only my mouth. Kris and Gen were as confused as I was.

"When—" She coughed, and crimson painted her lips. I released her hand to grab a cloth from the bowl of water on the bedside table. After wringing it, I gently wiped the blood from her lips. "Thank you, my honeybee."

I couldn't even summon a smile except for more tears.

"When Elynn was two years old," she continued, regardless of the pain she must be feeling, "she whispered something in a foreign language, and a faint light appeared around us. Two weeks later, I found out I was pregnant."

She coughed again, the heavier saliva of blood wetting the white bedding, unable to stop.

Gen and I exchanged wary glances.

The sentence hung between us, loud and clear.

The grim death was here, but Mum spoke nonetheless, her gaze fixed on me. "Kristian. You gave me Kristian. I ... I cannot express how grateful I am for—"

Another bloody cough interrupted her.

Gen's face reflected such heartache that I found her hand, giving it a supportive squeeze.

"For all of you." Mum tried to reach for something, and Kristian took her hand. A shadow of disturbance crossed his face, as if he only now realised she was leaving us. Tears welled up in his eyes. "I—"

"Shh." I tried not to choke on my tears as I dropped the cloth because there was no use of it anymore. "You need to rest now, Mum."

I extended my hand to Kris. He lowered his watery eyes to my proffered hand and took it. I joined my fingers with Mum's, and Gen laced hers through Kris's.

Mum opened her mouth as if to say something, but no sound came out. Her soul seemed to be drifting away from her eyes. Swallowing the lump in my throat, I leaned closer to her ear and whispered what I felt she needed to hear. "Someone told me you'd done a great job raising me, but you did the best job raising all of us, Mum. You're the best mother any child would be lucky to have." I pressed my lips against her cheek. "We all love you. Always and forever."

Gradually, her chest ceased rising. Her fingers stayed clammy and warm. A trace of a smile I hadn't spotted before lingered on her blood-stained lips, while her vacant eyes stared into nothingness.

"Mum?"

Gen gently shook her shoulder. She didn't react.

She drew in an unsteady breath. "Mum?"

I covered her hand with mine, and she met my gaze. As she read it in my eyes, she dropped her head onto our mother's still chest and let out a plaintive cry.

Kris's hand slipped away from mine as he stood up from the bed and left the room without saying a word.

I gazed out of the window into the night, wondering if stars, too, could mourn fallen angels as our hearts did.

Outside the cottage, I was puking blood.

It didn't glisten in the moonlight. It didn't change colour. It didn't flame up. Yet, it was my blood.

The headache had grown stronger, and every inch of my skull throbbed with pain.

This couldn't be my mother's illness. She hadn't vomited blood as I did. Whatever it was, I doubted I would last another day. I didn't think I had even half a day left.

If I died, I didn't want my siblings to witness it. They might assume I had gone outside to mourn the loss, which was why neither of them was searching for me. Or they might be lost in their own grief, unaware of my absence. Either way, it was for the better. Mum's death was already terrible to endure. They shouldn't have to cope with my passing on the same day, too.

Elynn? A distant voice echoed in my mind. It didn't belong to me. *Elynn?*

I released a shaky breath.

Elynn, can you hear me?

My stomach twisted, and a torrent of blood surged in my throat.

Elynn.

The same voice, the same owner, but when it echoed, as if coming from the end of a tunnel, I couldn't recognise it.

Elynn, please answer me.

I opened my mouth and emptied more blood onto the grass. My eyesight darkened, and the shapes of things around me lost their meaning.

Hells, no. This is not how you're going to die. You need to get out of there. Now!

I can't ...

I zoomed out, nearly losing my consciousness, the side of my head dropping against the wall. It felt as if somebody was keeping me from succumbing to grim death. As if my life hung on an invisible thread, a connection I could sense within me because of that someone.

Call your siblings, Elynn, it ordered, voice strict and unbending. *Now.*

Who are you?

Call. Your. Siblings.

It might be one of the three devils' voices, refusing to welcome me into one of the hells. Maybe outsmarting the rules wasn't a ticket to hell after all.

I opened my mouth, ready to yell.

"Gen." A whisper came out.

Louder. Another severe and insensitive demand. Yes, the voice definitely belonged to a devil.

"Gen," I murmured.

Come on. I'm sure you can do better than that.

Swallowing, although there was nothing to swallow, I tried to stand up on my limp legs. I drew in a long, deep breath, hopelessly searching for air to yell, but I coughed instead. A piece that looked like a lump of meat shot out of my throat, landing a foot away from me. I stared at it, terrified to even think of what it could be.

Elynn, for the Gods' bellow's sake!

I screamed from the excruciating pain that twisted my insides, sinking back to my knees. Tears gushed down my face as I curled up into a ball. I wrapped my hands around my abdomen to ease the pain, but it only grew worse.

I could barely see anything. The vision turned darker, darker and—

"Elynn?"

I felt a gentle touch.

"What's wrong?" she asked.

I couldn't answer her.

"KRIS!"

Gen helped me to my feet. "Come on," she said surprisingly calm, her voice offering a slight ease.

"What's—" a masculine voice spoke. "What's wrong with her?"

"Oh heavens, lift her. We need to carry her out of here. Be a man for once, Kris. Not a child."

I felt other arms around me, lifting me off the ground.

"She's a morph."

"I don't know *who* she is, but she doesn't belong here. The

Spell is going to kill her if we don't hurry up!"

"She's so light."

I coughed. Unstoppable.

"This is so not good," Gen observed.

"She won't survive," Kris concluded. "She's coughing pieces of her organs. If we get her further away from the Spell, she won't be ..."

Their voices became impossible to decipher, blending into one before dissolving into total silence.

Based on the earlier conversation between Gen and Kris, I could only speculate that they were carrying me out of the cottage's property.

I didn't feel the pain anymore. I didn't feel anything but the delightful music waltzing in the fringes of my mind, slowly drawing closer, growing louder. It was familiar, but I couldn't recall the name of the piece.

Is this it? The end?

Would I never be able to touch piano keys again? Would I never be able to hold a pencil and draw clothes? Would I never have a chance to learn how to dance? Would I never have a child to name Meira? Would I never get to tell my siblings how much I loved and appreciated them?

I couldn't even mourn my mother.

Perhaps, in death, I would meet her—both of my parents.

The cloud of obscurity was enveloping me. Time was slipping away. I knew my siblings were close by, and I wanted to tell them how much I loved them, but nothing came out.

Hold on. A whisper in my head. *Just hold on a little longer.*

It was easy to say.

Firm hands grasped me.

Drink, the voice ordered.

Drink? Drink what?

"Drink, Elynn," the gentle voice said. "Open your mouth. Please?" the same lovely voice asked. "Yes, just like that."

Something thick and bitter hit my tongue. Despite the foul flavour, my body begged for more. I couldn't stop slurping it.

"Just don't stop." A soothing stroke on my scalp, through my hair. "Keep drinking."

The voice might not belong to a devil after all.

Am I in heaven?

His chuckle caressed my ears.

My mouth continued sucking the liquid thirstily, the taste shifting from disgusting to refreshing—like a life source I desperately needed right now. The stranger kept stroking my hair until I regained my vision, and I could finally see who had saved me, *who* was holding me.

The most entrancing eyes gazed back at me before I fell into nothingness.

XXX

Something cold and oily touched my earlobe, causing me to shrink back. I immediately rubbed my ear against my shoulder and stretched my hands upward while yawning. I cracked my one eye open, only to be blinded by the sun.

I sat up and shaded my eyes, finding myself face to face with the eyes of a fish.

I screamed, and a snort sounded above me as I crawled away from the creature.

An alive fish was staring at me, wriggling in a hand that—

I slowly raised my eyes.

Once I saw *who* held the fish, another scream came out of me.

The Bloodsucker tilted his head. "Two screams in a row. Will it be three?"

My palm grazed something, and I yanked it away, glancing at the object I had touched. It was the fish's bones. Dozens of them were scattered around me, forming a circle, as if I were a part of some unholy ritual. My eyes fixated on the specific bones, unmistakably belonging to a piranha, its blank red pupils boring into mine.

I screamed again.

"Three," he whispered, smiling impishly. "A win-win."

I summoned all the curses I had learned throughout my lifetime, each one dedicated to him. His reaction differed with each curse that passed through my mind—some made him frown, some made him laugh, and others raised his eyebrows as he uttered *true*.

When the storm of curses ended, he glanced at the fish thrashing in his right hand. "Eat?" He gave me an inquiring glance.

I glared at him.

"I won't give it to you raw. I can warm it."

I gave him no answer.

"Your loss." He threw the fish into the ocean. It plunged, and at least it was out of the Bloodsucker's reach, unlike me.

I locked my shoulders, looking up at him with distaste and likely a hint of fear. "Explain," I demanded, and his golden eyes flicked to me, "*everything*."

He took a step closer and extended his hand. A chill crossed my skin at the thought of touching him.

His hands were smeared with blood. Although he wore gloves, and presumably, his palms beneath them were spotless, I knew better.

I stood up without his help and stumbled a bit when my vision darkened. His hand closed around my arm, keeping me steady while shapes and colours shifted back to their places. As I looked at him, he pulled his hand away, and I glanced at my arm that his hand had been on seconds ago. I was about to thank him when he said, "'Explain everything' won't do with me. You'll have to be more specific."

I closed my mouth, annoyed. After stretching my hands upward, I bent down, reaching for my bare toes with my fingertips to awaken my body from a profound but uncomfortable slumber.

He picked up a jacket that had been lying in the same spot I had woken up before encountering the fish, forcing me to leave my sleeping ground. Our eyes met, and we both looked away at the same time. His gaze dropped to his jacket, while mine travelled to the serene ocean.

I watched the waves lapping the shore. So calming, so

peaceful. It almost made me forget where I was, with *whom* I was. I slid my hands into my pockets, my fingers brushing against the paper that had entirely slipped from my mind.

Swallowing, I withdrew my hands from my pockets. "I'm not human, right?"

"No," he said, confirming what perhaps was obvious while slinging his jacket over his arm.

"How long have you known?"

"Twenty years."

I stood stunned for a moment. I had expected his answer to be ever since Fillan and Lupin's birthday, but twenty years?

"How did you learn about it?"

Of all creatures, why the Bloodsucker? Why the monster?

"I'll explain everything to you later," he said, but he must have seen the doubt on my face, for he added, "I promise. Now it's time to head home."

I frowned. "My home is in the Mortal Region."

"I meant my home, Elynn."

I took a step back, my heart racing.

He sighed deeply. "I'm not asking you to go with me or forcing you, either. You're allowed to weigh your options. You can stay here until some unfriendly morph finds you and feasts on you, or you can return to your home, where you'll die, or accept my help and come with me."

The more I stared at him, the harder it was to take him for a monster, especially when he was dressed in formal attire and spoke like an intelligent and distinguished man.

He had saved my life. Perhaps he wasn't as evil as tales had described him?

Now, did I actually believe that?

"Why are you helping me again?"

"If you come with me, I'll give you all the answers you need."

I stared at him, sceptical.

Although he had told me I could choose, there wasn't much to choose from. The last thing I wanted was to become a morph's dinner. I wasn't foolish to head back to the Mortal Region, now a lethal place for me. But going with the Bloodsucker into the unknown was also not the best choice. A terrible one, actually.

Yet it was the most reasonable option among the three, and I couldn't think of a better alternative. Still, I didn't know his true intentions. I couldn't trust him.

"How did I survive the Spell's effects?"

"I made you drink my blood."

An abrupt repulsion struck me. "Your what?!"

"Dragons' blood heals. Didn't you know that?" From my puzzled look, he could tell that, indeed, I didn't. "Are you humans taught anything in the Mortal Region, apart from reading tales about the world's most cruel monsters?"

I gritted my teeth but released them hastily. "For your information, we are taught many things, but humans usually avoid speaking about morphs, afraid that by mentioning them, they'll be summoned."

He snorted. "We aren't Gods, but I'm sure many morphs would be flattered to hear how intimidating they are that humans are afraid to speak of them."

"Are *you* flattered?"

"How can I not when tales are told about me?"

I rolled my eyes. "How long have I been here?"

"Five days," he said, but once he noted my astounded expression, he added, "Your body needed time to restore itself after my blood. I reckon it took you so long because your bracelet kept you from healing faster."

"Couldn't you just remove it?"

"No. It would have worsened your healing. It's been suppressing your abilities for two decades, and once everything is released, it won't be a delight. The sorceress infused the bracelet with potent magic, and it should be treated with great care."

I looked at the bronze bracelet on my wrist. Such a small, yet powerful thing. "How come I could live in the Mortal Region unaffected by the Spell all this time, and now I can't?"

"Because you wore your bracelet in the magical world for too long, and now it doesn't work against the Spell anymore."

I didn't want to think about it, about what his words meant, but running from the truth wouldn't do me any good.

I would never be able to return home. Not even for a brief visit.

I stifled the tears. "My abilities ... What are they like?"

"I'm not positive about them."

"Am I a morph?"

Please say no. Please say no.

"You could be."

"What do you mean I could be?"

"You're an interesting kind, Elynn. A love child of two kinds," he observed. "I'll explain it to you later if you come with me. Will you?"

"Do I have another choice?"

He offered me an apologetic smile before disappearing into a puff of crimson cloud, his jacket falling on the sand. Instead of a half-looking dragon, another dragon materialised, its mind-blowing size causing me to recoil and topple onto my bottom.

When he was this close, he seemed larger than at the twins' birthday, reminding me of how menacing he could be, as if I had forgotten. Perhaps I had. Drayard could breathe fire. He could *burn* me. Yet, I was still alive for some reason that I might learn if I went with him.

His ethereal eyes bore into mine. *Climb onto my back.*

Reluctantly, I rose to my feet and wiped the sand off my skirt. I raised my head, facing the dragon standing on his four legs before me. "I don't think I should."

All right, I can grab you with my talons and carry you all the way, and the trip is quite long, Elynn.

"Drayard, I'm not riding you," I answered fiercely.

Only after I said it, I realised how it sounded.

I prayed that my brown skin concealed my blushing cheeks.

What a shame, he sighed theatrically.

"That's not what I meant," I said, as if that would make him quit teasing me.

Again ... What. A. Shame!

Pressing my lips together, I tried not to avert my eyes, no matter how heavily I must be blushing. "No, but seriously, I'm not climbing on your back, Drayard."

All right then. Goodbye to you.

He shifted backwards, and I blurted out before I could stop myself, "No!" He hesitated. "Please. Wait. I ... I-I'll climb on you."

Although his dragon face showed no emotion, I had a hunch he was thrilled, perhaps even smirking in his calculating mind, knowing he had left me with no choice but to relent.

I took a sharp breath, steeling myself for the climb, and stepped closer to the dragon.

Put on my jacket first. It's going to be cold, he informed me. I lifted his jacket. *Go behind me and climb my tail until you reach my back. It'll be easier.*

I slipped my hands into the warm sleeves of his jacket while approaching his tail at a cautious pace, mindful of any sudden movements that might startle me. His giant height caused every muscle in my body to strain, much like a violin's strings when a musician tightened them while tuning the instrument.

I surveyed his long tail, bedecked with black spikes absent in his half-form. The journey to his back seemed lengthy. Once I got there, would I even be able to find a comfortable spot for the flight? Assuming flying on a dragon could ever be comfortable.

I touched the first spike. He didn't react. I didn't know why I had expected him to, anticipating another dirty comment.

I planted my foot on the spike and found my balance before I began mounting him.

How's it possible to shapeshift into such an enormous animal? I asked.

Ask the Gods if you meet them, he answered. *They created all creatures.*

But you're not as big when you turn into a human shape, right?

It was a silly question. I didn't even know why I had asked it.

As I reached his spine, I paused to examine my destination—a flat, narrow space between his wings. Each wing was adorned with three menacing horns capable of inflicting significant damage. I resumed my ascent, akin to a hiker climbing a sloping mountain, only in this case, it was a bloody dragon.

I'm two metres tall. Is that considered tall for a human?

Do your horns add up to the sum?

How do you know I have horns in my human form?

I paused, searching for a smart answer, but none came. *I ...*

uh, do they?

I hadn't even considered whether his horns disappeared when he turned into his real form or not. Animal-like features, such as horns or ears, didn't stay on any morph I'd seen at the Autumn Equinox. So, why had I assumed Drayard's horns were a part of his appearance once he transformed into a human-like shape?

No, he said, snapping me back to the present, *horns don't add up to the whole.*

Then yes, I thought, *it's tall for a human, so it doesn't apply to you.*

He huffed out a laugh. *You never let go of your sharp tongue, do you?*

As I felt myself smiling, I quickly dropped it. *Not when you're around, certainly.*

Eventually, I reached the space between his wings, settling in as comfortably as possible. I avoided looking down, as it might be my greatest mistake.

Hold onto my spikes tightly, and don't let go during the flight.

Following his advice, I gripped his spikes.

Ready? he asked.

No.

He snorted and shot into the sky without giving me a chance to brace myself.

The chilly breeze of autumn carried my scream away.

Part III

Notes of Fire & Friendship

XXXI

I couldn't lift my head to enjoy the sight, afraid that even a slight shift might cause me to fall off. Pressing my body against Drayard's hard-scaled back, I kept my eyelids clamped shut for most of the flight over the Indigo Ocean.

If someone had told me that I would be flying on a dragon one day, I'd have called them delirious. Ever since Mum started reading stories about Arragon, I never dreamed of meeting a single dragon, let alone riding one someday. Yet, here I was, on the most dangerous one alive, flying above the clouds.

This was *all* real.

Not a dream. Not a nightmare. But reality.

Mum would—

No, Mum would do nothing. She wasn't among the living anymore. She was *dead*.

Before sorrow could take hold of me, I pushed it away, choosing not to dwell on my mother's death. Not now, at least.

Hold tight, Elynn, Drayard warned me.

I opened my eyelids, gripping his spikes even firmer. I doubted he could feel them, despite my uncut nails sinking into the spikes. Perhaps, if I dared to cut one someday, he wouldn't feel any pain. It looked like the spikes were just decoration, but I might be wrong.

Drayard dived downwards, and I gritted my teeth to stifle the scream threatening to escape once again. When Drayard first sprang into the sky, and I screamed, he made a dirty pun in my head. Determined not to endure another one of his unseemly jokes, I forbade myself from letting out a single scream.

He returned to his normal flying state, and I dared to peer down.

Below, many colourful buildings varied in yellow, orange, and red hues, all crowned with brown roofs. As I peered closer, I discerned movement between them—morphs strolling the streets.

My lips parted as I recognised the City of Fire, yet another remarkable feature from tales.

To my disappointment, Drayard flew past it, and a much darker scenery unfolded miles away from the city. In front of a smoky chasm, seemingly half-filled with lava, two menacing dragon sculptures sat atop the columns, guarding engraved iron gates that led to the bridge. Beyond the bridge, a colossal black castle was ensconced on top of a dark mountain, taking my breath away.

The castle was built by my ancestors eight centuries ago, Drayard informed me before I could ask. *They burned the stone with their fire, turning it into hellrock.*

Hellrock. One of the books Mum had read mentioned that the dragons' palace was burned until it turned as black as a skillet. However, the book failed to mention the lava lines streaming through the fissures in the walls.

Those lava lines ... Are they real? I inquired.

Yes.

But how does it flow like that?

It's called magic, Honeylove.

Magic. Such beautiful, breath-taking magic.

We flew over a disruption in the bridge that created a large, impassable hole.

What happened to the bridge?

He didn't answer for a long moment, and as I thought he would ignore it, an emotionless reply came, *I destroyed it.*

But why?

As the silence settled, he didn't break it, and I took it as a sign that he wasn't going to elaborate further.

I was so immersed in admiring the ornate pillars that I failed to acknowledge the landing. When I did, we were already in the castle's courtyard.

Before I tried to climb off him, he disappeared into another crimson cloud. I fell but was caught before I could react. When I looked up, his eyes were already on me.

"How was your flight?" he inquired sweetly.

Unable to muster any reply, I stared at him, distracted by both his closeness and the unearthly heat seeping through his clothes.

I didn't want him to touch me.

He promptly planted me on the ground, as if he had heard my thoughts, which perhaps he had. I stepped back and hugged myself, feeling covert gratitude towards him for giving me his jacket. Without it, I would have turned to ice in the middle of our flight over the clouds.

"Can I ask you a question?" I tried.

"If it doesn't involve me, be my guest."

I hesitated before asking, "Where do your clothes go every time you shapeshift?"

"Ah," he said, tucking his hands into his pockets, "that's ... a secret."

"Why?"

"Because it is a mystery. I don't know where our clothes go every time morphs shapeshift, Elynn."

I surveyed the dark, empty yard, paved with stone and concealed by pillars from the citizens. No guards stood behind the massive gates and entrance doors shadowed by the high Gothic arch Drayard was already making his way to.

I caught up with him. "Why are there no guards?"

He halted before the door. "Guards would be unnecessary. Nobody can enter anyway."

"Morphs with flying ability can."

A hint of a smile appeared on his mouth. "Yes, but there aren't many of them around."

He creaked open the door, allowing me to enter first, but I hesitated. "Isn't it strange for a castle not to have anyone to guard it?"

"Might seem strange to those who are used to them, but not to me. Hellrock Castle has different rules."

As I walked inside, I scanned the foyer, unsurprised to find no guards or any other living creature this time. The door closed behind us, plunging the room into darkness, but the lights quickly sprang to life, undoubtedly touched by Drayard's ability.

Since candlelight couldn't reach every nook and cranny, and the place didn't have any windows, it remained mostly dark. Apart from two arched twin staircases joining in the landing and an impressive chandelier hanging above our heads, it was vacant, dreary, and silent. As if not a single living thing existed, other than Drayard and me.

I couldn't shake the growing sense of dread since the door had closed, making me more and more tense. It felt like a rotten presence permeating the air, yet I couldn't determine its source. It could be Drayard or something else. But what else could it be if not him?

I swiped my attention back to him, only to find him already staring at me. Again.

"What powers are you using?"

His eyebrows lowered, pretending to act clueless. "I beg your pardon?"

I backed away from him as he watched me with curiosity.

"This whole aura ..." I gestured with my hands to help me define what words couldn't. "It's awful. What are you doing?"

"I can assure you that I'm doing nothing. I'm just a half-breed."

"*Just.*" The word slid off my tongue like a tart candy. "You know what? I've changed my mind. I ... I want to leave."

"Don't you want to hear the reason you're feeling dreadful sensations?"

"Oh, I know," I declared boldly. "It's your power. Your evil nature."

A corner of his mouth quirked. *The bastard is clearly entertained by this.* "No, that's not me."

"Then what is it?"

"Look at the walls."

I didn't hesitate. At first, the walls appeared to be made of ivory-coloured stone, but as I looked more closely, everything inside me surged up into my throat.

"Oh, my heavens ..."

I backed away. Away from the wall, away from the *bones*.

The walls spun around me. I was on the edge of puking when he touched my arm, and I instantly shot back as if struck by lightning.

"You're a monster," I spat straight into his face, not hiding the intense revulsion I felt for him.

He casually shoved his hands into his pockets. "You agreed to come here."

"I'm leaving."

I turned and stomped towards the exit, but his calm voice, albeit irritating to the bone, rang behind me, bringing me to a halt.

"Don't get me wrong, Elynn. You're always allowed to leave, but I ought to remind you that you're in the world where morphs look like half-beasts, and your appearance is humanlike. As you may have figured out, morphs aren't fond of humans. If, hells forbid, you catch someone's eye, they won't hesitate to hurt you. Even if, by some miracle, you get away without them noticing you, are you sure you'll survive alone in the wild?"

I had never loathed someone as much as I loathed Drayard, nor had I ever felt so foolish for agreeing to let him bring me here, even though I had no choice. None of the options were worth considering, and once again, I found myself trapped in the same maze with only one choice—to stay and perhaps become one of the poor souls decorating these walls.

He had trapped me with minimal effort, like a marionette controlled by a mastermind. I knew I shouldn't have trusted him, yet at some level, I had anyway.

I glanced at him over my shoulder. "Did you enjoy tearing people's skin and decorating the walls with their bones?"

"You won't believe me if I said that it wasn't my work, will you?"

"No, you're right. I won't."

"Are you leaving?" he asked, sounding tired. "Or shall we proceed?"

Clenching my hands into fists, I kept the rage streaming

through my blood at bay. I released my fists, turning to him fully.

"Let's carry on, then," he concluded.

As he turned to the stairs, I pushed myself to follow his steps, attempting to dismiss the haunting image of people's bones in vain.

"Are they ..." My mouth turned dry, steps heavy as I mounted the stairs, but I forced myself to keep walking. I needed to get as far as I could away from here. "Are they remnants of humans?"

"Yes."

I stopped, clutching the banister. He hadn't even hesitated to reply.

Drayard paused a few steps higher, looking down at me. "Elynn?"

He must be delighting in seeing me this terrified. He fed on it. On people's fears, screams as he—

The light dimmed, and I swayed as the world slipped from under my feet.

When my eyelids parted one by one and I beheld a crimson canopy above the comfortable bed I lay upon, I believed what I'd seen was yet another nightmare. But it didn't take long for me to realise that I hadn't dreamed, nor was I delirious, as I sat up and found two of the most horrible-looking creatures at the foot of the bed, staring at me with their differently coloured eyes.

They were the same bats from the twins' birthday.

What kind of real-life nightmare had I gotten myself into this time?

"Wakey, wakey, sleeping beauty!" the one with navy eyes crooned. "What a journey, am I right?"

"She's scared, Baby," the lilac-eyed one noted as she stared at me, her features milder than her companion's. Was it concern?

She was right, but *scared* was not enough to define my current emotions. I was beyond terrified, not to mention revolted by the environment and disappointed in myself.

"Of course, she is." Baby approached me. *What a strange name.* "Listen, love, I know it's a lot to take in, but listen carefully because we're about to leave. Blossom and I have already drawn you a bath—"

"With bubbles," Blossom added. "Everybody likes bubbles, right?"

"Doesn't matter," Baby responded dismissively, and Blossom frowned. "Your bath is ready, but don't take too long cleaning yourself. His Highness is expecting you at dinner—"

"No."

How I had managed to release a voice, let alone form an actual word, was the question for the Universe to unfold.

A great silence settled over the room.

"Oh, the Gods are gracious! She has spoken!" Baby joined her hands together with a clap. "What an outstanding miracle that is! Her mutism has been cured!"

"No?" Blossom asked softly.

I shook my head.

"Why no?" Baby asked without sarcasm this time.

I attempted to speak, to push away the fear and rid myself of the sickening feelings. "I ..." Looking down, I took a deep breath, telling myself: *I will not be afraid.*

I held my chin up with all my remaining inner strength. "Tell him I won't dine with him."

Baby snorted, while Blossom remained concerned.

"Oh, that's out of the question, love," Baby said. "You see, he's the King. Now you're at *his* disposal. If you disobey, anything can happen. He can do whatever he wants with you, and he won't get punished. So take my advice"—she paused—"whatever your name is—"

"Elynn," I murmured.

"Hmm?"

I swallowed before I clarified louder and clearer, "My name is Elynn."

Perhaps I had made another mistake by telling her my name, but I didn't care. All I wanted was to be nowhere near the Bloodsucker ever again.

"All right, take my advice, Elynn. Follow his orders, don't disagree with him, and you'll be just fine."

"Just fine?" I couldn't believe my ears at the absurdity of the words. "He wants me for something evil. He will hurt me whether I obey him or not. He's *the Bloodsucker*."

Blossom opened her mouth. "He's actually not that—"

After Baby's unpleasant glance at Blossom, she shut her mouth. Baby looked at me, feigning peacefulness. "Take a bath not only to wash off the filth along with the reek but also to calm down. The bath helps—"

"The bath won't sort out any of my problems."

Baby pinched her nose as she dragged in a deep breath. I could tell she was trying her best not to surrender to the annoyance simmering inside her.

"Again," she said, "take a bath. You'll find us here in an hour, and we'll prepare you for—"

"I'm not—"

"Oh, hush!" she snapped at last with a tap of her foot. "We leave now. No objections, or else you know who will appear here earlier than he should."

I clenched my jaw and watched them leave. Just before the double ebony doors framed with gold closed, Blossom poked her head inside, smiling at me with the purest and most amiable expression I had ever seen a morph wear. Still, I wasn't fooled. They were all false creatures.

"Take a bath, Elynn," she said in a voice that equated to a light touch of wind on a blistering summer day. "And don't forget to—"

Before she could finish, someone—Baby—tugged her back, and the door shut with a decisive sound. Utter silence enveloped the room. I was officially left alone.

I surveyed the bedroom, amazed by its size—it was significantly larger than Asenah's quarters. The walls were half covered in wood planks and the other half decorated with brocaded dark-red wallpaper. The ceilings gleamed in gold, casting a warm glow across the room. In front of me, a grand set of double doors beckoned, flanked by two sweeping windows that offered a view of the ashen sky.

I slid off the bed and approached the doors, assuming they would be locked, but I swung them open without any hindrance. The sullen view across the balcony welcomed me, but I didn't step further, leaving the doors ajar for the fresh air to drift inside instead. I resumed studying more of the room until my eyes landed on the mirror, and I started.

A girl with a dress that struck more like a rag than a piece of clothing was staring at me. It was drenched with dirt and red stains. I wasn't sure whether they belonged to Mum or me, and I didn't want to think about it. My hair, neglected for weeks, had become a giant mess of knots. It would take a long time to comb out the nest and wash away the dirt along with dried blood. The gold in my hair was barely visible.

Mum had once told me that I'd inherited my looks from my grandmother, whom I had never met. She lied, but I didn't love her any less because of it.

Perhaps I had misunderstood? Perhaps it was all in my head because of the effects of the Spell? That my biological family wasn't the one I had grown up with?

I slipped my hand into my pocket and retrieved the letter. With trembling hands, I unfolded it, my heart pounding in my chest. I read it once, twice, but the text always remained the same.

I crumbled up the letter and tossed it into the dimly burning fireplace. I sank to my knees, embracing myself, and let the tears I had been holding back for a while finally leave.

I was sorry that I couldn't be at my mother's funeral to bid my final farewell.

I was sorry.

For everything I should feel sorry for but didn't know what for yet.

XXXII

After mourning my mother, I took a bath to cleanse my body and hair of dirt and blood using soap and whatever was in the bottles. My body was clean, and my blonde hair had regained its natural golden sheen. Physically, I felt better, but I couldn't say the same for my heart, mind, and soul. They were damaged and likely unrepairable.

I opened the gilded wardrobe, revealing a stunning collection of dresses in red, orange, yellow, and black shades, perfectly aligning with the Realm of Embers aesthetic of fire. I ran my fingers over their sleeves, appreciating the high-quality material. Under different circumstances, my heart would have cried out of joy.

I found a wine-red robe with gold embellishments and let a towel pool on my feet. I put on the robe, and as I reached for the towel, I paused. Two conflicting thoughts warred within me. One urged me to leave it as a mark of defiance, while the other, a sensible part that learned something from my days in the Realm of Bones, told me to pick it up. With a sigh, I chose the latter, folding it neatly on the bed before I lay on the nearby settee.

Baby and Blossom soon appeared, attempting to make me obey the King's orders, but I remained on the settee, impervious to their persistence.

I was playing with fire, and I didn't care. The sight in the entrance rendered me this way. Since I was here, my life was already doomed. Why bother pleasing someone who would kill me sooner or later?

"Where did he get this girl?" Baby complained. "Is he into stubborn women?"

If Baby wasn't a morph, I'd wither her with a look alone.

"Do you think he'll kill us if—"

But before Blossom could finish, the man's voice interrupted her.

"Leave the room, sweethearts."

I didn't look at him, continuing to stare at the ceiling. I wasn't terrified of him or convinced myself to believe that I wasn't, for I refused to behave like a timid doe in front of strangers.

Once his figure appeared in my periphery, I turned onto my left side, facing the settee's backrest. The colour reminded me of Mum's blood, and a knot formed in my chest.

"Aren't you thirsty or hungry?" he inquired in a gentle voice.

I didn't buy his concern. He was false—a murderer who, instead of constructing proper walls, displayed his achievements by using the bones of innocents he had killed. *Who does that?*

Right ... The Bloodsucker.

I didn't reply, despite feeling both hunger and thirst. But I had no intention of filling my belly with anything while stuck here.

"Aren't you interested in hearing who you are by birthright, Elynn?"

I turned my head to look at him. "No one's stopping you from speaking now."

He stuffed his hands into the pockets of his trousers. "I give orders, not you."

"I don't care." I sat up, adjusting my robe. "I'm not going into the room decorated with more human remnants."

"Only the entrance owns such a priceless decoration. The other parts of the castle don't have that finery."

"I don't—"

My stomach growled. Loud. I wouldn't be surprised if every living thing in the castle heard it.

He gave me a knowing look. "Are you going to eat? The food will go cold if you stall any longer."

"Wearing this?" I gestured at the robe.

He hastily eyed it. "Wearing this."

"Just like that?" I frowned, confused. "Aren't you going to demand that I change, saying it's inappropriate to wear a robe at the dining table?"

He stared at me with that inscrutable expression that vexed my nerves. "Wear whatever you like, Elynn. A robe, a towel, even nothing if you're comfortable with it."

Though the last sentence could be taken as an innuendo, it didn't sound like one. It was more like a statement of fact. I had thought nothing could ever amaze me again after the bones, but Drayard must have been the most unpredictable creature ever to exist, for he proved me wrong yet again. I expected him to order me to dress up, but he genuinely didn't care about my clothing. Or he just masked it well.

"I bet you'd be pleased if I wore nothing."

A smile, one of his seldom nice ones, made an appearance. "I'm sure I wouldn't be comfortable, but—"

"Don't you even dare to dream about it, you lecherous bastard." I rose to my feet. "I'm only going because I need answers, that's all."

Also, my stomach demanded food, and it had become impossible to ignore.

"Then hurry. I know how fast a runner you are. Delaying isn't your strongest suit."

Sudden fury lit up my blood, and I might have exploded if he hadn't turned away and moved towards the doors. With a deep, calming breath, I braced myself for spending dinner with the Bloodsucker and followed his footsteps into the corridor.

"Why did you tell me to run if you weren't planning to kill me?"

He glanced over his shoulder, wrinkles marring his forehead. "You shouldn't be walking behind me."

A scoff almost left me, but I held it back, keeping a straight face. "You're right, I shouldn't, but that's how society is, isn't it? Rulers are superior to the rest. Women are lesser than men.

Monsters are wearing crowns."

He looked away immediately, and I couldn't help but smirk. He was silent for the rest of the walk. We passed dimmed corridors, which, to my relief, weren't decorated with more human remains, and descended a staircase where more corridors followed. I craned my neck at the windows we passed, but it was dark outside, and I couldn't see a thing. At last, he halted before doors almost twice his height. He opened them into a dining room.

All the windows were covered by red velvet curtains. A lit chandelier hung over the table arrayed with plenty of food to satisfy and even overfeed one's stomach. But all the seats were empty, and the amount of food was excessive for two people. No matter how starved I was, I wouldn't be able to consume even half of it.

Drayard made it to the table and began picking his food.

"Won't Baby and Blossom be joining us?" I asked, trying not to reveal my curiosity.

"Why would they?" He placed some chicken wings on his plate. "They work for me, not you. So, don't be demure. Eat whatever you like instead of standing there like a pillar."

"Isn't that a bit too much for two mouths?"

He didn't answer. I stopped idling and focused on the table. I could choose whatever I wanted, and that's precisely what I did, selecting what my belly was craving, and, unsurprisingly, it asked for most of the food.

As I was putting potatoes on my plate, I caught Drayard sitting down and sipping on a dark red liquid. I froze.

Blood?

"No, not blood, Elynn," he reassured, cutting into a roast chicken nonchalantly.

"Drayard?"

He raised his eyes.

I forced a smile. "Stay away from my head."

I pivoted on my heel and chose the furthest seat from him—at the end of the table. As I settled into the chair, I eyed my plate with four slices of roasted pork, rice, part of the roast chicken, and potatoes. I cut the pork first.

"How can I when you're so willing to share your thoughts with me?" He put a bite of roast chicken into his mouth and half-smiled.

"I'm not willing, and I don't share my thoughts or anything with you." As I cut the pork with such force, it was a miracle I didn't slice through the plate. "You're the one who likes delving into my thoughts without an invitation, and when I happen to be in your mind by a complete *accident*, you turn into a beast, desperate to shoo me out." I took a bite, bottling up my annoyance.

"Your mind isn't half as noxious as mine. If you stayed in my head longer than you should, it would affect you more than it would me. I spared you from the nightmares."

I rolled my eyes. "What could be that bad inside your mind? Nefarious plans on how to kill this and that?" I gestured with my fork.

But I had caught a glimpse of what lurked in the deepest layers of his mind, heard something. Something I hoped never to hear again.

"I'm not answering questions that involve me, Elynn," he politely reminded me.

"Perhaps you should. I don't see any of your friends around, unless you don't have any because everyone's so terrified of you. All I saw were your whores who warm your bed, and, of course, the dead souls decorating your walls. So, tell me, Drayard." I leaned in. "Are you happy?"

His eyes were empty, devoid of any emotion. Despite my uneven heartbeat—I was positive he could hear—I maintained eye contact, finding his vacant stare more unsettling than any emotions he might be concealing.

"As much as it concerns you, yes, I'm happy."

For the first time, I recognised the lie in his tone, but I didn't bother to expose it.

For the next ten minutes or so, we ate in silence, which surprisingly wasn't uncomfortable. Both of us needed some time to savour the meal before wading into another conversation that would likely result in me hissing at him again, while he spoke with that calm, mature tone of his, aggravating me even more.

I took the time to consider the questions I needed answers to, ensuring they didn't involve Drayard's past, as he despised whenever I mentioned it. At last, I had my first question.

"Who are my biological parents?"

I wasn't sure if I wanted to know that, but only this way, I'd have a better knowledge of who I was by learning about my origins.

"They are traitors of both empires. I'm sure you have heard of them since their love story and treason are well known." He took a sip. "Tatyana Haroun and Aytigin Cresenbar are your parents."

I looked at the plate. The unknown people Imogen had refused to speak about were my birth givers.

Curiosity is what kills us humans. Her words drummed in my head. Little had we known, I was not human. Curiosity couldn't kill me. Gods knew what could, though.

At least Drayard needed no prompting to continue. "Your mother was a princess of the Empire of Beasts, and your father—an heir of the Empire of Skies. Your parents met at your father's family palace during negotiations for a treaty between morphs and enchanters. Cliché as it may sound, they fell in love at first sight." He winced, as if doubting love at first sight, which was something we had in common.

"Aytigin and Tatyana were meant to be enemies—a union between an enchanter and a morph posed a threat to our pureblood. However, they were soulmates, and no power of the Gods could intervene when they were destined to be together by the power of the supreme Universe. Do you know what soulmates are, Elynn?"

"Yes," I said without hesitation. "It's when two people are destined to be together, when separate souls, minds, bodies, and hearts belong together. Soulmates are extremely rare as there's one person dedicated to another. Either they find each other or they don't." I paused. "But it's a myth."

A subtle smirk graced the corner of his mouth. "It's not a myth."

I huffed, but he went on. "Your definition of a soulmate is debatable. While it fits your biological parents' case, there are exceptions. Soulmates aren't as rare as you claim, and they don't necessarily have to be in an eternal romantic relationship. Soulmates are those who understand each other instinctively, someone with whom one feels right and comfortable ..."

It clicked with me then.

My guardian parents were each other's soulmates.

I had never realised it until Drayard started defining my parents' relationship. They were the quintessence of what love should be—true equals. My dad never made less of Mum. He always consulted her before making important family decisions. But most importantly, when they were in the same room as me, their love radiated, as if they were meant to be. Like soulmates fortunate to have found each other.

I had lived with soulmates for more than half of my life, and I had no clue. And not only my guardian parents but even my biological ones had found theirs.

Did that mean I would find mine, too?

I let out a laugh at the thought.

"Are you done reflecting?" Drayard asked.

I nodded.

"As I was saying, soulmates do not always have to be romantically involved. They can simply be friends, even if one of them is in a relationship with someone else or has a mate."

"Mate?" I raised my eyebrows. "Like animals have mates and breed with them?"

"Something like that, yes. Morphs are the species most closely related to animals, as they are technically half animals, but we have more control. Morphs can find mates during mating seasons, but it's not a strict rule. For instance, certain morphs like wolves and dragons can find a mate for a lifetime, while others can have countless mates each mating season, just like in nature."

I was speechless. I had never heard about mates or soulmates before.

"What happened after Aytigin and Tatyana discovered they were soulmates?" I asked.

"Since Aytigin and Tatyana couldn't be together officially and legally, they ran away. They were selfish and unmindful of what it would cost to both empires because of their treason.

"As expected, their families became furious. The Emperor of Skies, your grandfather Tanwyn, sent an assassin to poison the Empress of Beasts, your grandmother Nathalie. In retaliation, the Emperor of Beasts, your other grandfather Rayko, murdered Tanwyn in his own bedchamber. Then Rayko was poisoned by the current emperor, Kalani, your uncle."

I frowned, struggling to keep track of who killed whom, bombarded with new names all at once.

"It was quite a bloodshed between two families," he observed. "Personally, I'm amazed that Tatyana's and Aytigin's treason didn't provoke another war."

I grasped my glass filled with Gods knew what and took a hefty gulp. To my relief, it turned out to be just wine. I finished it in no time and scanned the table in search of more.

As soon as I noticed the pitcher, Drayard pointed out, "The pitcher is in the middle."

I rose from my seat with the glass and made my way to the pitcher. I poured myself a drink, one that was meant for me for the first time and not for a morph.

"I know it's a lot to take in."

I gave him a pointed look over the rim. "You don't say."

He favoured me with a half-smile.

I returned to my seat. "But Tatyana and Aytigin were eventually discovered, right?"

"Yes, they hid for almost a year. Aytigin was caught by enchanters twenty years ago, and not long after, Tatyana returned to the empire. It became pointless for her to continue hiding when her loved one had been captured. However, instead of facing the music, she went to my father."

Drayard broke eye contact for the first time as he spoke in a hushed tone, as if the topic was unpleasant for him. "Tatyana and Arragon were good friends since childhood. They loved each other, but Father loved Tatyana more than a friend while she saw him as a brother. When she revealed her pregnancy, asking for his help to protect her unborn child from discovery, he, blinded by love, risked everything to help her."

Drayard looked at his plate, pausing his narrative until he resumed, "I assume with a sorceress's help, she drained magic from Tatyana, allowing her to enter the Mortal Region unaffected. Leaving you in the land protected from magic was the best idea they could think of."

"You *assume* with a sorceress's help?"

"I can't think of another way Tatyana entered the Mortal Region where it was deadly for her to be," he explained. "Before she gave birth to you in the Mortal Region and left you with humans, my father made a magical oath with her to protect you despite anything. To guarantee his loyalty, he put his entire kind at stake. Fourteen years later, enchanters marched into my realm and massacred the dragons, including my father. During that time, I was away, but I returned just in time to witness his death. He was alive long enough to pass on the oath to me. What a coincidence, huh?" His eyes twinkled with fire that wasn't meant for me—no, it was perhaps meant for his father and Tatyana.

"I'm sorry."

"You shouldn't be. It's not your fault my kind was decimated. I made peace with the dragons' unjust fate soon enough."

"But why would enchanters do this?"

"Because they're monsters."

I frowned. "I'm sure there was a reason they did what they did."

"People don't need to have a reason to be monsters, Elynn."

I took a sip, wanting to ask if he had a reason to be a monster, but it was about him. I held my tongue until I had another inquiry. "Did you save my life twice because of the magical oath?"

"Yes."

"Why did you take the oath?"

"As I've said before, I don't answer questions that include me."

I let out an irritated sigh. "This oath, then, is the reason I could hear your voice in the Mortal Region?"

He took another sip of wine. "Correct."

"Why did you tell me to run at the wedding?"

"Because Nayden with Nadira was going to make an appearance. They might have recognised you. I couldn't risk it as Nayden would have ended you."

"I'm related to them?"

"You're biologically their niece. Also, you have cousins."

I grimaced. "Ew, did they ..."

He smiled. "No. Nayden and Nadira don't have their own children. Your cousins are royals from the Realm of Wilds, such as Dara."

Oh, that sneaky panther.

The way she had stared at me at the twins' birthday ... What if she—

"Dara might know who I am," I said. "I was in the kitchen after the twins' birthday and felt her staring at me."

"Dara knows a lot. She might know who you've been ever since she saw you," Drayard confirmed my suspicions.

"Is she going to tell?"

"I wouldn't worry about her if I were you."

But I was thinking the opposite. "Why?"

"She's not a threat."

I watched him suspiciously. He was underestimating her, and I almost said that if I were him, I wouldn't brush off someone like her as harmless, but I stopped myself. There was no reason to tell him that.

"What kind do I belong to?"

"You might be a half-breed. Half-morph of a lion and half-enchantress."

"What powers do I have?"

"I cannot answer you because I'm not sure. There's a thing about half-breeds. They are rare. Enchanters and morphs can reproduce with each other, but it doesn't mean that their offspring will be a half-breed with both of their parents' abilities. It's a rare case when a baby is born with all the powers and not one of their parents' that dominated the most during the conception."

"You are that rare case," I thought aloud.

"I am."

"So, you don't have the slightest idea what powers might hit me once I remove my bracelet?"

"Aytigin was a Prince of Skies. He must have had great power, and Tatyana was the Princess of Beasts, a morph that could transform into a lioness with night vision and enhanced senses.

Both of your parents' genetics are powerful. There's a high chance you inherited both of their abilities. However, that's only based on my calculations, which have never failed me before."

Somehow, I didn't doubt him. He had the mind of a devil and a wise one. "What kills half-breeds?"

"The most dominant genetics during conception could only determine that. In my case, I'm more dragon than a bat, which makes any platinum weapon lethal to me. Gold can't kill me, only scar me. In your case, if Tatyana's DNA dominates yours, it's gold. If Aytigin's, it's iron. It can't be both. My guess is you have more morphs' abilities since you were affected by the Spell."

"Aren't enchanters affected by the Spell?"

"No. Only morphs can't go there. Enchanters can."

That was new.

"Is it as easy to kill half-breeds as any other species?"

"Yes."

I had no more questions, at least none that came to mind. I resumed eating, concentrating on the goal of filling my stomach.

"Is there something you need?" he asked after a while. "Because anything you require can be provided."

I looked at him, deadly serious. "I want freedom."

He showed no reaction. "The safest place for you right now is here, Elynn."

"Among the bones?"

"Among the bones."

The silence stretched out between us.

If I weren't so tired, I would fight him for my freedom, but I saved it for another time, sensing that I would be seeing him often. "I want a sewing machine and materials for it, as well as a sketchbook and colours to draw with."

"Servants will be right—"

"Slaves," I corrected him.

"No, not slaves. My realm doesn't engage in this whole sixteen-year-old slavery nonsense."

I blinked in utter surprise. Once again, he had managed to surprise me. How did he keep doing that?

"Morphs are working here, and they get paid for the jobs they do," he explained. "You can wander wherever you like, and if someone sees you, it won't matter. Nobody working here can ask questions since the contract they signed forbids it. However, for your own safety, leaving the castle is a high risk. My advice is that you stay here."

"I wouldn't be able to leave the castle with the bridge destroyed anyway," I grumbled.

He didn't say anything, and for a considerable time, I paused my inquiries, savouring the last bites of food.

I washed down the last bite with wine. "How long do I have to stay here?"

"This, I cannot answer." He dabbed his mouth with a handkerchief and dropped it onto the empty plate as he stood. "Will you be able to find your way back?"

I rolled my eyes. "How considerate of you."

"Will you?" he repeated.

"Yes."

I wasn't sure if I would, but I also didn't want him to stay here, watching me finish my meal.

He stared at me for a moment before saying, "Have a nice evening, Honeylove."

"I have another question."

He stopped in front of the doors and faced me. "Yes?"

"Why are you calling me Honeylove?"

A soft smile touched his mouth, and he lowered his gaze, tucking his hands into his pockets. With a slight bow of his head, he left. Sighing, I pressed my two fingers to my throbbing temple while swirling the glass of wine with my other hand, trying to absorb the mass of information he'd left me with.

I didn't sleep for long that night, as I had awakened from yet another nightmare. Surprisingly, it wasn't about the human remains downstairs or Fillan, Lupin, or Chase. Instead, it was something worse—a nightmare of my mother's death, where she died in a pool of her own blood.

As dawn broke, Blossom helped me choose today's clothes, and Baby styled my hair. I had breakfast in the dining room, this time alone.

Since my desired items hadn't arrived, I decided to explore the castle. With nothing else to do and Drayard assuring me that I could wander freely, I ventured to various doors on my floor, only to discover that all of them were locked. I wondered if there was a specific reason, especially a *bad* one, to lock them.

As I came across a narrow staircase, presumably intended for servants' use, I had two options: go upstairs or downstairs. However, aware of what the first floor offered and afraid of encountering the bones again, I didn't test my luck and chose to go upstairs.

When I reached the upper floor, I once again tried opening one door after another, but they, too, were locked. I scoffed at Drayard's words that I could wander wherever I liked. Of course,

I could when all the rooms were locked from wanderers like me.

I was on the verge of returning to my chamber to find another activity when the next doors I tried opened.

Aisles and aisles of shelves, laden with books, extended across two floors. Behind the winding stairs in the centre of the room stood a large ebony table and an unlit fireplace. Unlike the library in Asenah's mansion, this one was much bigger and grander.

I walked over to the windows nestled between the bookshelves and drew back the curtains, but the sun was covered by dark clouds, barely allowing any light inside. When I finished, I stood in the middle, marvelling at the hanging chandeliers, towering shelves, and thousands of books filling the spaces. Even the largest library in the city of the Mortal Region couldn't compare to the impressive design, assortment, and spaciousness of this one.

I lost track of time as I roamed through the aisles, selecting books and perusing the text until I came across the one that captured my attention the most—a tome about dragon tales.

A rush of excitement swept over me, but I couldn't pick it up with a stack of books in my hands. I hurriedly placed them on the table before I returned and pulled out the book with gilded edges. As I turned it over, the golden letters on the cover glistened in the light.

Tales of Dragons.

I opened it.

A sudden burn shot through my hand, causing me to release it. The book landed with a heavy thud, the sound echoing off the library's walls.

I couldn't move, frozen with fear spreading over me like a disease. Yet, it also awakened curiosity.

What is a platinum dagger doing in there?

I glanced around with a silly suspicion that I wasn't alone, but that was ridiculous. It was only me, the books, and ... the dagger, which elicited the same awful sensations as the sword hanging in Chase's armoury.

I collected myself and summoned the courage to face it. Squatting down, I found some outlandish strength within me to pick up the dagger by its handle. I analysed its shining blade, paying no attention to the instinctual voice urging me to put it back.

Platinum could kill dragons, which meant it could end the Bloodsucker. But why would a weapon lethal to dragons be here, within his property? Wasn't Drayard aware of its existence?

I returned the dagger to the book, closed it, and pushed the book back into the shelf with shaky hands. In case I needed it, I knew where to find it, but hopefully, that was my first and last encounter with *that* weapon.

Sitting at the table, I read a book about the dragon monarchy in the Realm of Embers. It offered both useful and interesting information, but eventually, I grew tired of it. Unlike Kristian, I couldn't spend an entire day with an informative book without wearing out my brain. As I closed the book, I pushed back the chair and stretched my back, only for the inconspicuous bookshelf enveloped in darkness in the corner to catch my attention.

I stood up and approached it, studying it carefully before reaching for a random book. Yet instead of grasping the spine, my fingers met a solid wall.

Even more intrigued now, I ran my fingers across its surface, fascinated by the books painted so realistically that they could easily mislead anybody.

But what was the purpose of it?

Suspecting it could be the door to a secret entrance, I touched every bit of the painting, including the edges, but nothing happened. Even if it appeared to be a painting, I couldn't remove it.

I would have left the painting alone if the unlit wall sconce hadn't caught the corner of my eye. I reached out, wrapping my fingers around it, and pulled it down.

The painting swung open slightly.

I cast a quick glance around to ensure I was alone before swinging open the camouflaged door wide. One by one, lights inside lit up, revealing a narrow passage ahead. Taking a deep breath, I stepped into the secret passageway, where cobwebs clung to the corners. My heart pounded with a blend of excitement and suspense.

Concealing the secret passage behind a painting of a bookshelf wasn't particularly wise, unless it was built many years ago when morphs who used libraries were less cautious. Or the library might not have been in frequent use, which could explain why.

I approached the winding stairs that disappeared into darkness. Swallowing the uncertainty of where they might lead me, I began my ascent. I reached another floor that branched into two corridors. Muffled voices seemed to come from the right. As I stepped into the corridor, lights flickered to life, as if sensing my presence.

With each step, the voices grew louder and more coherent. I hadn't made a mistake. After turning a corner, more cobwebs appeared, and I slowed down, having no desire to end up with them all over my face with spiders crawling in my hair.

"Why did you invite us here, Your Highness?" asked a man.

I halted and looked around. A single silver rectangle caught the reflection of my face, and I shifted it, uncovering two small holes.

"Perhaps for another mission to liberate the whores," another man said tauntingly, his voice as rough as gravel.

Pressing myself further, I braced my palms flat against the wall to get a better look.

Behind the peephole, the room reminded me of a study, spacious with an unusual arched ceiling. The overall theme was primarily dark, apart from the claret-red rug. To my left, Drayard stood behind the obsidian desk, the individuals sitting in the black leather armchairs obscuring most of him.

"Do you wish to return to your prison cell, Nathair?" Drayard directed his question to the man I presumed was the latter speaker. "Then think carefully before you speak."

Oh, the Bloodsucker clearly didn't like them. Who were those men anyway? Other workers of his?

"Why are we here, Your Highness?" the other one repeated.

Drayard set his gloved hands flat on the desk, leaning forward, helping me see him better. He maintained his unreadable expression, as usual. "When were you going to tell me about the alliance between morphs and enchanters to eradicate humankind?"

What?

Again, silence, broken only by Drayard's voice. "The plague?" He asked. "The plague spread in the Mortal Region to get rid of humans?"

I tried not to think about anything. Drayard could read my thoughts. He might figure out I was eavesdropping, judging by the look of it, on his meeting, and I had no desire to learn what he'd do once he realised I was here.

"Your Highness," the one whose name was unknown uttered with a hint of dread, "we swear by the Gods below, we are hearing about the plague for the first time."

Drayard surveyed his workers suspiciously. His radiating intensity could cut through a diamond, but it vanished like a puff, and the room's aura softened. He might have believed them, but I was inclined to doubt them.

"Very well." Drayard leaned away from the desk, clasping his hands behind his back. I released a quiet breath, finding it difficult to comprehend how these men could work for such a formidable creature, experiencing tension every time they were around him. "Kyrel, I need you to spy on Nayden's council." His gaze shifted from Kyrel to the next. "Nathair," he addressed him with a mixture of coldness and calmness, "find out the number of humans who died from the plague and bring the statistics to me. You have five days, not more." He paused. "That will be all. Dismissed."

The men stood, bowed to their King, and rushed out so quickly that I could barely register their proper appearance. Kyrel was a bat, and Nathair was a snake morph. From what I saw, Kyrel was as hideous as the bat girls, whereas Nathair's horrific appearance sent shivers trailing up my spine. I shrugged off the feeling, surprised that he had left on his feet instead of slithering out.

As the doors closed, Drayard made his way to the table, where a decanter stood with its stopper carved into a dragon's skull. His profile faced me as he opened it and poured whiskey into a glass. Frowning, I shut the metal cover and scurried back to the library. I closed the painting door, making sure it was well shut before I turned around. A fleeting flash of lightning illuminated the room, briefly revealing a figure at the table just before it thundered. I nearly jumped, clutching my chest.

"Bloody ...!"

A fire in the hearth suddenly ignited as rain began battering the windows.

Drayard sat on the edge of the table, paging through one of the books I had chosen, as if he had been there for a while.

"Eavesdropping is an act of offence." His eyes slowly shifted to me. "For a princess, it is an act of misconduct. Tell me, Elynn, what measures shall be taken for violating your rights as a princess?"

I crossed my arms over my chest, lifting my chin. "Says the one who listened to the siblings participating in illegal activities."

He brought the whiskey glass to his mouth. "How do you know sex between siblings is illegal?"

"You were surprised by it. I suppose it is."

"It's illegal between royal families, yes." He closed the book. "Though, it once wasn't."

"Oh?"

"It used to be encouraged, actually. It was believed that reproduction between kin kept the pure bloodline alive until more and more babies were born with defects. To prevent this, the law was established forbidding romantic relationships among relatives in royalty. Now, it's not only illicit but shameful."

I observed him with a frown as he took a sip. He noticed it. "What's the matter?"

"Nothing."

I didn't think he believed me, but he didn't question me either, taking another sip. I averted my eyes, staring at the bookshelves instead.

"You found one of the secret passages, I see," he observed.

I looked back at him, surprised. "One of the secret passages? There are more?"

"Of course, the castle is big."

"And all of them are hidden this foolishly? Behind doors that look like bookshelves?"

He smiled. "No, all passages are different. This one isn't very secret anyway."

"It leads to your study room, where servants might eavesdrop on things they shouldn't."

"I don't worry about that."

"Why?"

"They would be thrown into lava for trying."

There was no emotion in his countenance and tone as he said that. I wanted to comment, but instead, I asked, "Why are all the rooms locked?"

"Not all."

"Most of them are," I pointed out, and he didn't deny it. "Why?"

"Most rooms aren't used. I don't see a reason why they should be accessible when nobody lives in them."

But I remained sceptical. "How can I be sure there are no other morbid features like in the entrance of the castle?"

"You can't." He lifted one book after another, sorting them onto the same stack.

"You spoke about the plague in my land," I noted. "Explain it further."

"How brash of you, Honeylove."

"*The plague*, Drayard. I need more information about it."

At least he wasn't drinking anymore. The quarter-full glass rested on his right knee, and his entire focus was on me. "Your mother died from it. Did you know that?"

I hated that he brought up my deceased mother, especially after having a nightmare where she died over and over again. But come to think of it, Gen had warned me to be careful around her, insisting on wearing safety equipment. Her illness was contagious and fatal, yet I hadn't considered that other people in the Mortal Region might have been infected.

"Does it mean that it wasn't an illness that came out of the blue?"

I already knew the answer, having overheard him discussing it with his workers. I just wanted to make sure I had understood everything correctly.

"Morphs have two enemies: enchanters and humans. Of the two, they despise humans the most. If Nayden had to choose, he would side with the lesser enemy to wipe the most loathed from existence."

I couldn't stifle a laugh at how ridiculous it was. "Humans are your enemies? Seriously? We are weak and *human* compared to you."

It was only after I had finished speaking that I grasped the meaning behind my words.

We. I still deemed myself human, even though I wasn't. I had discovered that I belonged to two other kinds only yesterday. It felt like a far-off dream, and the realisation of my true identity hadn't fully settled in.

He smiled at my remark, appearing thoughtful. "Humans have hunters who wield weapons capable of bringing death to our kind. They also have witches and sorceresses who can destroy us, regardless of magic not working in the Mortal Region. While they can be killed more easily than us, if humans unite against morphs, they could be our downfall. Despite the differences between enchanters and morphs, as I gathered from the idea of the plague, they share a common goal—to eradicate humans from the Mortal Region. That's why they created a disease to spread through animals into human lands. I don't have the exact statistics of the deceased yet, but I'm sure it's working like a charm."

"How did you learn about the plague? Did you read someone's thoughts?"

"I don't need telepathy to know what's happening in my lands." There was no pride in his statement, just the fact that, as the King, he ought to know these things. "Also, your mother's illness and an everlasting animosity towards humans were clear indicators." He took yet another sip of his drink.

I clenched my jaw. "You can't stop drinking, can you?"

He lifted the glass for another sip, aggravating me even more. "Why should I when it sedates my demons?"

"Is that why you're so irritatingly calm all the time? Because of alcohol?"

Tiny lines appeared under his eyes as he pondered something. "Do I seem calm to you?"

Was he not self-aware? "You don't seem calm, you *are*."

"Isn't it interesting how our outside can be so different from our inside?"

Of course. I should have picked up on it sooner. His calm disposition was a mere facade, and he carried it well.

I was heading towards the table to gather the books and leave when the obvious struck me, rendering me still.

"My siblings. What if they catch the plague?"

"Well, according to my calculations," he said casually, "they die."

And another sip. But now I couldn't care less about it when my siblings' lives were in danger.

"No, no, no, no." I shook my head, feeling my heart race as I considered the numerous possibilities, the high chances of ... I brushed aside the thoughts of what-ifs. "You can't let them die, Drayard. Please, don't let them die."

I didn't care a whit about begging him. My honour or my beliefs didn't matter. When it came to my family, I would sell my soul for their well-being.

He tilted his head to the side, and I couldn't mistake it for anything but a villainous move. "What's in it for me if I happen to have a change of heart and find a way to protect them against the disease?"

Once again, he tossed me into yet another maze with only one way out, and whatever it was, it might revolt me. I could do anything for my family, but as I thought of what Drayard might want from me ...

"What do you want?" I asked. Miraculously, my voice didn't come out shaky, but the opposite—steady and unbending.

Mentally, I applauded myself for it.

"I don't know, Elynn. There's so much to choose from ..." He tapped his fingers against the glass, savouring the predicament I was in, playing with time and my nerves.

"Just spill it."

He swirled the glass in his hand thoughtfully before he downed it to the very last drop and set it down, his fingers remaining on the rim as his eyes fixed on me. "You're in debt, Elynn. I'll protect your siblings against the pandemic. Any more wishes, my *princess*?"

Now he was mocking me and finding it amusing, but I didn't let it get to me.

"Do you promise to do whatever it takes to prevent them from dying?"

He hesitated to reply, and I took it as a negative answer. If I knew how to do a magical oath, I would. It seemed a more reliable option than trusting someone I definitely shouldn't.

"Yes," he said impassively. "I promise. Now feel free to leave."

I didn't want to stay in the same room with him any longer either, but before I left, I took the pile of books with me.

Although his promise didn't reassure me, Thea had once mentioned that morphs took promises seriously. Drayard was a morph. Perhaps he'd keep his promise. He had to. But maybe that was only the naïve part of me striving to surpass the obvious.

I couldn't do anything to prevent the plague from catching my siblings—if it hadn't already—while I was stuck in the castle, managed by the most dangerous creature alive. The creature that had no reason to spare two human lives when his walls were built of thousands of their bones.

XXXIV

I didn't see Drayard for the rest of the week. Despite my concerns for my siblings' health, I was relieved he was staying away from me. Whether it was intentional or not, it didn't matter. Life in the castle was far better without encountering him, even with the constant reminder of bones lurking beneath every step I took.

Half of my days were spent in the library, while the other half were dedicated to sewing. As promised, I had received all the supplies and a sewing machine. For the first time, I had the freedom to create whatever I desired with high-quality fabric. And at night, when sleep eluded me, or I was interrupted by nightmares, I sketched.

Within a week, I grew accustomed to Baby's and Blossom's unappealing appearances. As I got to know them better, I learned they weren't as repulsive or sinister as I initially thought when they emerged on the twins' birthday. In fact, their company became rather pleasant, and I even taught Blossom the art of embroidery.

Occasionally, shadowy figures resembling people would flit through the corners, or eerie sounds would echo during quiet times. Each time, I dismissed them as mere tricks of light or figments of my imagination. But as the notion of ghosts became more compelling, I found myself reluctant to let the bat girls leave my room after they helped me prepare for the day. Instead, I asked them to hang out with me. Now, both lounged in my bedroom.

While I sat on the settee, stitching the gown I had been working on for a week, the bat girls occupied themselves with their own activities. Baby was contemplating her long and sharp talons, while Blossom was examining my sketched designs.

"Do you ..." I said into the silence, unsure how to ask it without suggesting that I might be descending into madness in this Gods' forsaken castle. "Do you sometimes hear strange ... funny noises?"

I caught them exchanging glances with each other before Blossom replied, "No."

"Do *you*?" Baby cocked a navy-blue eyebrow.

"Perhaps. But if you don't hear them, it's probably just my sleep-deprived mind conjuring up illusions."

Insomnia had been plaguing me since the horrors of Asenah's mansion, and it surely wouldn't disappear in the place where human bones adorned the walls.

"Are Baby and Blossom your real names?" I asked, eager to change the subject.

"No," Baby answered, not looking away from her talons. "We were given these names by the first men we had intercourse with."

"Didn't you have parents to name you?"

Blossom raised her eyes off the sketchbook. "No, we—"

Baby nudged her, and Blossom focused back on the sketches. I watched them suspiciously, meeting Baby's resolute gaze. I decided to drop the matter. I didn't care to learn more about some harlots anyway.

"How often do you satisfy Drayard's needs?"

Blossom grimaced as she turned the page, while Baby showed no reaction. "Almost daily, love. Why do you ask?"

My cheeks burned as I continued sewing, attempting to shrug it off as nonchalantly as possible. "For no reason at all. Just curiosity."

Baby smiled widely. "You're jealous."

"What?" I forced out a laugh. "That's ridiculous!"

Blossom glanced up from the sketchbook. "She *is* jealous."

Before I could deny it, Baby said, "Right? She's blushing like a little girl with a crush!"

They burst into laughter, and I clenched my jaw, choosing to ignore their teasing. Although I would have liked to shoo them out, doing so would only prove their point.

Finally, the laughter subsided, and Baby adopted a serious tone. "All right, but on a serious note ... we are not his whores, love."

I paused my sewing, bewildered by her statement.

"We aren't anyone's whores," she continued. "We live however we want, do whatever we want, shag whoever we want." Her smile grew bolder with each declaration.

"I don't understand. What about that incident in the Realm of Bones with Fillan and Lupin?"

Blossom adjusted herself into a sitting position. "It was all His Highness's idea."

"What?"

"He didn't go into details," Baby added. "All he did was tell us what we had to do, handing us syringes filled with something we were ordered to use on the twins' precious parts. We didn't question it. We aren't allowed. *But* he vaguely mentioned that they were abusers. How he knew that, only the Gods could tell."

"He knows everything," Blossom mused, impressed.

Not everything. I wanted to disagree with her but decided against it.

"Whether they were abusers or not," Baby said, "we came to spare those girls a few safe months at least. Blossom and I know what it's like to be abused, and well, that's been one of our proudest works, hasn't it, flower?" She glanced at Blossom expectantly.

Blossom nodded without looking at Baby.

I swallowed hard. "Thank you."

Baby's expression shifted from pride to shock.

Blossom raised her eyes from the sketchbook. "You were ..."

"Not only I, but the other maids were their victims. I've sworn to make them pay someday, even if it costs me my life."

Blossom slipped off the bed and approached me. She

perched beside me and tentatively placed her furry hand on mine. I managed a faint smile.

We sat like that for a little while until I asked, "If you're not Drayard's whores and you can choose to do whatever you want, then why are you still here?"

"Drayard freed the bats from centuries of whoring when he became king," Baby explained. "He gave us a choice: live a mundane life in the towns or work for him with the right to leave whenever we liked. Most chose an independent life, but a few, including Blossom and me, chose to work for the King."

"But why? He's horrible."

"The luxury was the main reason," Baby said. "We're whores for expensive things. Also, Blossom and I aren't family-oriented. Outside the castle, we'd have nothing to do apart from partying every day. And last but not least, Drayard isn't the Bloodsucker everyone fears." She paused, thinking with one eye closed. "Not most of the time, anyway. He's tolerable, indeed cold, but working for him isn't hell."

I hardly believed anything she'd said about Drayard was true. Perhaps they had been told to say that by Drayard himself. But I doubted he was the type of person who would try to prove his virtue through the bats that worked for him. He had never justified his actions, but I couldn't dismiss the possibility of him ordering the bats to speak well of him in my presence.

"If you're not whores," I said, "why keep the names men gave you?"

They both smiled knowingly, but it was Blossom who answered. "Those names never let us forget our past, all that we've been through. This way, we see what a long path we've come, forging us into the strong women we are today."

XXXV

I enjoyed breakfast alone in the dining room, savouring a plate of fruits and a glass of grape juice. I felt like a princess.

Technically, I was one of both empires, but I refused to think about my biological parents and the titles that belonged to me.

Perhaps I was more superior to humans and could live for a thousand years, but my heart was a stranger to this world. I had been raised as a human; my family were humans, and I had spent most of my life surrounded by them. They were my species, regardless of what others or Drayard might say.

"Good morning, Honeylove."

Could I have summoned the villain just by thinking about him?

I tensed as his deep voice rang behind me, disrupting the peaceful atmosphere. With his unexpected appearance, he effortlessly ruined my breakfast and the day ahead.

Drayard sauntered beside me and casually plucked a raspberry from my plate. I shot him a glare as he dropped it into his mouth.

"Why must you ruin my wonderfully passing week?" I didn't even try to conceal the bitterness in my tone.

"I haven't seen you in a while. Just making sure you're alive and well, and of course, I couldn't let you get too comfortable and forget to stay wary of my presence." He moved away from me. "Living like a princess, huh?"

I held back a frown at hearing that word again.

"But isn't that what I am?" I reached for my glass. "A princess?"

"You are," he agreed. "But nobody knows it other than me."

I took a sip, unable to suppress a smirk.

"Ah," he said with a sigh. "You've told somebody already, haven't you?"

"Of course. The bats ought to know with whom they're spending their days."

"You made friends?"

"Why does that come as a surprise?"

He pulled out a chair and sat down, surprisingly choosing a seat one space away from me and not at the head of the table.

"Do you trust them?"

"Do *I* trust them?" I raised my eyebrows, puzzled by his question. "They've been working for you for six years while I've known them for a *week*."

He stared at me for a moment, unsettling me, but then he smiled, and strangely, the tense atmosphere dissipated.

"You didn't sit doing nothing, I see."

"No, I did not," I admitted. "I have some questions to ask since you know a lot, and reading books takes too much time. It's easier to learn essential information from you."

"I believe you're not going to ask if unicorns exist."

"If? Of course, unicorns exist."

He gave me a droll look. "Do they?"

"Yes, they do." I met his gaze steadily, daring him to disagree with me.

"Hate to disappoint you, but I've travelled the world, and I haven't seen anything close to a unicorn."

"It's because you haven't searched for it."

"We don't always have to search to find something."

"Why?"

"Because we don't always know what we're looking for until it finds us."

I shook my head unconsciously.

"You don't agree with me?"

"How high do you stand in the hierarchy?"

One side of his mouth quirked at the sudden change of subject. He didn't call me out on it and proceeded to explain.

"At the highest is the emperor, followed by the King of kings and queens, and then the rulers of other realms. While I may not hold all the power, I still have a considerable amount of it."

Although all I had seen of Nayden was his back, I had sensed no power emanating from him, unlike Drayard. Perhaps it was because I was viewing him from Drayard's perspective, or maybe it was because, regardless of who wore the bigger crown, Drayard surpassed them all.

"If women are deemed lesser than men, then what does Nadira Haroun do?" I went on. "What authority does she hold as an empress?"

"Sleeping with her brother."

It was meant to be funny, but it only earned him a pointed look from me. He chuckled.

"Why is Nadira called an empress if she has less power than her brother?"

"Until Nayden doesn't find a wife—which I doubt he ever will—his sister will remain as an empress."

"Have you ever knelt before her?"

His expression turned serious. "I kneel before no one but myself."

I blinked several times. "You are full of pride, aren't you?"

"Hardly."

Liar.

He winced at that.

But before he could object, I pressed on, "Does that mean you've never knelt before Nayden, the emperor?"

"Like I said, I—"

"All right, all right, I understand. 'I kneel before no one but myself'," I mimicked him in a deep voice, and a smile tugged at his mouth as he rolled his eyes. I chose to ignore it, as well as the warm sensation in my belly. "But Asenah is a queen. How has she come to earn that position if the empire disapproves of female rulers?"

"Asenah's father was an interesting man." He leaned back in his chair. "He had a tendency to challenge the norms. When he fathered only one offspring—a daughter—he was expected to betroth her to one of the royal wolves of the empire, but he didn't. He believed his daughter was well-suited to lead their realm independently.

After his demise in the war, and with his daughter becoming a queen, naturally, a scandal ensued. Many insisted that her cousins should inherit the crown, but she dismissed their claims with laughter. Her cousins were immature fools, more interested in festivities than ruling. Besides, Lupin and Fillan didn't protest. Neither of them wanted to be a king. With no other male heirs in the high-blood wolf family, Asenah retained her crown. That's why she has remained a queen."

"But is she still expected to marry someday?"

"Yes, but she's about as interested in marriage as our dear emperor."

Indeed, Asenah wasn't interested in men to begin with, and marriage was out of the question.

"But I still don't understand why she flirted with you."

The mere memory of Asenah trying to seduce him while I was sweltering in the heat of the greenhouse summoned the same disgust I'd felt then.

"To find out my schemes."

A simple, nonchalant answer, which made sense. I simmered in silence, reluctant to ask another question. "Could you tell me more about how the empire was founded? How did morphs become rulers and all?"

I expected him to mock me, but instead, he nodded, his expression steady, as if he understood why I knew so little.

He remembered what I'd said near the ocean, and he wasn't judgmental. A weird feeling blossomed inside of me, and I wasn't sure what to make of it.

"Hundreds of years ago, your ancestor Macegan saved all three species in an ancient war against other continents, crowning himself and his future generation as eternal rulers," he began.

"But we, dragons, were seen as a threat to him and the Haroun dynasty. He bargained with my ancestors. Macegan would grant them an island and a title ranking them higher than the other kings in exchange for their promise never to try to usurp the empire. They signed a contract bound by magic to ensure their compliance.

"After a hundred and five years of war, when humans, enchanters, and morphs were no longer united, the Haroun family remained as the supreme rulers. They have the full power of all the realms except mine. Of course, if any burden falls on the empire, it also affects my realm, and the emperor can make drastic changes if the monarch of the Realm of Embers violates any term in the archaic contract."

"What are those terms?"

"The main one is that dragons can never breed with lion morphs."

"Phew." I wiped my hand across my forehead for emphasis. "I'm safe then."

He smiled, looking down at the table.

"What are the others?" I asked.

"The rest are inconsequential. The Realm of Embers will continue to be ruled by dragons, or a half-dragon now." A faint smile graced his face, but a hint of sadness appeared behind it.

I didn't question it, swirling the juice in my glass as I thought. "Hypothetically speaking, if one day I reveal myself as a daughter of Tatyana Haroun and morphs believe me, will I have the right to be an empress and rule all the"—I recalled the map I'd seen in the library of the Realm of Bone's mansion and counted the number of realms in the Empire of Beasts—"five realms?"

Drayard searched my face as though I was hiding something, his finger tapping the wood soundlessly. "You'd have the right by bloodline, yes," he said. "But it would be almost impossible."

"Why?"

"First of all, Nayden would never allow the daughter of his exiled sister to ascend to his throne. Second, even if Nayden were to vanish, morphs wouldn't accept a female ruler, particularly a half enchantress. And third, even if you were to become an empress, you'd be forced to marry a noble morph. Your future husband would hold more power than you. I know it sucks," he remarked, noticing the fire in my eyes that surely burned with indignation, "but that's how society is nowadays. Unless it changes, granting female leaders equality to male ones."

But I wasn't considering becoming an empress someday. Dear Gods, I didn't even regard myself as a princess of the Empire of Beasts. But the thought of having power, much greater than Drayard's, tempted me.

I snapped out of such absurd thoughts.

"What about my siblings? Are they all right?"

"Your sister and brother, to my knowledge, are both in good health. The plague hasn't affected them yet, unlike the other thousand humans who've recently died."

My heart sank. "That many?"

He nodded.

Rage towards the emperor and whoever ruled the Empire of Skies boiled within me. They were killing *my people.* The disease they'd spread over the Mortal Region had claimed my mother's life. Nayden and the emperor of the Empire of Skies were already a part of my ever-growing blacklist.

"How can you know my siblings are well if morphs can't enter the Mortal Region?"

"I have connections that some heads of authorities are unaware of."

I was sceptical, but he didn't seem to be lying. But then again, what did I know? I had no way of telling what lay behind his calm façade.

"If you have connections, then what if I wrote a letter to them? Would it reach them?"

He hesitated before replying, "I can arrange that."

I perked up. I hadn't expected him to agree, and his positive response brightened my day once again. "Really?"

"Yes."

I could have hugged him, or even kissed him out of sheer joy. Of course, I refrained, hiding my excitement.

"Do you know if Chase is infected?" It was a challenge to say his name out loud without gagging.

"Is he your former fiancé?" He asked, to which I nodded. "I

don't know, Elynn. Do you care about him that much?"

Huffing, I crossed my arms. "How did you know the twins were abusers?"

A flicker of surprise crossed his face before it transformed into annoyance. "The bats told you."

"Even if they did, don't you dare take your anger out on them."

His brows furrowed. "I wasn't planning to."

I watched him, suspicious. But then I returned to my questions, not trying to figure out whether he was lying. "So? How did you know the wolves were abusers?"

"I have sources."

"All right, then why disable them? What good did it bring you?"

"I wasn't invited to their birthday. I had to bring a gift."

His lie didn't impress me. "I need a real reason."

He fell silent. I waited, but he simply held my gaze. He wasn't going to answer.

I stood up, pushing back my chair with a scraping sound, and headed for the exit.

"I'm not done, Elynn."

His commanding voice made me pause. I glanced back at him over my shoulder, irritated to the bone. "You're speaking now?"

"How do you like Hellrock Castle?" He deflected my question. "I prefer honesty."

I turned to face him. "Why should I answer you if you refuse to answer my questions?"

"You've forgotten who—"

"Oh, spare me," I interrupted boldly. "For the record, no, I haven't forgotten who you are. You might be many people's walking nightmare, but you're not mine. I'm not scared of you. After all, you're bound by the magical oath to protect me. You can't harm me. So, tell me, Drayard, why should I answer you when you can't answer me? Where's the fairness in that?"

He reached for my glass, drained the juice to the dregs, and then set it down. "Just answer the question, please."

I let out a short laugh. "Burn in hell."

"I already did, making a home out of it."

Again, that same note of sadness, but I refused to be affected by it.

I bit the inside of my cheek.

Fine, I told myself. *I'll give in this time. But only this time.*

"This," I declared, sweeping my hand around the room, "is horror. I hate it with every inch of my flesh. I cannot even go downstairs because I'm terrified to see the bones again. The reminder that they're there haunts me. I despise this place, this atmosphere, everything."

Despite my unadulterated truth, his countenance remained serene, impassive, and unwavering as before.

"Pack your things," he said.

"What?"

"Pack your things," he repeated. "You have an hour."

"But why—"

"Elynn, please do as I say. The clock is ticking, and you have less and less time to—"

"All right, I get it!" I gave a mocking bow. "No questions asked, *Your Highness.*"

Drayard snorted as I spun on my heel and left the room. But instead of returning to my chamber, I hurried to the library, grabbing the book of dragon tales.

XXXVI

Baffled, I stared at the place where Drayard had brought me, wondering how much his brain was actually damaged.

"Why are we here?" I asked.

Instead of answering, he turned and strode forward. I stood for a moment, suitcase in hand, before hastening to catch up with him. There had to be more to this than landing at the foot of the colossal volcano.

Perhaps he had brought me here to throw me into the lava. He could have lied about the magical oath protecting me as much as he could have made up about my siblings being alive and healthy. Yet, I trusted him. Or wanted to at least.

"Is the volcano active?" I asked.

This time, he answered. "No."

That was a relief, at least.

After approximately twenty steps, he came to a halt, drawing a knife before I could realise. I took a step back. He regarded me with a slight frown and ...

... slashed his palm.

"Why did you—"

Before I could finish my sentence, he pressed his bleeding palm against the hardened lava. I blinked in utter confusion.

When he retracted his hand, a peculiar sound emerged, one I couldn't quite name—a mixture of grinding and hissing.

Drayard stepped back, and the wall began to slide open in front of us.

"What the ..." I trailed off.

As it opened, the eerie sound ceased. Cautiously, I stepped closer, finding a staircase descending into total blackness. Drayard extended his hand to me, and I looked at it, then at his eyes. "There's no way I'm going in there."

He smiled, a glint in his eyes, and I didn't think it was because of the afternoon sun. A spark caught my eye, drawing my attention back to the stairs. Where once had been all darkness, now torches were aflame, casting a glow on the stairs.

"Your choice." Drayard began his descent down the stairs.

I hesitated, and the same weird sound returned.

"You have five seconds to change your mind, or it's closing!" he warned me.

Without further hesitation, I rushed down the steps, the bright light fading rapidly. Fear gripped me, afraid to be crushed by the closing door that I didn't realise I was clutching onto something, digging my nails into something warm and firm. It wasn't until the entrance closed, leaving only the torches to light the stairs, that I felt it was Drayard's jacket sleeve I was clinging to as if my life depended on it.

Our gazes met.

I shot back, releasing his sleeve, and pressed the suitcase against my chest, my heart pounding.

He gave me the most self-satisfied smirk I'd ever seen. "I see where your trust lies."

"It doesn't ..."

His smirk broadened into a grin. "Right."

In his casual manner, he shoved his hands into his pockets and continued descending. I breathed in to collect myself and followed suit. The stairwell wasn't long, and soon we reached the ground of the narrow hallway, illuminated by torchlight.

No, not by torchlight, but by the glow of lava obstructing our path, forming a wall ahead.

Once again, Drayard performed the same ritual, pressing his bloody palm to the wall near the lava. To my amazement, the lava wall parted, opening a safe passage. He went through it, and I followed. After these magical discoveries, I didn't think anything would surprise me anymore.

But, if I were to be honest with myself, I might be proven wrong once again.

"Is it all magic?" I asked in undisguised awe.

"Yes."

But before I could continue my admiration, the floor switched beneath me. My heart dropped, knees wobbled, and unable to maintain my balance, I sank to the ground, releasing my grip on my suitcase. The solid stone beneath me transformed into a pool of lava. Despite my rising panic, I reasoned that it couldn't be real. But the image of kneeling on what seemed like a transparent platform over the lava hole did little to ease my nerves. And to my horror, the level of lava was rising.

"Drayard?"

He glanced over his shoulder. "Yes?"

I tried to move but found myself stuck. I couldn't budge or stand, not due to fear paralysing me, but because of some other supernatural reason. The lava continued to swell and rise, both puzzling me and scaring me. How was it possible?

"Don't panic," Drayard said calmly, making me feel more panicky. "Repeat these words: I surrender to fire."

"What do you mean? The lava is literally rising, Drayard!"

"Just repeat the words, Elynn."

"I surrender to fire. I surrender to fire! I—"

Everything was gone. The rocky walls and the rising lava were replaced by a completely different scene. Before me stood a staircase, carpeted in crimson, leading to a landing where two flights branched off to the left and right. The staircase matched the brocade walls of deep red and gold, which were half-panelled with dark wood.

On my left and right stood wooden double doors, sparking wonder about what lay behind them, as well as what awaited at the top of the stairs.

"What you saw was an illusion, meant to mislead any intruders who managed to pass the other obstacles," Drayard explained.

"That's ..." Somehow, I rose to my shaky limbs. My heart returned to its normal rhythm as I struggled to find the perfect word to define my current feelings. But words failed me, and I settled for a simple, "Whoa."

"It is," he agreed with a boyish smile. "Welcome to my humble abode, Elynn."

I gaped at him. "This is your home?"
Drayard nodded.
"And what about the castle? Isn't *that* your home?"
"Save those inquiries for later," he said. "I'm taking you out tonight. Be ready in"—he glanced at the Grandfather Clock on the left—"nine hours." He was about to leave when he halted before the stairs and threw me a glance back. "Don't go to the left side of the staircase. Other than that, you can roam wherever your heart desires."

With that said, he ascended the stairs and disappeared into the forbidden side, leaving me perplexed.

My attempts to gather my thoughts went for nought. I concentrated on my surroundings, checking what was behind the left doors first. When I opened them, mostly darkness greeted me, but I discerned a room reminding me of a dining room. It was much smaller and emptier than the one in the castle, with only a table and chairs for six people.

I closed the doors and approached the last room. Expecting darkness once again, I was surprised to find a burning fireplace inside. I snorted quietly at the irony of needing a separate source of warmth within the volcano.

But once I stepped foot inside the room, something caught my eye—a shape I could never have imagined encountering again. I froze, then slowly turned my head to the left.

My peripheral vision hadn't deceived me. The grand piano was utterly real.

Humble abode was not the phrase for a place with a grand piano.

Stirring with excitement, I approached the piano and placed my palm flat on its smooth, gleaming cover.

The piano's elaborate design closely matched the one I'd always dreamed of owning from my days of playing the old piano in the cottage. The dark wood tones, which complemented the room, were the only exception. Crafted for professional performances in front of thousands, it must have cost a fortune.

I settled onto the bench and lifted the lid carefully. Running my finger over the keys, the growing sound tipped its way to my music-missed ears. I felt myself beaming. It had been a while since I'd practised, but as I pressed the first notes of the song I knew like the back of my hand, my fingers remembered their way across the keys as though a three-month break from playing hadn't existed.

I didn't play for long since I had work to do, but I planned to return to it later. I retraced my steps back to the foyer and lifted the suitcase. As I looked up to ascend the stairs, I saw two girls standing on top of them.

My lips had made a secret deal to betray me because I smiled.

Later that day, I was in the new bedroom, which I believed was mine now. It wasn't as spacious as the previous one, but it held a better aura. I felt more comfortable in the smaller, still canopied four-poster bed, and I preferred the soft glow of the wall candles to the imposing chandelier. Being here just felt ... right.

I picked up a crimson crayon, biting my tongue in concentration as I coloured the sketched outline of a suit. A smile tugged at my lips as it gradually came to life before my eyes, just as I had imagined.

"Why aren't you dressed up?"

I flinched, looking up at the bat girls standing at the doorway.

"Dressed up?" I asked.

Baby took a step towards the bed. "Have you forgotten your date with Drayard?"

I winced. "A date?"

She leaned over, reaching for my sketchbook, but I pulled away.

"Not a date," Blossom corrected as she walked to the armoire and flung its doors wide open, revealing the array of clothes brought from the castle by the bats. It still amazed me that I had so many outfits to choose from when, merely three weeks ago, I'd been wearing a maid's uniform every day. "He wants to take you out somewhere and insists that you wear something more formal." She examined the dresses, dismissing them one by one with a frown.

To answer Baby's question, no, I hadn't forgotten what Drayard had said before he left. How could I? I just didn't want to go anywhere with him, especially when he didn't even bother to ask if I wanted to go or not. But I didn't have a choice, did I?

"Stand up, love," Baby ordered, her hands on her hips. "I need to fix your hair."

With a frustrated grunt, I clapped the sketchbook shut and put it in the drawer. I didn't need Blossom stumbling upon the drawing of a man's suit and bombarding me with questions I wasn't prepared to answer. I slid off the bed and approached the vanity where Baby awaited, ready to work her magic on my hair.

Blossom opted for the gown I had spent a week working on, rather than choosing one of the carefully selected ones from the wardrobe at Hellrock Castle. Baby lectured me about my behaviour in front of Drayard, but I ignored her advice to rein in my attitude, as I had no intention of doing so anyway.

Baby styled my hair into an elegant bun, adorning it with an antique comb that must have been expensive. Once she completed my hairstyle, she powdered my face without warning, causing me to sneeze. I shot her a pointed look, but she didn't bother to apologise, proceeding to paint my lips dark red to match the gown. Then, Baby and Blossom led me to the mirror to behold the masterpiece they had created. I couldn't help but marvel at the gown *I* had created without ever intending to wear it.

I had always known I was beautiful, but the woman staring back at me in the mirror caught me off guard. The puffed sleeves of the wine-red gown draped over my arms, revealing a glimpse of my cleavage and shoulders. The skirt was embroidered with darker patterns, and the slit on the right side tore through the layers of gossamer, opening a view of my slender leg. I hadn't worn anything of burgundy before, and I should have, for it complemented my honey-covered skin more than any other colour.

"She's radiant," Blossom marvelled, her chin propped on her knuckles. "Doesn't she look radiant, Baby?"

"Thanks to my skills as a beauty expert, she does," Baby replied with a hint of humour.

The corner of my lips twitched. I did look and even felt radiant. But there was one minor detail about this look that I disliked.

They had dolled me up like this for Drayard. If it weren't for him, I wouldn't be wearing this dress and looking like this. But for some reason, I didn't change into something less ... me.

The girls accompanied me downstairs. I struggled to avoid stepping on the skirt, fearing that a misstep would send me tumbling forward, providing amusement for the bats.

Baby would definitely laugh while Blossom might try to help me out.

Drayard, as always, appeared unexpectedly. I paused on the last step, as if his mere look rendered me still. He eyed me without any shame, making me feel uncomfortably exposed under his gaze. However, I returned the favour, studying his appearance.

I had never seen him wear such elegant clothes. I could tell he put thought into his attire. Perhaps *too* much thought. He rocked a black suit, an elaborate cravat, and something of the same colour was folded over his arm. The waistcoat matched my gown, which bothered me. I glanced at the girls, who had smug expressions on their faces.

I clenched my teeth.

"I don't recall anyone nowadays wearing anything as daring as you." He stretched his hand out to help me descend the last step, pretending to be a gentleman.

I stepped down the last step, disregarding his hand. "Of course, you don't. I designed it."

His eyebrows rose, but he banished the expression in no time, retracting his extended hand.

As I moved past him, his gloved hand closed over my arm, and his mouth appeared unsettlingly close to my ear.

"It suits you well. Burgundy in particular," he whispered. "You should wear this colour more often. You look as enchanting as the sky at dusk."

I looked up at him, our eyes locking.

My heart skipped a beat.

I swallowed.

"And you look as hideous as the beast you are," I stated, not forgetting to add, "If it was supposed to impress me, you failed pathetically."

He snorted, releasing my arm, and I pulled away from him. "Here, put this on." He handed me an ink-black cloak. I regarded it with disdain. "Elynn, please don't ruffle my feathers tonight."

I glanced back, but no one was on the stairs. The bat girls had left before I could even notice.

"I will, but first things first." I slid my two fingers into my cleavage, and Drayard averted his gaze. I drew out an envelope, battling a smirk. "If you promise this will reach my siblings, I'll be on my best behaviour tonight."

He searched my face for a lie, but I didn't give away anything.

At last, he took the envelope from my fingers and slipped it into his inner jacket pocket. Then he extended the cloak to me. "A promise is a promise."

"You didn't say if you promised."

He sighed. "I promise your letter will reach your siblings."

I narrowed my eyes. Instead of snatching the cloak as I'd planned, I accepted it with the grace of a well-mannered lady and draped it over my shoulders.

I wasn't prepared at all for what the night had in store for me. *But here goes nothing.*

"Where are you taking me?"

This time, Drayard didn't transport us by shapeshifting into a dragon. Instead, he flew us closer to the legendary City of Fire in his half-form, and now we were taking the route on foot. His fragrant smell lingered, as did the feeling of his touch when he'd carried me through the sky.

"It'll remain a secret for a little longer," he said.

I almost tripped on my long skirt, and I had no choice but to gather it up and gaze downwards to avoid collision with the ground. I wasn't used to wearing gowns, let alone my own. I should have shortened the skirt beforehand, but I didn't think about it until we left.

As we walked, I didn't notice when Drayard halted. He offered me his hand, causing me to pause and meet his gaze.

"Perhaps it's time to set aside your pride and take my hand, so your eyes won't be fixated on your feet," he suggested. "Shouldn't a princess walk with her head held high and her shoulders back?"

"A princess shouldn't be living under a volcano to start with," I retorted, "but in a castle, in a tower where chirping birds awaken her at dawn."

With that, I brushed past him, knocking away his hand as I went.

"You seem to have forgotten you were dwelling in a castle not long ago, and bats can fly, which is close to birds." He fell into step beside me. "Isn't that practically what you just described?"

I shot him a glare, but the hood obstructed most of my peripheral sight, making it difficult to see him. "Don't even get me started on the part where you tricked me and trapped me in the worst castle ever in the first place."

"I didn't trap you."

"No, that's *exactly* what you did, keeping me as your prisoner."

"Then what are you doing now if you consider yourself my prisoner? Not walking with your legs and hands free? With your mind free?"

"Yes, but with you as my chaperone."

He sighed. "You know I can't leave you wandering alone or else—"

I stepped on my skirt, tripping over it, but Drayard's reaction was as fast as lightning. He gently seized my arm, holding me until I regained my balance.

Swallowing, I looked up at him. "Thank you."

"No need to thank me. Instead, take my arm and spare yourself another fall as I might miss catching you next time."

"But you will always catch me, *my King*." I batted my eyelashes.

He didn't react to my playful tease but extended his arm, and I gave in, looping my arm through his. A pleased smile graced his mouth, tempting me to retract my hand, but I resisted, mindful of the promise I had made. I needed to prove to him I was trustworthy for potential future necessities.

We continued our stroll across the bridge as the sun half-set on the horizon. The sky shifted from ruby-red to amber, as though blood was seeping into molten gold, casting hues of dusk over the shimmering river. It was a sight unlike any I had seen before. If I were alone, I would stop to contemplate such beauty, but alas, I wasn't.

"I've been wondering ..." I began, indicating that I was about to ask a serious question. I knew he wasn't always in the mood to answer them.

"And what have you been wondering?"

"If the curse forces morphs to stay as beasts forever except at the equinoxes, why are you able to turn into this half-beast form?"

"It's called in-between form," he corrected me. "And unfortunately, no. There's no valid reason why we're not entirely animals. Some speculate that it's because the curse has flaws. Others think it's because the word *beasts* in the curse stands for in-between form, but most don't concern themselves with that."

As we approached the wooden sign with the carved letters reading 'The City of Fire', excitement surged within me. This was the city I had heard about since childhood. But I kept my emotions in check, biting the inside of my cheek.

As my gaze lowered to the stone-paved ground, memories of the experiences I'd rather forget flooded my mind. I scanned the path cautiously, half-expecting to find bones beneath my feet. To my relief, there were none.

"But don't those sorceresses living in the ... whatever the castle is called in the capital, know the real reason?"

"It's called Casidiarn Castle," he clarified. "Regarding the sorceresses in the castle, 'living' there isn't the right word for it."

"Then what is?"

He didn't answer, and I understood why.

We weren't alone anymore.

A few morphs were walking down the steep street as we made our way uphill. Orange-shaded three and four-story buildings were tightly packed together, making the street narrow enough to catch their whispers. Once the morphs saw Drayard, they hurried closer to the buildings to keep their distance from him, alarmed by who he was. Their reaction reminded me that my arm was hooked through the Bloodsucker's, yet it didn't terrify me as it perhaps should have. Apart from these few morphs, the city was quite deserted at this hour.

As we reached the highest point of the street, there were no morphs in sight.

I tilted my head towards Drayard. "Then what is the right word?"

"Sorceresses are imprisoned there," he said quieter now.

I scoffed at such falsehood. "They are traitors. Disgusting, disgusting traitors."

"Why do you think that?"

"Because they allow sixteen-year-olds to be offered, only for them to become slaves for the rest of their lives."

"Those sorceresses don't have a choice," he said in such a serene tone that my anger subsided. "They aren't Ascended. They don't have the power Ascended Sorceresses do. Also, they are Nayden's puppets. If they were to oppose him, they'd face torture. And any human would fear the morphs' methods of torture."

"What are their tortures like, then?"

"Believe me when I say you don't want to know."

"Perhaps I do."

"You don't."

Drayard took an abrupt turn into the dark alleyway, causing my heart to race. Despite the daylight, the shadows engulfed us, making it difficult to see anything.

"What are we doing here?" I whispered, not sure why. Perhaps it was an instinct to get quieter as it became dark.

"Hide your face behind the hood." His voice turned colder than usual. "And don't speak, or even look."

My heartbeat quickened as his words added to my unease. Once he stopped, it took me a moment to realise that we stood before the door. His three rhythmic knocks gave it away.

I lowered my gaze, pulling my hood down until it masked half my face.

As the door creaked open, my eyes were met by a pair of brown paws, resembling those of a bear. I tried to steady my heartbeat, aware that morphs' sensitive ears could pick up on it, and I couldn't afford to betray how nervous I was.

"Your Highness," the morph greeted Drayard, his voice masculine.

I was curious to observe him, but I forced myself to keep my gaze down. Despite my inquisitive nature, I knew when a line should and shouldn't be crossed.

Without a word, Drayard handed something to him. I heard

clanging, perhaps coins in a pouch.

"Please, let me show you and your date to your seats, Your Highness."

Merely the sound of the word *date* made me clench my teeth.

You know it's not a date, right? I warned him.

No answer came.

We stepped inside, the darkness effectively concealing my human-like features. Despite this, I kept my head low, unwilling to take any chances of being discovered. To their eyes, I was a human. That was why Drayard had instructed me to conceal my face in the alley. But why had he brought me here at all? Why risk his reputation?

When the morph opened the door, we entered the lit stairwell. With my free hand, I gathered the skirt to ascend the steps. Then we proceeded down a narrow passageway and soon halted before another door, which the morph opened for us.

"Enjoy the concert," he said.

Surprise rippled through me.

A concert?

I would have remained unmoving, but since Drayard's arm was entwined with mine, he pulled me inside. The door closed behind us, and I stood there, stunned by the sight before me.

A stage. A real *stage* with chairs and instruments lined up on it.

As I removed my hood, I met Drayard's gaze, a cheeky smile adorning both his face and eyes.

"A concert?" I marvelled, needing to confirm that my ears and eyes weren't deceiving me. It felt more like a dream than reality.

He nodded slowly.

I carefully pulled my hand from his arm and walked over to the balustrade, passing by two armchairs. The concert had yet to begin. Below me, some morphs were either searching for their seats or had already settled in, anticipating the start of the performance. I took in every detail of the concert hall: the balconies, the stalls, the intricate designs on the walls and ceiling, even morphs. Onstage, the instruments were neatly arranged, awaiting their musicians. I recognised them right away: flutes, cellos, violins, contrabasses ...

"Do you like it?"

I had been so captivated by the hall that I hadn't noticed when Drayard appeared beside me.

Instead of answering his question, I asked, "Why did you bring me here?"

"It's not a date," he reassured me. "I thought of giving you something you would appreciate. You deserve it. I've been unfair and heartless to you."

Now, he had my full attention instead of the hall.

"I know apologies won't fix anything, but I'm sorry for making you live in the castle for an entire week."

I blinked, baffled.

He turned to the stage and rested his arms on the balustrade. "Hellrock Castle has never been my home, Elynn."

He didn't elaborate further.

"I don't understand," I said.

He pursed his lips for a moment, then clasped his gloved hands together, lowering his gaze. "My father was born in it. I was born ... elsewhere. He spent his childhood in the castle. I spent mine on the battlefield. That castle isn't my home; I don't live there. I can't. I only make an appearance for meetings, and that's all."

"You don't live there just because you weren't born and didn't grow up in it?"

"No," he denied. "I don't live there because the hatred I feel for it is immeasurable."

"But why?"

He met my gaze. "Why do *you* hate that castle, Elynn?"

I frowned. "I told you. The bones, the aura ..."

Then it hit me, or so I believed, but that couldn't be right. He couldn't despise the castle for the same reason as I did.

"Is it possible that you can't live there because of the remains of ..."

I couldn't bring myself to finish without being reminded of the awful experience.

"It is one of the reasons, yes," he confirmed, and from the genuine look in his eyes, I struggled to convince myself his expression and words could be a trick. "When I was a boy, spirits of the dead haunted—or so I believed at the time—my every step in the castle. And they weren't friendly." He glanced at the stage and then snorted. "You must think I'm mad."

I didn't think he was mad because of that reason. I was more astounded that he was sharing something with me that had *him* involved.

His revelation reassured me that I wasn't losing my sanity by seeing ghosts in the castle when Baby and Blossom couldn't. But for some reason, I didn't relieve him by telling him I too could see them.

"Why did you bring me to the castle, then?" I asked. "To show me the bones, only to apologise for it later?"

"I was ... curious to see how you'd react."

"And did my reaction satisfy you?" I almost gritted out, feeling more repulsed by him than before.

He managed to face my glare. "I'm sorry."

I huffed, and gradually, the lights dimmed.

"It's starting." Drayard leaned away from the balustrade. "Take a seat next to me."

"No, I'll watch from here."

I was aware of my tone, sharp enough to slice through steel. I was playing with fire, but he had never reprimanded me for it before. Why would he now?

Only the stage lights remained alive as a group of morphs emerged from each side of the stage. Applause erupted from the audience, and though I hesitated at first, I joined in for the sake of art. As the performers took their seats, the hall descended into silence.

As they struck the first notes, the entire atmosphere shifted, whisking me away to a more serene place. I felt as though I was lifted off the ground and transported to a heavenly realm of music.

I closed my eyes, allowing myself to bask in paradise. A reminder of the last time I'd been somewhere similar twinged my heart. But it wasn't the same. Back then, it was just one man playing the piano, whereas now, the orchestra of morphs was wielding the instruments in flawless harmony.

As I opened my eyes, my gaze fell upon a scene below. A

morph couple was dancing away from the seats. The male spun his partner, drawing her close before gracefully dipping her. Her ashen hair brushed the floor before he lifted her back up.

Their dance wasn't perfect. Once in a while, they stepped on each other's feet or something else went wrong. But they laughed off each misstep, their broad, genuine smiles never faltering as they continued to dance.

Even from afar, I could sense the affection radiating from both, stirring a deep longing within me to dance as they did. But I didn't move, lacking a partner with whom I would want to dance like that and share my heart.

I didn't even know how to dance a simple waltz.

Why did I feel a sudden urge to cry?

Drayard had been watching me for quite some time, but it was only now that I noticed. Instead of taking a seat in the armchair, he remained by my side.

"What?" I asked.

His eyes shifted to the stage. "Nothing."

"Liar."

One side of his mouth quirked.

I rolled my eyes.

The song ended, and the sound of applause erupted. The couple returned to their seats, and another piece started.

A knot of sorrow swelled gradually in my chest with each immaculate piece. As the final notes of the fourth song rang out and the hall dissolved into a temporary silence, I couldn't bear it any longer.

They began another piece, but a lone tear was already sliding down my cheek. I needed to distract my mind before the music consumed me, along with the ghosts of the life I could never have. This environment felt like a cliff, and I teetered on its edge. It wouldn't be long before I plunged into a sea of tears.

But I couldn't cry. Not here. Not in front of anyone, certainly not Drayard.

"Once, my parents took me to a concert," I said, unsure if he was listening. Just in case, I pretended to push back my hair to disguise the wipe of the tear. "They brought Kristian and Gen along too. The orchestra hall wasn't something you'd find in our town, so my parents took us to the city. It was their gift to me for my fourth birthday. A professional pianist played that night, and it was the first time I heard someone who knew how to wield their instrument.

"Before I turned four, all I'd known about music were the lullabies my mum sang and the poor-quality instruments played in the streets. When I heard a piano for the first time at the concert hall, its sound spellbound me. I yearned to play like that pianist someday, even better. I asked my parents to buy me a piano, which they did. It wasn't the best quality, as pianos aren't the cheapest instruments for a family from a small town to afford, even if my parents didn't have to count every shilling back then. They could afford to hire a tutor for some time, and when they couldn't, I borrowed sheet music from the library. Since I'd learned how to read notes, I could continue to cultivate the skill."

I took a deep breath and glanced at Drayard, who was fully turned to me, all ears this whole time. "Music is the language my soul speaks," I said. "My salvation. My sanctuary. That's why I am grateful you brought me to the concert, regardless of the reason behind it. And not only for that. I thank you for putting the melody into my head when I was battling death. How did you do that, by the way?"

His smile was faint as he glanced at his hand resting on the balustrade. "Days of training."

"Days? You must be very talented, then."

Instead of confirming it, he asked, "If you hadn't offered yourself to the empire, would you have become a professional pianist like that man you saw playing in the city?"

I drew in a composing breath. "Becoming a pianist wouldn't have provided enough money for my family. It was too risky of a path. Besides, I would have had to live in the city, and it wouldn't have brought my family any fortune either. Just for the money, I would have married the wealthiest man in town. Even now, I know I wouldn't have pursued my dreams, as I'm not one to gaze at the stars and wish for something naïve to happen in my life. When I think deeper about it, it was my family who dreamed. I should have seen the difference all along, realised I was never one of them." I smiled incredulously. "I'm a realist raised in a family of dreamers."

XXXIX

The concert hall wasn't the only surprise Drayard had prepared for tonight. Once again, I hid my face beneath my hood as he guided me to another mysterious place. We entered another alley, and this time he handed a giraffe morph a pouch of coins. Without any questions asked, she escorted us upstairs, and we ended up on the balcony.

He had reserved a dinner under the moonlit sky, its soft glow seeping through breaks in the drifting clouds. Although it wasn't a date, it certainly felt like one. I watched him as he savoured roast chicken, confirming my suspicion that it was his favourite dish.

He caught me staring. "Is there something you want to ask me?"

There was indeed something on my mind, but I shook my head and took a sip of wine, focusing on pleasing my stomach instead.

After dinner, we left the city without haste. I didn't need to wear my hood this time as it was late, and not many morphs lingered in the streets once the sun descended. I trailed three steps behind Drayard, and neither of us exchanged words. He appeared distant, and I caught myself wanting to read his mind like he could read mine.

As the question I had been holding back at dinner resurfaced in my mind, I chewed nervously on the inside of my cheek. He came to a sudden halt on the bridge, turning to look at me. "What is it? You've been silent for a long time. It's unlike you."

It was indeed unlike me. Perhaps it was because what Drayard had done for me tonight was beyond anything I could have ever imagined—the concert, the dinner under the moonlight. I had expected nothing more than a decent evening, but I was taken by immense surprise. Despite the fatigue from many almost sleepless nights, I didn't want this night, with his kindness, to end.

"Have you ever tried to search for your mother?"

His shoulders tensed, and I braced myself for his typical deflection or a reminder that he didn't answer questions about himself. It was perhaps the most personal question of them all. I was entirely certain he wouldn't—

"No." He turned away and moved towards the balustrade.

I watched him, beyond astonished. He had actually answered. "Why?"

He gazed out over the tranquil river, and I approached to stand beside him.

"Why would I?" He turned to face me, his eyes shimmering with something I couldn't quite place. A deep redness overwhelmed the gold that I didn't know was possible. "It was her choice to leave me in my father's hands, and I respected it. Why would I search for someone who made it clear they didn't want anything to do with me?"

"But if you don't know who your mother is, and she's a bat, then what if you accidentally slept with her?"

Drayard grimaced, repulsed by question.

Asking something like that was indeed sickening to consider, but my curiosity got the better of me. After all, the bats had been whores six years ago. What if—

"Believe it or not, I haven't slept with any of the bats, and it's not because of who they used to be. I don't care about that. I simply don't like fooling around."

"You're not fond of the Sinner's Tango?"

His eyebrows shot up in surprise. "The Sinner's Tango?"

A chuckle escaped my lips, and I lowered my gaze, feeling the warmth spread across my cheeks. "It's what I call sexual intercourse."

"Why do you call it that?"

I shot him a knowing look. "Because it's a sin?"

He winced. "It's not a sin, Elynn. It's—"

I covered my ears. "Blah blah blah blah ..."

He emitted a short laugh. "To answer your previous question, I am very fond of *the Sinner's Tango*," he said. My smile broadened, and I couldn't force it away. "However, now, all I feel like doing is devoting myself to that one. My days of sleeping around with whoever I want are over."

"You sound like an old man."

"Yes, well, I am old compared to you and humans dying in their sixties, but in this world, I'm still considered a very young soul," he explained with an almost wistful smile.

"Yes, almost two centuries old still makes you a young soul. Sure."

His smile slightly widened.

As the hoot of an owl echoed through the air, my attention wandered to the few trees leaning over the river. Their drooping branches with leaves brushed against the glistening water. I'd observed before that the Realm of Embers wasn't the most wooded realm. It was mostly plain ground with old, yet well-maintained structures, and with distant mountains looming on the horizon. While it lacked lush greenery, it compensated with the soothing sounds of nature.

Despite scanning the surroundings for an owl, I couldn't find one, which left me somewhat disappointed.

"Have you found the one you'd want to pledge your devotion to?" The sudden question escaped my lips before I could stop it.

"What do you think?"

I searched his face, but his unreadable expression didn't reveal whether he'd laid his eyes on the future queen or not. Left with no other choice, I had to play a guessing game.

"Is it Asenah?"

I knew it wasn't her. There was just something about him that made me want to annoy him. I had asked him merely to see his reaction, which indeed met my expectations when he shot me an are-you-serious look.

My initial impression, while enduring the abnormal heat in the greenhouse, hadn't deceived me. I had surmised then that he wasn't fond of the Queen of Bones.

"Yes," Drayard responded in a serious tone. "She and I are a match made in heaven."

I was about to smile, but when I grasped the meaning of his words, I wasn't sure if it was appropriate.

The romantic relationship between him and Asenah couldn't exist, not only because she was interested in the opposite gender but also because he considered his life akin to hell. For me, life wasn't heaven, but it wasn't hell either. It was somewhere in between. So, how miserable did he have to be to think his life was equivalent to hell?

I pressed my index finger to my cheek and made a face, pretending to think carefully. I didn't forget to hum, which elicited a snort from Drayard.

"Oh, I know!" I exclaimed, pointing my finger up. "Is it Dara?"

Suddenly, all the fun vanished from his features as if it had never been there seconds ago. But it couldn't be her. Drayard was annoyed when Dara had interrupted his investigation in Casidiarn Castle. He didn't like her. But, if his mood changed at the mention of her, they must have some history.

"Did something happen between you and her?"

The seconds ticked by, and he remained silent. But I was patient.

I slept with her once, he confessed.

I stepped back, taken aback, though I should have expected it. But as I remembered Dara's small frame compared to Drayard's tall, sturdy build, and the fact that she was *my cousin*, I could understand why such a thought hadn't crossed my mind before.

Despite the discomfort, I asked. "Why do you have a problem with Dara? Why did she leave you to snoop around Casidiarn Castle after you threatened to reveal something to her future betrothed? What information do you have that could strip her of her title?"

He leaned away from the balustrade. "Here, royal girls don't have much to choose from. That includes their marriage and to whom they must yield their body first and forever."

Oh.

Since Drayard had an intimate interaction with her, Dara wasn't a *pure, untouched* princess anymore. If somebody learned she'd failed to fulfil her duties, she would get in deep trouble.

"But that's so unfair!" I exclaimed indignantly. "As much as I don't like Dara, she should have the right to do with her body whatever she pleases, not what others command."

"Yes." He eyed my gown, a smile pulling at the corners of his mouth. "I can very much see why you would think that."

My jaw dropped, and he laughed. Pressing my lips together to stifle a smile, I nudged his arm with my elbow. "Bastard."

When the fun ended, I inquired, "But don't you think people should have the right to do whatever they want with their bodies?"

"Elynn, this empire—the entire world—has tons of unfair convictions, laws, ancient conventions, and more. And if I must be truthful with you, women's privilege in arranged betrothals is the least of my concerns."

I frowned. "But it should be."

He didn't continue the topic, avoiding the argument that would have surely ensued between us. I didn't urge him to say more, even if I wanted to learn everything that concerned him, unless there was nothing. But there had to be. Why would he liberate morph bats from whoring, or command the bat girls to incapacitate the wolves' private parts if he had no concerns?

I rested my elbow on the balustrade, propping my chin on my palm. I didn't interrupt the silence between us, permitting the melodies of the owl, frogs, and crickets to fill the air.

Drayard straightened himself and turned to me. I watched him cautiously from the corner of my eye as he offered me his hand. "Dance with me?"

I snorted.

Undeterred, he repeated himself. "Dance with me, Honeylove?"

He was joking. He had to be. But his determined expression

told me otherwise. He was serious about this.

"Do you hear any music?" I asked. "Because I certainly don't. Besides, I can't see a reason why I should."

"But I do. I saw the way you were gazing at the couple dancing during the concert."

My heart stuttered. "And in what way was that?"

"Longing."

I wanted to look away from him, but I didn't allow myself to. If I did, he would know he was right, and that was the last thing I wanted.

"You don't know how to read my eyes at all, Drayard."

He smiled, and that was all it took for the weather to turn warmer. "Perhaps, but I assumed you might want to dance with somebody. Give it a try and see what it's like."

I looked at him, *truly* looked at him. Drayard wasn't *he*, the man from my trance. How could the Bloodsucker be the one I was perhaps meant to find and live happily ever—

I dismissed such thoughts. They were foolish, let alone naïve. Even if I was a princess, I didn't need Prince Charming. I didn't live in a fairy tale with a happy ending. If anything, I was a princess trapped by the monster. A prisoner, although I didn't feel like one when I should.

"All right, but longing?" I stalled, hoping he would give up and drop his hand, but he didn't.

There was a tiny part of me—the little girl who had listened to her mother read tales about dragons with her ears wide open—screaming at the opportunity to dance. And it was hard to silence her.

"You were thinking about somebody, weren't you?"

"No," I answered too fast, prompting a smile from Drayard. "I don't know how to dance anyway," I muttered, looking away.

"Consider yourself lucky. The best teacher out there is offering you his services for free."

I huffed. "Thanks, but I'll have to decline."

He moved closer. "What kind of princess will you be if you don't know how to dance, Honeylove?"

His warm breath tickled my skin, sending shivers skidding through me. I hadn't noticed how close he was to my face.

I bit the inside of my cheek harder than before, and a taste of blood touched my tongue. With effort, I released my cheek and whipped my head towards him, regaining control of myself. "I was never a princess. I am not one now, and I will never be. So, please, stop throwing that in my face."

He grasped my wrist before I could react, done with my resistance. As he tugged me towards his chest, I lost my breath from the unexpected touch. I looked up at him in surprise, meeting his gaze.

"You're *my* princess," he whispered, "but for your own safety, only the bats and I should know that."

For some time, I lost awareness of my surroundings as he guided me towards the middle of the bridge, dazed by the warmth of his touch, his closeness, his—

I forced myself to wake up.

"Oh, who are you trying to fool, Drayard? Even if I was wearing the hood, they saw my skin. Do you honestly believe other morphs won't have questions about why their King was going to a concert and having dinner with a human?"

He twirled me around and placed his hand on my waist. Strangely, I didn't feel the urge to push it away. His other hand's fingers laced through mine. Despite gloves separating our skin, his touch warmed something more than my hand.

"Put your left hand on my shoulder." His demand was mild—not one that belonged to the King or the Bloodsucker. That was why I didn't hesitate and obeyed, placing my hand on his shoulder.

"To answer your question, yes, there's a high chance they will, but why does it matter? What power do they have that I don't?"

"But can't gossip ruin your image?"

He gave me a meaningful look, and I realised how foolish my question was.

His reputation was already tainted. What harm would it do to him if the entire empire learned he was spending time with a human? Nothing. No one would take it seriously, assuming that the Bloodsucker would feast on her sooner or later.

"How are we supposed to dance without music anyway?"

A smile caressed his face, and a familiar tune began to play in my mind. I arched my brow in surprise. It was the same sonata he had sent me when I was dying in the Mortal Region.

As we began stepping in rhythm, I stared at our feet. He explained how to dance a simple waltz, but despite my efforts to follow his counting, I still managed to step on his feet. He usually acted like it hurt.

But when I had enough of his fake moans, I deliberately targeted his left foot with my heel. This time, he didn't fake a cry. Instead, he warned me that if I were to do it again, he would dispose of the piano in the living room. Such a barbarous threat turned me into a docile girl for the rest of the night.

As we moved step by step, the dance began to make sense. His patient counting guided me through each movement. His voice soothed me, and I hated that as much as his gloves.

"Why are you always wearing gloves?"

He ceased counting, and the music ended, but neither of us stopped dancing. "My hands are scarred."

"Are you ashamed of your scars?"

He was quick to answer. "No. I don't feel like exposing them to everyone, especially when I'm acting like a king. And the King shouldn't bare his real parts to the world, where there's always someone waiting for the shield to fall so they can strike."

Tonight was the first time Drayard was the most open with me. I wondered how long this would last. *If* it would last.

"But you don't have to act like a king when you're with me, do you?"

He spun me around before pulling me back to him. Silent.

"Drayard?" I prompted.

He sighed. "I'm afraid."

If we weren't close, I wouldn't have heard him. But I had. And I had expected anything but not this. What could he possibly be afraid of when he was the walking nightmare many feared the most in this world?

"Afraid of what?" I prompted.

Dancing became so natural to me that I hardly noticed when he had my full attention.

Although he didn't rush to answer, he did eventually. "I'm afraid if I show ... if I show more of what I am, there will be no way back."

He mystified me more than ever.

"Way back to what?"

"That's the thing, Elynn," he said. "It's already too late, I'm afraid."

I opened my mouth to speak, but he was faster. "Look at you dancing so well," he quipped, trying to lighten the mood. "Perhaps one day I'll teach you how to dance the tango as well." He winked playfully.

I couldn't help it. I threw back my head, laughing. But when I looked back at him, the smile reaching his eyes stole my laughter away. A smile like his could light up the Universe and outshine the stars if he just *wished*.

"Only if I let you," I whispered.

"Only if you let me," he whispered back.

I allowed myself to enjoy the moment and forget who he was. What devil, what title he wore. I forgot that the most terrifying tale had been written about him to scare children. I forgot he was in his in-between form, and something else flashed in his eyes, disappearing soon after.

But I had enough time to catch something rare and decent in his depraved soul.

Another nightmare invaded my sleep.

As usual, I woke up sweaty and out of breath, my eyes swollen from crying. I used my knuckles to wipe away the remaining tears.

I reminded myself that I was safe so far. Lupin and Fillan were in their realm, while Chase was in the Mortal Region. None of them could reach me here. Only the Bloodsucker could, but he didn't strike me as someone who would commit anything like those men.

As I crawled out of bed, I headed to the kitchen for a glass of water. Ever since the nightmares started plaguing my sleep, I doubted I would fall asleep again.

Before I reached downstairs, quiet music greeted my ears. I smiled at the recognition of the familiar melody. But my smile faltered when the wrong key was hit, followed by a string of swearing.

It restarted right from the beginning.

I tiptoed towards the living room and opened the door as quietly as I could, relieved that it didn't make a sound. I opened it wide enough to lean my head against the door frame and watch the creature who endeavoured his best to play the piece. The furrowed lines on his forehead, even visible from this distance, didn't suit his dragon-like face.

After starting over, he played decently until he reached the part where the melody intensified—the same part where he had failed earlier. I worried he might hit the wrong note again, but he navigated smoothly through the tricky part, and his wrinkles faded. He closed his eyes, as if confident that the rest of the melody would flow as smoothly as the beginning.

I closed my eyes as well, enjoying his playing, until I realised I was smiling. But my smile vanished, and my eyes shot open when he missed the right key again. He pressed multiple keys at once, creating a terrible sound that made my ears bleed.

"It's a higher chance you'll fail if you become so annoyed every time something goes wrong," I said.

He didn't respond, sitting with his eyes lowered, shoulders hunched, the tips of his wings and tail brushing against the floor.

"Tension doesn't help either," I added.

He straightened his shoulders. "Don't bother, Elynn. Go take what you've come here for and leave."

I stepped into the room and approached the piano instead. Leaning in, I rested my arms on its surface. Our eyes met, and I noticed tears tinged with redness before he quickly looked away.

He was crying. Actually *crying*.

But he didn't want me to see it. Perhaps he felt ashamed because I had caught a glimpse of the fragile boy within him—the boy abandoned by his mother outside the castle. Maybe that moment marked his breaking point, or maybe it was only one of many.

I couldn't allow myself to feel sorry for him or seek to understand the reasons behind his devilishness. Nobody was born wicked to the core, but I wouldn't dwell on why he had become the monster he was now either.

"Do you want to talk?" I heard myself asking.

I cursed my stupid heart. Anyway, he didn't answer.

"Drayard?"

He shot up to his feet and stormed out of the room. I stayed, fighting the urge to go after him. There was no way I was doing that. I had my own problems. I didn't need to care for the

Bloodsucker who had slaughtered thousands, if not millions.

Yet my legs carried me to him.

Traitors.

I saw him ascend the stairs, and I followed.

Stay away, Elynn. His voice sounded in my mind. *Don't bother yourself.*

I wish I could, but my innate kindness won't allow it.

He stopped on the stairs that led to his chambers, the side where I was forbidden to go for unknown reasons. I paused on the fourth step, but he didn't even glance in my direction.

"I'm not blind, Drayard. I can see that there's something wrong with you, and I'm not speaking about your corrupt nature. I don't know why it's like that, but I feel like ... I feel like I can *feel* you."

I wasn't sure why I was sharing this with him. Perhaps it was because I'd seen a glimpse of his soul when we danced. What I saw, merely a tiny fraction of him, intrigued me. I had no clue how it was possible to see one's soul, but I dared not question it.

"I feel like I can understand you, and perhaps I'll be unwise to say this, but whatever it is, you can tell me. Of course, if you don't want to reveal your heart to me, then perhaps there is someone else who is waiting for you to open up?"

I utterly doubted that to be the case. From what I had gathered during the times I saw him with someone else, he was cold towards them, speaking little or nothing if it didn't involve politics.

Drayard remained silent, but he didn't leave either.

I blamed my heart, which belonged to the human world and not here. In the world of beasts, my kindness, which I'd been taught to develop, could be my weakness.

"I feel like I'm communicating with the wall." I turned around, pushing myself to leave him alone. I'd tried to make him talk, but he refused. Whatever he was dealing with wasn't my problem anymore. In fact, it had never been my problem.

I headed into the kitchen, grabbed an empty glass, and filled it with water from the flask. Downing its contents in one swift motion, I hesitated before retracing my steps to the living room. There, I found Drayard seated on the bench again. Clenching my jaw, I proceeded towards the door.

Wait, his voice echoed in my mind.

I halted, but other than that, did nothing.

Stay, he said.

I debated. One part wanted me to stay, but the other, the wiser and colder one, told me to mind my own business.

"Please?" he asked, almost hopelessly.

Relenting, I turned around. He mustered a feeble smile and scooted over a little, making space for me. As I sat down, our shoulders touched, his body heat seeping through his shirt and warming me.

"Did you have a nightmare?" he asked, his tone suggesting he already knew the answer.

"Maybe."

"Do you want to talk about it?"

"Why should I talk about my demons if you refuse to talk about yours?"

"You don't need to worry about me."

"Oh, I'm not worried about you." I let out a short laugh. "But perhaps it would allow you to sleep better if you shared what's weighing on your chest."

"Would it make you sleep better if you shared your nightmares with me?"

I didn't answer.

"I see." His eyes fell on the piano keys.

Silence settled over the room, broken only by the rhythm of our breathing. I positioned my fingers on the correct keys and began playing the same song that Drayard had struggled with.

My fingers moved effortlessly across the keys, hitting each note with precision. After all, I'd been playing the piano for over fifteen years. I was a professional. I could perform in front of an audience without ever growing bored or tired because the music was my sanctuary.

When I finished, I met Drayard's gaze. His eyes, glowing like fire embers, held something I hadn't seen before. Something too good to be real.

Feeling suddenly shy, I looked away.

"Teach me how to play this song," he requested softly.

"I will if you tell me at least one reason why you're the way you are."

"What do you mean?"

"Why are you afraid to let anyone get to know you better?"

"I have trust issues."

I rolled my eyes. "Of course you do, but why?"

"I have trust issues. That's why I can't answer you." He gave me a silly smile.

"Fair enough." I looked at his hands. "If you want me to teach you, place your fingers on the keys."

As he did that, I was about to put my hands on his to guide him when a realisation struck me.

He wasn't wearing his gloves.

Of course, he wasn't. It would be weird if he wore them to bed, too.

There, on his ring finger, was a black ring adorned with a significant ruby. He must have hidden it under his gloves, along with the lighter lines on his red scales—*scars* he had mentioned once.

He then cleared his throat.

I'd been silent for too long.

I hastened to place my hands on his. Despite the dryness, his hands were warm and rough. *And* much too strained, like his body.

"Are you always this tense?"

"Yes."

"Try to relax. You can't play the piano with such tension, Dray."

His mouth curled into a smile, and I didn't understand why.

"What?"

"You called me Dray."

I hadn't even realised I'd shortened his name until he mentioned it. Feeling my cheeks flame, I looked down.

"You've never abbreviated my name before."

"I'm sorry. I shouldn't—"

"No, no," he burst out. "You can call me Dray. I don't mind."

His smile was so endearing that it brightened his eyes. I guided his fingers to the right keys, but they were still tense, although less so than before.

"Could you ..." He cleared his throat. "Say it again?"

"Say what?"

"My name?" he clarified, almost shyly.

The corner of my lips curved upwards, and I whispered while gazing deeply into his eyes, "Dray."

A new and intriguing emotion sparked in his eyes, one I hadn't seen before.

"Again." His voice dropped to a sensual tone, causing my heart to struggle to keep its normal rhythm. His face was so close to mine that there was almost no room left for oxygen.

"Oh," I breathed and bit my bottom lip, scarcely conscious of my actions, let alone the words about to escape. "Would you like me to scream it this time, perhaps?"

"Would you? Like to scream"—he leaned in even closer—"my name?"

I thought my heart would leap through my chest. My palms grew damp, and I was certain he could feel it, too. Despite my cheeks burning, I couldn't tear my gaze away from him, lost in his eyes. Then his eyes shifted to my lips.

I forced out a laugh, though it came out a bit strained, as I gently nudged his shoulder with mine, creating a healthy distance between us. At least he wasn't fixated on my mouth anymore, even though a part of me craved much more.

"Let's begin our lesson, shall we?" I suggested.

It was a miracle how my fingers remained steady on his hands despite the nervousness tingling throughout my body.

"If that's what you want, then I'm all yours to teach, Honeylove."

I pretended not to hear his innuendo. "First, you have to relax," I said, trying to keep my voice balanced, impervious to his charms, unlike my body. "And try not to dwell on anything. Let the music speak for you."

"All right," he complied. "Am I relaxed enough?"

"No."

"Do you want to know what could help me relax?"

I didn't need to be a mind reader to know what lurked in his mind flooded with darkness. All I needed was to see his suggestive expression, and I could guess.

"Knowing your perverted mind, I would rather not."

"Perverted mind?" He tilted his head to the side. "Since when is offering meditation considered a perversion?"

"Oh, do not lie!" I laughed, pushing him playfully. "That was not what you were going to say!"

His smile only grew. "And what did you think I was going to say, Elynn?"

As I shook my head, I noticed his hands felt softer under my touch.

"How interesting. You've relaxed."

He gave me a boyish smile.

I figured he could have relaxed sooner, but he found it amusing to toy with me first. But I didn't bother calling him out and began teaching him how to play, which lasted for the rest of the night. Most of the sonata he knew how to play himself, but some parts required my guidance. My hands remained on his until he felt comfortable playing on his own. In his first attempt, his fingers glided over the keys, not making a single mistake. Drayard was either a quick learner, or I was a good tutor. Perhaps it was a bit of both.

We didn't engage in heart-to-heart conversations, flirtation, jokes, or tears. No words needed to be spoken when the music spoke for us and our hearts.

But I wasn't sure if I should have heard any of that.

Dray wasn't home as often as I'd prefer. I had grown to treasure our sleepless nights, where I taught him how to play the piano or he taught me how to dance. Sometimes we talked, but neither of us spoke of our nightmares, nor did we ask about them.

"What's your biggest fear?" I asked Dray one night as I poured myself a glass of water, leaning against the counter. I watched him sitting on the kitchen floor, poring over my sketches.

"I don't have one." He flipped over the page to study another dress.

"I find it hard to believe." I took a sip. "Everyone has fears or phobias. Even terrifying men like you."

"But I'm not afraid of anything."

"You said otherwise when we danced on the bridge. You mentioned being afraid, but you didn't say of what."

He said nothing.

"Is it really the ghosts you're most afraid of?" I pressed.

He gave me a pointed look before continuing to inspect my creations. I recalled the words he had said at the concert. *And they weren't friendly.*

"What did you mean by saying ghosts hadn't been friendly?"

He hesitated before answering. "They haunted me. I was cautious in every room of the castle. They were also fond of messing with my head. Very much, if I must add."

"So, they're not your fear?"

He looked up at me, serious. "Elynn, I had many fears when I was a child, but I outgrew them. Like I said, I'm not afraid of anything anymore."

And there he was, lying to me.

"I'm claustrophobic," I admitted, hoping to encourage him to open up. "I'm afraid of small spaces."

He seemed to be contemplating something. "Interesting."

"Your turn," I prompted. "If you have a fear or phobia, you can tell me."

"I told you, I don't have either of those things."

"And yet, you're lying straight to my face."

He fell silent, and I ran my fingers through my hair, pushing them back from my forehead in frustration.

Unexpectedly, his voice echoed in my mind. *I'm not that fond of being left alone.*

His confession caught me off guard. I hadn't expected him to say anything at all, but it seemed he preferred not to say it out loud.

"But aren't you, like, always alone?"

"Am I alone now?"

"That's because you have me trapped in here."

His response to it was an eye roll.

I had noticed he began to roll his eyes more often as we spent more time together. Perhaps I had influenced him, but I didn't really mind when he rolled his eyes. It softened his features, making him seem less severe, tense, and cold-hearted. More ... real.

As I set my glass down, I settled in beside him, being careful not to touch his wings as I leaned against the wall. "I see ghosts, too."

I felt his astounded gaze on me.

"I saw the spirit of a boy in the Mortal Region," I explained. "Two days before the Summer Solstice. He helped me find a solution, a Conversion Potion, which turned me into Gen's lookalike. But I saw him because, before the Summer Solstice, spirits manifested themselves to human eyes, or so I thought until ghosts began haunting me in Hellrock Castle, scaring me with weird noises."

He chuckled incredulously, prompting a frown from me. "What's so amusing?"

Shaking his head, he continued flipping through the pages, practically beaming.

"What?" I urged, nudging him. "Tell me what it is!"

"It's nothing, Elynn. I just didn't expect that, that's all."

I studied his face, searching for a lie, but I couldn't detect one this time.

"What was it like in the war?" I managed to ask.

His shoulders tensed. "What do you think it was like?"

"Like a nightmare."

He smiled sadly. "Worse."

I swallowed, feeling my heartbeat quicken as I approached the question I'd been hesitant to ask ever since I saw a glimpse of decency in him. "Is it true? What the tale says about you?"

"I'm not even familiar with the tale humans have spun about me."

Summoning my courage, I recounted my favourite tale aloud for the first time. "'Once upon a time, the Bloodsucker was sent into the war camp. At first, he was a silent wolf and concealed his true nature. His peers went missing at night, and nobody knew why. Nobody dared to question the obvious. The Bloodsucker was feasting on them.'"

Lines appeared on his forehead.

"What?" I asked.

"Please, continue."

I hesitated before going on. "'As one night came, the battle began. Unable to hide his true nature any longer, he revealed his dark self. He sucked the blood of his enemies, set fire to those who tried to stop him, and even in the aftermath, still ravenous, he feasted on the fallen soldiers, tearing into their organs and consuming them whole.'"

I didn't include every detail, leaving out the part about stolen children. I wasn't sure if he would be willing to talk about his war crimes, and bringing up the children might discourage him from sharing anything at all.

He said nothing, his gaze distant as if he were elsewhere.

"Is any of it true?" I asked, bringing him back to the present.

"Yes."

But the emptiness in his tone contradicted it.

"You're lying."

He remained silent. For far too long.

"Why are you lying?"

My heartbeat raced as he stalled. I had hoped he would deny everything, reassuring me it was just a tale spun to frighten children who disobeyed their parents, but he didn't. He was lying. He must be. There was no way I'd been spending my nights with the same man described in the tale.

"I've never feasted on anybody's organs," he mumbled at last.

My heartbeat slowed down.

"But other than that, yes, I drained their life by sucking their blood. And it was indeed I who set aflame those who tried to stop me."

"But why be so cruel?"

"It's war, Elynn. It changes people. It leaves eternal scars not only on their bodies but inside their heads. It's something nobody can evade if they make it out alive. But none of us actually make it out alive." He sucked in a breath. "This one is a beautiful design. You are going to work on it, right?"

But I watched him as he poked at another dress.

"Dray—"

"No, please, Elynn." He met my concerned gaze, his eyes pleading. "Don't stir up those memories. I don't want to revisit anything from those times."

Questions formed on my tongue, ready to be voiced, but instead, I looked at the gown. I chuckled.

"What?" He arched his brow.

"It's a wedding gown."

He peered closer at it. "It's ... unlike any wedding gown I've seen before."

"I thought you had grown used to my scandalous fashion?"

His smile was faint. "*Grown used to* is not how I'd say it. More like I'm still adapting. But it is pretty. Are you planning to marry someone?"

"Yes." I puffed out my chest and deepened my voice. "I marry no one but myself."

He let out a snort. "I see ... I see. You're not only sharp-tongued but a mocker."

"And very beautiful," I added.

He laughed.

"What?" I feigned offense. "You forgot to add that!"

"You're gorgeous, Honeylove."

He averted his gaze, and I felt my cheeks flush.

He cleared his throat. "Are you planning to work on this dress?"

"I don't always bring my designs to life. Mostly, I'm just messing around. This dress is one of the many ideas I've played with."

"It doesn't look like messing around."

I said nothing, rising to fetch more water. My thirst had never been this intense at night before. I blamed the volcano, even though it was inactive.

As I drank water, a line formed between Dray's brows. I resisted the urge to step closer to see which design had caught his attention this time. He must not be fond of that one.

But he was staring at it so intently that I set my drink down and moved closer to him. As I saw the design, my heart stuttered.

I promptly seized the sketchbook, but he held onto it, raising a quizzical gaze at me. Without much effort, I wrested it from his grasp as he let go, allowing me to have it.

"Is the crimson suit considered messing around, too?"

My face burned. "It's not ..." I tried to find the right words to say, but either they didn't exist or I couldn't think of any.

The sketch wasn't supposed to be there. I had forgotten all about it. I should have reviewed my sketchbook, made sure there was nothing I wouldn't want him to see. But it was too late. Dray had already seen the sketch of a man's suit inspired by my trance.

He rose from the floor. "It's not what?"

"Ugh, nothing!" I attempted to pass him, but his fingers closed over my wrist.

"It isn't nothing if you're blushing. What are you hiding, Honeylove?"

I dropped my eyes to my slippers, feeling exposed. I should have handled this differently, but it was too late now. He had already seen my excessive reaction to what should have been no big deal, even though it meant a lot to me.

He grasped my chin tenderly and lifted it, searching my eyes.

"Elynn?" His voice was soft and concerned.

For some reason, I felt compelled to spill everything to him that had troubled me for four years. I felt like he was the only person who could understand, which was stupid as he might laugh at it, insisting that whoever the man from my trance was, he wasn't real. Dray didn't believe in unicorns ...

But he saw ghosts.

"Do you believe in trances?" I managed to meet his gaze.

He released my chin, and the heat left my skin. I ignored the knowledge of wanting it back.

"I do," he admitted.

I drew in a breath, steeling myself to reveal my secret I had kept from everyone until now. "A few years ago, while lost in music, I disconnected from my body and appeared in someone else's. It was almost like the time I accidentally entered your ..."

I halted mid-sentence, startled by a sudden realisation.

No, it couldn't be. I refused to believe it. Dray couldn't be *him*. When I was in his mind during the Autumn Equinox, I hadn't felt any presence of smoke, unlike in my trance. The likelihood of the Bloodsucker being my soulmate was perhaps none.

Perhaps.

But what were the chances that I had been spending time with my one all along?

"Almost like the time you accidentally entered my ..." he prompted.

"You know what? Forget it. It's stupid."

I left the kitchen, but his footsteps followed behind me. "I'm sure it's not stupid. Whatever it is, you can tell me."

I stopped, feeling a strong urge to tell him. Dray knew a lot. If he believed me, perhaps he could help me make sense of my trance. Maybe it meant nothing. Maybe it was just a figment of my imagination.

At last, I turned to face him. His expression was a blend of curiosity and concern.

I swallowed hard. "I turned into a man, saw the black sleeve of his suit as he was fixing it, and I felt him ... I felt the smoke. And then he said, 'I feel you too, stranger.'"

I braced myself for laughter and for him to dismiss my trance as nothing more than a dream or hallucination. However, he simply stared at me, his expression unreadable.

"Go ahead," I muttered. "Tell me how ridiculous it is."

But instead of agreeing with me, he asked, "You *felt* smoke?"

"Um ... yes."

"But did you smell it?"

I frowned. "Smell it?"

"You said you felt smoke, but perhaps you smelled it instead. You can't feel something like smoke without first smelling it."

"I don't understand why you're asking me this?"

He shrugged. "It's interesting because if you smelled smoke, you saw, as you call it, the trance of your mate."

I blinked incredulously. "What?"

Mate?

"Mates recognise each other by their distinct scents. If you smelled smoke, it means you felt your mate. And if that's true, then you have one."

Not only was I speechless but perplexed. Such a thought hadn't crossed my mind, but how could it when I had barely thought about my trance and had only recently learned about the existence of mates?

"I thought he was my soulmate, not mate," I mused. "My one."

If I hadn't sounded naïve before, I definitely did now.

"Maybe he is."

"Do you truly believe me?"

Bewilderment flickered across his face. "Why wouldn't I believe you?"

I looked down. "It just sounds unrealistic."

"It seems like you don't believe what you saw or felt yourself,

Elynn."

In that moment, as he said it, it struck me that he could be right. The likelihood of my trance being real was improbable because if the stranger was my mate, he would have found me already. Morphs were the only species that had mates, and I was in the world swarming with them.

And here, one of them stood right in front of me.

When I raised my eyes at him, my pulse raced, my legs felt numb, but I managed to form the words. "I know this may sound even more insane, but ... but is it possible that you could be *him*?"

Stupid, stupid, stupid! my inner voice yelled.

The longer he took to answer, the more I wanted to dig a hole and bury myself in it.

Finally, he spoke. "Do you feel the smoke now? Or smell it?"

I swallowed, trying to focus despite everything. I had never felt—or smelled—smoke around him before, and I didn't smell one now.

"No."

"Then you have your answer."

Dray wasn't him.

But relief didn't come.

"But I don't quite understand ..." I said. "Why can you enter my mind from such a great distance? And how could I have entered yours while asleep? I don't think that's how telepathy works."

"The oath binds me to you," he replied flatly.

Right. *That* magical oath.

"But why are you still protecting me? The part of the bargain your father agreed to no longer exists. Your kind is dead."

Arragon and his kind were dead, and only the half-breed Drayard remained after the enchanters' raid. It was pointless for him to keep the oath, and yet he did.

"But I'm not," he said. "If I don't keep the oath, I die."

Oh.

"Is there any way to free you from it?"

"There are two ways. First, all parties bound by the oath must mutually agree to terminate it. The second way involves Ascended Sorceresses or Witches. Their power can unbind it.

And the final option is if someone included in the bargain dies. But Tatyana is very much alive, exiled somewhere, which means I'm bound to protect you no matter what forever."

If Dray was *him*, he would have said it. Why keep it a secret? Was it to avoid repulsing or scaring me away? I was the one who confronted him, after all. And I thought I'd made it obvious that I wasn't revolted by the idea of him being my one. But in the end, everything indicated Dray couldn't be *him*, and I was holding on to someone who didn't exist.

"Good night, Dray."

I was about to retire to my room and try to sleep for an hour or two when he stopped me once again. "Before you go, I have something for you."

He reached into his pocket and withdrew an envelope.

"Your siblings wrote back."

Dear Elynn,

Kristian and I are relieved to hear you're safe and well. You deserve to be happy.

To reassure you, we are both healthy and safe. We burned our mother's body, and we both missed your presence at the funeral, but we understand why you couldn't be with us.

To be honest, Elynn, sometimes I get angry. Worse than before. Sometimes I feel lost, unsure of what to do with myself. But overall, I'm managing alright.

Sometimes I'm angry at you. Angry that you left us here. Angry that you got into that world in the first place. Angry that you're now a part of it. Angry that you've always been a part of it, and none of us had a clue.

But I also miss you. We both do. This can't last forever. Startels are stronger together. Regardless of whether your blood is a stranger to ours, you are not and will never be a stranger to us.

Hope you're still doing well,

Love,
Kris and Gen

I couldn't look away from the letter. I kept reading it over and over, hoping for more. After all, I had written two pages in mine. I expected more than this.

Despite its shortness, I was relieved that the letter wasn't forged. I could never forget Gen's distinctive handwriting.

At least they were both healthy, although unhappy. But how could they be when our mother had recently passed away? Happiness would find its way to them eventually.

I fell asleep for an hour and woke up with a heavy feeling of foreboding in my chest.

However, I dismissed it, choosing to forget.

XLII

For the first time, I woke up not from a nightmare but from the shaking. My bed and other furniture trembled, shifting from their positions.

I had never experienced an earthquake before.

Or perhaps it wasn't an earthquake but a volcanic eruption.

Could Dray have been wrong about the volcano being inactive? I trusted him, but what if there was an earthquake and we ended up trapped here?

Out of the blue, a growl thundered in my head, rattling my brain cells. I winced. Such a growl could only belong to one morph who had access to my mind.

I left the bed, using it for support until I found my balance. Then I hurried out of the room, leaving the doors wide open behind me.

Are you all right? I asked him, but no answer came.

As I descended the flight of stairs, the ground stopped shaking. I lurched to a halt on the landing and looked up at the stairs leading to his rooms—the side where he had forbidden me to go.

Only then it occurred to me that perhaps it wasn't an earthquake. But it would be ridiculous to assume Dray could cause all this. How could he make the ground tremble? It didn't seem possible. Or did it? After all, he had mastered telepathy, which morphs didn't have ...

"Elynn?"

I turned my head back, finding Blossom at the top of the stairs.

The ground began trembling anew, and I nearly lost my balance, but I grasped onto the newel just in time to avoid falling. I glanced back at the stairs in front of me.

One part of me screamed to check if he was all right, even though it was evident he wasn't. Perhaps there was something I could do to help him. But a more reasonable voice urged me to return to bed, hide under the covers, and hope whatever it was would pass.

Yet, I stepped towards the stairs.

"Elynn, no!"

I glanced back at Blossom. "Why?"

Concern was visible on her face. "It's a full moon, and he's a dragon. Full moons affect all morphs, but dragons in particular. He might hurt you."

He might hurt me ...

But I pushed the thought away. In the days we'd spent together, he had shown me he would never harm me. However, my past trauma reminded me not to trust anyone, as I could always be deceived.

"He won't," I reassured myself, though my voice sounded more confident than my brain.

I hastened up the stairs, straight into the forbidden zone. My mind was already criticising me for likely handing myself to the claws of death, while my heart whispered otherwise.

He will not hurt me. He will not ...

The hallway was like mine, with deep red walls and golden patterns. But in the semi-darkness, the red appeared more like blood than anywhere else. Taking a calming breath, I continued down the hallway, relying on the wall for support.

As I continued, the more it trembled. Maintaining balance became difficult, but I refused to give up. The longer it took me to find him, the emptiness in my chest grew, making it harder and harder to breathe. I couldn't explain why I felt this way. Not when my mind was elsewhere.

A few days ago, Dray had confessed his fear. He wasn't fond of being left alone. Perhaps what he needed right now was someone next to him, to hold him and whisper that he wasn't alone. Not anymore, at least.

The ground stopped shaking. It became as silent as the forest in the Realm of Bones. But this silence unsettled me even more.

Perhaps it was over, and I should retrace my steps back to my bedroom.

But I kept going.

I'd definitely gone mad.

At last, I reached two slightly open doors. Despite my fear of encountering Dray, possibly at his worst, I looked inside. What I saw shouldn't have surprised me, yet it did.

The floor was cluttered with painted canvases, scattered paint tubes, and splatters of paint everywhere. The easel lay in two cracked pieces on the floor.

I didn't even know Dray was a painter. He'd never told me that.

I entered the room, looking for him, but he wasn't here.

On my way towards the door, I tripped over one of the paintings. Squatting down, I brushed my fingertips over it. The painting was mostly dark, but the scratched middle revealed a smudge of maroon. I pushed the peeled-off pieces back in place and recognised a cowering child with burgundy hair and horns—

I fell as a sudden roar and shaking startled me, causing the painting to slip from my grasp. Then, everything quickly stopped, leaving behind an unsettling silence. Perhaps he was in another room?

When I stood back up, I exited the painting room and cautiously approached the other open doors. I peered inside, afraid he might not be pleased to find me where I shouldn't be. But he wasn't in his bedroom either.

Like the painting room, his bedroom didn't escape unharmed. Talon scratches marred the burgundy wallpaper, as well as his pillows and blanket. Feathers were strewn across the room. In one corner, the mirror lay shattered, its glass shards littering the floor, some smeared with blood.

I heard heavy breathing nearby. I peeked around the door and found Dray. He held his head in his hands, appearing to battle a terrible headache, while his bare chest rose and fell with laboured breathing. He wore nothing but his drawers.

If his eyes didn't have a peculiar expression, I would have looked away. It was as though he didn't see me. His body was here, but his consciousness was absent.

A hair-rising growl rumbled from his throat. Once again, the ground trembled, and the furniture shook violently. I tightened my grip on the door handle, trying to maintain my balance.

"Leave. Me. Alone," he snarled through gnashed teeth. For a second, I thought it was directed at me, but that wasn't it. He wasn't even conscious of me, despite standing so close to him. "Please ..." His voice faltered.

He was hurting. Why, I had no clue, but it stung to see him like this. I'd rather see him cold, demanding, and monstrous than this weeping, utterly destroyed creature.

I released the handle and dropped to my knees before him. Many distressing emotions crossed his eyes, tightening my heart. He stared into nothingness, ensuring that he didn't see me here, on my knees in front of him.

"I'm here," I breathed out, as if my lungs were starved of air. I grasped his knees and gently spread them apart to create room for myself between them as I drew closer to him.

He was shaking his head non-stop, muttering incomprehensible words under his breath.

I touched his nape. His skin felt unusually hot and damp, as if burning with fever.

"Dray, you're not alone. I'm here. I'm here ..."

What was he trying to fight? What demons did he have that made the formidable Bloodsucker be in such a tormented state?

He continued to ignore me. I tried a different approach, taking his hand and placing it on my chest, right where my heart was thumping.

"Listen to my heartbeat," I implored. "Listen to my heart, Dray."

"Leave me alone," he cried, his voice dripping with pain.

I shut my eyelids, and when I reopened them, I found myself engulfed in the darkness. Horror washed over me, and I screamed, the sound echoing throughout the space, fading into the void.

Where was I?

It was so cold, so terrifying, so—

You're weak, a voice whispered.

I cast around the black-pitch area frantically but didn't see anyone.

My son cannot be weak.

A cry thundered through the darkness, and I felt a sudden ache to cry.

I'm sorry, Father, a much younger voice apologised, and somehow, I knew it belonged to the man in whose head I was trapped.

Gradually, the blackness ebbed away, giving way to a clearer environment.

In front of me stood a towering man, staring down at me. His eyes were golden with bits of red, like Drayard's, but the man wasn't in his in-between form. Despite his human-like body, wings peeked from his shoulders, and familiar twisted horns protruded from his head. His face bore cruel and cold features.

But it wasn't Dray. I knew it and felt it.

That was Arragon.

"Step aside, Drayard," Arragon demanded.

Little Dray shook his head. "No, Father. You can't hurt him. Please don't do it."

Arragon's face contorted with displeasure. Fear washed over me like nothing I had ever felt before.

His expression suddenly softened. "All right, I won't."

Dray's eyes widened. "You ... you won't?"

"No," Arragon said, his tone firm, "but you will."

Dray's heart pounded as he glanced at the person behind him—a human. Tears streamed down the human's face as he whispered prayers under his breath.

"Father, I can't." He whipped his head back to Arragon.

"This is war, Drayard. They are our enemies. We must send the message." Arragon's expression remained as sharp as a knife. "Kill him."

Dray took a cautious step back. "No, we—"

"Kill him!"

Dray flinched. I could feel every emotion coursing through him and hear thoughts I wished I didn't.

He wasn't a killer. He knew that, and his father—more than anyone—was aware of it too. Arragon didn't like his son's tender heart because it weakened him. And no dragon, especially not the sole heir to the throne, should be *weak*.

"Kill him," Arragon insisted.

I loathed him. If I could access the memory, I would make Arragon pay for tormenting his son like that, even if I stood no chance against him.

Dray's eyes locked with the human's sky-blue ones, silently pleading with him not to do this. He swallowed hard, his pounding heart threatening to jump out of his chest. I didn't want to hear his thoughts, but they flooded into me anyway.

Kill him. Kill him. Father will love you. Kill him. Kill him. He'll be proud of you. It's so simple. Just kill him. Kill him. And it will be over.

He will love you.

He closed his eyes. He didn't see what was happening, and neither did I, but we both heard a scream that split through my soul. *His* soul.

Once he stopped screaming, a merciless silence settled in. As Dray slowly opened one eye, all that remained were the ashes of the man's bones and the unpleasant smell of burnt flesh.

And as if the invisible replay button was pressed, the memory repeated, right from its start.

I couldn't bear this any longer. I did everything to leave his mind, to escape the dark talons of the void. To my relief, I succeeded, and I was once again left with my own demons, which were angels compared to what was lurking in Dray's head.

His hand remained on my chest as I'd left it. I placed my hand on his shoulder and shook him gently.

Dray, it's over, I pleaded. *Please come back. Your father is dead. It's over.*

Despite my efforts, he didn't react.

I'm here. Elynn is here. You are safe.

If the memory was repeating in his head non-stop, it would drive him insane. I didn't know how frequently he experienced something like that because it couldn't be a one-time thing. If he suffered like this every full moon, it would be admirable how he stayed this composed and somewhat sane every day.

Or perhaps it was his façade that fooled me, when in reality, he was a drowning ship inside.

His face was streaked with tears, and I could feel my own cheeks becoming wet and taste the salt on my lips. I must have been a crying mess, but at that moment, I didn't care.

Listen to my heart. I closed my eyes. *Please.*

Elynn?

His voice echoed in my mind, and for the first time, it was an immense relief to hear it there.

I opened my eyes and found him already staring at me.

He *saw* me.

I smiled, nodding to assure him that it was me. "I'm here, Dray."

He wrapped his hands around my waist and pulled me even closer, resting his face against my chest. Unsure of how to handle his closeness, I slipped my arms around his neck.

"How are you?" I whispered.

He raised his head and tucked my hair behind my ear. Tear-stained eyes gazed at me as if I was a ray of light in the dark.

Better when you're here, he said.

My heart cracked a little.

You don't have to talk if you don't want to. I unconsciously traced my fingers over his nape, his head. *But know that I'm here, and you're not alone.*

His smile was weak. *I know.*

But if you do want to talk, I'm here to listen too.

I know.

He pulled me onto his lap, and I snuggled against his heaving, bare chest, feeling the rise and fall of his breath. Eventually, his breathing steadied, and a sense of calm enveloped us in its cocoon.

I was curious to learn more about his past, but I wasn't sure if he knew I was inside his mind. Also, I didn't want to pressure him after learning about the past horrors he battled. It was up to him whether he wanted to open up, and tonight didn't seem like the right time to share his deepest thoughts or the demons eating him piece by piece.

Now, I wished to understand him even more. There was more to him than he let others see. There was more than *A Tale of the Bloodsucker*. There was an entire novel I craved to explore.

But would he allow me to understand what war he was fighting in his mind or not?

XLIII

Drayard was avoiding me. During my sleepless nights, I didn't find him at the piano, trying to play something. It felt like we'd taken a step back, or maybe more. And I thought our relationship had progressed after that night, but I was tremendously mistaken.

I wondered why. Perhaps reaching out to him that night was a mistake. But he was hurting, and I wouldn't have been able to rest if I hadn't gone there and tried to find out what was wrong. And perhaps I stumbled upon something by accident—a fragment of what had shaped him into who he was now. His father was undoubtedly one of the reasons. I saw with my own eyes how he had broken his child. It disgusted me.

As I played one of the piano pieces Drayard had given me, my body detached from my mind. It took only one minute of relaxation before I was pulled back into the void, into the depths of the Bloodsucker's mind, where horrors lurked.

This time, however, it was different. I wasn't trapped in his mind because he was conscious of his surroundings.

As I recognised the study room in the dreadful Hellrock Castle, I felt an urgent need to escape. But I hesitated once I saw two unsightly males sitting across from Drayard.

"As you may be aware, the Winter Solstice is coming," Drayard spoke with the bone-chilling voice of the King.

That kind of voice reminded me of his father, who had looked at his son with cold eyes, demanding that he kill an innocent human—

I shook off the memory.

"And yet we remain as beasts." Nathair sighed disappointedly.

"I miss my love's true beauty," Kyrel muttered.

"And I miss *my* true beauty," Nathair quipped.

Kyrel snorted, but not even a muscle twitched on Drayard's face. He stayed silent, listening to his advisors' complaints about their lives as beasts.

After a few shared laughs between the two men, Kyrel turned to Drayard. "Why are we here, again, Your Highness?"

With his hands clasped behind his back, Drayard went and stood before the window overlooking the entire City of Fire, the volcano looming behind it like an ominous haze. "I need you two to bring me a few sorceresses."

But his mind was elsewhere, preoccupied with thoughts of the impending Winter Solstice and the approaching sacrifice that—

His thoughts vanished. I couldn't hear them anymore.

Did he know I was here?

"But all the sorceresses are in Casidiarn, Your Highness," Kyrel noted cautiously.

"I am aware. That is why you must bring them to me."

"With all due respect, Your Highness, how are we supposed to do that?" Nathair asked, confused. "Steal them from under the emperor's nose?"

"No, negotiate," Drayard stated nonchalantly. "An affair between royal siblings is illicit. If Nayden doesn't cede you the sorceresses, threaten to disclose his incestuous relationship with the empress to the empire."

"Hold on a minute," Nathair said. "Nadira and Nayden are ... banging?"

Drayard's silence spoke volumes. Kyrel cringed, while Nathair appeared incredulous.

"And I thought they were just two boring, self-centred siblings." Nathair leaned back in his seat before quickly straightening up as if remembering he shouldn't slouch in the King's presence. "But why not threaten them yourself? You're better at blackmail than we are."

"I have other matters to attend to," Drayard replied.

I expected the men to ask him about his affairs, but to my immense disappointment, they didn't.

"For what reason do you need sorceresses, Your Highness?" Kyrel inquired.

Drayard took a seat in the armchair in the corner, pressing his forefinger to his mouth. "I figured out how to break the curse."

Silence sank in the room.

Kyrel and Nathair stared at him, their mouths hanging open in disbelief, while Drayard remained impassive. I was as surprised as his advisors were, yet not entirely so.

Drayard was the wisest person I knew. He could shift pawns to his advantage and see important details that eluded others.

A few months ago, he stumbled upon Nadira and Nayden together, and now he was going to use their relationship to acquire sorceresses for an unknown reason. And I had no doubt he would get all the sorceresses he needed.

I wanted to clap, but if he hadn't already realised, he shouldn't know I had revisited his mind.

"H-how?" both men asked in unison.

Drayard didn't bother answering.

"But who is lost and found?" Kyrel recalled the words of the curse.

And only one word, one name, echoed in Drayard's mind. *Elynn.*

The meant to be, yet doomed to fall, shall bear lost and found whose blood shall be spilled once the longest night falls.

Only then, may humanity take over their shapes for life.

I once asked Drayard what sick game he was playing, and all he said was *many*. Only now did I realise I played a significant role in one of his major games.

Tatyana and Aytigin were soulmates, but as their relationship neared its end, they fled to prevent it. Though destined to be together, they were condemned to part eventually, making them meant to be yet doomed to fall. And when I was born, I became their lost and found—the answer to the curse.

I had to be sacrificed at the Winter Solstice as soon as night fell, exactly one month from now. Then, the curse would be lifted.

That was why Drayard had welcomed me under his wing. It wasn't because of the magical oath. It was pointless since his kind was already dead. He lied that breaking it would result in his death.

He saved me from the Spell twice, not because of the oath, but because I had to die for a purpose on a specific day and time. That was why he kept his distance after that night. Aware of my impending sacrifice, he chose not to form an emotional bond with me. That was, if he was even capable of getting close to someone at all.

I glanced at my bracelet. Taking it off would unleash my powers, and I might fall victim to the curse and become a beast. Even with the powers of an enchantress, I doubted they would thwart Drayard long enough to—

The book! The one with the dagger inside!

As I played different melodies, I made a plan. Fuelled by determination, I started to implement it before Drayard returned. But first, I needed to ask Baby and Blossom when he would be back. This way, I would have enough time to prepare myself to kill the most terrifying morph in the world.

After learning about the significant role his father played in shaping his diabolical personality, any sympathy I once felt for him vanished into thin air. He had been playing with me all along, but that ended now. He would not sacrifice me at the Winter Solstice. I would make sure of it.

Drayard might have started the game, and the rules were his, I could still outsmart them. I might have been just a pawn, unaware of my role, which made me weak, but not anymore.

If he hadn't felt me in his mind, he didn't know I knew everything, and such knowledge gave me an advantage.

And even if he had felt me, I wouldn't back down when my

life was at stake.

I learned from the bat girls he was likely to return from his "business trip" tomorrow. In the meantime, I slept, waited, schemed, and waited again.

I couldn't deny how disappointed and upset I was. I genuinely thought what we had was special—something hard to describe but definitely worth cherishing. I thought our relationship was leading somewhere. Perhaps he would have ended up with a friend, but he ruined everything by turning me into his pawn.

As night fell, I donned my boldest creation—a scarlet dress with two daring slits, accentuated by a loose golden star belt. The dress clung to my body, barely containing my breasts and leaving little to the imagination. Although I hated using my body this way, I knew my beauty was one of my greatest strengths. If using my looks could save my life, I was willing to swallow my pride. After all, I had nothing to lose.

Before I left my room, I double-checked that the dagger was strapped to my right thigh. Then I walked to the dining room with my head held high and shoulders back, feeling nervous tingles all over.

As I pushed open the doors, I found no one there. I exhaled in relief and relaxed as I surveyed the food on the table. It was exactly what I had asked the bat girls to get from the city yesterday—strawberries, roast chicken...

But where was that bastard?

"I'm here, Honeylove."

My heart leaped, and I grasped at my chest as I whipped my head around to find him standing behind me. "Heavens!"

He smiled with his distinct charm and walked around me, inspecting me from head to toe. When his eyes reached my chest, I wanted to cover myself, but I resisted. It was all part of the plan.

"Interesting," he said. "Did you dress this shamelessly pretty for me?"

I opened my mouth to give a sarcastic response, but instead, my words came out in a seductive tone. "Who else would I bare this much skin for if not for you, Dray?"

The look in his eyes changed. He had noticed it wasn't my typical response. Nevertheless, I bit my lip and offered a smile that used to make all human men go wild when I was eighteen. It had always worked miracles, but Drayard didn't seem to pay any attention. Either it didn't affect him, or he didn't show it, as he quickly focused on the table and its assortment.

"For what special occasion is all this?" he asked.

I released my lip. "I've never expressed my gratitude for saving my life twice. I thought it was about time to do so."

It wasn't an absolute lie, at least.

"Huh," he said, as if unaware of my lie. Then he casually walked to the table, grabbed his plate, and chose his food.

I looked over the food, trying to decide what to eat without appearing like a wild animal. I needed to choose something that would make me look attractive and desirable. Strawberries with whipped cream seemed perfect, so I picked those. And, of course, I didn't forget about the roast chicken, knowing how much he loved it. Perhaps seeing me eat it would pique his interest.

If not, I had other advantages. Although Drayard was older and more experienced than me in almost everything, he was still a man with certain needs that a woman could satisfy, even if only once in a while. My plan had to work.

As expected, Drayard claimed his seat at the head of the table.

I settled beside him, noticing the quizzical look he gave me. I anticipated him asking about my uncharacteristic behaviour, but to my surprise, he removed his gloves and placed them neatly on the table before concentrating on his meal.

After a moment of silence, I gathered the courage to speak. "Where were you all week?" I glanced down at my plate, feigning shyness. "I kind of ... missed you."

"I was on a business trip. Didn't Baby and Blossom inform you?"

"They must have forgotten." I flashed him an innocent smile.

Drayard observed me sceptically, his gaze unwavering as he bit into a chicken leg.

I raised a strawberry, dipped it into whipped cream, and tasted it with the tip of my tongue. He continued chewing, watching intently as I savoured the fruit slowly. As we both swallowed our bites at the same time, he averted his gaze.

He cleared his throat. "How was your day?"

I stifled a smirk, sensing a newfound tension in the air. Hesitating to answer, I slid my foot out of my heel and leaned over the table, drawing closer to him. Propping my chin on my palm, I sought his gaze, but he remained focused on his food. Undeterred, I raised my leg and lightly touched Drayard's shin.

Once his eyes met mine, I drawled, "Awfully, awfully boring without you, Dray."

I brushed my toes against his leg with a smile, but he kept eating, unmoved by my flirtation.

"You must have done something," he said after swallowing another bite.

I continued lazily caressing his leg. "I did."

"And what did you do?"

"Not much." I licked my lips as he lifted a glass of wine to his mouth. "I played the piano, tried on some black undergarments in front of the mirror, and ... played with myself."

He choked on his drink, and I covered my mouth to stifle a laugh. He pounded his chest and used a handkerchief from his black suit to dab his mouth. While I continued tracing circles on his leg with my toes, he grabbed my ankle and locked eyes with me. The touch of his bare skin against mine stirred inappropriate feelings within me.

"I don't think you're here just to dine with me, Honeylove." His voice turned husky, sending a trail of shivers through me.

His coarse thumb stroked my once-injured ankle, spreading almost therapeutic warmth over my skin. My heart began to race, and butterflies fluttered in my stomach.

Focus, focus, focus, Elynn!

I mustered a half-smile. "And you would be right."

The heat on my skin disappeared as he leaned back in his chair. His eyes travelled down my neck, pausing on my deep cleavage. Surprisingly, I didn't feel uncomfortable or the need to cover myself as I had before. His intense gaze, likely the fiery spark in his eyes, not only warmed the atmosphere but also me.

"Elynn." My name slid off his tongue like a far-off, forbidden siren melody. "Demonstrate to me how you played with yourself while I was away."

I snapped back to my senses and blinked, puzzled by his sudden desire. "Now?"

"Now."

Oh, heavens ...

I searched my brain for ideas to get myself out of this situation, but it was utterly blank. Still, I had to say something. Anything.

"It's hard to reach it while wearing a dress," I said with a slight smile. "Why don't *you* play with me instead?"

I didn't expect him to agree. There was no doubt in my mind.

But a disarming smile graced his face, and he patted his thigh. "Come here, Honeylove."

Crap.

I had underestimated him.

Of course, he would want that. He was a *man,* and *I* was seducing him. What else did I expect? That he would lean in for a kiss while I secretly drew the dagger to slash his neck?

Without hesitating any longer to arouse unnecessary suspicion, I gracefully rose. But before I could straddle him, he stood up. His towering height forced me to raise my head, trapping me not only with his glowing gaze but his body. The back of my thighs bumped against the table, leaving me with no choice but to crawl over it to escape him.

That was *if* I wanted to escape.

I gripped the edge of the table, trying to resist his charms and stay focused on my role. But when he took my hand and pressed a tender, warm kiss on my palm, all my plans vanished from my mind.

"You are displaying wonders of your beauty to the wrong eye, Elynn." He gazed at me with such intensity that I was surprised I remained intact. "Showing parts of your skin to someone you should be exposed to the least. But no matter how hard I try to resist, I can't tear my eyes off you. You enchant me."

My breathing hitched. "I ... enchant you?"

As he came closer, I shifted away on the table, making space by nudging the dishes with my rear. Positioned properly on top, his gaze fixed on mine.

"Yes," he breathed.

He was as lost as I was, if not more. I could do it now—pull out the dagger and plunge it into his monstrous heart—if I wasn't interested in learning where our coquetry would lead us.

Hooking my unarmed leg over his hip, I pulled him closer, eliminating the gap between us. His mouth quirked up as I rested my palm on his strong, slightly rising chest. His delightful scent, with a promise of sin, engulfed my senses—I longed to drown in it.

"Elynn?"

I looked at him from under my lashes. "Yes, Dray?"

"What game are you playing with me?"

My heartbeat quickened.

Before I could muster a clever response, his scaled hand slipped under my thigh, igniting a fire within me, yet not nearly enough.

"When did you start looking at me differently? What did I do to deserve the kindness you've shown me in these past months? Please, tell me why."

Our latest memories bombarded me, but I tried to fend them off. I tried to ignore the sting in my eyes and everything else that should be ignored until they faded away.

This man wanted to *kill* me. He wasn't my friend. He was *a monster*.

He had been toying with my feelings since the day we met, and now he was doing it again. I couldn't let any of this affect me. All I needed to do was to focus on my game and ensure I emerged as the victor.

"Because I'm attracted to you," I said, trying to convince myself it was just another lie. "You tell me, how wicked must I be to be attracted to a scheming devil like you?"

He smiled. "On what scale?"

"One to ten."

"It would be a thousand, then."

An honest chuckle broke through, betraying me. My cheeks burned, but I hastily schooled my features, reminding myself that I was acting. Merely act—

He caressed my cheek, brushing aside the golden waves from my face, and moved closer until his face was a hair's breadth away from mine. I clenched the edge of the table harder, surprised it didn't break.

"But you're not as wicked as I am, Elynn." He lifted my leg above his hip, a thumb drawing circles over my sensitive skin, sending tingles to my forbidden area. "I'm afraid if you stay, I'll break you."

I grasped his shirt, refusing to swoon, and drew him closer, holding onto him as if he were my willpower or perhaps my most dangerous weakness. Our lips were barely an inch away from touching, as I demanded against his mouth, "Then break me."

An unadulterated confusion crossed his face. He hadn't expected that. Neither had I, but I had him wrapped around my finger. It was time to move on to the next stage before delivering the final blow.

I closed my fingers around the nape of his neck and drew myself closer, my lips almost brushing against his ear. "Break me into a thousand shards, if you must," I whispered. "Break me however you like. But before you do that, set me aflame." As I looked into the eyes of the man who believed everything I said, doubt crept in, and I began to wonder if there could be some truth to my words after all. "Let me burn, Dray. Let me burn with you."

He didn't avert his gaze. Neither did I.

What was he thinking? Did my words sound believable? They must have, or else he wouldn't be gazing at me as if I were a ruby in the rough.

Then he leaned in.

My heart turned into a wild tempest.

Just as our lips were about to touch, I reached for the dagger. I ignored my shaking fingers while I searched for the only weapon that could close the Bloodsucker's eyes for eternity.

But my heart stilled along with my hand on the strap.

The dagger wasn't there.

It wasn't there.

The dagger wasn't there!

I knocked his glass of wine off the table, causing Drayard to draw back, his black trousers now wet with wine.

"Oh, clumsy me!" I exclaimed.

He looked at me mutely.

As I reached for the handkerchief on the table, another "accident" occurred, and a fork clattered to the floor.

"Oh, dear!"

I hopped off the table and quickly kicked the fork under it. Then I crouched down and crawled beneath the table, checking under my dress. The leg strap was indeed empty. I must have lost the dagger. But how? It wasn't on the floor! Yet, I could sense its suffocating presence. But where?

However, I had already lost. Drayard had been under my spell, and now it was all gone.

Swallowing my defeat, I picked up the fork and concealed my disappointment as I emerged from under the table. Once I stood up, I brushed my hair aside. "I don't think I'm feeling—"

When I looked at him ... Oh, when I looked at him! There he stood with one hand casually resting on the table, his gaze fixed on the dagger in his right hand.

My dagger.

His eyes snapped to me.

Clouded with nothingness.

Shivers erupted all over my body as he stared at me. He didn't need to speak. No words were necessary to realise ...

I had never played Drayard.

Drayard had played *me*.

XLV

My voice was lost somewhere because it surely wasn't with me. I stood there in total disbelief, staring at Drayard and the dagger he held. *My dagger*, which he had stolen right from under my nose.

He tilted his head, dragging his finger across the blade like a villain.

But that was who he was. A villain.

"Pray, do tell me, Elynn. What was a princess planning to do with such a dangerous dagger strapped to her thigh?"

Anger surged through me, and my ability to speak returned as I gritted out, "I'm not a princess."

"You are right. Princesses don't carry weapons. That is why I'm asking what you were planning to do with it. You might have hurt yourself. And my heart would have shattered if something bad had happened to you."

What a false bastard.

"Liar," I hissed, clutching the fork tighter.

"I beg your pardon?"

"Liar!" I exclaimed, seething with anger. Even without the ability to control fire, I felt like I was burning. "You played me! Is that what it was all along? A game for you?"

He didn't answer.

He had played me while I, like an utter fool, believed I held the reins. But it had been him all along. It was always him, and it would forever be him. Who was I compared to the Bloodsucker? Nothing. Inferior. *Female.*

But a female with nails.

"You like to play, don't you, Bloodsucker?" I took a deliberate step towards him. He remained silent. "Answer me, you bloody bastard!"

He didn't even flinch at my raised tone. "I think we both like to play, Elynn."

I scoffed, tracing my thumb along the handle of the fork. I wouldn't wound him with it, let alone kill him, but I could try to pluck out his eyeball.

"You knew I was planning this," I said.

"Indeed."

"How?"

"You are fond of my tale. Your admiration for it helped me to understand what books you like. You stumbled across the only book of tales about dragons in the library. Intrigued, you looked inside, and you took it. And with that move of yours, you failed."

"You set it all up," I said, both disgusted and amazed. "But why? For your own amusement?"

"No," he replied. "I did it to see if you would use a weapon against me."

"It was a test?"

"Yes."

"What kind of test?"

His shoulders slumped, and suddenly all pretence vanished, revealing a broken man. He let go of the dagger, which clattered to the floor. I stole a glance at it, calculating my chances of reaching it and plunging it into where it was supposed to be now—in Drayard's rotten heart.

"I wanted to trust you, Elynn," he said, capturing my full attention. His eyes looked ... shattered. "I wanted to trust someone because you know I don't trust anyone. I don't trust anyone other than myself. And I thought perhaps you would be someone I could put my trust in, but that will never be the case, will it?"

He lied shamelessly to me. Boiling my blood. Breaking my heart. Summoning tears.

Although sadness alternated with anger, the rage overpowered them both. I lunged at him with the fork, but he grabbed my wrist, stopping it an inch from his eye. Unfazed, he tilted his head and raised an eyebrow, as if asking what I was trying to achieve here.

Clenching my teeth, I swung my fist, but he caught it before it reached his face. He effortlessly lifted my hands above my head, spun me around, and pulled me close, while keeping my hands in front of me. I struggled against his hold, trying to break free. As I realised escape was futile, I snapped my head towards him and spat, aiming for his eye but hit his mouth instead.

Instead of wiping it off like a normal person, he licked it off. The bastard licked it off.

But I was too livid to be surprised.

"That wasn't very ladylike of you, Honeylove."

"Ladylike?" I spat with undisguised animosity. "Release me, and I'll show you exactly how my father taught me to deal with sick bastards like you, in the *ladylike* manner you deserve."

He dared to smirk. "As much as I would like to see that, it is neither the time nor the place for it." He began prying the fork from my tight grasp. "Now, what was it you lost in my head this morning?"

"You are going to kill me," I whispered.

His movements went still. He met my gaze, a new emotion flickering in his eyes. "Kill you?"

"You're planning to sacrifice me at the Winter Solstice."

He stared at me for a while, as if stricken by the truth.

Liar. Liar. Lying bastard.

"Elynn ..." He sighed. "I don't think you understood the curse right."

"Oh, I understood it perfectly!" I surged forward, causing him to release his grip, but he still held the fork. I spun around like a whirlwind of emotions I couldn't contain any longer. "'*The meant to be, yet doomed to fall, shall bear lost and found whose blood shall be spilled once the longest night falls.*' You said it was me. You *thought* of me. I am the one who was meant to be sacrificed all along. You're not keeping me safe and sound because of that oath, which, by the way, you made up. It's because you're planning to slaughter me like a bloody lamb in a month!"

His look was unreadable. "Yes, you *are* lost and found. But you forgot one of the most important parts of the curse. '*The meant to be, yet doomed to fall, shall bear them lost and found whose creation's blood shall be spilled once the longest night falls.*'" He stepped towards me. "*Whose creation's blood,* Elynn."

I had forgotten that part of the curse. It changed things drastically.

But he was lying. He had to be.

If I was lost and found, and it was my creation's blood that should be sacrificed ...

"But how can I be lost and found?" I asked, though I already knew the answer. I felt it with every bit of my heart. Soul, even. "I've never been lost. And what isn't lost can't be found. How can I be lost and found, Drayard?"

He glanced meaningfully at the platinum dagger lying on the floor behind me. "It doesn't matter now, does it?"

I clenched my fists. "Yes, indeed, it doesn't matter. It never will, because if I am lost and found, then you are keeping me trapped here to bear a child you'll sacrifice later on, aren't you?"

He stared at me as if unable to believe it. Then, his expression softened, and he rested his chin on his fist, letting out a deep, theatrical sigh.

"How are you even planning to do that?" I continued, casting thunders at him as he remained silent. "Send strangers to rape me over and over again until one of them gets lucky?"

Another sigh left him.

"Or would you assault me yourself until I become pregnant, only to sacrifice your own baby? But no ..." I shook my head, glancing down. "You wouldn't sacrifice a part of the dragon. They are far too precious," I whispered before lifting my gaze back at him. "Then what? Do you really think those sorceresses you're planning to get from the emperor will magically implant a child into my womb and make me give birth before the Winter Solstice?"

It was actually impossible. Even if it took a week or so to conceive, no one could speed up the process of having a baby in less than a fortnight. Even in a magical world like this, it defied reality.

He sighed once more. "Are you finished now?"

I didn't respond.

I hate you. I hate you. I hate you!

"Good," he said with a faint but wicked smile. "Yes, you understood the curse correctly. Your child could break it. And at first, I thought once you had that hunter's child, I'd take it away and ... sacrifice it. But then you offered yourself to the Empire of Beasts, and those two lunatics abused you. I assumed maybe you'd carry one of their offspring, but you didn't. I delved deeper into the terms of the curse, reconsidered your life story to see if I'd missed something, and indeed, I had. But you won't like the price of lifting the curse either."

"If it isn't my unborn child, what should I worry about?"

"Your mother, before she died, had given you the answer."

I frowned. "What are you talking about?"

"You can't have children, Elynn."

My lips parted in disbelief at the unexpected, utterly impossible, and absurd news. "Excuse me?"

His eyes held a hint of sympathy, but I couldn't trust it. He was one broken male, and I felt disgusted for even considering helping him bear the pain inflicted by his past. Why should I care for someone who showed no interest in caring for me? At least not in the same way I had when I held him and whispered that I was there for him.

And yet ...

"Your human mother couldn't have children, but after you whispered a magical sentence in the language of dryads, you passed on your gift to her," he explained. "Two weeks later, she became pregnant with your brother. It wasn't a coincidence. But unfortunately, the power you gave to your mother died with her."

I shook my head, refusing to believe it. Mum had mentioned before she died that she'd dreamed of me carrying a baby.

Or perhaps it was a hallucination caused by her illness, I reminded myself.

"How ... How do you know all of this?" I asked.

"Does it matter?"

No, it didn't. Not now.

I wrapped my arms around myself, feeling tears prickling my eyes, but I held them back. Drayard stepped closer, as if to embrace me, but I stepped back.

"What's the answer to the curse?" I asked, trying to sound as strong as possible. Judging by the sound of my voice, I had succeeded.

He looked at me with the same apologetic expression and said, "Either one of your siblings."

Time passed. Long, slow, and ticking.

What the ...

I couldn't believe his words until the realisation finally sank in. Then, a surge of anger engulfed me like a wildfire. I lunged for the fallen dagger, but Drayard was faster. He kicked it, sending it skidding across the floor to the far corner of the room. He also blocked my passage, standing tall and superior.

"Seriously, Elynn? I—"

"Don't you even!" I fumed. "You are not sacrificing either of them! What are you even thinking?"

"I don't have another choice," he said flatly.

"Yes, you do! To. Not. Sacrifice. Them. Find another way."

"There is no other way. I wish there was, but a sacrifice must happen. Someone must be killed to break the curse and save morphs."

"Save morphs?" I scoffed. "They can all go to hell, you included."

He pinched the bridge of his nose. "Morphs are a part of your kind, Elynn."

"No, they are not!" I stepped closer to him, unafraid to close the distance between us. "Humans are *my* kind. Genette and Kristian are *my* family. And morphs are *my* enemies. The curse shall remain. And that's final."

"You're playing with dangerous fire," he warned, stepping

closer until our chests were almost touching. "Besides, I never asked for your permission."

I gritted my teeth, meeting his fiery gaze with determination. "I. Am. Your. Princess."

"Are you now?" He raised his eyebrows ironically. "What happened to all that talk about how you weren't a princess before and would never be one?"

I gripped my burning bracelet in desperation, threatening to peel it off and show him whatever powers I had.

He glanced briefly at it. "If you remove it, you will turn into a lion forever."

"Perhaps not. I'm a half-enchantress. Have you forgotten about that?"

"You are, but are you sure you want to take that risk?"

He knew I wasn't going to, yet I toyed with his nerves, holding his challenging stare. My fingers lingered on my bracelet, a silent warning that I could remove it at any moment. But after a moment of intense staring, I stepped back and released the bracelet. I was sick of playing games with him.

"Burn in hell, Drayard," I spat, turning on my heel and stomping towards the exit.

"I am already burning. According to you, I'm the devil here," he shot back.

I paused, glancing at him over my shoulder. "Barely. You're far worse than them. They were, after all, exiled from the heavens while you were a mistake of your father's seed."

And just like that, I stormed out of the dining room, knowing my words had struck his corrupted heart.

Inside my room, I slammed the door shut. I didn't know where I'd found the strength, but the slap made the entire room shake. Unable to hold back the tears any longer, they poured down like a waterfall as I swept everything off the vanity.

The perfume bottles and cosmetics crashed and spilled their scented liquid on the floor. Most of the cosmetics remained unharmed, except for the eyeshadows and rouge.

I sank to my knees, burying my face into my palms.

No children. I would never be a mother.

If what Drayard said was true ... If I had given that power to my mother ... But such a decision, made when I was just an infant, shouldn't have been allowed! Besides, if the Mortal Region was shielded from magic, how could such a thing even work? Didn't it require magic to give the ability to have children to another human being?

I shuddered as I drew in a deep breath.

A hand landed on my quivering shoulder, but I quickly shoved it away.

"Go away!"

Go away. Go away. Go away! I yelled at him.

"It's us," Baby said.

I lowered my hands from my face, meeting Blossom's face in front of me.

No doubt, *he* had sent them here so I wouldn't feel alone. Perhaps he felt obliged to repay me for being there for him on his worst night.

I hate you, I told him, but no answer came. Of course, I didn't expect one.

"Would you like a cup of tea?" Blossom offered with a kind smile, extending the cup towards me.

Frowning, I smacked it from her hands. It fell onto her lap, hot liquid spilling onto her skirt. With a yelp, she sprang to her feet.

Morphs could get hurt by hot water. *Noted.*

I felt Baby's deadly stare piercing into my back.

"Leave. Me. Alone," I stated firmly.

Baby and Blossom hadn't done anything wrong to deserve such treatment. But they were working for Drayard, who was determined to sacrifice one of my siblings for his own gain. If Baby and Blossom were on his side, they were just as much my enemies as Drayard was.

"With pleasure," Baby said, clutching Blossom's hand as she dragged her towards the door. Blossom glanced at me with deep concern instead of anger or fear before disappearing from my sight.

I turned to the mirror and looked at the reflection of the weeping, defeated girl. I pressed my lips together, trying to repress the sobs that threatened to come.

I wanted to trust you, Elynn.

I inhaled shakily, blinking away the sting of the tears as I whispered, "And I already trusted you."

I spent the rest of the week in bed. I couldn't even muster the strength to go downstairs and play the piano.

Baby brought me food, but I could hardly eat anything. I couldn't stomach it. Just a single glance at it made me sick. Still, I forced it down. I had no wish to starve to death yet.

Nightmares only added to my misery. Like claws, they tore open my wounds, prohibiting them from healing once and for all. I doubted the day would come when nightmares bid me their final farewell.

As the Winter Solstice drew nearer, I felt hopeless about stopping the sacrifice. I had no idea who Drayard would choose. Although I had once saved Gen from being offered to the empire, I couldn't protect her or Kris from Drayard's stubbornness. I was powerless when it came to him.

And I hated it.

Ever since that dinner, I hadn't spoken to him, and he hadn't reached out either. The regret of calling him a mistake of his father's seed gnawed at me, even though it shouldn't. After all, he was eager to slaughter one of my siblings in three weeks. Why should I apologise for my sharp mouth?

But one night, I thought I heard his voice, like a faint whisper in my ear. "*I wish we had met before I became the King,*" he said. "*Everything would have been different then.*"

When I opened my eyes, nobody was there. I could only feel the pain in my finger, and when I licked it, I tasted blood.

Since the entire night was a haze, I doubted any of it was real. It was possible I pricked my finger on a splinter of wood from the bed frame.

I hugged the pillow, staring at nothing when Drayard contacted me. The smell of my sweat burned my nose, but I didn't feel like getting up for a bath. The bed held me captive in its cosy and calming embrace.

Can I come in? he asked.

No.

You're hurting, Elynn, he remarked. *You can't dig a deeper hole for yourself, one you won't be able to get out of later. Let me help you.*

Don't sacrifice my siblings, and I'll consider your offer to help.

You know I can't. It's for the good of the entire empire. Just one life in exchange for ending the decades-old curse. I'm sorry it had to be one of your siblings' lives.

Although he sounded genuine, I didn't care.

Have you already chosen the victim? Did the counting-out rhyme?

Yes.

Who?

He spoke after a moment of silence. *Your sister.*

I gritted my teeth and slowly squeezed the pillow, sinking my uncut nails deeper and deeper.

Can I come in? he tried again.

Go to hell.

Drayard made multiple attempts to invade my thoughts, but I pushed him out each time. I had learned how to do that. When you were brimming with hatred and drowning in heartache, anything was possible. Even forcing a demon from your mind before he could say a single word.

The week after that, I got out of bed. I asked Baby to draw me a bath, where I not only scrubbed off the week-old sweat but also relaxed and gathered my thoughts. The Winter Solstice was less than three weeks away, and I still hadn't figured out a way to save my sister's life.

The only solution that came to mind was to remove my bracelet. But if I turned into my beast form, I wouldn't be able to save her. I couldn't take the risk without a guarantee that it would ensure Gen's rescue. Yet, not taking that chance wouldn't save her either.

I felt like I was trapped in a dark maze.

But I never gave up, always seeking solutions, no matter how dark or impossible things seemed. There was always a way. Just as the boy's spirit once guided me to the right book, there had to be something now too.

After getting out of the bathtub, drying myself, and putting on a robe, I went back to the bedroom. There, I found Baby with a tray of food. She placed it on the bedside table and shot me a hostile look before turning to leave.

"Baby, wait," I said.

She paused, then turned to me, arms crossed over her chest. She must still be upset with me for behaving like a brute and spilling hot tea on Blossom.

I had no regrets. I hated them almost as much as I hated Drayard. But after a week of doing nothing and being left alone with my own poisonous mind, I felt enough guilt to realise that the least I could do was apologise.

"Well?" She tapped her foot impatiently. "What do you want?"

"Can you tell Blossom to come here?"

"Why? So you can smash a plate into her face?"

"No," I responded, keeping my voice level. "I want to apologise to you and her."

She scrutinised my face, searching for any sign of trickery.

"I swear," I added.

Baby stared at me for a while, then without another word, she spun on her heel and left.

I had tried. If she didn't believe me, there was nothing more I could do about it.

I knelt down to open the first drawer of the armoire. After searching for something to wear, I chose a white shirt and a floor-length skirt.

As I brushed my wet hair, the two girls walked in. Baby kept a watchful eye on me, while Blossom regarded me with caution.

I attempted to smile at them, hoping to reassure them, but their expressions remained unchanged.

I rose from the chair. "Is it too late for me to say sorry?"

Baby narrowed her eyes, but Blossom's expression softened, and she smiled warmly. "No, not at all."

"Then I'm sorry for mistreating you when all you wanted to do was to help me. I'm sorry for spilling hot tea on you, Blossom."

The alertness faded away from Baby's eyes. Taking a wide step towards them, I embraced them carefully, mindful not to touch their wings. Blossom hugged me back right away, but Baby hesitated before eventually giving in.

As the days passed, I focused on plotting, but I kept hitting a wall. Two weeks. I had *two weeks* to come up with a plan. Last time, I had managed to come up with one just two days before the Summer Solstice. I was close to selling my soul when the miracle came out of the blue. Perhaps this time, I would be lucky again, and it would come out of nowhere. But overcoming the Summer Solstice offering was one thing; tricking Drayard was another. My previous attempts made it crystal clear—fooling him was as impossible as trying to outrun death.

I prayed in vain. As time went by, no solution appeared. I couldn't afford to wait for a miracle. I had to act before it became too late. Yet, I found myself at a dead end.

But my parents hadn't raised a quitter.

Gen was likely already in the empire, brought there by the sorceresses that Drayard had surely received from the emperor. I wondered how she was being treated.

But I didn't want to know.

I could remove my bracelet and see where my caged powers would lead me. But before grasping at straws, I decided to try something else first. I doubted it would work, but it was worth a try.

I ventured into the forbidden hallway and headed straight for the painting room, knowing he'd be there. How I knew, I wasn't entirely sure. I chalked it up to a hunch.

The room looked much better since my last visit, with the floor free of clutter and randomly scattered canvases. Although most of the paint had been washed off, some traces still clung to the walls, giving the room a messy yet artistic touch. A brand new easel stood in the room, and sitting before it was none other than the devil himself.

His hand with the paintbrush froze when he saw me.

"Elynn," he said, surprised. "What are you doing here?"

He must not have heard me coming, so immersed was he in his art.

I tried to keep my focus on his face, ignoring everything else. Behave as if I wasn't affected by his black shirt, its top three buttons undone, revealing a glimpse of his red-scaled chest, and the crimson brocade waistcoat emphasising his fine physique. Behave as if his legs propped on the stool, with the cuffs of his trousers unrolled, showcasing his powerful calves, had no sway over me. Or pretend not to notice the dash of yellow paint on the tip of his nose, portraying him as a handsome beast and an adorable half-dragon caught unaware.

I tried to ignore all those things, lifting my chin to show confidence and strength. "I came to make a bargain with you."

His eyebrows furrowed. "A bargain?"

"Yes."

He set down his palette and a paintbrush on the nearby table. "What kind of bargain?"

I hesitated to make sure it was what I truly wanted. But when my sister's life was at stake, there couldn't be any doubts about the opportunities to save her.

"If you don't sacrifice my sister, I will sell you my soul."

I was fully aware that selling my soul meant the same thing to morphs as it did to humans. If I sold my soul to him, I would be entirely his, bound to him in every way. I would never be able to deny him, and he could use me however he pleased. I suspected he might exploit my title to gain whatever he desired. Drayard wasn't interested in my body or having me as a shoulder to cry on. His focus was on saving his kind and changing the emperor. Perhaps my title would provide him with easier access to the latter if he intended to pursue it someday.

But he sighed. "Elynn, I don't need your soul. I don't want a pretty, mindless doll, blindly following my every command and believing my every word."

"Then what *do* you want?" I asked impatiently. "What could change your mind about sacrificing my sister, Drayard? Please, tell me. I beg of you."

I would have knelt if that was what he wanted. If stroking his ego could save Gen's life, I was willing to do it. But if he had no interest in controlling me, my grovelling wouldn't sway him. It wouldn't change his stubborn mind.

"I don't want anything from you. Forgive me, but your sister must be," he paused, as if it pained him to say, "killed tomorrow night."

What a false bastard.

"But there must be another way," I pleaded, close to falling and begging on my knees.

Drayard must have sensed my despair because he quickly stood up and gently grabbed my arms, preventing me from further humiliating myself. His touch disgusted me, but I didn't push his hands away. Not yet.

"Elynn, I told you, I—"

"Please, Drayard, you can't take my sister away from me," I interrupted, maintaining a soft tone despite the fire awakening in my veins. "The plague inflicted by your kind and enchanters killed my mother. Don't take my sister's life too." I locked my eyes with him, desperately trying to reach his hardened heart. "Please, Dray. I'm begging you."

His mouth parted but then closed. What he said next, I knew wasn't what he had initially planned to say. "I'm sorry, but there's nothing I can do."

I pulled back from his arms, consumed by a surge of anger. My palm met his cheek. As the sound echoed in the quiet room, I realised what I had done.

His face turned from the force of the blow. I hadn't expected to strike him, yet I felt no regret afterward. He deserved it. He deserved far worse than a slap.

When Drayard looked at me, his eyes had lost their warmth,

replaced by an abyss of emptiness. He rolled back his shoulders and dropped his mask, revealing the monster his father had made of him.

"If I'm the devil, my home is hell. Then you must know you are testing wildfire," he said calmly, but with a hint of threat. "Are you sure you want to stoke that?"

"I'm not scared of you."

I knew who I was playing with and that I should stop before the flames caught and consumed me. But I didn't care. I didn't want to stop.

He moved closer, as if to prove me wrong, to intimidate me. But I stayed calm, unmoved. He gripped both of my wrists, while his other hand caressed my cheek. His sharp talons brushed against my skin, but not hard enough to draw blood. I met his icy gaze, feeling goosebumps rise on my skin, lowering the temperature even more.

Or perhaps he could indeed manipulate temperature.

His talons lingered on my bare skin, and my pounding heart betrayed my fear. I tried to reassure myself that he couldn't hurt me—the magical oath forbade it. But he might still take the risk and make me regret slapping him.

"Oh, don't be scared, my sharp-tongued beauty," he drawled, tilting his head as his talon brushed across my chin. "I have no wish to see you bleed. Because when you bleed, I bleed with you. And I've already bled enough."

He dragged his single talon down my neck. I held my breath, fearing that even the slight movement could make it sink into my skin, despite his reassurance. He was still a liar.

As his talon reached my neckline and brushed downward over my shirt, my body tensed like a taut string. I let out a breath through my slightly parted lips, unable to hold it any longer. He glanced down at my rising chest, a devilish smile curling his mouth as his talon traced down my shirt, slicing it open. It slid between my breasts, lower and lower...

"What are you doing?" I breathed.

"What you crave me to do."

"I don't ..."

His talon paused just above my navel. Warmth spread through

my cheeks as shivers ran down my spine. I couldn't hide it, and I had only myself to blame.

He cupped my chin, his talons pressing against my skin like a threat. "You tell me you despise me, but your body sings the opposite, Elynn," he whispered in a husky tone, causing my legs to weaken. "If I'm sacrificing your sister, you should feel contempt, not lust. Perhaps I'm not the only one broken in this room."

I clenched my teeth, pulling myself together. "You're the monster, not me."

"So let's hope it stays that way." He released my chin and wrists. "Now, leave my room."

I immediately pulled away. Glancing down, I noticed a tear in my shirt, exposing part of my skin. He had ripped it with his single talon. Quickly, I tugged at the fabric to shield myself from his gaze, even though he wasn't looking at me but at the wall behind.

"You will regret not taking my offer," I warned before stalking off.

Part IV

Notes of Curse & Winter

XLVII

It was the Winter Solstice Day.

Only eight hours remained until nightfall—the time when my sister would be sacrificed to break the four-decade curse.

Drayard had left, likely already at the unknown location where the ritual would take place.

"After only an hour of sleep, I refreshed myself with a cold bath and prayed to the Gods for their blessings on the journey ahead."

Feeling clean and lighter from my prayers, I returned to my bedroom and changed into the outfit I had already picked out. As I sat at the vanity, I braided my hair to keep it from bothering me later. I had no clue what would happen tonight, but there was a high chance that ... I might die.

My plan wasn't perfect, but I had thought it through as best as I could. There was no better alternative. I was prepared for anything, even willing to sacrifice myself to save Gen.

After eating, I sat at the piano and played, perhaps for the last time.

This could be the last time my fingers danced across the keys, the last chance to savour the music. As sorrow built in my chest,

I pushed it away. I didn't have time for that.

After I finished playing, only a few hours were left until nightfall. I walked down the hallway, passing my room and heading towards the smaller room where the bat girls lived.

Some days, when boredom overwhelmed me, I would join them in their room, chatting about trivial matters and sharing laughs. The thought that such moments might never happen again pained my heart.

In the volcano's house, there wasn't much to do. I spent my time playing, sketching, sewing, eating, getting on Drayard's nerves, chatting with the bat girls, and repeating the cycle because it was too dangerous to venture outside. But today, everything was about to change.

I opened the door without knocking, instantly realising my mistake.

From their bed, Baby and Blossom looked at me with wide eyes, dressed in undergarments I couldn't stand to wear, their chests touching.

Baby frowned. "Elynn, what the hells?"

All I wanted was to leave and forget I'd walked in on something ... private. But instead, I held Baby's glare, despite the immense awkwardness in the air.

"Are you going to join us, or are you just going to stand there?" Baby cocked her brow.

Blossom looked down shyly.

I swallowed the awkwardness. "Get dressed. I need your help."

With a scoff, Baby stood up from the bed. "Drayard warned us not to help you with anything if you asked."

"Well, I don't see that bastard anywhere, do you?"

"He will kill us," Blossom murmured, smoothing out the covers without making eye contact.

"Not if I do it first," I declared, meeting Blossom's unbelieving gaze. I ignored the pang in my chest.

Baby scowled, glaring at me.

"It's up to you whether you help me willingly or not. But if you defy me, things will turn ugly." I raised my wrist, the bracelet dangling threateningly.

"You wouldn't," Baby said in a low voice.

"Try me."

"You're going to regret this, Elynn."

I already did, but I had no choice.

Both girls dressed in appropriate attire, while Baby glared at me the entire time. I had undoubtedly made an enemy, perhaps even two, as Blossom usually followed Baby's lead. But that was the least of my concerns. I didn't expect to make it until the next day anyway.

"Where's the sacrifice taking place?" I asked, my tone cold. I didn't like acting like a witch, but being gentle wouldn't help me get crucial information. "In the capital?"

As we left the room, the bat girls trailed behind me. They could have attacked me and easily defeated me, but for some reason, they hadn't.

"No," Blossom replied. "In the Realm of Bones."

The terrible memories of that place struck me like lightning, but I refused to let them frighten me enough to reconsider my mission. Tonight, they could cause my downfall, and I couldn't allow it.

Baby and Blossom must have noticed my tremor, although they didn't mention it. I still had unfinished business with those three wolves. If they were there tonight—which I was confident they would be—I'd make time to kill them, not just for my own sake, but Thea's, Imogen's, Jill's, and even Clare's.

"You're going to fly me there, then," I stated.

"Oh, hells, no!" Baby objected.

I stopped at the foot of the stairs and turned to them. "Don't test me, Baby."

The Indigo Ocean surrounded the Realm of Embers. Even if I removed my bracelet and transformed into a lion, crossing the ocean in feline form would still be impossible. I needed the bats as my transportation.

I expected Baby's glare to scorch a hole in my forehead, but it never did.

"What Baby meant to—"

"Blossom, don't," Baby interrupted.

Blossom gave her an apologetic glance before addressing me.

"There's no need for us to fly you there when we have portals."

My eyebrows went up. "Portals?"

Blossom nodded, trying to force a smile that faltered once she noticed Baby looking at her disapprovingly.

"Where are those portals?" I inquired.

"In the volcano." Blossom descended the remaining stairs. "Concealed as well as this place."

As she reached the plain wall, she retrieved a vial of blood from her pocket.

Getting out of the volcano was simpler than getting in since there were no traps to worry about. But we couldn't leave without Drayard's blood, which was the key for both entering and exiting. Luckily, the bat girls had saved some of his blood. He had left it with them in case they wanted to go to the city, which ended up being convenient for me.

Blossom opened the vial and spilled the blood onto the wall. It absorbed it, and the double doors gradually appeared before us. Blossom opened them, revealing a dark tunnel, and we all went inside.

I couldn't see anything all the way to the end. I assumed Blossom used another vial of blood because a distinct sound came before the doors opened.

After the sound stopped, we went up the stairs and stepped into daylight. Squinting, I shielded my eyes from the sudden brightness. It had been a while since I'd been outside, and it took me some time to adjust. As I drew in a deep breath of fresh, mildly cool air, I anticipated seeing snow on the ground, but it remained unchanged—dark and obsidian, just as before. Of course. We were in the Realm of Embers. No snow fell here.

Blossom led the way while Baby followed behind me, her gaze piercing my back like daggers. Irritated, I stopped and turned to her. "What's your problem?"

"What's *my* problem?" she shot back. "You threatened us to achieve something. That's what Drayard does. He uses threats to manipulate. You're turning into him."

I winced at her absurd accusation. "I'm nothing like him. Drayard is a monster. We're nothing alike."

Baby walked past me, deliberately bumping into my shoulder.

I staggered back and tightened my jaw, then relaxed. Now was not the time to be angry.

Despite my efforts, the words spilled out as I followed her. "I must save my sister. She's innocent, and you're all sacrificing her!"

"Some sacrifices must be made," Baby said, throwing a glance back over her shoulder. "Deal with it."

I stopped in disbelief, feeling anger simmer beneath my skin as my bracelet seemed to burn my skin. The powers inside me demanded to be set free, but I resisted, not yet ready to unleash them.

I strode after her. "She's my sister!"

"I had a younger sister, too," Baby said bitterly. "She was killed for no reason, unlike your sister, whose death will serve a purpose. Be proud of her."

I was on the verge of tackling her and punching her ugly face.

Blossom and Baby stopped at the opposite side of the volcano, and I followed suit. Blossom drew a spare vial of Drayard's blood from her pocket, glancing in my direction. Seeing the anger contorting my face, her eyes turned kind, and she subtly shook her head, as if telling me to calm down.

And I did, refocusing on my mission and ignoring Baby's hurtful words, no matter how wrong they were.

As another stairwell opened below us, they began descending while I stayed behind. It was dark, and since none of us could manipulate fire, the torches remained unlit. But the bats could navigate in darkness. I wished I had their night vision right now.

Blossom paused on the stairs and offered me a helping hand, which I gladly took.

The air was strangely frigid here, with a scent reminding me of the sea. I nearly stumbled, but Blossom steadied me. If Baby had been guiding me, she would have let me fall. She despised me now.

Dim rays of various colours spilled through the arched passage. As we entered the cavernous space, five arches with different hues formed a crescent shape in the centre—*portals*.

The portal on the left contained a transparent black fluid. Next was forest green, then yellow, similar to the one that had taken me to the Empire of Beasts. Perhaps this one led there too. The fourth was white, and the last one was fawn brown, likely taking to the Realm of Bones. I had worn a brown maid uniform when I was a slave. Brown might symbolise the Realm of Bones.

I couldn't stand the thought of returning there, but I didn't have much of a choice.

"You're coming with me," I commanded.

Blossom nodded, while Baby remained silent.

"Baby?" I addressed her.

"Do I have another choice?"

"You always have a choice."

Something flickered in her eyes, too fleeting for me to identify.

Blossom approached the brown portal and vanished in an instant. I turned to Baby, who lingered in my shadow.

"Planning to stab me when I'm not looking?" I quipped.

"I would, but I'm not sure what could kill you."

I regarded her suspiciously before walking to the portal. As I stepped into it, I fell into a pit of cocoa.

XLVIII

Just like the last time, my landing was terrible. I fell into the snow, feeling lightheaded, but it quickly passed. My knees felt cold.

Baby laughed behind me, but I paid no attention as I stood up and brushed the snow off my knees.

She and Blossom had landed beautifully, standing on their legs with ease and grace. They must have been more accustomed to travelling through portals than I was. After all, it was only my second time.

At least I hadn't lost my vision this time.

As I surveyed the area, I recognised it as the same silent pine forest that brought back unpleasant memories: the wolf and dryad attack, fleeing from the Bloodsucker, and meeting Gen, who was with Chase.

A chill settled in my limbs, and I shoved my hands into my coat pockets.

"What's your next move, Elynn?" Baby mocked, but I ignored her.

My plan was already mapped out in my mind. Coerce the bat girls into bringing me to the Winter Solstice ritual. *Check.* Be at the sacrifice location. *Che–*

No, I still wasn't there.

"Where's the sacrifice ritual?" I asked, hoping it wouldn't be at the mansion.

"In the mansion's garden," Blossom replied, as if she had sensed my fear.

Fantastic.

"I guess we're off to the sacrifice ritual." Baby linked her arm with Blossom's. "Hopefully, the bastard won't gut us."

Blossom's violet eyes met mine. "Good luck," she said as if she meant it, then added, "And please, don't die."

In a heartbeat, they turned into bats and flew over my head.

Blossom's words pinched my heart. It seemed like she genuinely didn't want me to die.

I braced myself for whatever lay ahead and followed the bat girls. Without knowing where the mansion was, I couldn't risk getting lost again.

As I walked, I felt warmer. Distant music grew louder with each step. When the mansion from my nightmares emerged from behind the trees, I stopped. The bat girls paused briefly before disappearing behind the pines, leaving me with only a slim chance to save my sister.

Hiding behind the thick trunk, I tried to listen, stealing occasional glances at the garden.

It became clear that morphs were having a good time: sharing laughs, dancing, mingling ... It disturbed and irritated me to the core, even though their carefree nature shouldn't have fazed me.

The bracelet stung my skin, tempting me to remove it and transform into what I had feared my whole life—a morph. But I resisted, surveying the garden instead. A tall platform amid the garden caught my eye. I was certain it was the place where my sister would be sacrificed if my plan failed.

But failure wasn't an option.

Drayard and Gen were nowhere in sight. Perhaps they would bring her later for the final entertainment of the night. The mere thought reignited my anger.

"Why aren't you joining them, Princess Elynn?"

The voice startled me, and I spun around to face the creature. It was Juniper, the dryad. I had helped him find his parents, only for his father to almost cripple me.

"Princess Elynn?" I asked, confused.

"Most of us back home call you Princess Elynn because you saved the heir of the forest's nymphs from morphs."

I furrowed my eyebrows, but then it dawned on me. "You're the heir?"

He smiled shyly and nodded.

I never believed in coincidences, but this year's events made it hard to continue doubting them. The dryads owed me for saving their heir, and it seemed that I was well-known there, even being called a princess. Perhaps I could use this to my advantage.

"I've heard the curse will be broken today."

"It might not if I save my sister in time," I said, and Juniper stared at me, puzzled. I clarified, "My sister's death is the answer to breaking the curse."

The silence settled between us, punctuated only by the distant music and the chatter of morphs.

"Did you come here to save her by yourself?"

"I'll try."

Juniper pressed his wooden fingers to his lips, gnawing on one. "Do you need ... help?"

I considered the dryads' role in my mission and concluded they would likely make things more complicated. However, I could still use Juniper's help.

"You rule the forest, right?"

He frowned. "No, my father does. I'm too young to rule it yet."

"But could you somehow quiet the sounds in the forest?"

A proud smile spread over his face. "That's easy."

My heart pounded as I fumbled for the clasp on the bracelet. "If I scream or make any noise, silence everything that comes out of my mouth."

"Understood."

Confident I could trust him, I focused on the bracelet. I hesitated to remove it, fearing the creature I might become. Once it was off, there would be no turning back.

But I was also curious to discover my powers and what kind of creature I was.

As I prepared to unclasp the bracelet, a firm hand gripped my arm and spun me around.

A deep voice pierced the air, low and serious. "What do you think you're doing?"

I stared into his steely gaze.

Juniper hid behind me as if I could protect him from the Bloodsucker. Judging by his expression, he was anything but pleased to find me here.

"Let me go." I attempted to free my wrist from his tight grip, but to no avail. At least my right hand was free.

"Whatever plan you have in that pretty little head of yours, it won't work," he stated. "It's not safe for you here, especially if you remove your bracelet."

I tried to free myself again, but it was futile.

"Who brought you here?" he demanded, but I didn't answer. "Baby and Blossom, right?"

As the sky darkened, I had less and less time to save my sister. I needed to act *now*, but Drayard was thwarting me.

But Juniper stayed close behind me, and I was the only one who could understand him. Although I had no clue why I knew the language of dryads, it wasn't important now.

But what if Drayard also knew the dryad language? It wouldn't be surprising, given his many skills. If he did know it, my plan would fail.

There is only one way to find out.

"Remove my bracelet, Juniper," I gently commanded.

Drayard frowned. I didn't think he understood. Smiling, I leaned closer to make sure he couldn't see Juniper.

"I've dreamed of you," I whispered into his face. "You said you wished we had met before you became the King, and things would have been different. But here's the thing: I don't dream. So, tell me, what did you mean by that, and why did you prick my finger?"

His grip slackened on my wrist, but I didn't pull away yet.

My heart raced as he remained silent, yet I still wanted to hear his answer. I had no idea how many secrets he had—perhaps a gazillion. But at least I knew I could expect anything from him, and nothing would shock me anymore.

His throat bobbed as he swallowed. "Elynn, I—"

"I don't know how to remove this thing!" Juniper whined behind me.

Drayard's eyes flicked towards him, but I grasped his chin and brought his focus back to me, smashing my lips against his.

I hadn't thought this through, but it was the only idea I had to distract him from Juniper.

Neither of us parted our mouths, but I kept my lips pressed against his anyway. He didn't pull away either. For a brief moment, I caught myself hoping he would open his mouth—a thought I quickly suppressed.

Meanwhile, Juniper was still trying to solve the mystery of how to unclasp the simple bracelet.

"Just yank it, Juniper," I muttered against Drayard's mouth.

Drayard promptly drew back. "What are you ..."

Juniper yanked off the bracelet, and I winced as it tore. Drayard glanced at my now bare wrist.

His eyes went wide. I felt an overwhelming surge of pride, which made me giddy. I even had the audacity to smile at him. For the first time, I achieved something without Drayard getting in my way.

He seized my wrist and pulled me closer, clasping my chin with his fingers to force me to look at him. His whispered words sent a chill down my spine. "You've made a huge mistake, Elynn."

His touch on my bare skin felt slightly different without the bracelet. It flooded me with warmth, like standing in front of a crackling fire on a cold night. I forgot that I was supposed to be shivering from the cold.

Despite this, I didn't feel any other changes. No power was trying to escape the cage it'd been in since my birth. Perhaps Drayard had lied, and I was human after all. The bracelet was nothing more than an accessory that tended to burn my wrist every now and then for no reason.

"We'll see," I said.

"I'm serious. If you have enchantress powers, the moment they manifest, morphs will be warned of your presence. The Empire of Beasts is protected from enchanters with magic. It only takes one to step into our territory and use their powers for the high morphs to be alerted. It's a part of the treaty your grandfather travelled to the Empire of Skies to negotiate. I won't be able to save you."

"Perhaps I don't need to be saved any—"

Pain slashed through me, and I clenched my teeth. Glancing at Juniper over my shoulder, I mouthed, "Now."

I could only hope he understood, as I couldn't tell if he was silencing my moans. Hopefully, he was.

Another wave of pain hit my knees. If it weren't for Drayard holding me, I would have fallen. I winced from the burning pain as his hand held onto my waist, preventing me from falling.

"Oh Gods, Dray, make it stop!" I dug my nails into his coat. "Please!"

I sank down, and Drayard followed me into the snow. If he said anything, I couldn't hear him over my screams.

The ground trembled beneath us as my body burned, yet there were no flames in sight. As the trembling ceased, icy-cold water hit me, then wind swirled around me—us—like a mini-tornado. Drayard never let go of me, holding me tightly the whole time. His voice echoed in my mind, offering reassurance and comfort. *I'm here. I'm here.*

I disappeared from his arms, reappearing a few feet away.

The pain in my body gradually ebbed away. Panting, I looked up at the two startled beings in front of me. I tried to stand, but my knees buckled, and I fell. But instead of hitting the snow, I fell into Dray's arms.

Various thoughts, strange and unfamiliar, flooded my mind. They didn't belong to me.

Morphs' thoughts.

I winced.

But it all went quiet as soon as I caught Drayard's eyes. He looked utterly dazzled, as if seeing me in a new light.

"Have I changed that much?" I teased, smiling. My voice sounded the same, it seemed.

"No ..." he breathed, a smile tugging at the corners of his mouth. "Your beauty has always been enchanting. With or without a touch of magic, Honeylove."

My cheeks flushed with heat. As a smile tugged at my lips, it felt like my lungs began to shrink. The ground rushed towards me, as if I was shrinking too. My hands transformed into tawny legs with broad paws, and colours changed in front of me.

Once the pain subsided, I lifted my head to meet Drayard's gaze. He cursed under his breath.

The curse had caught me. I had shapeshifted into a lioness.

But that was all part of my plan. I had seen it coming.

As the drums thundered in the garden, I saw it as my cue.

It was time to rescue my little sister from the clutches of the morphs once again.

Lynn, Drayard's voice echoed in my mind as I ran away, *whatever you're planning, don't.*

I didn't listen to him, using my enhanced vision to look for a tree to climb, but they were all pines. It was impossible to climb any of them, even for a wild animal skilled in climbing.

Abandoning that idea, I sneaked over to a bush and observed the garden. My senses were heightened, sharpening my vision and making colours appear strange. I could hear the quietest conversations and catch the aroma of Imogen's cooking all the way from the kitchen.

For the first time, I felt free, as if a part of my true self had been hidden for too long. With that part of me unleashed, I finally felt alive. If not for my mission to rescue my sister, I'd have run through the forest, climbed the mountains, and connected with nature in its best ways.

If being a morph improved my senses, how would it feel like to be in my human form again? Would I smell everything? Hear everything? Feel everything? But I might never know if I died tonight.

Morphs had already gathered before the platform. I spotted

Baby and Blossom watching from the shadow of a tree, but Drayard was nowhere to be seen.

Thea stood among the maids, looking just as I remembered. I wondered if she missed me or had any inkling about their scheme to sacrifice my sister, who I had disguised as. Of course, Asenah was here too, standing in the first row with her cousins. My fur bristled.

The drums rose to a crescendo, and two high-blood-looking morphs stepped onto the platform. The man wore a gilded crown adorned with lions in motion, but not the woman in a long blue dress. Their fur matched mine, and I instantly knew they were the emperor and empress of the Empire of Beasts, Nayden and Nadira, my biological uncle and aunt.

They met in the centre, and as they turned to the audience, the drums fell silent. Nadira lowered her eyes to her feet, taking a step back from her brother.

Nayden extended his hands wide, a broad smile spreading across his lion-like face, exposing his shiny maws. "Good evening, my lords and ladies, kings and queens," he greeted, clasping his hands together. "Tonight, we've come together to finally end the four-decade curse."

The sounds of cheering and clapping broke out, causing me to dig my claws into the snow. As the applause ended, Nayden announced, "Thanks to the King of kings and queens, Drayard Emyur, a human girl is our answer. Alas, he won't be here to witness the sacrifice with us, but we hope his prediction is correct."

What did he mean Drayard wasn't here? Drayard *was* here. Then why did Nayden say he wasn't? Had Drayard not made his dramatic entrance yet, or was he watching from a distance, with no intention of joining them?

"Bring her here," Nayden ordered, to no one in particular.

As all eyes shifted in the same direction, I followed their gaze. My sister, *my little sister*, was forcefully dragged out of the mansion by two hawk-like guards. I clenched my teeth. Despite the manacles on her wrists, she appeared unharmed, with healthy skin and hair. It was difficult to believe she had been imprisoned, if at all.

Dara, the panther, stepped onto the platform. I tensed. I would never forget how she had tripped me at the twins' birthday party, and how morphs found it amusing.

Dara replaced the guards and forced my sister to kneel. As the emperor approached, Dara grabbed my sister's hair with one hand and yanked it down, making Gen's head tilt back.

I wanted to kill her.

Nayden chuckled, looking down at my sister like she was a funny jester. It further fuelled my existing fury.

"What an adorable little thing," he said. "What's your name, human?"

In response, Gen spat on his foot.

Nayden sneered, but one of the guards acted quickly, dropping to a crouch and using his sleeve to wipe off the spit from the emperor's foot.

Heavens ...

The crowd stayed as silent as the dead. If I could, I would have laughed.

As the guard stood up and retreated, Nayden's smile returned, and he exclaimed, "What a remarkable day! Suddenly, an earthquake struck and an enchanter was spotted nearby. But don't fret. My men are handling it," he reassured the worried murmurs of the crowd. "Despite these unforeseen events, we're ready for the sacrifice. *'The meant to be, yet doomed to fall.'* Whatever that means." He waved his hand dismissively. "Go ahead, Dara. It's almost dark."

After his encouragement, he walked off the platform, followed by Nadira, who kept her head low.

Dara pulled Gen to the centre of the platform by her hair, causing her to cry out. I fought the urge to leap over the bush and murder Dara for hurting Gen, but it wasn't the right moment. Not yet.

Then when will the right moment be, Elynn? I chided myself. But I didn't know. Perhaps never.

Then Dara began intoning, "*Shapeshifters of the empire turn into beasts ...*"

The crowd echoed the beginning of the curse like a prayer.

"*... but shall return to their true form when days last as long as* *nights."*

I couldn't understand why they recited the curse. It said nothing about quoting it during the sacrifice. Perhaps it was for dramatic effect.

"*The meant to be, yet doomed to fall, shall bear them lost and found ...*"

What should I do?

As time passed, my nervousness grew. I didn't have a solid plan for what to do after taking off the bracelet. I didn't expect to come this far.

"*... whose creation's blood shall be spilled once the longest night falls.*"

Dara glanced up at the setting sun. Mere minutes remained until the darkness descended upon the grounds. I had less and less time to save Genette because of my unexplained stalling.

"*Only then, may humanity take over their shapes for life!*"

Something glistened in Dara's hand.

My stomach dropped.

A dagger.

As morphs repeated Dara's words, I jumped over the bush and sprinted onto the platform with the speed of a lioness. Despite the crowd's warnings, it was too late. My jaws were already around Dara's neck.

"Tatyana ... Tatyana is here!" exclaimed the morphs in awe.

"What is she doing here?"

"How ...?"

Dara's dagger fell, leaving Gen alone. I couldn't tell her to run in words, so I roared.

Gen lifted her head, and her eyes met mine. They narrowed. "Lynn?"

Yes, it's me, Gen! It's me! I wanted to tell her, but Dara transformed into a panther and slipped out from under me. She poised to attack, threatening me with her sharp feline teeth. I took a cautious step back, but she pounced on me before I could prepare. As her teeth sank into my leg, I cried out in pain.

I tried to break free, but it was futile to fight a more experienced opponent. Wherever she could reach, she bit me with her sharp teeth. Shockingly, I also managed to hurt her.

I bit her ear.

I couldn't attack her elsewhere. It was clear I wouldn't survive this. How could I, when I was inexperienced in a fight *and* in this body?

From the glimpses I caught of the garden, chaos reigned. Roots sprang from the ground, grasping every morph they encountered. Some morphs cried out for help, while others fought against the roots controlled by an invisible power.

But I knew exactly what that power was and who it belonged to.

The dryads were helping me without my request, filling me with warmth.

Yet the trees didn't catch the two morphs I most wanted to see harmed. The twins stood behind my sister, restraining her. I hated their hands on her, but I was busy fighting Dara.

As Dara attacked me with her teeth and claws, I found myself calling for Drayard's help in my mind. I was sure I was bleeding in many places, but the adrenaline coursing through my veins numbed the pain.

Drayard didn't respond, and I didn't spot him either. He was gone.

Coward.

Finally, Dara pinned me down. Baring her teeth, she threatened to attack my neck and end this childish game. I tried to fight her off, but I was too weak and injured.

Suddenly, I smelled smoke, and Dara paused. Her nostrils widened as she sniffed the air. Then she sprang back as if lightning had almost struck her. Dara seemed as bewildered as I was until her jet-black fur caught fire. With a yelp, she began rolling on the ground to put it out.

It reminded me of Fillan rolling on the grass after releasing my ankle, as if his fur was—

Memories from that night flooded my mind. The pine forest had seemed lifeless to me, devoid of birds and animals, except for those Chase had slaughtered. But I distinctly remembered seeing a bat before encountering the glosse.

There was no one else who could control fire. No one else but Drayard.

Why hadn't I made the connection sooner? It had been *his* voice that told me to run and guided me to the oak. Drayard hadn't saved my life twice. He had saved me three times, and now four.

And now, all I could feel was the smoke.

I stood on my own four legs, trying to regain my balance. All of me ached—my body, my heart, and my head. My sensitive ears picked up every morph's scream. It wasn't just their screams that caused the pain, but their thoughts, which swelled into a painful clamour.

Tatyana Haroun was the only name in their minds.

But I wasn't Tatyana. I was Elynn. Completely lost and not a found soul.

I didn't know who I was looking for in the crowd or what I was doing. Everything became a blur until I locked eyes with someone with grey-blue eyes coming towards me. Her determined stare and thoughts revealed that she knew exactly who I was—not Tatyana, the woman she loved. She knew my true identity and birthright.

But before Asenah could reach me, a small branch pulled her away. I saw Juniper behind her, who winked at me before vanishing.

Finally, I focused on the twins holding my sister. I prowled towards them, eager to tear their throats out and disembowel them for everything they had done.

Just as I was about to attack, a blade zipped past me, burying itself in my sister's chest. The twins released her, and she collapsed onto her knees.

I went still.

"You've failed, cousin." Dara's voice sounded behind me.

I glanced back at her, and she flashed me the most wicked grin.

Despite the temptation to kill her, I ran towards my sister's lifeless body. Her eyes, wet with tears, met mine.

No, no, no, no, no.

I placed my paws on her chest, which was blooming with blood, but I couldn't pull out the weapon. I couldn't stop the blood from spreading. I couldn't stop anything!

"It hurts, but it's okay," she whispered with a trembling smile, a tear trickling down her pale cheek. For a split second, I saw our mum in her, on her deathbed. "It's okay, Lynn."

Her fingers reached up towards my nose, but they fell limp with her last breath.

A blast of wind sent me flying from Gen to the other side of the platform. I didn't care whether it hurt or where the explosion had come from. I didn't care about anything but Gen.

I rushed back towards her, but warm hands came around my waist and dragged me away. I screamed and kicked until they let go. I scrambled back and held her still-warm body in my arms. Only then did I realise I was back to my normal self—not a lioness.

Drayard was right. My sister's death was the answer to the curse. He hadn't made a mistake. Of course, he hadn't.

But she couldn't be dead. It was too quick. It couldn't be real, even if my hands were covered with her blood.

"You're not dead," I whispered, rocking her body, naively hoping she would wake up, and we would laugh at this absurdity. "You're not dead, Gen. Wake up. Wake up! Now is not the time for playing games. Please. P-please—"

Tears choked me as I buried my face in the warmth of her neck.

It's okay, Lynn. Her last words echoed in my mind like a heart-wrenching song.

But it was not okay.

I hated that I hadn't been able to speak. All I had managed was a growl before being flung across the platform.

It's just another nightmare, I convinced myself. *She's alive. I'm about to wake up as usual. I have to wake up.*

This isn't real.

It can't be ...

"Elynn," a deep voice hissed behind me, "we have to go."

I didn't budge.

He tried to haul me away from Gen again, but I clung to her body. I couldn't leave her. Not here. Not with *them*. Not with those who felt no sympathy for the innocent girl.

I didn't need to look to know that the dryads were gone and everyone was staring at me. Their loud thoughts squeezed my head.

Thoughts that wanted me dead.

Lupin and Fillan were standing nearby, wide-eyed and staring at me like the dorks they always had been, but I paid no attention to them.

"Elynn—"

"No." I sniffled. "She's not dead. S-she can't be. She can't. I'm not leaving her."

The smell of smoke threatened to drown me, but I refused to focus on anything I saw, felt, or smelled.

"Elynn, please ..."

I didn't listen to what he had to say. I closed my eyes and pressed my lips to my sister's forehead. Like a desperate child, I held onto memories of her, like the time when I finally made her laugh after a long, long while.

Kris had been in the library, while Mum had been confined to her bed since our father passed away. As I played the piano, Gen started sharing her favourite memories of our father, encouraging me to do the same.

I would give anything to return to that day, to relive the moment when we laughed and cried and laughed again. Gen had made peace with the fact that he wasn't coming back, and *I* was the one who helped her reach that point.

Because I always found a way to make things better.

But now ... I'd failed.

I felt like throwing up, even though the strangers' thoughts had vanished. When I opened my eyes, we weren't on the platform in the Realm of Bones anymore. Instead, we were by a glowing fireplace.

I knew this place ...

I was back home.

"Oh, mother of ... Elynn!" Drayard exclaimed in frustration.

Gen was in my hands. At least I hadn't left her in that realm. I'd brought her home despite the cost.

I buried my face back in her neck and sobbed loudly.

She was *dead*.

He pulled me away from her, and I didn't fight him. I was too tired to fight.

As he got me standing, he spun me around, and I met his face.

His human-like face.

My heart dropped.

His hair ... it glistened like burgundy wine. The warmth of the firelight made his copper skin glow, casting a soft radiance on the right side of his well-defined face. The same twisted horns were on full display, unchanged, just like his golden eyes twinkling with ruby dust. He didn't remind me of his father, but of someone else.

Every memory hit me hard, like a whip.

Every moment I had disregarded.

Every detail I'd chosen to ignore.

Now, everything was as clear as him standing before me in his real, unmasked form.

I yanked my hand from his grasp and stumbled backwards, tripping over Gen's body. I almost fell, but his warm hand firmly grasped my wrist, keeping me from falling.

"I know you're angry and your mind is fogged with hostile feelings, but we have to go," he said. "Unless you want to join your sister, I'm not stopping you."

I recognised that voice long before I met him.

His eye and hair colour, as well as other details, were different, but he was unmistakably the same man I had drawn years ago. Yet, instead of joy, all I felt was infinite anger.

"Let go of me."

"If I let go, you'll fall."

"Better than *you* catching me."

He pulled me to him, pinched my chin and made me, even gently, look at him. He inspected my face and neck, his face creasing with concern. The roughness of his fingers stung my neck, but I would be lying if I said it didn't sting everywhere.

"You're bleeding," he said.

Inside and out. "No hells."

His eyes flicked to mine. "Hate me after we get out of here, but now we—"

I spat into his eye. He scowled and let go of me. As he pulled out a handkerchief, I seized my chance to run. But once I left the living room, I almost collided with a man in the hallway.

"Elynn?"

I wanted to smile at the sight of my brother, safe and sound in front of me, but it wasn't the time for a family reunion. Even if he was the only one left.

"Kristian, you need to ... you need to run!" I tried to form the words, despite my frantic heart and thoughts. "Gen is ... Gen is ..."

"Calm down, Elynn." He grimaced. "First, what are you doing here?"

"I..."

He looked up, and my body went numb. I expected Kristian's face to drain of colour, but his facial expression was nothing like it. He was ... confused?

I whipped my head back. Drayard was staring at me. Very annoyed. "Elynn, I'll not repeat myself—"

"Shut up!" I seethed. "You killed her! You ..." My eyes darted back to Kris, who stood motionless, perhaps stunned by the unexpected "guest". "He killed Gen," I told him. "She's in the living room. She's ..." I bit my tongue, unable to voice the word as tears blurred my sight.

But Kris looked at Drayard. "You didn't—"

As I looked back at the Bloodsucker, he had his finger to his lips, but he promptly dropped it when he caught me staring.

Everything inside me stopped functioning. Something ...

something was off.

"He didn't ..." I turned to Kris. "He didn't what?"

Kris stared at me like he was sorry.

"Nothing, Honeylove," answered the Bloodsucker. "Now we—"

"Do not call me that!" I spun to him, balling my hands into fists. "What the hells is going on?" I looked back at Kris. "How can *you* be so calm when Gen's dead body is lying in the living room? Is this another nightmare, or am I losing my mind? I must be losing my mind because you ..." I laughed, motioning towards Drayard. "Oh ... hells ..." I held my head and took a deep breath.

"Lynn—"

"Kristian," Drayard warned.

Perplexed, I looked between Kristian and Drayard as I lowered my hands. "You know each other ..." I trailed off. "But how ... What ... What the hells is going on? Can someone tell me, for heavens' sake?"

"Elynn, I can assure you it's not a nightmare, and you're not losing your mind," the villain said. "It's all real, and the longer we stay here, the greater our chances of dying. We have to go. Please."

Please.

"Without me, you won't leave the Spell," Kris said.

"You are right," the killer agreed. "I suppose, no horses?"

Kris shook his head. "Waiting for—"

"Kristian," Drayard interrupted. "Two hours."

What the ...?

I stepped back. Back. And back until I hit the wall. I didn't understand what was happening. Neither of them answered me. Kris seemed to try, but the monster silenced him every bloody time.

Why didn't Kris show concern that our sister was dead?

Two hours of what?

Something was placed on me, but I didn't notice what. I was trying to hold on to my sanity, trying not to succumb to my emotions. All I wanted was to scream and scream and—

"Elynn?"

I didn't realise someone was calling me or that I was being

pulled away.

An owl hooted in the dark, snapping me out of my stupor. Something weighed on my neck, and as I looked down, I saw a black necklace. *What ...*

The snow crunched under our feet. Kris led the way, and ahead of me, a winged man walked, his hand—

I dug my heels into the snow, putting all my remaining strength into my legs to stop him from moving me like a doll. Drayard paused.

"I'm not going anywhere until you tell me how you two know each other," I insisted.

Kristian pursed his lips while Drayard looked at me as if I was a stubborn child. I tried to pull my hand from his grasp, but he held it firmly.

"Too bad, Elynn," he said, stepping closer. "That's too bad."

He lifted me as if I weighed nothing and tossed me over his shoulder.

"Let go of me, you sick, sick bastard!"

"Sick bastard. Something new."

"Oh, do you want more? Monstrous, filthy, blood-sucking bastard!"

"Doesn't she have a sharp tongue?" Drayard asked in a biting tone. "Your sister?"

"To be frank," Kristian said, "I'm hearing her say something like this for the first time."

"Do you even know who he is?" I snapped at my brother. "He's the Bloodsucker! He's real, and you are letting him get away with Gen's murder?"

"I know who he is, Lynn."

I was robbed of my voice for a moment. "W-what?"

His eyes shifted to Drayard, as if seeking his permission. *What is going on ...?*

"I'm sorry, Lynn," Kristian said. It seemed like the Bloodsucker prevented him from saying more. It felt like they were both hiding something from me. "Just ... it all happens for a reason."

I scoffed at such an unreasonable thought. "It all happens for a reason? How can you say that? Our sister is dead, Kris! And you dare to say—"

"Ely?"

Drayard came to a sudden stop.

I lifted my head.

Among the trees stood my former fiancé, armed with golden weapons, ready for a hunt, as always. I wasn't sure whether it was the effects of the Spell or his mere presence, but my stomach churned.

When Drayard turned around, he covered my view of Chase.

Next to me, Kristian crossed his arms and glared at Chase.

"Who are you?" I heard Chase ask.

Drayard put me back on my feet and pushed me behind him. "Drayard Emyur," Drayard replied.

I stood on my tiptoes to catch Chase's expression over Drayard's shoulder. The name seemed to mean nothing to him as he held his most precious sword—Goldy.

Drayard sighed. "Better known as the Bloodsucker."

Still no reaction. "The Bloodsucker?"

He doesn't know who you are, you idiot, I said.

What an uncultured prick, Drayard crooned back.

"If you attempt to use your weapons, it will be very foolish of you, huntsman," Drayard said serenely. "You allow us to go, and no harm will come to any of your precious body parts."

"You're a dragon," Chase noted, as if Drayard's wings and horns hadn't made it obvious. Then, his eyes shifted to mine, and his lip curled. "You're one of them."

"We're leaving," Drayard announced.

But Chase had other plans. "A dragon, really, Ely? And here I didn't listen to what your girlfriends had to say about you. I should have believed them. You *are* a slut."

Drayard was about to lunge at him, but I grabbed his wrist. He looked over at me, his eyes fiery. I shook my head, and the fire in his eyes dampened.

"What did you just call her?" Kristian inquired, his tone sharp.

Drayard and I looked at Kristian in unison.

"Kristian, I like you, man. I really do. But forgive me when I speak the truth that your sister is one big—"

"We are leaving, and if you follow us, consider yourself dead,"

Drayard interrupted.

He took my hand, lacing his fingers through mine, and turned around.

"Kristian," Drayard called.

It took a while for Kristian to tear his glare away from Chase and follow us. Wondering if Chase had left, I glanced back, but he was still there, unsheathing his Goldy.

Dray ...

He paused, casting a glance back at Chase. He snorted. "What a fool." He released my hand and turned to Chase. "Come on then, huntsman. Let's see what kind of fragile clay you're made of."

Chase did, surprising me. As he charged at Drayard, I knew Chase's minutes were numbered, if not seconds. It hadn't occurred to me until now that if I had stayed in the Mortal Region, I would have married the imbecile of the century.

Drayard *screamed* danger. Even unarmed, he was a walking threat. But Chase was too ignorant to realise he'd just signed his death warrant.

As Chase approached, I stepped back. He swung his sword at Dray, who effortlessly dodged it. Chase grunted and tried again, but his second attempt was also unsuccessful. Dray was toying with him and even had the audacity to yawn.

Chase's face turned puce with rage. "You took my fiancée." Another lunge; another failure. "You ruined her, and you turned her into one of you. *A monster.*"

Drayard opened his mouth to speak, but I beat him to it. "A monster?"

As Chase's attention turned to me, Drayard captured his hand holding Goldy and twisted his arm behind his back. "She's not your fiancée, you fool," he hissed near his ear. "Apologise for insulting her with nonsense words, or say goodbye to your tongue."

"I have nothing to say to her," Chase spat with disgust.

"Nothing?" My hands formed into tight fists. "You have nothing to say to me after taking your anger out on my body, leaving me with bruises?"

I felt Drayard's astounded look on me. Before he could say

anything, I pushed his voice out of my mind.

And then Chase said the fatal, "You deserved it, *slut.*"

He cut off the last thread of my self-control. I moved to strangle him, but Drayard was quicker. He forced Chase to his knees and grabbed his hair, yanking it back.

I paused, curious to see his next move.

"I've tasted huntsman's blood before," Drayard revealed, two sharp fangs glinting behind his lips. "They usually have the worst flavour, but perhaps newer descendants taste better. Doubtful, but I'll drain you dry regardless. I haven't had time to eat today."

Terror was etched into every line of Chase's face as Drayard lifted him, sinking his fangs into his neck.

Chase winced while Drayard drank his blood. My heart thumped, reminded of Drayard's true nature.

He was a *bloodsucker. A killer. A bastard.* And yet, the sight of him in all his unmasked glory didn't intimidate me. Instead, I felt ... drawn to it.

Drayard was right. He wasn't the only one who was broken.

But a sudden, sharp pain in my stomach snapped me back to my senses. I looked down.

An arrow stuck out from my stomach.

I touched it cautiously, and when I raised my fingers, they were stained with red.

"Elynn!" Kristian called out.

One last time, I looked at Drayard. At the man who had murdered my sister. At the man who was plotting something behind my back. At the man who, despite all his faults, lured my heart out and crowned it as his.

"Dray?" I whispered.

He glanced up from Chase's neck, his pupils dilated and eyes bloodshot. I fell, but he caught me before I hit the snow.

EPILOGUE

Death was natural.

Death sooner or later came for everyone.

Death could not be avoided, let alone outwitted.

But these rules didn't apply to him. Not to a man who deflected its blows like wildfire, destroying everything it touched. While death always found him, it said hello as quickly as it said goodbye. Death refused him, as if the Gods below found him too fiendish to welcome into their kingdom.

Now, as death approached *her*, he wouldn't let it take her away.

He lifted her and brushed aside the loose waves of her honey-blonde hair. "Elynn?"

Her eyelids parted slightly.

"Try to remain conscious." His voice was as calm as the sea before a storm, unlike his roaring heart. "I'll get us out of here."

She didn't respond, so he cradled her head against his chest, striding towards the end of the Spell. Its effects ate away at his insides, but his attention was solely on Elynn's life, not his own. Despite the enchanted necklace around her neck, she was still dying, poisoned by the gold in her bowels. He couldn't allow that.

He *would not* allow it.

The taste of copper lingered in his mouth, reminding him of the huntsman's blood. He hated it. Hated his blood *and* the huntsman. Yet, not as much as he hated himself.

He craved to avenge her, to tear the huntsman apart and leave his remains for animals to feast on, but he resisted his animalistic urges. He blamed himself and only himself for letting this happen—for allowing her to be struck by the golden arrow in the first place.

How could he have missed the crossbow?

"Why didn't you tell her?" Her brother's voice jolted him from his thoughts.

He had forgotten Kristian was here, struggling to keep up with his quick pace.

As Drayard didn't answer, Kristian looked down, scratching his nape. "You will save her, right?"

"She is not dying," Drayard almost hissed.

He glanced at her again. Her eyes were closed.

"Elynn?"

No reaction.

He gently patted her cheek. "Elynn?"

Her eyes barely opened, and her lips parted slightly, but she said nothing.

"Just hold on," he whispered, pressing her closer to his chest. "Hold on a little longer, Honeylove."

He considered feeding her his blood but quickly dismissed the idea. It might harm her more while they were in the Spell's area. He couldn't risk that. His priority now was to get her out of here, then deal with the rest.

As they neared the river, the smell of freedom teased his senses. It was so close, within arm's reach, but as he took another step forward, he bumped into an invisible wall.

The Spell.

He glanced at Kristian, who passed through effortlessly.

Drayard hesitated, then took a cautious step forward. This time, he didn't hit the wall. The nausea vanished, and his powers surged back into his veins, as familiar as home—if he had one. He hurried forward until he was free from the Spell's ill energy.

He collapsed by the river with Elynn in his arms. "Elynn?"

But she lay still, her skin feverish against his touch. Swallowing his fears and possibilities that could send him to misery and rage, he sliced his wrist with his fangs and pressed it to Elynn's hot lips, ignoring Kristian's grimace.

She didn't open her mouth.

Desperation swelled within him, yet he resisted the urge to act on it. Not before trying everything he could.

He looked up at Kristian. "I need you to hold her for a

moment."

Kristian swallowed, his hands shaking.

"Kristian, I need you to hold her and stop the bleeding," Drayard repeated, this time with more urgency.

His patience wore thin, and Kristian sensed Drayard's growing frustration. Out of fear, he knelt down and carefully took Elynn from his arms, putting his hand on the bleeding wound. Once Drayard's hands were free, he hastily removed his coat and laid it on the snow.

"Lay her on it gently," he instructed. "And keep your hand on the wound."

Kristian complied as Drayard unsheathed his daggers. Kristian's eyes widened at the sight of them. "What are you going to do with those?"

"Remove your hand, Kristian," he ordered, ignoring his question.

After Kristian did it begrudgingly, Drayard carefully widened Elynn's wound with his daggers. Kristian watched in horror as Drayard, like a skilled physician, removed the barbed golden arrowhead using only his sharp blades. He then discarded both the arrow and his weapons.

"Put your hand back on the wound," Drayard told Kristian before puncturing his wrist with his fangs again and pressing it to Elynn's lips.

Drink, Elynn, he urged in her mind, but, as before, she didn't.

He pulled her back to his chest, replacing Kristian's hand with his own. He implored her to drink over and over again, both in her mind and aloud, but she didn't listen.

Nearby, a dryad child appeared, followed shortly by a taller one draped in moss. Drayard recognised the little one as the same dryad who had removed Elynn's bracelet, but not the female.

Lately, dryads had been getting on his nerves. The entire Empire of Beasts had learned about Elynn's existence because of the kid. Sooner or later, they would demand her head, and it was all because of the dryad.

"Princess Elynn," the female dryad spoke in his native language, offering him a vial. "To Princess Elynn."

Drayard furrowed his eyebrows but took the vial, not willing to take any chances despite his scepticism. He knew that dryads, especially females, were well known for their healing ability, while males were prone to tearing apart those who harmed their kind. Perhaps the liquid in the vial would help Elynn.

As the female dryad blessed him with a kind smile and placed her hand on the boy's shoulder, they disappeared in a small whirlwind of pine needles within a moment.

He turned his attention back to Elynn, opened the vial, and poured the liquid into her dry mouth until the last drop. He watched as it slowly dissolved on her tongue.

It had to work. He didn't understand why the dryads cared for Elynn so much as to consider saving her life, let alone how Elynn knew their language. But at this exact moment, he couldn't care about it. This had to work. This *must* work.

But she stayed feverish, her breathing gradually slowing down.

Drayard's muscles went stiff, his eyes burning with unshed tears. "Elynn?"

Her chest stopped rising.

As Drayard was about to curse the dryads, Elynn suddenly gasped for air, her eyelids snapping open for a second before shutting again.

The marks Dara's teeth and claws had left in her skin healed along with the wound in her abdomen, leaving an everlasting scar in its wake. But at least she was breathing. She was *alive*.

A sigh of immense relief escaped Drayard as he relaxed his tense shoulders, resting his forehead against Elynn's. Her scent of honey and sweat calmed his racing heart.

"You care about her," Kristian broke the silence. He had been kneeling across from Drayard this whole time, but Drayard had forgotten about him once again. "But why bother caring for someone if you're going to be their villain?"

Drayard raised his head, gently brushing Elynn's hair from her damp face. Her skin was coming back to its normal temperature only because he was the one keeping it in balance.

"Don't you have another sister to look after?" Drayard asked.

"About that ..." Kristian began. "I don't understand why you didn't tell Elynn anything, making her believe that ... Unless you want to be a villain?"

"I'm not a villain, but I must be one in her story."

"Why?"

Drayard dropped his eyes back to Elynn, gently stroking her hair. He restrained himself from smelling it, despite her scent already dominating his air. "I'll be a villain in her story because there's no way I'll let her fall for someone like me."

Because she deserves a thousand times better, he thought and meant it.

"How can you be so sure she hasn't already fallen for you?"

Drayard's heart skipped a beat, but he quickly dismissed the idea. It wasn't possible. Not for him. "She strongly believes I killed Genette."

"Yes, but before ... Before she even met you, she'd already been captivated by stories about dragons, but not in the same way she was with *A Tale of the Bloodsucker*. It had her under its spell, but didn't want to admit it, given the tale's horrifying events. And she'd often gaze into the fire on winter nights. Sometimes she smiled as if she saw something in the flames."

"Fires have that influence."

"No, she believed in something. Do you know what she said before she offered herself to the Empire of Beasts? She said that it felt right. And Elynn is a huge liar. She lies to protect. But she wasn't lying then."

Drayard swallowed hard.

"I see you're doing something similar," Kristian went on. "But you can't hurt her, Emyur."

"I already did."

"You could fix that by telling her—"

"No," Drayard stated firmly. "I may not be a villain, but *I am a monster*. I must lie. She must hate me. If not ..."

His attention shifted back to Elynn. The gentle wind tousled her hair, veiling half of her face. He brushed it behind her ear with a delicate, almost hesitant, touch.

"How many secrets are you hiding?" asked Kristian.

"Too many that I'm not willing to share."

Kristian's eyes narrowed, much like Elynn's did when she was pondering his secrets, but he wouldn't be able to guess them. Few knew what he was hiding, and he intended to keep it that way.

Kristian adjusted his glasses. "You know, if she likes stories about monsters, it doesn't mean you have to be one in her story."

Drayard wanted to disagree, but he figured it would be wiser to stay silent.

"When did you fall for her?" Kristian persisted.

A bitter smile graced Drayard's lips. "Does it matter?"

"Yes, because she's my sister. I don't care that biologically she isn't. So yes, it matters when you first laid eyes on her."

"If I don't tell, you know it's pointless for you to try anything against me, right?"

Kristian rolled his eyes. "We'll have to talk about this later. Just ..." He glanced up at the clear midnight-blue sky, resting his hand on his knee. "I believe it had to be this way and not the other. She had to return home so that you would save her from the Spell's effects. *Twice.* Every time she walked away from you, she faced difficulties, which ended up almost costing her life. Her every path has been leading to you, which makes me think—"

"That's enough," Drayard cut him off. "Go back home and wait. Your sister is my priority now. Her health, her happiness is my priority. Nobody will hurt her as long as she's with me. I promise."

Nobody will hurt her anymore, except for me. But he didn't voice this part aloud.

"I know," Kristian said, standing up. "I saw it with my own eyes. That she's safe. Only read why the world fears you." He shoved his hands into his pockets. "Maybe I shouldn't leave her with you, but I trust you. Besides, I believe it all happens for a reason."

Which could be your mistake, Drayard thought.

He watched as he walked away until he disappeared behind the trees. Immediately, his shoulders sagged, and he drew Elynn closer, listening to her steady heartbeat as if it was the most beautiful melody.

He pressed a gentle kiss on her temple and rested his forehead against hers. "For a second, I thought I'd lost you," he whispered. "And that was the scariest second of my life. Don't scare me like that, Elynn. Hells, I—"

The sound of clapping interrupted him.

He looked up and saw the last person he expected to see here.

A stranger in a royal blue cloak stepped out from behind the trees, clapping his hands with a smile that melted hearts.

"My, oh my, isn't that a touching sight?" the stranger observed.

Drayard tensed. "What are you doing here?"

The stranger's smile widened as he noticed Elynn in Drayard's arms. "Isn't she lovely?"

"What are you doing here?" Drayard's tone grew more intense as he repeated himself.

The stranger crouched in front of them and extended his hand, as if he was going to touch Elynn's face. Drayard instinctively pulled her away.

The stranger chuckled. "I'm not her enemy, dragon boy."

Drayard stayed cautious. "Are you?"

To that, the stranger offered no response. "Well, it seems I'm not welcome here." He straightened up, adjusting his cloak. "My apologies for interrupting your sweet moment. I hope I didn't spoil any plans you had, like ... hmm ... What was it? Oh, right. Saying something like 'I feel you too, stranger?'"

Drayard concealed all the emotions trying to surface. Although many thoughts and questions came to mind, he knew it was wiser not to voice them. Instead, he stayed silent, his expression unchanged.

It drew a smirk from the stranger. "Well, goodbye for now. We'll meet again soon." With a parting glance at Drayard, he added, "Oh, and don't forget to cut your hair. It suits you better than"—he eyed Drayard's flowing hair distastefully—"whatever that is."

He disappeared where he'd come from.

Drayard looked down at Elynn, now peacefully asleep in his arms, oblivious to what had just happened.

Then Drayard's eyes shifted back to where the stranger had disappeared.

It felt like the Gods and the Universe were mocking him, *laughing* at his situation. And somewhere deep in his mind, Drayard could hear the boy's laughter echoing the loudest of all.

THE SEQUEL
LULLABY OF THE LOST PRINCESS

**The sequel to Anthem of the Cursed Empire ponders the question ...
Love or Revenge?**

Elynn's sacrifice was for nothing. She's lost every member of her family. Everyone wants her dead. Thanks to the King of Embers, Drayard Emyur—the man she thought she could trust and perhaps even love.

Now she loathes him with her entire being.

Brought into the Isle of Sage, she has no choice but to stay there and learn to protect herself. The only one who could teach her that is her number one foe—Drayard.

Stuck with him on the remote island, undeniable feelings keep growing until she can't deny them. She's attracted to him, but she also wants him dead.

What's going to prevail in the end? *Love or ... revenge?*

Coming October 2024 ...

An enemies-to-lovers romance set in 1960s France, featuring a woman with amnesia ...

Before She Remembers

She doesn't remember.
Teodora wakes up to a reality she can't recognise after surviving the fire she can't remember. Worst of all, she can't remember the man who claims to be her husband, Ettore.

Not his wife.
Ettore, involved in a dangerous criminal organisation, believes her to be Vittoria, his wife from an arranged marriage. Yet her personality doesn't match with the cruel and selfish woman he married. But if she isn't Vittoria, who is she?

Enemies but they don't know it.
As Teodora struggles to remember her past, she knows nothing about Ettore and his criminal life, yet he is her safety. Her feelings grow towards him, and he finds himself attracted to her too. But what if she remembers who she truly is and is the only capable of destroying everything he believes in?

Author's Note

This book almost didn't happen.

When I first got the idea, I was writing the second book in my first fantasy series. I really didn't want to leave it unfinished, but the new idea was so intriguing...

As you might have already guessed, I'd relented. I remember plotting the book during almost every lesson, biology class in particular. I couldn't wait to go home afterwards. And when it took an hour to get home, the anticipation only grew, and therefore, I finished the first draft in less than a month.

I named it the Empire of Beasts.

In July, I started publishing it on Wattpad. It was my first story written in English I'd published there. A month passed... No reads. Two passed... NO reads. I knew the story was good. I never stopped believing in it, but I was planning to take it down until... one reader appeared.

It really takes one person to make a difference, huh.

That one person inspired me, and I wasn't even close to being popular on Wattpad. I never thought I would be since not only did the book have many errors, but it wasn't your ordinary Wattpad story. I've always known it was bigger than that, and it had to go bigger, too. With as less errors as possible.

Before I graduated, I decided to unpublish it from Wattpad along with two books of a series and rewrite the book for publication. Three months or so passed, and I received a DM.

It was a poem about Drayard & Elynn from a reader.

First of all, I thought my book had been long since forgotten, so imagine my surprise when I received a poem. A poem from a reader! About the two characters *I* had created! The sensitive girl I am, I exploded into tears. It's been a year, and if that person is reading this, I remember you and I appreciate you. You motived me to finish that rewrite, needless to say, made not only my day, but my year.

Free from school at last, I sent the letters to some agents. Although I received rejection after rejection, I wasn't discouraged. If anything, I was more driven to let this story out into the world.

It has changed a lot in the past two years. Now, when I look back, I can boldly say that from bad things, good things arise. If I hadn't experienced an awful downfall in the music department when I was truly considering suicide (which was stupid, but I was in a bad place), this book wouldn't exist.

Elynn wouldn't exist.

Drayard wouldn't exist.

This entire world wouldn't exist if over two years ago, a hopeful seventeen-year-old girl wouldn't have stood on the stage only to experience an ultimate let down.

Bad things bear good things.

No matter how dark everything might seem to be, there will always be a ray of light in the darkness. You might not see it yet, but it's there. Just hold on a little longer because, trust me, it's going to be worth it.

Love,
Austea

About The Author

Born and raised in Lithuania, Austea hasn't had a chance to explore the world beyond it yet. To make up for it, she now creates worlds while dreaming about savouring tea in Scotland. Currently, she's a mother of three endearing kitties writing about everything she finds intriguing: witches, dragons, enemies-to-lovers trope, soulmates, strong and admirable women, etc.

Follow her journey on Instagram! @austea.kette

www.ingramcontent.com/pod-product-compliance
Lightning Source LLC
LaVergne TN
LVHW040036080526
838202LV00045B/3360